'A novel so exquisitely written that at times it feels almost as if it could dispense with plot and characters and exist on a plane of pure perception and connotation. It doesn't, of course, and it ably depicts the high-days of a boom society and the ambiguous charm of being both insider and cuckoo in the nest. But its delights and rewards extend beyond its comic or documentary achievements and are to be found in its author's almost uncanny apprehension of the world he observes'
Alex Clark, *Sunday Times*

'A novel which, though richly textured, has the ring of simple human truth. The book is Jamesian in the best sense; indeed, in some ways, Hollinghurst surpasses his master. His prose is both super-elegant and super-succinct' David Robson, *Sunday Telegraph*

'Magnificent . . . There are literally thousands of impeccably nuanced touches. Hollinghurst is living proof that the vaulting claims made by the Master on behalf of the novel – "the force and beauty of its process" – still hold good today'
Geoff Dyer, *Daily Telegraph*

'There is something memorable on every page . . . there is much to savour in *The Line of Beauty*, not least its humour, a shivering yet morally exacting satire that leaves no character untouched'
Henry Hitchings, *Times Literary Supplement*

'Hollinghurst writes beautifully. His sentences seem at times sculptural, carved with a care and craft that it's possible to delight in. He can illuminate character with the briefest of glances'
Keith Ridgway, *Irish Times*

'One cannot help admiring the sheer classiness of writing is the literary equivalent of leather upholstery and a walnut board. Settling ourselves in the comfortable grip of Hollingh flawless prose, we are taken on a ride through 1980s London t smooth, unhurried and utterly captivating'
Andrew Crumey, *Scotland on Sunday*

THE LINE OF BEAUTY

Alan Hollinghurst is the author of five novels, *The Swimming-Pool Library*, *The Folding Star*, *The Spell*, *The Line of Beauty* and *The Stranger's Child*. He has received the Somerset Maugham Award, the James Tait Black Memorial Prize for Fiction and the 2004 Man Booker Prize, for *The Line of Beauty*. He lives in London.

Also by Alan Hollinghurst

ALAN HOLLINGHURST
THE LINE OF BEAUTY

PICADOR

FOR FRANCIS WYNDHAM

First published 2004 by Picador

This edition published 2005 by Picador
an imprint of Pan Macmillan
20 New Wharf Road, London N1 9RR
Associated companies throughout the world
www.panmacmillan.com

ISBN 978-0-330-48321-6

37 39 38 36

A CIP catalogue record for this book is available from
the British Library.

Typeset by SetSytems Ltd, Saffron Walden, Essex
Printed and bound by
CPI Group (UK) Ltd, Croydon, CRO 4YY

I am very grateful for the hospitality of Yaddo,
where part of this novel was written.

A. H.

'What do you know about this business?' the King said to Alice.

'Nothing,' said Alice.

'Nothing *whatever*?' persisted the King.

'Nothing whatever,' said Alice.

'That's very important,' the King said, turning to the jury. They were just beginning to write this down on their slates, when the White Rabbit interrupted: '*Un*important, your Majesty means, of course,' he said in a very respectful tone, but frowning and making faces at him as he spoke.

'*Un*important, of course, I meant,' the King hastily said, and went on to himself in an undertone, 'important – unimportant – unimportant – important –' as if he were trying which word sounded best.

Alice's Adventures in Wonderland, chapter 12

THE LOVE-CHORD
(1983)

I

Peter Crowther's book on the election was already in the shops. It was called *Landslide!*, and the witty assistant at Dillon's had arranged the window in a scaled-down version of that natural disaster. The pale-gilt image of the triumphant Prime Minister rushed towards the customer in a gleaming slippage. Nick stopped in the street, and then went in to look at a copy. He had met Peter Crowther once, and heard him described as a hack and also as a 'mordant analyst': his faint smile, as he flicked through the pages, concealed his uncertainty as to which account was nearer the truth. There was clearly something hacklike in the speed of publication, only two months after the event; and in the actual writing, of course. The book's mordancy seemed to be reserved for the efforts of the Opposition. Nick looked carefully at the photographs, but only one of them had Gerald in it: a group picture of 'The 101 New Tory MPs', in which he'd been clever enough, or quick enough, to get into the front row. He sat there smiling and staring as if in his own mind it was already the front bench. The smile, the white collar worn with a dark shirt, the floppy breast-pocket handkerchief would surely be famous when the chaps in the rows behind were mere forgotten grins and frowns. Even so, he was mentioned only twice in the text – as a 'bon viveur', and as one of the 'dwindling minority' of Conservative MPs who had passed, 'as Gerald Fedden, the new Member for Barwick, so obviously has', through public school and Oxbridge. Nick left the shop with a shrug; but out in the street he felt delayed pride at this sighting of a person he knew in a published book.

He had a blind date at eight that evening, and the hot August day was a shimmer of nerves, with little breezy interludes of lustful dreaming. The date wasn't totally blind – 'just very short-sighted', Catherine Fedden said, when Nick showed her the photograph and the letter. She seemed to like the look of the man, who was called Leo, and who she said was so much her type; but his handwriting made her jumpy. It was both elaborate and impetuous. Catherine had a paperback called *Graphology: The Mind in the Hand*, which gave her all sorts of warnings about people's tendencies and repressions ('Artist or Madman?' 'Pet or Brute?'). 'It's those enormous ascenders, darling,' she said: 'I see a lot of ego.' They had pursed their lips again over the little square of cheap blue writing paper. 'You're sure that doesn't just mean a very strong sex drive?' Nick asked. But she seemed to think not. He had been excited, and even rather moved, to get this letter from a stranger; but it was true the text itself raised few expectations. 'Nick – OK! Ref your letter, am in Personnel (London Borough of Brent). We can meet up, discuss Interests and Ambitions. Say When. Say Where' – and then the enormous rampant L of Leo going halfway down the page.

Nick had moved into the Feddens' big white Notting Hill house a few weeks before. His room was up in the roof, still clearly the children's zone, with its lingering mood of teenage secrets and rebellions. Toby's orderly den was at the top of the stairs, Nick's room just along the skylit landing, and Catherine's at the far end; Nick had no brothers or sisters but he was able to think of himself here as a lost middle child. It was Toby who had brought him here, in earlier vacations, for his London 'seasons', long thrilling escapes from his own far less glamorous family; and Toby whose half-dressed presence still haunted the attic passage. Toby himself had never perhaps known why he and Nick were friends, but had amiably accepted the evidence that they were. In these months after Oxford he was rarely there, and Nick had been passed on as a friend to his little sister and to their hospitable parents. He was a friend of the family; and there was something about him they trusted, a gravity, a certain shy polish, something not quite apparent to Nick himself, which had helped the family agree that he should become their lodger. When Gerald had won Barwick, which was Nick's home constituency, the arrangement was jovially hailed as having the logic of poetry, or fate.

Gerald and Rachel were still in France, and Nick found himself almost resenting their return at the end of the month. The housekeeper came in early each morning, to prepare the day's meals, and Gerald's secretary, with sunglasses on top of her head, looked in to deal with the imposing volume of post. The gardener announced himself by the roar of the mower outside an open window. Mr Duke, the handyman (His Grace, as the family called him), was at work on various bits of maintenance. And Nick was in residence, and almost, he felt, in possession. He loved coming home to Kensington Park Gardens in the early evening, when the wide treeless street was raked by the sun, and the two white terraces stared at each other with the glazed tolerance of rich neighbours. He loved letting himself in at the three-locked green front door, and locking it again behind him, and feeling the still security of the house as he looked into the red-walled dining room, or climbed the stairs to the double drawing room, and up again past the half-open doors of the white bedrooms. The first flight of stairs, fanning out into the hall, was made of stone; the upper flights had the confidential creak of oak. He saw himself leading someone up them, showing the house to a new friend, to Leo perhaps, as if it was really his own, or would be one day: the pictures, the porcelain, the curvy French furniture so different from what he'd been brought up with. In the dark polished wood he was partnered by reflections as dim as shadows. He'd taken the chance to explore the whole house, from the wedge-shaped attic cupboards to the basement junk room, a dim museum in itself, referred to by Gerald as the *trou de gloire*. Above the drawing-room fireplace there was a painting by Guardi, a capriccio of Venice in a gilt rococo frame; on the facing wall were two large gilt-framed mirrors. Like his hero Henry James, Nick felt that he could 'stand a great deal of gilt'.

Sometimes Toby would have come back, and there would be loud music in the drawing room; or he was in his father's study at the back of the house making international phone calls and having a gin-and-tonic – all this done not in defiance of his parents but in rightful imitation of their own freedoms in the place. He would go into the garden and pull his shirt off impatiently and sprawl in a deckchair reading the sport in the *Telegraph*. Nick would see him from the balcony and go down to join him, slightly breathless, knowing Toby quite liked his rower's body to be looked at. It was the easy charity of beauty. They would have a beer and Toby would say, 'My sis all right? Not too mad, I hope,' and Nick would say, 'She's fine, she's fine,' shielding his eyes from the dropping August sun, and smiling back at him with reassurance, among other unguessed emotions.

Catherine's ups and downs were part of Nick's mythology of the house. Toby had told him about them, as a mark of trust, one evening in college, sitting on a bench by the lake. 'She's pretty volatile, you know,' he said, quietly impressed by his own choice of word. 'Yah, she has these moods.' To Nick the whole house, as yet only imagined, took on the light and shade of moods, the life that was lived there as steeped in emotion as the Oxford air was with the smell of the lake water. 'She used to, you know, cut her arms, with a razor blade.' Toby winced and nodded. 'Thank god she's grown out of all that now.' This sounded more challenging than mere moods, and when Nick first met her he found himself glancing tensely at her arms. On one forearm there were neat parallel lines, a couple of inches long, and on the other a pattern of right-angled scars that you couldn't help trying to read as letters; it might have been an attempt at the word ELLE. But they were long healed over, evidence of something that would otherwise be forgotten; sometimes she traced them abstractedly with a finger.

'Looking after the Cat' was how Gerald had put it before they went away, with the suggestion that the task was as simple as that, and as responsible. It was Catherine's house but it was Nick who was in charge. She camped nervously in the place, as though she and not Nick was the lodger. She was puzzled by his love of its pompous spaces, and mocked his knowledgeable attachment to the paintings and furniture. 'You're such a snob,' she said, with a provoking laugh; coming from the family he was thought to be snobbish about, this was a bit of a facer. 'I'm not really,' said Nick, as if a small admission was the best kind of denial, 'I just love beautiful things.' Catherine peered around comically, as though at so much junk. In her parents' absence her instincts were humbly transgressive, and mainly involved smoking and asking strangers home. Nick came back one evening to find her drinking in the kitchen with an old black minicab driver and telling him what the contents of the house were insured for.

At nineteen she already had a catalogue of failed boyfriends, each with a damning epithet, which was sometimes all Nick knew them by: 'Crabs' or 'Drip-Dry' or 'Quantity Surveyor'. A lot of them seemed almost consciously chosen for their unacceptability at Kensington Park Gardens: a tramplike Welshman in his forties whom she'd met in the Notting Hill Record Exchange; a beautiful punk with FUCK tattooed on his neck; a Rastafarian from round the corner who moaned prophetically about Babylon and the downfall of Thatcher. Others were public schoolboys and sleek young professionals on the make in the Thatcher slump. Catherine was slight but physically reckless; what drew boys to her often frightened them away. Nick, in his secret innocence, felt a certain respect for her experience with men: to have so many failures required a high rate of preliminary success. He could never judge how attractive she was. In her case the genetic mixture of two good-looking parents had produced something different from Toby's sleepy beauty: Gerald's large confidence-winning mouth had been awkwardly squashed into the slender ellipse of Rachel's face. Catherine's emotions always rushed to her mouth.

She loved anything satirical, and was a clever vocal mimic. When she and Nick got drunk she did funny imitations of her family, so that oddly they seemed not to have gone away. There was Gerald, with his facetious boom, his taste for the splendid, his favourite tags from the *Alice* books. 'Really, Catherine,' protested Catherine, 'you would try the patience of an oyster.' Or, 'You recall the branches of arithmetic, Nick? Ambition, Distraction, Uglification, and Derision . . . ?' Nick joined in, with a sense of treacherously bad manners. It was Rachel's style that attracted him more, as a code both aristocratic and distantly foreign. Her *group* sounded nearly Germanic, and the sort of thing she would never belong to; her *philistine*, pronounced as a French word, seemed to cover, by implication, anyone who said it differently. Nick tried this out on Catherine, who laughed but perhaps wasn't much impressed. Toby she couldn't be bothered to mimic; and it was true that he was hard to 'get'. She did a funny turn as her godmother, the Duchess of Flintshire, who as plain Sharon Feingold had been Rachel's best friend at Cranborne Chase school, and whose presence in their lives gave a special archness to their joke about Mr Duke the odd-job man. The Duke that Sharon had married had a twisted spine and a crumbling castle, and the Feingold vinegar fortune had come in very handy. Nick hadn't met the Duchess yet, but after Catherine's impression of a thoughtless social dynamo he felt he'd had the pleasure without the concomitant anxiety.

Nick never talked to Catherine about his crush on her brother. He was afraid she would find it funny. But they talked a good deal about Leo, in the week of waiting, a week that crawled and jumped and crawled. There wasn't much to go on, but enough for two lively imaginations to build a character from: the pale-blue letter, with its dubious ascenders; his voice, which only Nick had heard, in the stilted cheerful chat which finalized the plans, and which was neutrally London, not recognizably black, though he sensed a special irony and lack of expectation in it; and his colour photograph, which showed that if Leo wasn't as handsome as he claimed he still demanded to be looked at. He was sitting on a park bench, seen from the waist up and leaning back – it was hard to tell how tall he was. He was wearing a dark bomber jacket and gazed away with a frown, which seemed to cast a shadow over his features, or to be a shadow rising within them. Behind him you could see the silver-grey crossbar of a racing bike, propped against the bench.

The substance of the original ad ('Black guy, late 20s, v. good-looking, interests cinema, music, politics, seeks intelligent like-minded guy 18–40') was half-obliterated by Nick's later dreamings and Catherine's premonitions, which dragged Leo further and further off into her own territory of uncomfortable sex and bad faith. At times Nick had to reassure himself that he and not Catherine was the one who had a date with him. Hurrying home that evening he glanced through the requirements again. He couldn't help feeling he was going to fall short of his new lover's standards. He was intelligent, he had just got a first-class degree from Oxford University, but people meant such different things by music and politics. Well, knowing the Feddens would give him an angle. He found the tolerant age range comforting. He was only twenty, but he could have been twice that age and Leo would still have wanted him. In fact he might be going to stay with Leo for twenty years: that seemed to be the advertisement's coded promise.

The second post was still scattered across the hall, and there was no sound from upstairs; but he felt, from a charge in the air, that he wasn't alone. He gathered up the letters and found that Gerald had sent him a postcard. It was a black-and-white picture of a Romanesque doorway, with flanking saints and a lively Last Judgement in the tympanum: 'Eglise de Podier, XII siècle'. Gerald had large, impatient handwriting, in which most of the letters were missed out, and perhaps unnegotiable with his very thick nib. The author of *Graphology* might have diagnosed an ego as big as Leo's, but the main impression was of almost evasive haste. He had a sign-off that could have been 'Love' but could have been 'Yours' or even, absurdly, 'Hello' – so you didn't quite know where you stood with him. As far as Nick could make out they were enjoying themselves. He was pleased to have the card, but it cast a slight shadow, by reminding him that the August idyll would soon be over.

He went into the kitchen, where Catherine, it must be, had made a mess since Elena's early morning visit. The cutlery drawers tilted heavily open. There was a vague air of intrusion. He darted into the dining room, but the boulle clock ticked on in its place on the mantelpiece, and the silver safe was locked. The brown Lenbach portraits of Rachel's forebears stared as sternly as Leo himself. Upstairs in the drawing room the windows were open on to the curving rear balcony, but the blue lagoon of the Guardi still gleamed and flashed above the mantelpiece. A low cupboard in the break-fronted bookcase stood open. Funny how mere living in a house like this could have the look of a burglary. He peered down from the balcony, but there was no one in the garden. He went more calmly up the further three flights of stairs, and when his nerves about Leo took hold of him again they were almost a relief from the grown-up anxieties of guarding the house. He saw Catherine moving in her room, and called out to her. A breeze had slammed his door and his own room was stifling, the books and papers on the table by the window curled up and hot. He said, 'I thought we'd had a break-in for a moment' – but the fear of it had already gone.

He picked out two possible shirts on their hangers, and was looking in the mirror when Catherine came in and stood behind him. He sensed at once her desire to touch him and her inability to do so. She didn't meet his eye in the mirror, she simply looked at him, at his shoulder, as though he would know what to do. She had the bewildered slight smile of someone only just coping with pain. Nick smiled back more broadly, to make a few seconds of delay, as if it might still be one of their jokes. 'Blue or white?' he said, covering himself with the shirts again, like two wings. Then he dropped his arms and the shirts trailed on the floor. He saw night falling already and Leo on his racing bike racing home to Willesden. 'Not too good?' he said.

She walked over and sat on the bed, where she leant forward and glanced up at him, with her ominous hint of a smile. He had seen her in this little flowered dress day after day, it was what she strode about the streets in, something off the Portobello Road that looked just right for the district or her fantasy of it, but now, armless, backless, legless, seemed hardly a garment at all. Nick sat beside her and gave her a hug and a rub, as if to warm her up, though she felt hot as a sick child. She let it happen, then shifted away from him a little. Nick said, 'What can I do, then?' and saw that he was hoping to be comforted himself. In the deep, bright space of the mirror he noticed two young people in an undisclosed crisis.

She said, 'Can you get the stuff out of my room. Yeah, take it all downstairs.'

'OK.'

Nick went along the landing and into her room, where as usual the curtains were closed and the air soured with smoke. The dense red gauze wrapped round the lampshade gave off a dangerous smell, and filtered the light across a chaos of bedclothes, underwear, LPs. Drawers and cupboards had been gone through – the imaginary burglary might have reached its frustrated climax here. Nick peered around and though he was alone he mugged a good-natured readiness to take control. His mind was working quickly and responsibly, but he clung to his last few moments of ignorance. He made a low quiet concentrating sound, looking over the table, the bed, the junk heap on the lovely old walnut chest. The cupboard in the corner had a wash-basin in it, and Catherine had laid out half a dozen things on the tiled surround, like instruments before an operation: a heavy carving knife, a curved two-handled chopper, a couple of honed-down filleting knives, and the two squat little puncheons that Nick had seen Gerald use to grapple and turn a joint with, almost as though it might still get away. He gathered them up in an awkward clutch, and took them carefully downstairs, with new, heavy-hearted respect for them.

She was adamant that he shouldn't call anyone – she hinted that worse things would follow if he did. Nick paced about in his uncertainty over this. His ignorance of what to do was a sign of his much larger ignorance about the world in which he'd recently arrived. He pictured the sick shock of her parents when they found out, and saw the stain on the record of his new life with the Feddens. He was untrustworthy after all, as he had suspected he was, and they had not. He had a dread of being in the wrong, but was also frightened of taking action. Perhaps he should try to find Toby? But Toby was a non-person to Catherine, treated at best with inattentive politeness. Nick was shaping the story in his head. He persuaded himself that disaster had been contemplated, stared at, and rejected. There had been a ritual of confrontation, lasting an hour, a minute, all afternoon – and maybe it would never have been more than a ritual. Now she was almost silent, passive, she yawned a lot, and Nick wondered if the episode had already been taken away, screened and isolated by some effective mechanism. Perhaps his own return had always played a part in her design. Certainly it made it hard for him to refuse her when she said, 'For god's sake don't leave me alone.' He said, 'Of course I won't,' and felt the occasion close in on him, suffocatingly, from a great distance. It was something else Toby had mentioned, by the lake: there are times when she can't be alone, and she has to have someone with her. Nick had yearned then to share Toby's duty, to steep himself in the difficult romance of the family. And now here he was, with his own romance about to unfold in the back bar of the Chepstow Castle, and he was the person she had to have with her. She couldn't explain, but no one else would do.

Nick brought her down to the drawing room and she chose some music by going to the record cupboard and pulling out a disc without looking and then putting it on. She seemed to say she could act, but that deliberations were beyond her. It came on jarringly. The arm had come down in the wrong place, as if looking for a single. 'Ah yes . . . !' said Nick. It was the middle of the scherzo of Schumann's Fourth Symphony. He kept an eye on her, and felt he understood the way she let the music take care of her; he saw her drifting along in it, not knowing where she was particularly, but grateful and semi-interested. He was agitated by indecision, but he went with it himself for a few moments. The trio returned, but only for a brief airing before the magical transition to the finale . . . based, very obviously, on that of Beethoven's Fifth: he could have told her that, and how it was really the second symphony, and how all the material grew from the opening motif, except the unexpected second subject of the finale . . . He stood back and decided, in the bleak but proper light of responsibility, that he would go downstairs at once and ring Catherine's parents. But then, as he left the room, he thought suddenly of Leo, and felt sure he was losing his only chance with him: so he rang him instead, and put off the call to France until later. He didn't know how to explain it to Leo: the bare facts seemed too private to tell a stranger, and a watered-down version would sound like an invented excuse. Again he saw himself in the wrong. He kept clearing his throat as he dialled the number.

Leo answered very briskly, but that was only because he was having his dinner and still had to get ready – facts which Nick found illuminating. His voice, with its little reserve of mockery, was exactly what he had heard before, but had lost in the remembering. Nick had only begun his apologies when Leo got the point and said in an amiable way that he was quite relieved, and dead busy himself. 'Oh good,' said Nick, and then felt almost at once that Leo could have been more put out. 'If you're sure you don't mind . . .' he added.

'That's all right, my friend,' said Leo quietly, so that Nick had the impression there was someone else there.

'I'd still really like to meet you.'

There was a pause before Leo said, 'Absolutely.'

'Well, what about the weekend?'

'No. The weekend I cannot do.'

Nick wanted to say 'Why not?' but he knew the answer must be that Leo would be seeing other hopefuls then; it must be like auditions. 'Next week?' he said with a shrug. He wanted to do it before Gerald and Rachel got back, he wanted to use the house.

'Yeah, going to the Carnival?' said Leo.

'Perhaps on the Saturday – we're away over the bank holiday. Let's get together before then.' Nick longed for the Carnival, but felt humbly that it was Leo's element. He saw himself losing Leo on their first meeting, where a whole street moves in a solid current and you can't turn back.

'The best thing is, if you give us a ring next week,' said Leo.

'I most certainly will,' said Nick, pretending he thought all this was positive but feeling abruptly miserable and stiff in the face. 'Look, I'm really sorry about tonight, I'll make it up to you.' There was another pause in which he knew his sentence was being decided – his whole future perhaps. But then Leo said, in a throaty whisper,

'You bet you will!' – and as Nick started to giggle he hung up. So that little pause had been conspiratorial, a conspiracy of strangers. It wasn't so bad. It was beautiful even. Nick hung up too and went to look at himself in the high gilt arch of the hall mirror. With the sudden hilarity of relief he thought how nice-looking he was, small but solid, clear-skinned and curly-headed. He could see Leo falling for him. Then the colour drained from him, and he climbed the stairs.

When it had cooled Nick and Catherine went down into the garden and out through the gate into the communal gardens beyond. The communal gardens were as much a part of Nick's romance of London as the house itself: big as the central park of some old European city, but private, and densely hedged on three sides with holly and shrubbery behind high Victorian railings. There were one or two places, in the surrounding streets, where someone who wasn't a keyholder could see through to a glade among the planes and tall horse chestnuts – across which perhaps a couple would saunter or an old lady wait for her even slower dog. And sometimes in these summer evenings, with thrush and blackbird song among the leaves, Nick would glimpse a boy walking past on the outside and feel a surprising envy of him, though it was hard to know how a smile would be received, coming from the inside. There were hidden places, even on the inside, the path that curled, as if to a discreet convenience, to the gardeners' hut behind a larch-lap fence; the enclosure with the sandpit and the children's slide, where genuine uniformed nannies still met and gossiped with a faint air of truancy; and at the far end the tennis courts, whose overlapping rhythms of serves and rallies and calls lent a calming reminder of other people's exertions to the August dusk.

From end to end, just behind the houses, ran the broad

gravel walk, with its emphatic camber and its metal-edged
gutters where a child's ball would come to rest and the first few
plane leaves, dusty but still green, were already falling, since the
summer had been so hot and rainless all through. Nick and
Catherine strolled along there, arm in arm, like a slow old
couple; Nick felt paired with Catherine in a new, almost formal
way. At regular intervals there were Victorian cast-iron benches,
made with no thought of comfort, and between them on the
grass a few people were sitting or picnicking in the warm early
twilight.

After a minute Nick said, 'Feeling a bit better?' and
Catherine nodded and pressed against him as they walked. The
sense of responsibility came back to him, a grey weight in his
chest, and he saw them from the point of view of the picnickers
or an approaching jogger: not a dear old couple at all but a pair
of kids, a skinny girl with a large nervous mouth and a solemn
little blond boy pretending he wasn't out of his depth. Of course
he must ring France, and hope that he got Rachel, since Gerald
wasn't always good with these things. He wished he knew more
about what had happened and why, but he was squeamish too.
'You'll be all right,' he said. He thought that asking her about it
might only reopen the horror, and added, 'I wonder what it was
all about,' as if referring to a mystery of long ago. She gave him
a look of painful uncertainty, but didn't answer. 'Can't really
say?' Nick said, and heard, as he sometimes did, his own father's
note of evasive sympathy. It was how his family sidled round
its various crises; nothing was named, and you never knew
for sure if the tone was subtly comprehensive, or just a form of
cowardice.

'No, not really.'

'Well, you know you always can tell me,' he said.

At the end of the path there was the gardener's cottage,
huddled quaintly and servilely under the cream cliff of the
terrace. Beyond it a gate gave on to the street and they stood

and looked out through its iron scrolls at the sporadic evening traffic. Nick waited, and thought despairingly of Leo at large in the same summer evening. Catherine said, 'It's when everything goes black and glittering.'

'Mm.'

'It's not like when you're down in the dumps, which is brown.'

'Right . . .'

'Oh, you wouldn't understand.'

'No, please go on.'

'It's like that car,' she said, nodding at a black Daimler that had stopped across the road to let out a distinguished-looking old man. The yellow of the early street lights was reflected in its roof, and as it pulled away reflections streamed and glittered in its dark curved sides and windows.

'It sounds almost beautiful.'

'It is beautiful, in a sense. But that isn't the point.'

Nick felt he had been given an explanation which he was too stupid, or unimaginative, to follow. 'It must be horrible as well,' he said, 'obviously . . .'

'Well, it's poisonous, you see. It's glittering but it's deadly at the same time. It doesn't want you to survive it. That's what it makes you realize.' She stepped away from Nick, so as to use her hands. 'It's the whole world just as it is,' she said, stretching out to frame it or hold it off: 'everything exactly the same. And it's totally negative. You can't survive in it. It's like being on Mars or something.' Her eyes were fixed but blurred. 'There you are, that's the best I can do,' she said, and turned her back.

He followed her. 'But then it changes back again . . .' he said.

'Yes, Nick, it does,' she said, with the offended tone that sometimes follows a moment of self-exposure.

'I'm only trying to understand.' He thought her tears might be a sign of recovery, and put an arm round her shoulder – though after a few seconds she made another gesture that meant freeing herself. Nick felt a hint of sexual repudiation, as if she thought he was taking advantage of her.

Later on, in the drawing room, she said, 'Oh, god, this was your night with Leo.'

Nick couldn't believe that she'd only just thought of that. But he said, 'It's all right. I've put him off till next week.'

Catherine smiled ruefully. 'Well, he wasn't really your type,' she said.

Schumann had given way to The Clash, who in turn had yielded to a tired but busy silence between them. Nick prayed that she wouldn't put on any more music – most of the stuff she liked had him clenched in resistance. He looked at his watch. They were an hour later in France, it was too late to ring them now, and he welcomed this rational and thoughtful postponement with a sense of cloudy relief. He went over to the much-neglected piano, its black lid the podium for various old art folios and a small bronze bust of Liszt – which seemed to give a rather pained glance at his sight-reading from the Mozart album on the stand. To Nick himself the faltering notes were like raindrops on a sandy path, and he was filled with a sense of what his evening could have been. The simple Andante became a vivid dialogue in his mind between optimism and recurrent pain; in fact it heightened both feelings to an unnecessary degree. It wasn't long until Catherine stood up and said, 'For god's sake, darling, it's not a fucking funeral.'

'Sorry, darling,' said Nick, and vamped through a few seconds of what they called Waldorf music before getting up and wandering out on to the balcony. They had only just started calling each other darling, and it seemed a nice part of the larger conspiracy of life at Kensington Park Gardens; but outside in the cool of the night Nick felt he was play-acting, and that Catherine was frighteningly strange to him. Her mirage of the beautiful poisonous universe shimmered before him again for a moment, but he couldn't hold it, and it slipped quickly away.

There was a supper party in a nearby back garden, and the talk and light clatter carried on the still air. A man called Geoffrey was making everyone laugh, and the women kept calling out his name in excited protest between the semi-audible paragraphs of his story. Out in the communal gardens someone was walking a small white dog, which looked almost luminous as it bobbed and scampered in the late dusk. Above the trees and rooftops the dingy glare of the London sky faded upwards into weak violet heights. In summer, when windows everywhere were open, night seemed made of sound as much as shadow, the whisper of the leaves, the unsleeping traffic rumble, far-off car horns and squeals of brakes; voices, faint shouts, a waveband twiddle of unconnected music. Nick yearned for Leo, away to the north, three miles up the long straight roads, but possibly anywhere, moving with invisible speed on his silver bike. He wondered again in which park the photo of him had been taken; and of course what person, routinely intimate with Leo, had taken it. He felt hollow with frustration and delay. The girl with the white dog came back along the gravel path, and he thought how he might appear to her, if she glanced up, as an enviable figure, poised against the shining accomplished background of the lamplit room. Whereas, looking out, leaning out over the iron railing, Nick felt he had been swept to the brink of some new promise, a scented vista or vision of the night, and then held there.

2

'Something for everybody!' Gerald Fedden said, striding into the kitchen with a rattling brown-paper carrier bag. 'All must have prizes!' He was tanned and tireless, and a lost energy came back into the house with him, the flash of his vanity and confidence – it was almost as though the words of the returning officer were fresh in his ears and he were responding to applause with these high-spirited promises. On the side of the bag was the emblem of a famous Périgueux delicatessen, a blue goose with its head through what looked like a life-saving ring, its beak curling Disney-wise in a complacent smile.

'Yuk, not foie gras,' Catherine said.

'In fact this quince jelly is for the Purring One,' said Gerald, taking out a jar in a gingham cap and bow and sliding it across the kitchen table.

Catherine said, 'Thanks,' but left it there and wandered away to the window.

'And what was it for Tobias?'

'The . . . um . . .' Rachel gestured. 'The *carnet*.'

'Of course.' Gerald rummaged discreetly before passing his son a small notebook, bound in odorous green suede.

'Thanks, Pa,' said Toby, who was sprawling in shorts on the long banquette and obliquely reading the paper while he listened to his mother's news. Behind him, the wall was a great hilarious page of family history, with numerous framed photographs of holidays and handshakes with the famous, as well as two wicked caricatures of Gerald, which he had made a point of buying from the cartoonists. When Gerald was in the kitchen, guests always found themselves contrasting him with his grinning, hawk-nosed cartoon image; the comparison was obviously to his advantage, though it couldn't help stirring the suspicion that under his handsome everyday mask this predatory goon might indeed be lurking.

Now, in linen shorts and espadrilles, busying back and forth from the car, he was full of anecdotes about life at the manoir, and mentioned particular local characters to stir up amusement and regret in his children. 'It's such a shame we couldn't all be there together. And you know, you really should come down one year, Nick.'

'Well, I'd love to,' said Nick, who had been hovering with an encouraging but modest expression. Of course it would have been grand to summer with the Feddens at the manoir, but less marvellous, he couldn't help feeling, than staying in London without them. How different the room looked now, with all of them noisily and unnoticingly back in it. Their return marked the end of his custodianship, and his real pleasure in seeing them again was stained with a kind of sadness he associated with adolescence, sadness of time flying and missed opportunities. He was keen for a word of gratitude to ease the mysterious ache. Of course his main achievement, in the crisis with Catherine, went unmentioned. It seemed an omission which could still be redeemed, by a quick firm gesture of good conscience, and Catherine herself looked nervously aware of the unstated subject; but Nick saw, in the unsuspecting presence of her parents, that he had somehow sided with her, and that it was never going to be declared.

'However,' said Gerald, 'it was simply great for us that you could be here to look after the Cat that Walks by Herself. I hope she wasn't any trouble?'

'Well . . .' Nick grinned and looked down.

As an outsider, he had no pet name, and was exempt from the heavy drollery of the family lingo. His own gift was a small knobbly bottle of cologne called 'Je Promets'. He took an appreciative sniff, and read into it various nice discriminations on the part of the donors; certainly his own parents would never have given him anything so fragrant or ambiguous. 'I trust it's all right,' said Gerald, as if to say he'd made a generous stab at something outside his competence.

'It's wonderful – thank you so much,' said Nick. As an outsider he found himself floating again in a pleasant medium of social charm and good humour. Toby and Catherine could frown and sulk, and exercise their prerogative not to be impressed or amused by their parents. Nick, though, conversed with his hosts in an idiom of tremendous agreement. 'Did you have glorious weather?' 'I must say we had *glorious* weather.' 'I hope the traffic wasn't too frightful . . .' '*Frightful!*' 'I'd love to see the little church at Podier.' 'I think you'd *love* the little church at Podier.' So they knitted their talk together. Even disagreements, for instance over Gerald's taste for Richard Strauss, had a glow of social harmony to them, of relished licence, and counted almost as agreements transposed into a more exciting key.

There was a lot of wine in the back of the Range Rover and Nick offered to help Gerald carry it in. He couldn't help noticing the almost annoying firmness of the MP's backside, pumped up no doubt by daily tennis and swimming in France. The suntanned legs were a further hint of sexual potential that Nick would normally have thought impossible in a man of forty-five – he thought perhaps he was so excited by the prospect of Leo that he was reacting to other men with indiscriminate alertness. When the last case was in, Gerald said, 'We were stung for a hell of a lot of duty on this stuff.'

Toby said, 'Of course if trade barriers were lifted in the EC you wouldn't have to worry about that sort of thing.'

Gerald smiled thinly to show he wasn't rising to the bait.

There were a couple of bottles for Elena, who was involved in an anxious transfer of household powers to Rachel, and put them aside in her black shopping bag, to take home. Elena, a widow in her sixties, was treated with affection and a careful pretence of equality by the family, so it was revealing to see her nervousness as she accounted for what she had done in their absence. Nick couldn't quite rid himself of a sense of embarrassment with her, the ghost of an elaborate but misdirected courtesy. On his first visit to Kensington Park Gardens, he'd been welcomed by Toby and then left briefly alone in the house, with the warning that his mother would soon be home. Hearing the front door open and close, Nick went downstairs and introduced himself to the good-looking woman with jet-black hair who was sorting out the mail on the hall stand. He spoke excitedly about the painting he'd been looking at in the drawing room, and it was only slowly, in face of the woman's smiling deference and heavily accented murmurings, that he realized he wasn't talking to the Honourable Rachel but to the Italian housekeeper. Of course there was nothing wrong in being charming to the housekeeper, and Elena's views on Guardi were probably just as interesting as Rachel's and more so than Gerald's, but still the moment which she seemed to remember for its charm Nick recalled as a tiny faux pas.

Even so, sliding on to the seat beside Toby, taking in the soap and coffee smell of him, pressing briefly against his bare knee as he reached for the sugar, he felt what a success he had had. That was a year ago, and now everything was rich with association. He picked up the notebook, which had barely been looked at, and stroked the soft pile of its cover, to make up for Toby's lack of appreciation and remotely, too, as if he were thumbing some warm and hairy part of Toby himself. Toby was talking of becoming a journalist, so the gift was vaguely insulting, a lazy attempt at aptness, the sense of mere duty in the givers disguised by the stinking costliness of the production. The notebook wouldn't open flat, and a few addresses or 'ideas' would have filled it. It was certainly hard to imagine Toby using it as he visited a picket line or jostled for an answer from a camera-mobbed minister.

'You heard about Maltby, of course,' said Toby.

Immediately Nick felt the air in the room begin to tingle, as if at the onset of an allergic reaction. Hector Maltby, a junior minister in the Foreign Office, had been caught with a rent boy in his Jaguar at Jack Straw's Castle, and had rapidly resigned from his post and, it seemed, from his marriage. The story had been all over the papers last week, and it was silly of Nick to feel as self-conscious as he suddenly did, blushing as if he'd been caught in a Jaguar himself. It was often like this when the homosexual subject came up, and even in the Feddens' tolerant kitchen he stiffened in apprehension about what might care-lessly be said – some indirect insult to swallow, a joke to be weakly smiled at. Even the case of the absurd fat Maltby, a real-life cartoon of the greedy 'new' Tory, seemed to Nick to allude to his own quiet case and, in a brief twinge of paranoia, to raise a question about his closeness to Toby's beautiful brown leg.

'Silly old Hector,' said Gerald.

'I don't think we were terribly surprised,' Rachel said, with her characteristic tremor of irony.

'You must have known him?' Toby asked, in a ponderous new 'interview' style he had.

'A bit,' said Rachel.

'Not really,' said Gerald.

Catherine was still gazing out of the window, indulging her dream of not being connected to her family. 'I really don't see why he has to go to jail,' she said.

'He's not going to jail, you daft old puss,' Gerald said. 'Unless you know something I don't. He was only caught with his trousers down.' By some half-conscious association he looked to Nick for confirmation of this.

'As far as I know,' said Nick, trying to make the five little words sound both casual and judicious. It was horrible to imagine Hector Maltby with his trousers down; and the disgraced MP didn't seem after all to merit much in the way of solidarity. Nick's taste was for aesthetically radiant images of gay activity, gathering in a golden future for him, like swimmers on a sunlit bank.

'Well, I don't see why he had to resign,' Catherine said. 'Who cares if he likes a blow-job now and then?'

Gerald smoothed this over but he was clearly shocked. 'No, no, he had to go. There was really no alternative.' His tone was ruffled but responsible, and the sense of his own voice submitting to the common line and formula of politics was vaguely disturbing, though Catherine laughed at it.

'It may all do him good,' she said. 'Help him to find out who he really is.'

Gerald frowned, and pulled a bottle from the cardboard crate. 'You have the oddest idea of what might do people good,' he said, musingly but indignantly. 'Now I thought we might have the Podier St-Eustache with dinner.'

'Mm, lovely,' Rachel murmured. 'The thing is, darling, quite simply, that it's vulgar and unsafe,' she said, in one of her sudden hard formulations.

Gerald said, 'You'll dine with us tonight, Nick?'

Nick smiled and looked away because the generous question raised a new uncertainty about his status on subsequent nights. How much and how often would he be sharing with them? They had mentioned he might sometimes be called on to make up numbers. 'I'm terribly sorry, but I can't tonight,' he said.

'Oh . . . what a shame, our first night back . . .'

He wasn't sure how to put it. Catherine watched his hesitation with a fascinated smile. 'No, Nick can't because he's got a date,' she said. It was annoying to have her frankness applied to his tender plans, and a treacherous reward for his silence about her affairs. He coloured, and felt a further crackle of social static pass through the room. Everyone seemed to be humming, doubtful, encouraging, embarrassed, he couldn't tell.

Nick had never been on a date with a man before, and was much less experienced than Catherine imagined. In the course of their long conversations about men he had let one or two of his fantasies assume the status of fact, had lied a little, and had left some of Catherine's assumptions about him unchallenged. His confessed but entirely imaginary seductions took on – partly through the special effort required to invent them and repeat them consistently – the quality of real memories. He sometimes had the sense, from a hint of reserve in people he was talking to, that while they didn't believe him they saw he was beginning to believe himself. He had only come out fully in his last year at Oxford, and had used his new licence mainly to flirt with straight boys. His heart was given to Toby, with whom flirting would have been inappropriate, almost sacrilegious. He wasn't quite ready to accept the fact that if he was going to have a lover it wouldn't be Toby, or any other drunk straight boy hopping the fence, it would be a gay lover – that compromised thing that he himself would then become. Proper queens, whom he applauded and feared and hesitantly imitated, seemed often to find something wrong with him, pretty and clever though he was. At any rate they didn't want to go to bed with him, and he was free to wander back, in inseparable relief and discouragement, to his inner theatre of sexual make-believe. There the show never ended and the actors never tired and a certain staleness of repetition was the only hazard. So the meeting with Leo, pursued through all the obstacles of the system which alone made it possible, was momentous for Nick. Pausing for a last hopeful gaze into the gilt arch of the hall mirror, which monitored all comings and goings, he found it reluctant to give its approval; when he pulled the door shut and set off along the street he felt giddily alone, and had to remind himself he was doing all this for pleasure. It had taken on the mood of a pointless dare.

As he hurried down the hill he started focusing again on his Interests and Ambitions, the rather surprising topic for the meeting. He saw that interests weren't always a sexy thing. A shared passion for a subject, large or small, could quickly put two strangers into a special state of subdued rapture and rivalry, distantly resembling love; but you had to hit on the subject. As for ambitions, he felt it was hard to announce them without sounding either self-deluding or feeble, and in fact unambitious. Gerald could say, 'I want to be Home Secretary,' and have people smiling but conceding the possibility. Whereas Nick's ambition was to be loved by a handsome black man in his late twenties with a racing bike and a job in local government. This was the one thing he wasn't going to be able to admit to Leo himself.

He fixed his thoughts for the hundredth time on the little back bar of the Chepstow Castle, which he had chosen for its shadowy semi-privacy – a space incuriously glanced into by people being served in the public bar, but barely used on summer evenings when everyone stood outside on the pavement. There was an amber light in there, among the old whisky mirrors and photographs of horse-drawn drays. He saw himself sitting shoulder to shoulder with Leo, their hands joined in secret on the dusty moquette.

As he approached the pub he registered a black man at the edge of the crowd of drinkers, then knew it was Leo, then pretended he hadn't seen him. So he was quite small; and he'd grown a kind of beard. Why was he waiting in the street? Nick was already beside him and looked again, very nervously, and saw his questioning smile.

'If you don't want to know me . . .' Leo said.

Nick staggered and laughed and stuck out his hand. 'I thought you'd be inside.'

Leo nodded, and looked down the street. 'This way I can see you coming.'

'Ah . . .' Nick laughed again.

'Besides, I wasn't sure about the bike, in this area.' And there the bike was, refined, weightless, priceless, the bike of the future, shackled to the nearest lamp-post.

'Oh, I'm sure it will be fine.' Nick frowned and gazed. He was surprised that Leo thought this a bad area. Of course he thought it was rather dangerous himself; and three or four corners away there were pubs he knew he could never enter, so bad were their names, and so intense the mana of their glimpsed interiors. But here . . . A tall Rastafarian strolled by, and his roll of the head was a greeting to Leo, who nodded and then looked away with what seemed to Nick a guarded admission of kinship.

'We'll have a little chat outside, eh?'

Nick went in to get the drinks. He stood at the counter looking through to the back bar – where in fact there were several people talking, perhaps one of those groups that meet in a pub, and the room was brighter than he remembered it or would have wanted it. Everything seemed to be a bit different. Leo was only having a Coke, but Nick needed courage for the evening and his own identical-looking drink had a double rum in it. He had never drunk rum before, and was always astonished that anyone liked Coke. His mind held the floating image of the man he had longed to meet, whom he had touched for a moment and left outside in all his disconcerting reality. He was too sexy, he was too much what he wanted, in his falling-down jeans and his tight blue shirt. Nick was worried by his obvious intention to seduce, or at least to show his capacity for seduction. He took the drinks out with a light tremble.

There wasn't anywhere to sit down, so they stood and leaned against a brown-tiled window sill; in the opaque lower half of

the window the word SPIRITS was etched in fancy Victorian
capitals, their serifs spiralling out in interlacing tendrils. Leo
looked at Nick frankly, since that was what he was here for, and
Nick grinned and blushed, which made Leo smile too, for a
moment.

Nick said, 'You're growing a beard, I see.'

'Yeah – sensitive skin . . . it's a bloodbath when I shave.
Literally,' said Leo, with a quick glance that showed Nick that
he liked to make his point. 'Then if I don't shave, I get these
ingrowing hairs, fucking murder, have to pick the ends out with
a pin.' He stroked his stubbly jaw with a small fine hand, and
Nick saw that he had those shaving-bumps he had half-noticed
on other black men. 'I tend to leave it for four days, say, five
days, maybe, then have a good shave: try and avoid both problems that way.'

'Right . . .' said Nick, and smiled, partly because he was
learning something interesting.

'Most of them still recognize me, though,' said Leo, and gave
a wink.

'No, it wasn't that,' said Nick, who was too shy to explain his
own shyness. His glance slipped up and down between Leo's
loose crotch and the neat shallow cushion of his hair, and
tended to avoid his handsome face. He was taking Leo's word
for it that he was handsome, but it didn't quite cover the continuing shock of what was beautiful, strange, and even ugly
about him. The phrase 'most of them' slowly took on meaning
in his mind. 'Anyway,' he said, and took a quick sip of his drink,
which had a reassuring burn to it. 'I suppose you've had lots of
replies.' Sometimes when he was nervous he asked questions to
which he would rather not have known the answers.

Leo made a little puff of comic exhaustion. 'Yeah . . . yeah,
I'm not answering some of them. It's a joke. They don't include
a picture, or if they do they look horrible. Or they're ninety-
nine years old. I even had a thing from a woman, a lesbian

woman admittedly, with a view to would I father her child.' Leo frowned indignantly but there was something sly and flattered in his look too. 'And some of the stuff they write. It's disgusting! It's not like I'm just looking for a bonk, is it? This is something a bit different.'

'Quite,' said Nick – though bonk was a troublingly casual way of referring to something which preoccupied him so much.

'This dog's been round the block a few times,' Leo said, and looked off down the street as if he might spot himself coming home. 'Anyway, you looked nice. You've got nice writing.'

'Thanks. So have you.'

Leo took in the compliment with a nod. 'And you can spell,' he said.

Nick laughed. 'Yes, I'm good at that.' He'd been afraid that his own little letter sounded pedantic and virginal, but it seemed he'd got it about right. He didn't remember it calling for any great virtuosity of spelling. 'I always have trouble with "moccasin",' he said.

'Ah, there you are . . .' said Leo, with a wary chuckle, before changing the subject. 'It's nice where you live,' he said.

'Oh . . . yes . . .' said Nick, as if he couldn't quite remember where it was.

'I went by there the other day, on the bike. I nearly rang your bell.'

'Mm – you should have. I've had the place virtually to myself.' He felt sick at the thought of the missed chance.

'Yeah? I saw this girl going in . . .'

'Oh, that was probably only Catherine.'

Leo nodded. 'Catherine. She's your sister, yeah?'

'No, I don't have a sister. She's actually the sister of my friend Toby.' Nick smiled and stared: 'It's not my house.'

'Oh . . .' said Leo. 'Oh.'

'God, I don't come from that sort of background. No, I just live there. It belongs to Toby's parents. I've just got a tiny little room up in the attic.' Nick was rather surprised to hear himself throwing his whole fantasy of belonging there out of the window.

Leo looked a bit disappointed. He said, 'Right . . .' and shook his head slowly.

'I mean they're very good friends, they're a sort of second family to me, but I probably won't be there for long. It's just to help me out, while I'm getting started at university.'

'And I thought I'd got myself a nice little rich boy,' Leo said. And perhaps he meant it, Nick couldn't be sure, they were total strangers after all, though a minute before he'd imagined them naked together in the Feddens' emperor-size bed. Was that why his letter did the trick – the address, the Babylonian notepaper?

'Sorry,' he said, with a hint of humour. He drank some more of the sweet strong rum and Coke, so obviously not his kind of drink. The refined blue of the dusk sky was already showing its old lonely reach.

Leo laughed. 'I'm only kidding you!'

'I know,' Nick said, with a little smile, as Leo reached out and squeezed his shoulder, just by his shirt collar, and slowly let go. Nick reacted with his own quick pat at Leo's side. He was absurdly relieved. A charge passed into him through Leo's fingers, and he saw the two of them kissing passionately, in a rush of imagination that was as palpable as this awkward pavement rendezvous.

'Still, your friends must be rich,' Leo said.

Nick was careful not to deny this. 'Oh, they're rolling in money.'

'Yeah . . .' Leo crooned, with a fixed smile; he might have been savouring the fact or condemning it. Nick saw further questions coming, and decided at once he wouldn't tell him about Gerald. The evening demanded enough courage as it was. A Tory MP would shadow their meeting like an unwelcome chaperon, and Leo would get on his bike and leave them to it.

He could say something about Rachel's family, perhaps, if an explanation was called for. But in fact Leo emptied his glass and said, 'Same again?'

Nick hastily finished his own drink, and said, 'Thanks. Or maybe this time I'll have a shot of rum in it.'

After half an hour more Nick had slid into a kind of excited trance brought on by his new friend's presence and a feeling, as the sky darkened and the street lamps brightened from pink to gold, that it was going to work out. He felt nervous, slightly breathless, but at the same time buoyant, as if a lonely responsibility had been taken off him. A couple of places came free at the end of a picnic table with fixed benches, and they sat leaning towards each other as though playing, and then half-forgetting, some invisible game. For Nick the ease and comfort of the rum were indistinguishable parts of the intimacy which he felt deepening like the dusk.

He found himself wondering how they looked and sounded to the people around them, the couple beside them at the table. It was all getting noisier as the evening went on, with a vague sense of heterosexual threat. Nick guessed Leo's other dates would have met him in a gay pub, but he had flunked that further challenge. Now he regretted the freedom he would have had there. He wanted to stroke Leo's cheek and kiss him, with a sigh of surrender.

Nothing very personal was said. Nick found it hard to interest Leo in his own affairs, and his various modest leads about his family and his background were not picked up. There were things he'd prepared and phrased and turned into jokes that were not to be heard – or not tonight. Once or twice he took Leo with him: into a falsely cheerful dismissal of the idea that Toby, though fairly attractive, was of any real interest to him (Leo would think him a weirdo to have loved so long and pointlessly); into a sketch of Rachel's banking family, which Leo interrupted with a sour smile, as if it was all proof of some general iniquity. He had a certain caustic preoccupation with money, Nick could see; and when he told Leo that his father was an antiques dealer the two words, with the patina of old money and the flash of business, seemed to combine in a dull glare of privilege. Among his smart Oxford friends Nick managed to finesse his elbow-patched old man, with his Volvo estate full of blanket-wrapped mirrors and Windsor chairs, into a more luminous figure, a scholar and friend of the local aristocracy. Now he felt a timid need to humble him. And he was wrong, because Leo's long-time boyfriend, Pete, had been an antiques dealer, on the Portobello Road. 'Mainly French work,' Leo said. 'Ormolu. Boulle.' It was the first clear thing he had said about his private past. And then he changed the subject.

Leo was certainly quite an egotist – Catherine's graphological analysis had been spot on. But he didn't expound his inner feelings. He did something Nick couldn't imagine doing himself, which was to make statements about the sort of person he was. 'I'm the sort of guy who needs a lot of sex,' he said, and, 'I'm like that, I always say what I think.' Nick wondered for a moment if he'd inadvertently contradicted him. 'I don't bear grudges,' Leo said sternly: 'I'm not that kind of person.' 'I'm sure you're not,' Nick said, with a quick discountenancing shudder. And perhaps this was a useful skill, or tactic, in the blind-date world, even if Nick's modesty and natural fastidiousness kept him from replying in the same style ('I'm the sort of guy who likes Pope more than Wordsworth,' 'I'm crazy about sex but I haven't had it yet'). It added to the excitement of the evening. He wasn't here to share quickly matched intuitions with an Oxford friend. He loved the hard self-confidence of his date; and at the same time, in his silent, superior way, he thought he heard how each little brag was the outward denial of an inner doubt.

With the third drink Nick grew warm and half-aroused and he looked undisguisedly at Leo's lips and neck and imagined unbuttoning the shiny blue short-sleeved shirt that cut so tightly under his arms. Leo hooded his eyes for a second, a signal, secret and ironic, and Nick wondered if it meant he could see he was drunk. He wasn't sure if he should somehow signal back – he grinned and took another quick sip. He had the feeling that Leo had drunk Coke since he was a child, and that it was one of the nearly unnoticed facts of life to him, beyond choice or criticism. Whereas in his family it was one of a thousand things that were frowned on – there had never been a can or bottle of it in the house. Leo couldn't possibly have imagined it, but the glass of Coke in Nick's hand was a secret sign of submission, and afterwards the biting sweetness of the drink, like flavouring in a medicine, seemed fused with the other experiments of the night in a complex impression of darkness and freedom. Leo yawned and Nick glanced into his mouth, its bright white teeth uncorrupted by all the saccharine and implying, Nick humbly imagined, an almost racial disdain for his own stoppings and slants. He put his hand on Leo's forearm for a moment, and then wished he hadn't – it made Leo look at his watch.

'Time's getting on,' he said. 'I can't be late getting back.'

Nick looked down and mumbled, 'Do you have to get back?' He tried to smile but he knew his face was stiff with sudden anxiety. He moved his wet glass in circles on the rough-sawn table top. When he glanced up again he found Leo was gazing at him sceptically, one eyebrow arched.

'I meant back to your place, of course,' he said.

Nick grinned and reddened at the beautiful reversal, like a teased child abruptly reprieved, rewarded. But then he had to say, 'I don't think we can . . .'

Leo looked at him levelly. 'Not enough room?'

Nick winced and waited – the truth was he didn't dare, he just couldn't do that to Rachel and Gerald, it was vulgar and unsafe, the consequences unspooled ahead of him, their happy routines of chortling agreement would wither for ever. 'I don't think we can. I don't mind going up to your place.'

Leo shrugged. 'It's not practical,' he said.

'I can jump on the bus,' said Nick, who had studied the London *A–Z* in absorbed conjecture about Leo's street, neighbourhood, historic churches, and access to public transport.

'Nah—' Leo looked away with a reluctant smile and Nick saw that he was embarrassed. 'My old lady's at home.' This first hint of shyness and shame, and the irony that tried to cover it, cockneyfied and West Indian too, made Nick want to jump on him and kiss him. 'She's dead religious,' Leo said, with a short defeated chuckle.

'I know what you mean,' said Nick. So there they were, two men on a summer night, with nowhere to call their own. There was a kind of romance to that. 'I've got an idea,' he said tentatively. 'If you don't mind, um, being outside.'

'I don't care,' said Leo, and looked lazily over his shoulder. 'I'm not dropping my pants in the street.'

'No, no . . .'

'I'm not that sort of slut.'

Nick laughed anxiously. He wasn't sure what people meant when they said they'd had sex 'in the street' – even 'on Oxford Street', he'd once heard. In six months' time perhaps he would know, he'd have sorted out the facts from the figures of speech. He watched Leo twist and lift a knee to clamber free of the bench – he looked keen to get on with it, and he acted of course as if Nick knew the procedure. Nick followed him with a baked smile and a teeming inward sense of occasion. He was consenting and powerless in the thrust of the event, the rich foregone conclusion of the half-hour that opened ahead of them: it made his heart race with its daring and originality, though it also seemed, as Leo squatted to unlock his bike, something everyday and inevitable. He ought to tell Leo it was his first time; then he thought it might bore him or put him off. He gazed down at his strictly shaved nape, the back of a stranger's head, which any minute now he would be allowed to touch. The label of Leo's skimpy blue shirt was turned up at the collar and showed the temp's signature of Miss Selfridge. It was a little secret given away, a vanity exposed – Nick was light-headed, it was so funny and touching and sexy. He saw the long muscles of his back shifting in its sleek grip, and then, as Leo hunkered on his heels and his loose jeans stood away from his waist, the street lamp shining in on the brown divide of his buttocks and the taut low line of his briefs.

He unlocked the gate and let Leo go in ahead of him. 'Cycling isn't permitted in the gardens, but I dare say you can walk your bike.'

Leo hadn't learnt his mock-pompous tone yet. 'I dare say bumshoving isn't permitted either,' he said. The gate closed behind them, an oiled click, and they were together in the near-darkness of the shrubbery. Nick wanted to hold Leo and kiss him at once; but he wasn't quite certain. Bumshoving was unambiguous, and encouraging, but not romantic exactly . . . They strolled cautiously forward, leaning against each other for a step or two as they steered for the path. There was the slightest chill in the air now, but Nick shivered wildly in a spasm of excitement. His fingers felt oddly stiff, as though he was wearing very tight gloves. Even in the deep shadow he wanted to conceal his weird smirk of apprehension. He did so hope it would be him who got to do the shoving, but didn't know how you arranged that, perhaps it all just became clear. Perhaps they both had to have a go. He led Leo through on to a wide inner lawn, the bike bouncing out beside them, controlled only by a hand on its saddle – it seemed to quiver and explore just ahead of them. To the right rose a semicircle of old planes and a copper beech whose branches plunged to the ground and made a broad bell-tent that was cool and gloomy even at midday.

Away to the left ran the gravel walk, and beyond it the tall out-
line of the terrace, and the long, intermitted rhythm of glowing
windows. As they skirted the lawn Nick counted confusedly,
searching for the Feddens'. He found the first-floor balcony,
the proud brightness of the room beyond the open French
windows.

'Yeah, how far is it?' said Leo.

'Oh, just over here . . .' – Nick giggled because he didn't
know if Leo's grumpiness was real. He went ahead a bit,
anxiously responsible. As his eyes adjusted to the semi-darkness
nowhere seemed private enough – there was more show-
through from the street lights, voices on the pavement were
unnervingly close. And of course on a summer night there were
keyholders still at large, picnickers charmed into long late rem-
iniscence, walkers of white dogs. He stooped under the copper
beech, but the branches were rough and confusing and the mast
crackled underfoot. He backed out again, bashing into Leo and
gripping his waist for a moment to steady himself. 'Sorry . . .'
The feel of his warm hard body under the silky shirt was almost
worryingly beautiful, a promise too lavish to believe in. He
prayed that Leo didn't think he was a fool. The other men in
Leo's life, anonymous partners, answerers of ads, old boyfriends,
old Pete, massed impatiently behind him – as if a match had
flared he saw their predatory eyes and moustaches and hardened
sex-confidence. He led the way quickly to the little compound
of the gardeners' hut.

'All right, this'll do,' said Leo, propping his bike against the
larch-lap screen. For a moment it seemed he was going to chain
it up again, then he stopped himself and left it there with a
regretful laugh. Nick tried the door of the hut even though it
was padlocked. Beside it there was a shadowy area where a flat-
bedded barrow was kept, and a broken bench; there were
laurels, and a yew tree hanging over; the dusty sour smell of the
yew was mixed with the muted sweetness of a huge compost

heap, a season's grass cuttings mounded high in a chicken-wire coop. Leo came up to Nick and hesitated for a second, looking away, trailing his fingers over the warm cuttings. 'You know, these composts get really hot inside,' he said.

'Yes . . .' Nick had known this all his life.

'Too hot to touch – like a hundred degrees.'

'Is that right . . . ?' He reached out like a tired child.

'Anyway,' Leo said, letting Nick's hand slide round his waist, putting his arm, his elbow, round Nick's neck to pull him close against him. 'Anyway . . .' His face slipped sideways across Nick's as he breathed the word, the unguessed softness of his lips touched his cheeks and neck, while Nick sighed violently and ran his hand up and down on Leo's back. He pushed his mouth towards Leo's, and they met, and hurried into a kiss. To Nick it felt simply like a helpless admission of need, and the shocking thing was the proof of Leo's need, in the force and thoroughness with which he worked on him. They pushed apart, Leo faintly smiling, Nick gasping and tormented just by the hope that they would do it again.

They kissed for a minute more – two minutes, Nick wasn't counting, half-hypnotized by the luscious rhythm, the generous softness of Leo's lips and the thick insistence of his tongue. He was gasping from the rush of reciprocity, the fact of being made love to. Nothing at the pub, in their aimless conversation, had even hinted at it. He'd never seen it described in a book. He was achingly ready and completely unprepared. He felt the coaxing caress of Leo's hand on the back of his head, roaming through the curls there, and then lifted his other hand to stroke Leo's head, so beautifully alien in its hard stubbly angles and the dry dense firmness of his hair. He thought he saw the point of kissing but also its limitations – it was an instinct, a means of expression, of mouthing a passion but not of satisfying it. So his right hand, that was lightly clutching Leo's waist, set off, still doubting its freedom, to dawdle over his plump buttocks and then squeeze them through the soft old denim. The prodding of Leo's angled erection against the top of Nick's thigh seemed to tell him more and more clearly to do what he wanted, and get his hand inside his waistband and inside the stretched little briefs. His middle finger pushed into the deep divide, as smooth as a boy's, his fingertip even pressed a little way into the dry pucker so that Leo let out a happy grunt. 'You're a bad boy,' he said.

He moved away from Nick, who clung to him, then let him go with a sulky laugh. 'I'm coming back,' Leo said, and edged off past the shed. Nick stood for a little while, holding himself and sighing, alone again, aware of the unending soft roar of London and a night breeze hardly dipping the dark leaves of the laurel. What was Leo doing? He was getting something from the slim side pannier of his bike. He was amazing with his habits, he was fabulous, but then Nick's skin prickled for a moment at the thought of himself out here in the dark with a stranger, the risk of it, silly little fool, anything could happen. Leo felt his way back, shadow among shadows. 'I think we might be needing this,' he said, so that the rush of risk flowed beautifully into the mood of adventure.

Next day Nick wandered for lost half-hours through what he'd done, taking the tube of gel, that was folded back neatly, three-quarters empty, and peering at it in the gloom with relief and embarrassment; turning Leo round in his arms and unbuttoning his jeans as if they were his own, and prising his broad blunt hard-on from his pants as he eased them down, and pushing him forward to hold on to the bench as he knelt behind him and paid the kind of homage with his tongue and lips that he'd dreamed of paying for years to a whole night-catalogue of other men. He loved the scandalous idea of what he was doing more perhaps than the actual sensations and the dull very private smell. He twisted his own pants down to his knees, and smiled at the liberated bounce of his dick in the cool night air, and kissed his smile into Leo's sphincter. Then when he fucked Leo, which was what he did next, a sensation as interesting as it was delicious, he couldn't help laughing quietly. 'I'm glad you think it's funny,' Leo muttered. 'No, it's not that,' said Nick; but there was something hilarious in the shivers of pleasure that ran up his back and squeezed his neck, and ran down his arms to his fingers – he felt he'd been switched on for the first time, gently gripping Leo's hips, and then reaching round him to help unbutton his shirt and get it off and hold his naked body against him. It was all so easy. He'd worried a lot the night before that there might be some awful knack to it –

'Mind that shirt,' Leo said: 'it's my sister's.'

That made Nick love him much more, he couldn't say why. 'Your arse is so smooth,' he whispered, while his hands stroked hungrily through the short rough hair on his chest and belly.

'Yeah . . . shave it . . .' said Leo, between grunted breaths as Nick got quicker and bolder, 'get arse-knit . . . fucking murder . . . on the bike . . .' Nick kissed the back of his neck. Poor Leo! With his arse-knit and his ingrowing beard he was a martyr to his hair. 'Yeah, like that,' he said, with a sweet tone of revelation. He was leaning forward on one arm now, and masturbating in a pounding hurry. Nick was more and more seriously absorbed, but then just before he came he had a brief vision of himself, as if the trees and bushes had rolled away and all the lights of London shone in on him: little Nick Guest from Barwick, Don and Dot Guest's boy, fucking a stranger in a Notting Hill garden at night. Leo was right, it was so bad, and it was so much the best thing he'd ever done.

Later Nick sat for a minute on a bench by the gravel walk, while Leo took a piss on the lawn. It wasn't clear whether the tall stooping figure in white shirtsleeves had seen this. Leo sat down beside Nick and there was a sense that some last, more formal part of their date was to be enacted. Nick felt abruptly heavy-hearted, and thought perhaps he had been silly to let Leo

see how happy he was – he couldn't stifle his sense of achieve-
ment, and his love-starved mind and body wanted more and
more of Leo. The air seemed to jostle with nothing but the
presence and names of Nick and Leo, which hung in a sad sharp
chemical tang of knowledge among the sleeping laurels and
azaleas. The tall man walked past them, hesitated, and turned.

'You do know it's keyholders only.'

'I'm sorry?'

The mingled light from the backs of the houses revealed a
flushed summer-holiday face, soft and weak-chinned, perched
at an altitude under thin grey hair. 'Only this is a private
garden.'

'Oh, yes – we're keyholders,' the phrase subsuming Leo, who
made a little grunt, not of lust this time but of indignant
confirmation. He set his hands on his knees in a proprietary
attitude, his knees wide apart, sexy and insolent too.

'Ah, fine . . .' The man gave a squinting half-smile. 'I didn't
think I'd seen you before.' He avoided looking at Leo, who was
obviously the cause of this edgy exchange – and that for Nick
was another of the commonplace revelations of the evening, of
being out with a black man.

'I'm often here, actually,' Nick said. He gestured away behind
him towards the Feddens' garden gate. 'I live at number 48.'

'Fine . . . fine . . .' – the man walked on a couple of steps,
then looked back, doubtful but eager. 'But then you must mean
at the Feddens' . . .'

Nick said quietly, 'Yes, that's right.'

The news affected the man visibly – in the softly blotted
glare, which reminded Nick for a moment of plays put on in
college gardens, he seemed to melt into excited intimacy.
'Goodness . . . you're living there. Well, isn't it all splendid! We
couldn't be more delighted. I'm Geoffrey Titchfield, by the way,
number 52 – though we only have the garden flat, unlike . . .
unlike some!'

Nick nodded, and smiled noncommittally. 'I'm Nick Guest.' Some solidarity with Leo kept him from standing up, shaking hands. Of course it was Geoffrey's voice he had heard from the balcony on the night he had put Leo off, and Geoffrey's guests whose regular tireless laughter had heightened his loneliness, and now here he was in person and Nick felt he'd got one past him, he'd fucked Leo in the keyholders' garden, it was a secret victory.

'Aah . . . aah . . .' went Geoffrey. 'It's *such* good news. We're on the local association, and we couldn't be more thrilled. *Good old Gerald.*'

'I'm really just a friend of Toby's,' Nick said.

'We were saying only the other night, Gerald Fedden will be in the Cabinet by Christmas. He knows me, by the way, you must give him all the very best from both of us, from Geoffrey and Trudi.' Nick seemed to shrug in acquiescence. 'He's just the sort of Tory we need. A splendid neighbour, I should say at once, and I fancy a splendid parliamentarian.' This last word was played out with a proud, fond rise and fall and almost whimsical rubato in its full seven syllables.

'He's certainly a very nice man,' Nick said, and added briskly, to finish the conversation, 'I'm really more a friend of Toby and Catherine.'

After Geoffrey had wandered off Leo stood up and took command of his bike. Nick didn't know what to say without making matters worse, and they walked along the path together in silence. He avoided looking up at the Feddens', at his own window high up in the roof, but he had a sense of being noticed by the house, and the verdict of 'vulgar and unsafe' seemed to creep out like a mist and tarnish the triumph of the evening.

'Well,' said Leo under his breath, 'two sorts of arse-licking in ten minutes' – so that Nick laughed and hit him on the arm and immediately felt better. 'Look, I'll see you, my friend,' Leo said, as Nick opened the gate. They came out a bit shiftily on to the street, and Nick couldn't tell if the sentence really meant its opposite. So he was clear about it.

'I want to see you,' he said, and the five light words seemed to open and deepen the night, with the prickling of his eyes, the starred lights of the cars rushing past them and down the long hill northwards, towards other boroughs, and neighbourhoods known only from their mild skyward glare.

Leo stooped to fit on his lamps, front and back. Then he leant the bike against the fence. 'Come here,' he said, in that part-time cockney voice that shielded little admissions and surrenders. 'Give us a hug.'

He stepped up to him and held him tight, but with none of the certainty of minutes before, beside the compost heap. He pressed his forehead against Leo's, who was so much the right size for him, such a good match, and gave him a quick firm kiss with pursed lips – there was a jeer and a horn-blast from a passing car. 'Wankers,' murmured Leo, though to Nick it felt like a shout of congratulations.

Leo sat on the bike, one foot straight down like a dancer's to the pavement, the other in the raised stirrup. A kind of envy that Nick had felt all evening for the bike and its untouchable place in Leo's heart fused with a new resentment of it and of the ease with which it would take him away. 'Look, I've got a couple more to see, yeah?' At which Nick nodded dumbly. 'But I'm not letting you go.' He settled back on the saddle, the bike wobbled and then he rode round in ratcheting circles, so that Nick was always facing the wrong way. 'Besides,' said Leo, 'you're a damn good fuck.' He winked and smiled and then darted out across the road and down the hill without looking back.

3

Nick's birthday was eight days after Toby's, and for a moment there had been an idea that the party for Toby's twenty-first should be a joint celebration. 'Makes obvious sense,' Gerald had said; and Rachel had called it 'a fascinating idea'. Since the party was to be held at Hawkeswood, which was the country house of Rachel's brother, Lord Kessler, the plan almost frightened Nick with its social grandeur, with what it would confer on him and demand from him. Thereafter, though, it had never been mentioned again. Nick felt he couldn't allude to it himself, and after a while he allowed his mother to make arrangements for his own family party at Barwick a week later: he looked forward to that with queasy resignation.

Toby's party was on the last Sunday in August, when the Notting Hill Carnival would be pounding to its climax, and when many local residents shuttered and locked their houses and left for their second homes with their fingers crossed: since the race riots of two summers earlier the carnival had been a site of heightened hopes and fears. Nick had lain in bed the night before and heard the long-legged beat of reggae from down the hill, mixed in, like the pulse of pleasure, with the sighing of the garden trees. It was his second night without Leo. He lay wide-eyed, dwelling on him in a state beyond mere thought, a kind of dazzled grief, in which everything they'd done together was vivid to him, and the strain of loss was as keen as the thrill of success.

Next morning at eleven they gathered in the hall. Nick,

seeing Gerald was wearing a tie, ran up and put one on too. Rachel wore a white linen dress, and her dark hair, with its candid streaks of grey, had the acknowledged splendour of a new cut and a new shape. She smiled her readiness at them, and Nick felt their fondness and efficiency as a family unit. He and Elena stowed the overnight luggage in the Range Rover, and then Gerald drove them out, past blocked-off streets, through gathering crowds. Everywhere there were groups of policemen, to whom he nodded and raised his hand authoritatively from the wheel. Nick, sitting in the back with Elena, felt foolish and conceited at once. He dreaded seeing Leo, on his bike, and dreaded being seen by Leo. He imagined him cruising the carnival, and yearned to belong there in the way that Leo did. He saw him dancing happily with strangers in the street, or biding his turn in the dense mutating crowds at the underground urinals. His longing jumped out in a little groan, which became a throat-clearing and an exclamation: 'Oh I say, look at that amazing float.'

In a side street a team of young black men with high yellow wings and tails like birds of paradise were preparing for the parade. 'It's marvellous what they do,' said Rachel.

'Not very nice music,' said Elena, with a cheerful shiver. Nick didn't reply – and found himself in fact at one of those unforeseen moments of inner transition, when an old prejudice dissolves into a new desire. The music shocked him with its clear repetitive statement of what he wanted. Then one vast sound system warred happily with the next, so that there were different things he wanted, beautiful jarring futures for him – all this in forty or fifty seconds as the car slipped out and away into the ordinary activity of the weekend streets.

Still, if he couldn't be with Leo it was best to be somewhere quite different. Gerald drove them out along the A40, at a somehow preferentially high speed, as if led by an invisible police escort. Soon, however, they came into massive roadworks, and a long unimpressionable tailback, as you did everywhere these days. Here they were taking out the last old roundabouts and traffic lights and forcing an unimpeded free-way across the scruffy flat semi-country. Nick gazed out politely at the desert of digging and concrete, and beyond it a field where local boys were roaring round and round on dirt-bikes in breakneck contempt for the idea of actually going anywhere. They didn't care about the Carnival, they'd never heard of Hawkeswood, and they'd chosen to spend the day in this field rather than anything else. Beside them perhaps a mile of solid traffic stood stationary on the motorway of the future.

As always, Nick felt a need to make things all right. He said, 'I wonder where we are. Is this Middlesex, I suppose?'

'I suppose it's Middlesex,' Gerald said. He hated to be thwarted and was already impatient.

'Not very nice,' said Elena.

'No . . .' said Nick, hesitantly, humorously, as if considering a defence of it, to pass the time. He knew Elena was anxious about the party, and about her role for the evening. She had asked a couple of questions already about Fales, who was Lionel Kessler's new butler, with whom she was about to find herself pressed into some unspecified relation.

'If Lionel's giving us lunch,' said Gerald, 'we'd better stop somewhere and ring ahead. We'll be late.'

'Oh, Lionel won't mind,' said Rachel, 'we're just taking pot luck.'

'Hmm,' said Gerald. 'One doesn't as a rule find the words Lionel and pot luck used in the same sentence.' The tone was mocking, but suggested a certain anxiety of his own about his brother-in-law, and a sense of obligation. Rachel settled back contentedly.

'Everything will be fine,' she said. And in fact the traffic did then make a move, and an optimistic attitude, which was the only sort Gerald could bear, was cautiously indulged. Nick thought about the old-fashioned name Lionel. Of course it was related to Leo; but Lionel was a little heraldic lion, whereas Leo was a big live beast.

Five minutes later they were at a standstill.

'This fucking traffic,' said Gerald; at which Elena looked a bit flustered.

'As well as everything else,' Nick said, with determined brightness, 'I can't wait to see the house.'

'Well, you're going to have to,' said Gerald.

'Ah, the house,' said Rachel, with a sighing laugh.

Nick said, 'Or perhaps you don't like it. It must be different for you, having grown up there.' He felt he was rather fawning on her.

'I don't know,' Rachel admitted. 'I hardly know if I like it or not.'

'You'd have to say, I think,' said Gerald, 'that it's the contents that make Hawkeswood. The house itself is something of a Victorian monstrosity.'

'Mmm . . .' In Rachel's conversation a murmured 'mmm' or drily drawn-out 'I *know* . . .' could carry a note of surprising scepticism. Nick loved the upper-class economy of her talk, her way of saying nothing except by hinted shades of agreement and disagreement; he longed to master it himself. It was so different from the bounding effort of Gerald's conversation that he sometimes wondered if Gerald himself understood her. He said,

'I think I'll like the house as well as the contents.'

Rachel looked grateful, but remained vague about the whole thing, and Nick felt slightly snubbed. Perhaps it was impossible to describe a place one had known all one's life. She didn't disparage Nick's interest, but she showed she couldn't quite be expected to be interested herself. It had been her fortune not to describe but to enjoy. She said, 'You know of course there's modern art, as well as the Rembrandts,' with a brief smile at having retrieved a notable detail.

Hawkeswood had been built in the 1880s for the first Baron Kessler. It stood on an artificially flattened hilltop among the Buckinghamshire beech woods, which had since grown up to hide all but its topmost spirelets from outside view. The approach, after trailing through the long linked villages, entering past a lodge and a cattle grid and climbing the half-mile of drive among grazing deer, was a complex climax for Nick; as the flashing windows of the house came into view he found himself smiling widely while his eyes darted critically, admiringly – he didn't know what – over the steep slate roofs and stone walls the colour of French mustard. He had read the high-minded but humorous entry in Pevsner, which described a seventeenth-century château re-imagined in terms of luxurious modernity, with plate-glass windows, under-floor central heating, numerous bathrooms, and running hot water; but it had left him unprepared for the sheer staring presence of the place. Gerald pulled up in front of the *porte cochère* and they got out and went in, Nick coming last and looking at everything, while Fales, a real butler in striped morning trousers, materialized to meet them. There they were, already, in the central hall, the great feature of the house, two storeys high, with an arcaded gallery on the upper level, and a giant chimneypiece made from bits of a baroque tomb. Nick felt he'd stepped into the strange and seductive fusion of an art museum and a luxury hotel.

Pot luck turned out to be an exquisite light lunch served at a round table in a room lined with rococo *boiseries* that had been removed wholesale from some grand Parisian townhouse, and painted pale blue. On the ceiling, in a flowered ellipse, two naked females held a wreath of roses. Nick saw at once that the landscape over the fireplace was a Cézanne. It gave him a hilarious sense of his own social displacement. It was one of those moments that only the rich could create, and which came for Nick all wrapped up in its own description, so that he was already recounting it to some impressionable other person – a person, that is, as impressionable as himself. He didn't know whether he should refer to it, but Lord Kessler said as he sat down, 'You see I've moved that Cézanne.'

Rachel peered at it briefly and said, 'Oh yes.' Her whole manner was comfortable, almost sleepy; she made a charming shrug of welcome, of dissolved formality, gesturing Nick to his place. Gerald looked at the painting more critically, with a sharp way he had of scanning any document which might come in useful later on.

Nick thought he could say, 'It's very beautiful.' And Lord Kessler said, 'Yes, isn't it a nice one.'

Kessler was perhaps sixty, shorter and stouter than Rachel, bald, with an alert, not quite symmetrical face. He had on a dark grey three-piece suit which made no concession to fashion or even to the season; he looked warm in it, but seemed to say that this was simply what one wore. He ate his salmon and drank his rather sweet hock with an indefinable air of relished routine, an admission of lifelong lunching in boardrooms and country houses and festival restaurants all over Europe. He said, 'So Tobias and Catherine are coming down when?'

'I wouldn't want to put too precise a time on it,' said Gerald. 'Toby is driving down with a girlfriend, Sophie Tipper, who's a daughter of *Maurice* Tipper, incidentally, and a very promising young actress.' He looked to Rachel and she said,

'No, she's awfully promising . . .' – the remark hesitating towards something she seemed to see in the middle distance but which, as so often, she left amiably unexpressed. Nick sometimes felt that being people's children was the only claim that some of his friends had on the attention of their preoccupied elders. He observed Lord Kessler's snuffle and murmur at the name of Maurice Tipper, the incalculable ironies of different kinds of rich people about each other. The Sophie Tipper thing had been dragging on pointlessly since the second year at

Oxford, as if Toby were pliably fulfilling expectations by dating the daughter of a tycoon.

'As for Catherine,' Gerald went on, 'she's being brought down by a so-called boyfriend whose name escapes me and whom I'm bound to say I've never met.' He smiled broadly at this. 'But I expect a late arrival and burning rubber. Actually Nick probably knows more on this front than we do.'

Nick knew almost nothing. He said, 'Russell, you mean? Yes, he's terribly nice. He's a very up-and-coming photographer' – in a successful imitation of their manner and point of view. Russell had only been announced as a boyfriend the day before, in a helpless reaction, Nick felt, to his own success with Leo, which of course he'd had the pleasure of describing to Catherine, entirely truthfully. He hadn't in fact met Russell, but he thought he'd better say again, 'He's awfully nice.'

Lord Kessler said, 'Well, there are umpteen bedrooms ready here, and Fales has made bookings at the Fox and Hounds and the Horse and Groom, both perfectly decent, I'm told. As to the precise arrangements, I avert my eyes.' Kessler had never married, but there was nothing perceptibly homosexual about him. Towards any young people in his social orbit he maintained a strategy of enlightened avoidance. 'And we're not getting the PM,' he added.

'We're not getting the PM,' Gerald said, as if for a while it had really been likely.

'A relief, I must say.'

'It is rather a relief,' said Rachel.

Gerald murmured in humorous protest, and retorted that various ministers, including the Home Secretary, very much were still expected.

'Them we can handle,' Lord Kessler said, and shook the little bell to call in the servant.

*

After lunch they strolled through several large rooms that had the residual hush, the rich refined dry smell of a country house on a hot summer day. The sensations were familiar to Nick from visits he made with his father to wind the clocks in several of the great houses round Barwick – they went back to childhood, though in those much older and remoter houses the smells were generally mixed up with dogs and damp. Here there was a High Victorian wealth of everything, pictures, tapestries, ceramics, furniture – it made Kensington Park Gardens look rather bare. The furniture was mostly French, and of astonishing quality. Nick straggled behind to gaze at it and found his heart beating with knowledge and suspicion. He said, 'That Louis Quinze escritoire . . . is an amazing thing, sir, surely?' His father had taught him to address all lords as sir – bumping into one had been a constant thrilling hazard on their clock-winding visits, and now he took pleasure in the tone of smooth submission.

Lord Kessler looked round, and came back to him. 'Ah yes,' he said, with a smile. 'You couldn't be more right. In fact it was made for Mme de Pompadour.'

'How amazing!' They stood and admired the bulbous, oddly diminutive desk – kingwood, was it? – with fronds of ormolu. Lord Kessler pulled open a drawer, which rattled with little china boxes stowed away inside it; then pushed it shut. 'You know about furniture,' he said.

'A bit,' Nick said. 'My father's in the antiques business.'

'Yes, that's right, jolly good,' said Gerald, as if he'd confessed to being the son of a dustman. 'He's one of my constituents, so I should know.'

'Well, you must look around everywhere,' Lord Kessler said. 'Look at anything and everything.'

'You really should,' said Gerald. 'You know, the house is never open to the public, Nick.'

Lord Kessler himself took him off into the library, where the books were apparently less important than their bindings, which were as important as could be. The heavy gilding of the spines, seen through the fine gilt grilles of the carved and gilded bookcases, created a mood of minatory opulence. They seemed to be books in some quite different sense from those that Nick used and handled every day. Lord Kessler opened a cage and took down a large volume: *Fables Choisies de La Fontaine*, bound in greeny-brown leather tooled and gilded with a riot of rococo fronds and tendrils. It was an imitation of nature that had triumphed as pure design and pure expense. They stood side by side to admire it, Nick noticing the pleasant smell of Lord Kessler's clean suit and discreet cologne. He wasn't allowed to hold the book himself, and was given only a glimpse of the equally fantastic plates, peopled with elegant birds and animals. Lord Kessler showed the book in a quick dry way that was not in itself dismissive but allowed for Nick's ignorance and perhaps merely polite interest. In fact Nick loved the book, but didn't want to bore his host by asking for a longer look. It wasn't clear if it was the jewel of the collection or had been chosen at random.

'It's all rather . . .' Lord Kessler said.

After a moment, Nick said, 'I *know* . . .'

After that they browsed for a minute or two in a semi-detached fashion. Nick found a set of Trollope which had a relatively modest and approachable look among the rest, and took down *The Way We Live Now*, with an armorial bookplate, the pages uncut. 'What have you found there?' said Lord Kessler, in a genially possessive tone. 'Ah, you're a Trollope man, are you.'

'I'm not sure I am, really,' said Nick. 'I always think he wrote too fast. What was it Henry James said, about Trollope and his "great heavy shovelfuls of testimony to constituted English matters"?'

Lord Kessler paid a moment's wry respect to this bit of showing-off, but said, 'Oh, Trollope's good. He's very good on money.'

'Oh . . . yes . . .' said Nick, feeling doubly disqualified by his complete ignorance of money and by the aesthetic prejudice which had stopped him from ever reading Trollope. 'To be honest, there's a lot of him I haven't yet read.'

'You must know that one, though,' said Lord Kessler.

'No, this one is pretty good,' Nick said, gazing at the spine with an air of judicious concession. Sometimes his memory of books he pretended to have read became almost as vivid as that of books he had read and half-forgotten, by some fertile process of auto-suggestion. He pressed the volume back into place and closed the gilded cage. He had a sense, which was perhaps only his own self-consciousness, of some formal bit of business, new to him but deeply familiar to his host, being carried out in a sociable disguise.

'You were at school with Tobias?'

'Oh . . . no, sir.' Nick found he'd decided not to mention Barwick Grammar. 'We were at Oxford together, both at Worcester College . . . Though I read English and Toby of course read PPE.'

'Quite . . .' said Lord Kessler, who perhaps hadn't been sure of this fact. 'You were contemporaries.'

'Yes, we were, exactly,' said Nick, and the word seemed to throw a historic light across the mere three years since he had first seen Toby in the porter's lodge and felt a sudden obliviousness of everything else.

'And you took a First?'

Nick loved the murmured challenging confidence of the question because he could answer 'Yes'. If it had been no, if he'd got a Second like Toby, he felt everything would have been different, and a lie would have been very ill-advised.

'And how do you rate my nephew's chances?' said Lord Kessler with a smile, though it wasn't clear to Nick what contest, what eventuality he was alluding to.

'I think he'll do very well,' he said, smiling back, and feeling he had struck a very subtle register, of loyal affirmation hedged with allowable irony.

Lord Kessler weighed this for a moment. 'And for you, what now?'

'I'm starting at UCL next month; doing graduate work in English.'

'Ah . . . yes . . .' Lord Kessler's faint smile and tucked-in chin suggested an easily mastered disappointment. 'And what is your chosen field?'

'Mm. I want to have a look at *style*,' Nick said. This flashing emphasis on something surely ubiquitous had impressed the admissions board, though Lord Kessler appeared uncertain. A man who owned Mme de Pompadour's escritoire could hardly be indifferent to style, Nick felt; but his reply seemed to have in mind some old wisdom about style and substance.

'Style *tout court*?'

'Well, style at the turn of the century – Conrad, and Meredith, and Henry James, of course.' It all sounded perfectly pointless, or at least a way of wasting two years, and Nick blushed because he really was interested in it and didn't yet know – not having done the research – what he was going to prove.

'Ah,' said Lord Kessler intelligently: 'style as an obstacle.'

Nick smiled. 'Exactly . . . Or perhaps style that hides things and reveals things at the same time.' For some reason this seemed rather near the knuckle, as though he were suggesting Lord Kessler had a secret. 'James is a great interest of mine, I must say.'

'Yes, you're a James man, I see now.'

'Oh, absolutely!' – and Nick grinned with pleasure and defiance, it was a kind of coming out, which revealed belatedly why he wasn't and never would be married to Trollope.

'Henry James stayed here, of course. I'm afraid he found us rather vulgar,' Lord Kessler said, as if it had been only last week.

'How fascinating!' said Nick.

'You *might* be rather fascinated by the old albums. Let me

see.' Lord Kessler went to one of the cupboards beneath the bookcases, turned a scratchy-sounding key and bent down to take out a pair of large leather-bound albums, which he carried over to a central table. Again the inspection was hurried and tantalizing. He stopped now and then, as the heavy pages fell, to display a Victorian photograph of the gardens, with their wide bald views over newly planted woods, or of the interiors, almost comically crowded with chairs and tables, vases on stands, paintings on easels, and everywhere, in every vista, the arching, drooping leaves of potted palms. Now the house seemed settled and seasoned, a century old, with its own historic light and odour, but then it was ostentatiously new. In the second album there were group photographs, posed on the steps of the terrace, and annotated in a tiny florid script: Nick wanted days to read them, countesses, baronets, American duchesses, Balfours and Sassoons, Goldsmids and Stuarts, numerous Kesslers. The gravel was bizarrely covered with fur rugs for the group that centred on Edward VII in a tweed cape and Homburg hat. And then, May 1903, a gathering of twenty or so, second row, Lady Fairlie, The Hon. Simeon Kessler, Mr Henry James, Mrs Langtry, The Earl of Hexham . . . a cheerful informal picture. The Master, with his thumb in his striped waistcoat, eyes shaded by a traveller's widebrimmed hat, looked rather crafty.

'So what do you think of the house?' said Catherine, coming across the lawn.

'Well . . . obviously, it's amazing . . .' He was tingling to the point of fatigue with the afternoon's impressions, but was cautious as to what to say to her.

'Yeah, it's fucking amazing, isn't it!' she agreed, with a bright, brainless laugh. She didn't normally talk like this, and Nick supposed it was part of the persona she was showing to Russell. Russell wasn't actually present (he was busy with his camera somewhere) but it would have taken an unnecessary effort to get out of role. Other elements of the performance were a strange dragging walk and a stunned, vaguely cunning, smile. Nick assumed these were meant to convey sexual satiation.

'How was your journey?'

'Oh, fine – he drives *so* dangerously.'

'Oh . . . We were held up for ages by the roadworks. Your dad got in quite a state about it.'

Catherine gave him a pitying glance. 'He obviously went the wrong way,' she said.

They wandered on among the formal gardens, where rose scents were mixed with the cat's-piss smell of low box hedges, and the round ponds reflected a summer sky now faintly scrimmed with high white cloud. 'God, let's sit down,' said Catherine, as though they'd been walking for hours. They went to a stone bench supervised by two naked minor deities. Marvellous the great rallies of the undressed that rich people summoned to wait on them. Lord Kessler at home must be almost constantly in view of a sprawling nymph or unselfconscious hero. 'Russell should be finished soon, then you can meet him. I wonder if you'll like him.'

'I've already told everyone how charming he is, so I rather feel I've got to.'

'Yeah . . . ?' said Catherine, with a grateful, intrigued smile. She felt for cigarettes in her spangled evening bag. 'He's doing lots of stuff for *The Face* at the moment. He's a brilliant photographer.'

'I told them that too. They all take *The Face*, of course.'

Catherine grunted. 'I suppose Gerald was mouthing off about him.'

'He was just saying he didn't have an opinion about him because he'd never met him.'

'Mm . . . That doesn't normally prevent him. In fact that doesn't sound like him at all.' She clicked her lighter and took in a first deep drag of smoke – the breathing out accompanied by a little toss of the head and a comforted settling back. 'At all, at all, at all,' she went on, meaninglessly assuming an Irish accent.

'Well . . .' Nick wanted everyone to get on, but for once he couldn't be bothered to work at it. He wished he was in a position to speak about Leo as freely as she spoke about Russell – he thought if he did bring the subject up she would say something upsetting and possibly true. She said,

'Did my mother show you round the house?'

'No, actually, your uncle did. I felt rather honoured.'

Catherine paused and blew out smoke admiringly. 'What do you make of him, then?'

'He seems very nice.'

'Mm. What do you think, he's not gay, is he?'

'No, I didn't feel anything like that,' Nick said, a little solemnly. He knew he was supposed to be able to tell; in fact he tended to think people were when they weren't, and so lived with a recurrent sense of disappointment, at them and at his own inadequate sensors. He didn't tell Catherine, but his uncertainty on the house tour had actually been the other way round. Had his own gayness somehow put Lord Kessler off and made him seem unreliable and lightweight in the old boy's eyes? Had Lord Kessler even registered – in his clever, unimpressionable way – that Nick *was* gay? 'He asked me what I was going to do. It was a bit like an interview, except I hadn't applied for a job.'

'Well, you may want a job one day,' said Catherine. 'And then he's bound to remember. He's got a memory like an ostrich.'

'Perhaps . . . I'm not quite sure what he actually does.'

She looked at him as if he must be joking. 'He's got this *bank*, darling . . .'

'Yes, I know—'

'It's a big building chock-a-block full of money.' She waved her cigarette arm around hilariously. 'And he goes in and turns it into even more money.'

Nick let this simple sarcasm pass over him. 'I see, you don't know what he actually does either.'

She stared at him and then gave another neighing laugh. 'Haven't a clue, darling!'

There was a shaking in the trimmed beech hedge away to the right, and then a tall man came hopping out of it sideways, holding up a camera that was strung round his neck. They watched him as he strolled towards them, Catherine leaning back on one hand with a nervously triumphant expression. 'Yeah, hold that,' he said, and took a couple of exposures very quickly, as he was still moving. 'Lovely,' he said.

So Russell was one of her older boyfriends, thirty perhaps, dark, balding, with the casual but combative look of the urban photographer, black T-shirt and baseball boots, twenty-pocketed waistcoat and bandolier of film. He passed in front of them, clicking away, cheerily exploiting this little episode of his arrival, Nick's awkwardness and Catherine's hunger for the spontaneous, the outrageous. She lolled backwards, and touched her upper lip with her tongue. Was it good when her men were older, or not? He could be Protector or Abuser – it was a great deep uncertainty, like the ones in her graphology book. He pulled her up and gave her a hug and then Catherine said, almost reluctantly,

'Oh, this is Nick, by the way.'

'Hello, Nick,' said Russell.

'Hello!'

'Did you meet anyone?' asked Catherine, showing a hint of anxiety.

'Yeah, I've just been talking to the caterers round the back. Apparently Thatcher's not coming.'

'Oh, sorry, Russell,' Catherine said.

Nick said, 'We are getting the Home Secretary, though,' in his mock-pompous tone, which Russell, like Leo, failed to pick up on.

'I wanted Thatcher doing the twist, or pissed.'

'Yeah, Thatcher pogoing!' said Catherine, and laughed rather madly. Russell didn't look especially amused.

'Well, I wouldn't want her at my twenty-first,' he said.

'I don't think Toby really wanted her,' Nick put in apologetically. The touching thing was that Catherine had clearly taken her father's fantasy as the truth, and then used it to lure Russell. The dream of the leader's presence seeped through to an unexpected depth.

'Well, Toby would have been perfectly happy with a party at home,' she said. She wasn't quite sure whose side she was on, when it came to a difference between her father and her brother; Nick saw that she wanted to impress Russell with the right kind of disaffection. 'But then Gerald has to get hold of it and invite the ministers for everything. It's not a party, darling, it's a party conference!'

'Well . . .' Russell chuckled and dangled his long arms and clapped his hands together loosely a few times, as if ready to take them on.

'We've got an enormous house of our own,' Catherine said. 'Not that Uncle Lionel's isn't fantastic, of course.' They turned and frowned at it across the smooth lawn and the formal scrolls of the parterre. The steep slate roofs were topped with bronze finials so tall and fanciful they looked like drops of liquid sliding down a thread. 'I just don't think Uncle Lionel will be all that pleased when Toby's rowing friends start throwing up on the whatsits.'

'The whatnots,' Nick made a friendly correction.

Russell blinked at him. 'He's a fruit, is he, Uncle Lionel?' he said.

'No, no,' Catherine said, faltering for a moment at the expression. 'Nothing like that.'

*

Nick's dinner jacket had belonged to his great-uncle Archie; it was double-breasted and wide on the shoulder in a way that was once again fashionable. It had glazed, pointed lapels which reached almost to the armpits, and shiny silk-covered buttons. As he crossed the drawing room he acknowledged himself with a flattered smile in a mirror. He was wearing a wing collar, and something dandyish in him, some memory of the licence and discipline of being in a play, lifted his mood. The only trouble with the jacket, on a long summer night of eating and bopping, was that when it warmed up it gave off, more and more unignorably, a sharp stale smell, the re-awoken ghost of numberless long-ago dinner-dances in Lincolnshire hotels. Nick had dabbed himself all over with 'Je Promets' in the hope of delaying and complicating the effect.

Drinks were being served on the long terrace, and when he came out through the French windows there were two or three small groups already laughing and glowing. You could tell that everyone had been on holiday, and like the roses and begonias they seemed to take and hold the richly filtered evening light. Gerald was talking to a somehow familiar man and his blonde-helmeted wife; Nick knew from his smiles and guffaws that he was being recklessly agreeable. None of his particular friends was here yet, and Toby was still upstairs with Sophie, interminably getting dressed. He took a flute of champagne from a dark-eyed young waiter, and strolled off into the knee-high maze of the parterre. He wondered what the waiter thought of him, and if he was watching him in his solitary meandering over trimmed grass and pea gravel. He had worked as a waiter himself, two Christmases ago, and stood about with a tray in a similar way at two neighbouring hunt balls. It was not impossible that he would do so again. He felt he might look like a person with no friends, and that the waiter might know that he didn't really belong to this looking-glass world. Could he even tell, any more than Lord Kessler could, that he was gay? He felt there had been a flashing hint, in their moment of contact, of some more luxurious understanding, of a longer gaze, full of humour and curiosity, that they might have shared . . . He thought at the second contact, the refill, he would make it all right. The curlicue of the path brought him round to a view of the house again, but the waiter had moved off, and instead he saw Paul Tompkins ambling towards him.

'My dear!'

At Oxford Tompkins was widely known as Polly, but Nick said, 'Hello, Paul,' because the nickname seemed suddenly too intimate or too critical. 'How are you?' He realized that in the romantic retrospect of his undergraduate life Paul was a figure he had painted out.

'I'm extremely well,' Paul said meaningly. He was large and round in the middle and seemed to taper away, in his tight evening suit, towards narrow feet and a tall, jowly head. He had been a noise, a recurrent clatter of bitchery and ambition, a kind of monster of the Union and the MCR, throughout Nick's years in college. He had come out just below the top in the Civil Service exams, and had recently started in some promising capacity in Whitehall. He looked pop-eyed already from the tussle between pompous discretion and a natural love of scandal. He raised his glass. 'My compliments to wicked old Lionel Kessler. The waiters here are sheer heaven.'

'I know . . .'

'That one with the champagne is from Madeira, which is rather funny.'

'Oh, really . . .'

'Well, better than the other way round. Now, however, he lives in Fulham: really awfully close to me.'

'You mean that one there.'

'Tristão.' Paul gave Nick a look of concentrated mischief. 'Ask me more after our date next week, my dear.'

'Ah.' Nick's face was tight with regret for a second, the pinch of his own incompetence. It was a mystery to him that fat old Polly, who was rutted with acne scars and completely lacking in ordinary kindness, had such a conspicuous success with men. In college he had brought off a number of almost impossible seductions, from kitchen boys to the solemnly hetero Captain of Boats. Nothing that lasted, but startling triumphs of will, opportunism and technique, even so. Nick was slightly frightened of him. He walked on a pace or two, round the plinth of a large urn, and looked across the roses at the assembling guests. A famous TV interviewer was exerting his charm over a group of flattered girls. Nick said, 'It's rather a distinguished crowd.'

'Mmm.' Paul's murmur had a note of scepticism in it as well as a suggestion that here too there were opportunities. He got out, and lit, a cigarette. 'That depends very much on your idea of distinction. But aren't the wives marvellous, since the last election? It's as if any doubts they had the first time round have now been completely discounted. The men did something naughty, and got away with it, and not only did they get away with it but they've been asked to do it again, with a huge majority. That's so much the mood in Whitehall – the economy's in ruins, no one's got a job, and they just don't care, it's bliss. And the wives, you see, all look like . . . her – they've all got the blue bows, and the hair.'

'Well, Rachel hasn't,' said Nick, who rather doubted that Paul could sum up the mood in Whitehall when he'd only been there five minutes.

'No, dear, but Rachel's got a lot more class. Jewish class, but still class. And her husband's not called Norman.'

Nick had some further objections to what Paul was saying, but didn't want to seem humourless. 'No, or Ken,' he said.

Paul inhaled tolerantly and blew the smoke out in a long sibilant jet. 'I must say Gerald is looking quite delicious this evening.'

'Gerald Fedden . . . ?'

'Absolutely . . .'

'You're pulling my leg.'

'Now I've shocked you,' Paul said unapologetically.

'Not at all,' said Nick, to whom life was a series of shocks, more or less well mastered. 'No, I can see he's . . .'

'Of course now you're living in his house you've probably grown accustomed to his sheer splendour.'

Nick laughed and together they watched the MP as he wound up a story (which was all chortling patter with booming emphases) and the blue-dressed women around him rippled and staggered about slightly on the fine gravel. 'I wouldn't deny that he's very charming,' Nick said.

'Aha . . . So who is it at the house, just you and them and the Sleeping Beauty?'

Nick loved hearing Toby described like that, the praise in the mockery. 'I'm afraid the Sleeping Beauty isn't there much any more, you know he's been given his own flat. But there's Catherine, of course.'

'Oh, yes, I love Catherine. I just caught her smoking a joint about a yard long with a very dodgy-looking man. She's quite a girl.'

'She's certainly a very unhappy one,' Nick said, swelling for a moment with his portentous secret knowledge of her.

Paul's eyebrow suggested that this was a wrong note. 'Really? Every time I see her she's got a new man. She really should be happy, she must have everything a girl could want.'

'You sound just like her father, I've heard him say exactly the same thing.'

'Ah, there you are!' said Paul. He grinned and stamped out his half-smoked cigarette on the path. 'There's Toby now.' He nodded towards the door from the drawing room, where Toby was emerging with Sophie on his arm, more like a wedding than a birthday party. 'Christ, the jammy *bitch*!' Paul murmured, in an oddly sincere surrender to the sheer dazzle of the couple.

'I know, I do hate her.'

'Oh, she's marvellous. She's good-looking, she's as thick as a jug – and of course she's a highly promising actress.'

'Exactly.'

Paul smiled at him, as if at a country cousin. 'My dear, don't take it so seriously. Anyway, they're all tarts, these boys, they've all got a price. Get Toby at two in the morning, when he's had a bottle of brandy, and you'll be able to do what you want with him. I promise you.'

This idea was so wildly, almost grimly, exciting to Nick that he could hardly smile. It was clever of old Polly to tamper so intimately with his feelings. Nick said, 'Mm, this is rather a festival of the girlfriend, though, I'm afraid.'

And it was true that as the crowd quickly doubled and trebled on the terrace it took on more and more the air of an efficiently reproductive species. The boys, most of them Nick's Oxford contemporaries, all in their black and white, glanced across at politicians and people on the telly, and caught a glimpse of themselves as high- achieving adults too – they had that canny glint of self-discovery that comes with putting on a disguise. They didn't mingle unnecessarily with the girls. It was almost as if the High Victorian codes of the house, with its smoking room and bachelors' wing, still guided and restrained them. But the girls, in a shimmer of velvet and silk, and brilliantly made up, like smaller children who had raided their mothers' dressing tables, had new power and authority too. As the sunlight lowered it grew more searching and theatrical, and cast intriguing shadows.

Paul said, 'I should warn you, Wani Ouradi's got engaged.'

'Oh, no,' said Nick. It was such a snub, an engagement. 'He might have thought about it a bit longer.' He could picture a happy alternative future for himself and Wani – who was sweet-natured, very rich, and beautiful as a John the Baptist painted for a boy-loving pope. His father owned the Mira supermarket chain, and whenever Nick went into a Mira Mart for a bottle of milk or a bar of chocolate he had a vague erotic sense of slipping the money into Wani's pocket. He said, 'I think he's coming tonight.'

'He is, the old tart, I saw that vulgar motor car of his in the drive.' Tart was Paul's word for anyone who had agreed to have sex with him; though as far as Nick was aware, he had never got anywhere with Wani. Wani, like Toby, remained in the far pure reach of fantasy, which grew all the keener and more inventive to meet the challenge of his unavailability. He felt the loss of him as though he had really stood a chance with him, he'd gone so far with him in his mind, as he lay alone in bed. He saw the great heterosexual express pulling out from the platform precisely on time, and all his friends were on it, in the first-class carriage – in the wagons-lit! He clung to what he had, as it gathered speed: that quarter of an hour with Leo by the compost heap, which was his first sharp taste of coupledom. 'Are you and I the only homos here?' he said.

'I doubt it,' said Paul, who didn't look keen to become Nick's partner for the night on the strength of that chance connection. 'Oh my god, it's the fucking *Home Secretary*. I must wiggle. How do I look?'

'Fantastic,' said Nick.

'Oh, I knew it.' He knuckled his hair, with its oily fringe, like a vain schoolboy. 'Gotta go, girl!' he said, silly but focused, an outrageous new seduction in view. And off he went, eagerly striding and hopping over the little low hedges. Nick saw him reach the group where Gerald was introducing his son to the Home Secretary: it was almost as if there were two guests of honour, each good-humouredly perplexed by the presence of the other. Polly hovered and then pushed in shamelessly; Nick caught his look of unironic excitement as the group closed round him.

*

'So what's he like?' said Russell. 'Her old man. What's he into?'
He glanced at Catherine, across the table, before his eyes drifted
back down the room to Gerald, who was smiling at the blonde
woman beside him but had the fine glaze of preoccupation of
someone about to make a speech. They were in the great hall,
at a dozen tables. It was the end of dinner, and there was a
mood of noisy expectancy.

'Wine,' said Nick, who was drunk and fluent, but still wary
of Russell's encouraging tone. He twirled his glass on the rucked
tablecloth. 'Wine. His wife . . . um . . .'

'Power,' said Catherine sharply.

'Power . . .' – Nick nodded it into the list. 'Wensleydale
cheese he's also very keen on. Oh, and the music of Richard
Strauss – that particularly.'

'Right,' said Russell. 'Yeah, I like a bit of Richard Strauss
myself.'

'Oh, I'd always prefer a bit of Wensleydale cheese,' said Nick.

Russell blinked at him in a way that suggested he didn't
understand him or was about to punch him in the face. But then
he smiled reluctantly. 'So he's not into anything kinky at all.'

'Power,' said Catherine again. 'And making speeches.' As the
glass tinkled and the hubbub quickly died a lot of people heard
her saying, 'He loves making speeches.'

Nick pushed his chair back to get a clear view of Gerald, and
also of Toby, who had coloured up and was looking round with
a tight grin of apprehension. There were ten minutes of oddly
relished ordeal ahead of him, being teased and praised by his
father and cheered by his drunk friends – his contemporaries.
Nick grinned back at him, and wanted to help him, but was
powerless, of course. He was blushing himself with the anxiety
and forced eagerness of awaiting a speech by a friend.

Gerald had donned his rarely seen half-moon spectacles, and
held a small card at arm's length. 'Your Grace, my lords, ladies,
and gentlemen,' he said, offering the old formula with an ironic

negligence which had the clever effect of making you think –
yes, the Duchess, of course, and her son were here, as well as
Lord Kessler and fat young Lord Shepton, a Martyrs' Club pal
of Toby's. 'Distinguished guests, family and friends. I'm very
happy to see you all here tonight, in this truly splendid setting,
and very grateful indeed to Lionel Kessler for giving the
Worcester College First XV the run of his world-famous porcelain collection. Well, as the sign in Selfridge's says, or used to
say, "all breakages must be paid for".' This drew a few titters,
though Nick wasn't sure it struck the right tone. 'We're honoured by the presence of statesmen, and film stars, and I suspect
Tobias is thoroughly flattered that so many members of Her
Majesty's government were able to be here. My witty daughter,
I understand, has said that it's "not so much a party as a party
conference".' Uncertain laughter, through which, with good
timing: 'I only hope I get to play an equally important role
when we meet at Blackpool in October.' The MPs chuckled
amiably at this, though the Home Secretary, who'd taken the
epithet of statesman more gravely than the rest, smiled
inscrutably at the coffee cup in front of him. Russell said 'Good
girl!' quite loudly, and clapped a couple of times.

'Now, as you may have heard,' Gerald went on, with a
delayed quick glance in their direction, 'Toby is twenty-one
today. I had been going to give you Dr Johnson's well-known
lines on "long-expected one-and-twenty", but when I looked
them up again last night I found I didn't know them quite as
well as I thought, or indeed as well as many of you, I'm sure,
do.' Here Gerald looked down at the card in a marvellously
supercilious way. '"Lavish of your grandsire's guineas," says the
Great Cham, "Bid the slaves of thrift farewell . . . When the
bonny blade carouses, Pockets full, and spirits high, What are
acres? What are houses? Only dirt, or wet and dry." So: *far* from
suitable advice to the grandson and nephew of great bankers, or
for any young person coming of age in our splendid property-

owning democracy. And the question of wet versus dry, of course, is one on which indecision is no longer acceptable.'

Through the generous laughter Nick caught Toby's eye again, and held it for two or three long seconds, giving him perhaps a transfusion of reassurance. Toby himself would be too nervous to listen to his father's speech properly, and was laughing in imitation of the others, not at the jokes themselves. It was typical of Gerald not to have realized that Dr Johnson's poem was a ruthless little satire. Nick surveyed the room, and was reminded of a college hall, with Gerald and the more influential guests elected to the high table. Or perhaps of some other institution, such as houses like this had often turned into. Up in the arcade of the gallery one or two servants were listening impassively, waiting only for the next stage of the evening. There was a gigantic electrolier, ten feet high, with upward-curling gilt branches opening into cloudy glass lilies of light. Catherine had refused to sit under it, which was why their whole table had apparently been demoted to this corner of the room. If it did fall, Nick realized, it would crush Wani Ouradi. He began to feel a little anxious about it himself.

Gerald was now giving a facetious review of Toby's life, and again it made Nick think of a marriage, and the best man's speech, which everyone dreaded, and the huge heterosexual probability that a twenty-first would be followed soon enough by a wedding. He could only see the back of Sophie Tipper's head, but he attributed similar thoughts to it, transposed into a bright, successful key. 'As a teenager, then,' Gerald said, 'Tobias a) believed that Enoch Powell was a socialist, b) set fire to a volume of Hobbes, and c) had a large and mysterious overdraft. When it came to Oxford, a degree in Politics, Philosophy and Economics was the irresistible choice.' There was more laughter – and Gerald was leading them along very ably: they were drunkish and amenable, even gullible, since making a speech was a kind of trick. At the same time there was a bond among the young people, who were old enough to know that speeches were allowed, and perhaps even supposed, to be embarrassing, and who were rowdy and superior at once, in the Oxford way. Nick wondered if the women were responding more warmly, if they were picking up, as Polly did, on their host's 'splendour'; perhaps their laughter would seem to him a kind of submission. Nick himself was lazily exploring the margin between his affection for Gerald and a humorous suspicion, long resisted, that there might be something rather awful about him. He wished he could see Lord Kessler's reactions.

'And now, as you know, Tobias has opted,' Gerald said, 'at least for the moment, for a career in journalism. I'm bound to admit this made me anxious at first, but he assures me he has no interest in becoming a parliamentary sketch writer. There's been puzzling talk of the *Guardian*, which we hope will blow over, though for the time being I'm thinking hard before answering any of his questions, and have decided to strenuously deny everything.'

Nick glanced round, in a little shrug of amusement, and saw that Tristão, the waiter from Madeira, was standing in the doorway behind him, following the proceedings with a vacant stare. As a caterers' waiter he must have to listen to an abnormal number of speeches, each of them built around private jokes and allusions. What was he thinking? What was he thinking of all of them? His hands were huge and beautiful, the hands of a virtuoso. His dressy trouser-front curved forwards with telling asymmetry. When he saw that Nick was looking his way he gave him the vaguest smile and inclined his head, as if waiting for a murmured order. Nick thought, he doesn't even realize I like him, he thinks I'm just one of these toffs who never look at waiters for their own sake. He shook his head and turned back, and his disappointment was practised and invisible. He saw that Catherine was stuffing things into her bag and flashing irritable looks at Russell, who mouthed, 'What?' at her, and was getting irritable in his turn. 'So, Toby,' Gerald said, raising his voice and slowing his words, 'we congratulate you, we bless you, we love you: happy birthday! Will you – all – please raise your glasses: to Toby!'

'Toby!' the overlapping burble went up, followed by a sudden release of tension in cheers and whistles and applause – applause for Toby, not for the speaker, the heightened, unreal acclaim of a special occasion, amongst which Nick lifted his champagne glass with tears in his eyes, and kept on sipping from it to hide his emotion. But Catherine had jumped her little gilt chair back from the table and hurried out, past Tristão, who followed her for a second, to see if he could help. Then Nick and Russell stared at each other, but Toby was getting to his feet, and Nick was damned if he was chasing after her this time, he really did love Toby, more than anyone in this high magnificent room, and he was going to be with him as he spoke.

'No,' said Toby, 'I'm afraid Pa got that a bit wrong. I *tried* to get him an interview with the *Guardian*, but they just weren't interested!' This wasn't quite a witticism, but it drew a loud laugh from his friends, and Gerald, who'd assumed a self-congratulating air, was forced to make a quick moue of humility. '"Wait till he does something big," they said.' He turned to his father. 'Of course I told them they wouldn't have to wait long.'

There was something artless in Toby's delivery; he was working in the family tradition of teasing, but he was too relenting and couldn't yet match Gerald's heavy archness. When he had stood up he was strikingly pale, like someone about to faint, but when he relaxed a little the colour suddenly burned in his cheeks, and his grin was a nervous acknowledgement of his blush. He said, 'I'm not going to say much – ' vague groans of disappointment – 'but above all I want to thank my dear sweet generous Uncle Lionel for having us all here tonight. I can't imagine anything more wonderful than this party – and I have a horrible feeling that after this the rest of my life is going to be one long anticlimax.' This brought cheers and applause for Lord Kessler, who was surely used to being thanked, but not to such public declarations of love. Again the family note was strong and sentimental, and a little surprising. Nick was smiling at Toby in an anxious trance of lust and encouragement. It was like watching a beautiful actor in a play, following him and wanting him.

'I'm also really touched,' Toby said, 'that my old friends Josh and Caroline have come all the way from South Africa. Oh, and I understand they're also squeezing in a wedding ceremony while they're here.' There was good-natured applause, though no one really knew who Josh and Caroline were. Nick found himself listening almost abstractly to Toby's voice, hearing its harmless pretensions, which were the opposite of Gerald's. Gerald was a knowing, self-confident speaker, trained at the Oxford Union, polished at innumerable board meetings, and his tone combined candour and insincerity to oddly charming effect. Toby, like many of his friends, spoke in the latest public-school accent, an inefficient blur of class denial. Now he was a bit drunk, and under pressure, and older vowels were showing through as he said that it was 'awfully good of' his parents to have tolerated him. He too seemed not to know what the point of his speech was; he came over like a cross between a bridegroom and the winner of an award, with a list of people to thank. His boyish technique was to deflect attention from himself onto his friends, and in this he was also the opposite of his father. He made various jokes such as 'Sam will need two pairs of trousers' and 'No more crème de menthe for Mary,' which clearly alluded to old disgraces, and began to bore the MPs. Nick sensed a touching nostalgia for the Oxford years, on which a door, an oak perhaps, seemed gently but firmly to have closed. He himself was not referred to; but he took this as a sign of intimacy. His gaze embraced Toby, and from behind his helpless grin and raised applauding hands he saw his dream-self run forwards to hold him and kiss his hot face.

Up in his room Nick slipped out of his jacket, and sniffed at it resignedly: time for a further dowsing in 'Je Promets'. He went into his bathroom, and opened the little turret dormer; he splashed cold water on his cheeks. It was the toasts that had done for him – there was always one glass that tipped him over, unfairly and joltingly, into being drunk. And there were hours of the party still to come. It was a great ritual of fun, a tradition, a convention, which everyone was loving for its lavishness and truth to form. Now there was going to be a move to the dance floor, and all the couples would be allowed to make love to each other with their hips and thighs and sliding hands. Nick gazed in the mirror and saw someone teeteringly alone. The love he had felt for Toby ten minutes before migrated into a sudden hungry imagining of Leo, his transfiguring kisses, his shaving rash, and the wonderful shaved depth between the cheeks of his arse. The exactness of memory, the burning fact of what had happened, blinded him and held him for a while. When he came back, perhaps only seconds later, to the image in the mirror, he saw the flush in his cheeks and his mouth gasping in re-enacted surrender. He re-tied his tie, very perfectly, and ran a hand through his hair. There was a kind of tenderness for himself in the movement of his hand through his curls, as if it had been taught a lesson by Leo. The mirror was a chaste ellipse in a maplewood frame. The washstand was a real Louis Seize commode cut and drilled to hold a basin and a pair of tall hoarse-throated taps. Well, if you owned a Louis Seize commode, if you owned dozens of them, you could be as barbarous with them as you liked; and a commode after all was meant for ease. And after all it was marvellous to be staying in a house like this, a friend of the family, not the son of the man who wound the clocks.

As he trotted down the stairs he saw Wani Ouradi coming

up. Nick sometimes greeted Wani with a friendly grope
between the legs, or a long breathless snog, and he'd once had
him tied up naked in his college room for a whole night; he had
sodomized him tirelessly more often than he could remember.
Wani himself, glancing back to see if his girlfriend, his
intended, was following, had no idea of all this, of course;
indeed, they hardly knew each other.

'Hi, Wani!' said Nick.

'Hi!' said Wani warmly, perhaps not able to remember his
name.

'I believe I have to congratulate you . . .'

'Oh . . . yes . . .' Wani grinned and looked down. 'Thank you
so much.' Nick thought, as he had thought before, in the slow
hours of the seminar room, that a view of the world through
such long eyelashes must be one extraordinarily shadowed and
filtered. They both suddenly decided to shake hands. Wani
glanced back again with a murmur of exasperation so fond and
well mannered that it seemed to include Nick in some harmless
conspiracy. 'You must meet Martine,' he said. A provoking thing
about him was the way his penis always showed, a little jutting
bulge to the left, modest, unconscious, but unignorable, and a
trigger to greedy thoughts in Nick. He checked for it now, in a
woozy half-second. He was rather like a pop star of the 60s, with
the penis and the dark curly hair – though the look was quite at
odds with the bemused courtesy of his manner.

'I hope it will be a long engagement,' Nick heard himself
saying.

'Ah, here she is . . .' – and they looked down together at the
young woman who was climbing the shallow red-carpeted stairs
towards them. She was wearing a pearl-coloured blouse and a
long, rather stiff black skirt, which she held raised a little with
both hands, so that she seemed to curtsey to them on each step.
She created a sober impression, well groomed but not fashion-

able. 'This is Martine,' Wani said. 'This is Nick Guest, we were at Worcester together.'

Nick took Martine's cool hand, smiling at Wani's knowing his name, and feeling himself to be briefly the subject of humorous suspicion as an unknown friend from her fiancé's past. He said, 'I'm pleased to meet you, congratulations.' All this congratulating was giving him a vague masochistic buzz.

'Oh – thank you so much. Yes, Antoine has told you.' She had a French accent, which in turn suggested to Nick the unknown networks of Wani's family and past, Paris perhaps, Beirut . . . the real life of the international rich from which Wani had occasionally descended on Oxford to read an essay on Dryden or translate an Anglo-Saxon riddle. Antoine was his real name, and Wani, his infantile attempt at saying it, his universal nickname.

'You must be very happy.'

Martine smiled but said nothing, and Nick looked at her wide pale face for signs of the triumph he would have felt himself if he had become engaged to Wani.

'We're just going to our room,' Wani said, 'and then we'll be down for the bopping.'

'Well, you will be bopping perhaps,' said Martine, showing already a mind of her own, but with the same patient expression, which registered with Nick, as he went on down the stairs, as decidedly adult. It must be the face of a steady happiness, a calm possession, that he couldn't imagine, or even exactly hope for.

He needed some air, but there was a clatter in the hall as people ran back indoors. Outside, from an obscured night sky, a fine rain had started falling. Nick watched it drifting and gleaming in the upcast light of a large globed lantern. Out in the circle of the drive a couple of chauffeurs were sitting in the front of a Daimler with the map-light on, waiting and chatting. And there was Wani's soft-top Mercedes, with its embarrassing number plate WHO 6. A voice brayed, 'Right! Everyone on the dance floor!' And there was a ragged chorus of agreement.

'Hoorah! Dancing!' said a drunk Sloanish girl, staring into Nick's face as though with an effort she might remember him.

'Where is the ruddy dance floor?' said the braying boy. They had wandered back into the hall, which was being cleared with illusionless efficiency by the staff.

Nick said, 'It's in the smoking room,' excited by knowing this, and by suddenly taking the lead. They all straggled after him, the Sloaney girl laughing wildly and shouting, 'Yah, it's in the smoking room!' and sending him up, as the funny little man who knew the way.

A friend of Toby's had come down from London to do the disco, and red and blue spotlights flashed on and off above the paintings of the first Baron Kessler's numerous racehorses. Most of the group started grooving around at once, a little awkwardly, but with happy, determined expressions. Nick lounged along the wall, as if he might start dancing any moment, then came back, nodding his head to the beat, and walked quickly out of the room. It was that song 'Every Breath You Take' that they'd played over and over last term at Oxford. It made him abruptly sad.

He felt restless and forgotten, peripheral to an event which, he remembered, had once been thought of as his party too. His loneliness bewildered him for a minute, in the bleak perspective of the bachelors' corridor: a sense close to panic that he didn't belong in this house with these people. Some of the guests had gone into the library and as he approached the open door he took in the scant conversational texture, over which one or two voices held forth as if by right. Gerald said words Nick couldn't catch the meaning of, and through the general laughter another voice, which he half-recognized, put in a quick correcting 'Not if I know Margaret!' Nick stood at the doorway of the lamplit room and felt for a second like a drunken student, which he was, and also, more shadowy and inconsolable, a sleepless child peering in at an adult world of bare shoulders, flushed faces, and cigar smoke. Rachel caught his eye, and smiled, and he went in – Gerald, standing at the empty fireplace in the swaggering stance of someone warming himself, called out, 'Ah, Nick!' but there were too many people for introductions, a large loose circle who turned momentarily to inspect him and turned back as if they'd failed to see anything at all.

Rachel was sitting on a small sofa, apart from the others, with a wrinkled old lady dressed in black, who made Rachel in her turn seem a beautiful, rather mischievous young woman. She said, 'Judy, have you met Nick Guest, Toby's great friend? This is Lady Partridge – Gerald's mother.'

'Oh no!' said Nick. 'I'm delighted to meet you.'

'How do you do,' said the old lady, with a dry jovial look. *Toby's great friend* – there was a phrase to savour, to analyse for its generosity, its innocence, its calculation.

Rachel shifted slightly, but there was really no space for him on the sofa. In her great spread stiffish dress of lavender silk she was like a Sargent portrait of eighty years earlier, of the time when Henry James had come to stay. Nick stood before them and smiled.

'You do smell nice,' Rachel said, almost flirtingly, as a mother sometimes speaks to a child who is dressed up.

'I can't bear the smell of cigars, can you?' said Lady Partridge.

'Lionel hates it too,' murmured Rachel. As did Nick, to whom the dry lavatorial stench of cigars signified the inexplicable confidence of other men's tastes and habits, and their readiness to impose them on their fellows. But since Gerald himself was smoking one, frowning and screwing up his left eye, he said nothing.

'I can't think where he picked up the habit,' Lady Partridge said; and Rachel sighed and shook her head in humorous acknowledgement of their shared disappointments as wife and mother. 'Do Tobias and Catherine smoke?'

'No, thank heavens, they've never taken to it,' Rachel said. And again Nick said nothing. What always held him was the family's romance of itself, with its little asperities and collusions that were so much more charming and droll than those in his own family, and which now took on a further dimension in the person of Gerald's mother. Her manner was drawling but vigilant, her face thickly powdered, lips a bold red. There was something autocratic in her that made Nick want to please her. She sounded grander than Gerald by the same factor that Gerald sounded posher than Toby.

'Perhaps we could have some air,' she said, barely looking at Nick. And he went to the window behind them and pushed up the sash and let in the cool damp smell of the grounds.

'There!' he said, feeling they were now friends.

'Are you staying in the house?' Lady Partridge said.

'Yes, I've got a tiny little room on the top floor.'

'I didn't know there were any tiny rooms at Hawkeswood. But then I don't suppose I've ever been on the top floor.' Nick half admired the way she had taken his modesty and dug it deeper for him, and almost found a slur against herself in it.

'I suppose it depends on your standard of tininess,' he said, with a determined flattering smile. The faint paranoia that attaches to drunkenness had set in, and he wasn't certain if he was being rude or charming. He thought perhaps what he'd said was the opposite of what he meant. A waiter came up with a tray and offered him a brandy, and he watched with marvelling passivity as the liquor was poured. 'Oh that's fine . . . that's fine . . . !' He was a nice, conspiratorial sort of waiter, but he wasn't Tristão, who had crossed a special threshold in Nick's mind and was now the object of a crush, vivid in his absence. He wondered if he could have a crush on this waiter too – it only needed a couple of sightings, the current mood of frustration, and a single half-conscious decision, and then the boy's shape would be stamped on his mind and make his pulse race whenever he appeared.

Rachel said, 'Nick's also staying with us in London, where he really does have a tiny room in the roof.'

'I think you said you had someone in,' said Lady Partridge, again without looking at Nick. It was as if she had scented his fantasy of belonging, of secret fraternity with her beautiful grandson, and set to eradicate it with a quick territorial instinct. 'Toby's certainly enormously popular,' she said. 'He's so handsome, don't you think?'

'Yes, I do,' said Nick lightly, and blushed and looked away as if to find him.

'You'd never think he was Catherine's brother. He had all the luck.'

'If looks *are* luck—' Nick was half-saying.

'But do tell me, who is that little person in glasses dancing with the Home Secretary?'

'Mm, I've seen him before,' said Nick, and laughed out loud.

'It's the Mordant Analyst,' said Rachel.

'Morton Danvers,' Lady Partridge noted it.

Rachel raised her voice. 'The children call him the Mordant Analyst. Peter Crowther – he's a journalist.'

'Seen his things in the *Mail*,' Lady Partridge said.

'Oh, of course . . .' said Nick. And it was true he did seem to be dancing with the Home Secretary, wooing him, capering in front of him, bending to him with new questions and springing back with startled enlightenment at the answers – a procedure which the Home Secretary, who was heavy-footed and had no neck, couldn't help but replicate in a clumsy but courteous way.

'I don't think I'd be quite so excited,' said Lady Partridge. 'He talked a lot of rot at dinner on . . . the *coloured* question. I wasn't next to him, but I kept hearing it. *Racism*, you know' – as if the very word were as disagreeable as the thing it connoted was generally held to be.

'A lot of rot certainly is talked on that subject,' Nick said, with generous ambiguity. The old lady looked at him ponderingly.

They turned and watched Gerald come forward to rescue the Home Secretary, with a solicitous smile on his lips and a flicker of jealousy in his eyes. He led him away, stooping confidentially over him, almost embracing him, but looking quickly round like someone who has organized a surprise: and there was a flash and a whirr and another flash.

'Ah! The *Tatler*,' exclaimed Lady Partridge, 'at long last.' She patted her hair and assumed an expression of . . . coquetry . . . command . . . welcome . . . ancient wisdom . . . It was hard to say for sure what effect she was after.

Catherine was hurrying Nick and Pat Grayson along the bachelors' corridor towards the thump of the dance music.

'Are you all right, darling?' Nick said.

'Sorry, darling. It was that ghastly speech – one just couldn't take any more!' She was lively, but her reactions were slow and playful, and he decided she must be stoned.

'I suppose it was a bit self-centred.'

She smiled, with a condescension worthy of her grandmother. 'It would have been a marvellous speech for his own birthday, wouldn't it. Poor Fedden!'

Pat, who must have been the person described in the speech as a film star, said, 'Ooh, I didn't think it was all that bad, considering'; though considering what, he didn't specify. Nick had seen him as the smooth eponymous rogue in *Sedley* on TV, and was struck by how much smaller, older and camper he was in real life. *Sedley* was his mother's favourite series, though it wasn't clear if she knew that Pat was a whatnot. 'Ooh, I don't know about this, love . . .' he said as they came into the room. But Catherine pulled him into the crowd and he started rather nimbly circling round her, flicking his fingers and frowning sexily at her. She seemed to love everything that was uncool about this, but to Nick Pat was an unwelcome future, a famous man who was a fool, a silly old queen. He slipped away across the room, and found he was being shouted and smiled at by people and roughly hugged as if he was very popular. The brandy was having its way. But for a minute he was ashamed of snubbing Pat Grayson, and pretending to be part of this hetero mob. He felt pretty good, and grinned at Tim Carswell, who came across the floor and seized him and whirled him round till they were both stumbling and Tim's damp breath was burning his cheek, and Tim shouted 'Whoa!' and slowly pulled away, still slamming from side to side and then backing into the crowd with a Jaggerish raised arm. 'How's the bonny blade?' said Nick, and Sophie Tipper looked at him over her shoulder with faint recognition as she danced annoyingly with Toby – Nick kissed them both on the cheek before they could stop him, and shouted 'How are you?' again, beaming and heartbroken, and Toby put out a fist with a raised thumb, and shortly after that they moved away. Nick danced on, his collar was tight and he was sweating, he undid his jacket and then did it up again – ah, a window was open at the far end of the room and he jigged around in front of it for a while, turning his face to that rainy garden smell. Martine was sitting on the raised banquette that ran along the wall, and in the beam of green light that flashed on every few seconds her patient profile looked haggard and lost. 'Hi-i!' Nick called, stopping and half-kneeling beside her. 'Isn't Wani with you?' She looked round with a shrug: 'Oh, he's somewhere . . .' And Nick really wanted to see him, suddenly certain of a welcome like the ones he gave him in his fantasies, and there was a twist of calculation too – he could press himself, heavy and semi-incapable, into Wani's arms. Three girls were doing disco routines in a line, turning round and touching their elbows. Nick couldn't do that. The girls danced better than the boys, as if it was really their element, where their rowdy partners were making twits of themselves. Nick didn't like it near the door, where some of the older couples had wandered in and were trotting to and fro as if quite at home with Spandau Ballet. The ultraviolet light made Nat

Hanmer's dress shirt glow and the whites of his eyes were thrillingly strange. They held hands for a few moments and Nat goggled at him for the freaky effect, then he shouted 'You old poof!' and slapped his back and gave him a barging kiss on the ear before he moved off. 'Your eyes!' Mary Sutton gasped at Nick, and he goggled too. It was easy to trip over the raised edge of the hearthstone if you were bopping near the fireplace, and Nick fell against Graham Strong and said, 'It's so great to see you!' because he'd sometimes hungered for Graham too, he hardly knew him, and he said, 'We must have a dance together later,' but Graham had already turned his back, and Nick fetched up with Catherine and Russell and Pat Grayson, where he was very welcome since they were an awkward threesome.

He opened a door from the hall into a small drawing room where a man in shirtsleeves got up and said, 'I'm sorry, sir,' and came towards him unsmilingly.

'I'm so sorry,' Nick said, 'I'm on the wrong side,' and he went out again and pulled the door closed with a boom.

He could hear the music in the distance, and the burble and laughter from the library, and a high ringing in his own ears. Up above, the hundred lilies of the electrolier glowed and twitched – there was a hesitant animation to things, all beating to his own pulse. He went sidling and parading through a suite of lit rooms, abandoned, amusing, a bolster or pulled-back curtain like a glimpse of a person in hiding. Stopped and stooped now and then to appreciate a throbbing little bronze or table that revolved as you looked away from it. Leant caressingly, a little heavily, on the escritoire of the dear old Marquise de Pompadour, which creaked – he was a lover of that sort of thing, if anyone was watching . . . He went into the dining room where they'd had lunch, found the light switches and looked very closely at the landscape by Cézanne, which pulsed as well, with secret geometries. Why did he talk to himself about it? The imaginary friend was at his shoulder, the only

child's devoted companion, needing his guidance. The compo-
sition, he said . . . the different greens . . . He had a keen idea,
which he was cloaking and avoiding, and then licensing step by
step as he opened a side door into a brown passageway, that
turned a corner, and had other doors off it, and then came in a
quickening cool draught to an open back door with the service
yard beyond, glittering in drizzle. The glare was bright and
unsentimental here. No enriching glow of candles or picture
lights. Men in jeans were stacking and crashing things, and
carried on shouting to each other as they passed Nick, so that
he felt like a ghost whose 'Thanks!' and 'Sorry!' were inaudible.
Tristão was washing glasses in a pantry and he walked in behind
him with his heart suddenly thumping, smiling as if they were
more than friends, and aware none the less that Tristão was
working, it was one in the morning, and he himself was just a
bow-tied drunk, a walking wrong note of hope and need.

'Hi there!'

Tristão looked round and sighed, then turned back to his
work. 'You come to help?' The glasses came in on metal trays,
half full, lipstick smeared, fag ends in claret, jagged edges on
stems.

'Um . . . I'm sure I'd break everything,' Nick said, and gazed
at him from behind with wonder and a sense of luck and again
the suspicion of a rebuff.

'Oof . . . ! I'm tired,' Tristão said, and came across the room
so that Nick felt in the way. 'I been up on my feet nine hours
now.'

'You must be,' said Nick, leaning towards him with a friendly
stroke or pat, which fell short and was ignored. He wondered if
he might be going to fall over. 'So . . . When do you finish?'

'Oh, we go on till you go off, baby.' He dried his hands on a
tea towel, and lit himself a cigarette, half offering one to Nick
as an afterthought. Nick hated tobacco, but he accepted at

once. The first sharp drag made his head fizz. 'You enjoying the party, anyway?' Tristão said.

'Yeah . . .' said Nick, and gave a shrug and a large ironical laugh. He wanted to impress Tristão as a Hawkeswood guest, and to mock at the guests as well. He wanted to suggest that he was having a perfectly good time, that the staff, certainly, could not have done more, but that he could take it or leave it; and besides (here he half closed his eyes, suavely and daringly) he had a better idea about how to have fun. Tristão perhaps didn't get all that at once. He looked at Nick moodily, as at a kind of problem. And Nick looked back at him, with a simmering drunk smile, as if he knew what he was doing.

Tristão had lost his bow tie, and the top two buttons of his shirt were open over a white singlet. His sleeves were rolled up, there were streaked black hairs on his forearms, but from his heart to his knees he wore a white apron tied round tight, which made a secret of what had been such a heavy hint before. The pantry was lit by a single fluorescent tube, so that his tired sallow face was shown without flattery. He looked quite different from what Nick had remembered, and it took a little effort of lustful will to find him attractive – there seemed almost to be an excuse for giving up on him and going back to the party. 'A lot of people here, yeah?' said Tristão. He glanced sourly at the trays of glasses and debris, and blew out smoke in that same critical sibilant way that Polly had, like a sign of some shared expertise. And then Nick found himself bitterly jealous at the idea of Polly getting Tristão, and knew that he had to stay. 'Yeah, he got a lot of friends, this Mr Toby . . . I like him. He's like a hactor, no?' – and Tristão made a gesture, long fingers spread like a fan beside his face to indicate the general éclat of Toby's features, bone structure, complexion.

'Yes, he is,' said Nick, with a chuckle and a puff of smoke. Toby's face seemed to hover for a moment in front of the waiter's, which was less beautiful in each respect . . . But wasn't the fact that he didn't admire Tristão so much a part of the lesson, what he thought of as the homosexual second-best solution? This backstairs visit was all about sex, not nonsensical longings: he wasn't going to get what he wanted elsewhere. There was a challenge in the boy's deep-set eyes and something coded in his foreignness – were Madeirans in fact susceptible to casual sex? Nick couldn't see why they shouldn't be . . .

'So how much you had to drink?' Tristão said.

'Oh, masses,' said Nick.

'Yeah?' said Tristão.

'Well, not as much as some people,' said Nick. He smoked, and held his cigarette by his lapel, and felt that his smoking was unpractised and revealing. Of course the wonderful thing about his date with Leo had been that it was a date – they both knew what they were there for. Whereas the Tristão thing might well be all in his own head. He wasn't sure if the thinness of their conversation showed how futile it was, or if it was a sign of its authenticity. He suspected chat-ups should be more colourful and provocative. He said, 'So you're from *Madeira*, I gather,' with the flicker of an eyebrow.

Tristão narrowed his eyes and gave his first little smile. 'How you know that?' he said. Nick took the moment to hold his gaze. 'Oh, I know, the big guy tell you.'

'Huge,' said Nick – 'well, round the middle anyway!'

Tristão looked inside his packet of cigarettes, where he'd stowed Polly's card. 'That him?' he said. Nick glanced dismissively at the card but felt he'd been taught a lesson by it. *Dr Paul Tompkins, 23 Lovelock Mansions* . . . so established already, like a consulting room, with the boys coming through. He turned the card over, where Polly had scribbled *Sep 4, 8pm sharp!* 'Why he say sharp?' said Tristão.

'Oh, he's a very busy man,' said Nick, and feeling it was the moment he made a sudden movement forwards, two steps, his arms out, and a smirk of ineffable irony about Polly on his lips.

'Sorry, mate—': a red-faced man looked in at the door, then tucked in his chin and gave a confident dry laugh. 'Wondered what was going on there for a moment!' Nick reddened and Tristão had the proper provoking presence of mind to snort quietly and say, 'Bob, how's things?'

Bob gave him some instructions about the different rooms, 'his lordship' was referred to a couple of times, with servants' irony as well as pitying respect, and Nick swayed from side to side with a tolerant smile, to convey to the men that he knew Lord Kessler personally, they'd had lunch together and he'd shown him the Moroni. When Bob had gone, Tristão said, 'What am I going to do with you?' without much warmth or sense of teasing.

'I don't know,' said Nick, chirpily, half numbed by drink to the looming new failure.

'I got to go.' Tristão tugged his bow tie out of his pocket, and fiddled with the elastic and the clip. Nick waited for him to take his apron off. 'Look, OK, I see you, by the main stairs, three o'clock.'

'Oh . . . OK, great!' said Nick, and found a happy relief in both the arrangement and the delay. 'Three o'clock . . .'

'Sharp,' said Tristão, with a scowl.

He looked in at the door of Toby's bedroom. A group of his friends had come up here when the music stopped at two, and they seemed lazily to assess him. 'Come in and close the door, for god's sake,' said Toby, beckoning from the vast bed where he was propped up among sprawling friends. He had been given the King's Room, where Edward VII had slept – the swags of blue silk above the bedhead were gathered into a vaguely comic gilded crown. On the opposite wall hung a comfortable Renoir nude. Nick picked his way between groups sitting on the floor in front of an enormous sofa where fat Lord Shepton was lying with his tie undone and his head on the thigh of an attractive drunk girl. The curtains were parted and a window open to carry the reek of marijuana far away from the nose of the Home Secretary. Somehow they had recreated the mood of a college room late at night, girls' stockinged feet stretched out across boyfriends' knees, smoke in the air, two or three voices dominating. Nick felt the charm as well as the threat of the group. Gareth Lane was holding forth about Hitler and Goebbels, and his lecturing drone and yapping laughs at his own puns brought back something dreary from the Oxford days. He was said to be the 'ablest historian of his year', but he had failed to get a first, and seemed now to be acting out some endless redemptive viva. The talk went on, but there felt to Nick's tingling drunk ears to be a residual silence in the room, on which his own movements and words were an intrusion . . . and yet left no trace. Several of his other pals were here, but the two months since term had distanced them more than he could explain. Some simple but strong and long-prepared change had occurred, they had taken up their real lives, and left him alone in his. He came back and perched on the edge of the bed and Toby leaned forward and passed him the joint.

'Thanks . . .' Nick smiled at him, and at last some old sweetness of reassurance glowed between them, what he'd been waiting for all night.

'God, darling, you smell like a tart's parlour,' Toby said. Nick carried on gazing at him, paralysed for the moment by the need to hold in the smoke, a tickle in his throat, blushing with shame and pleasure. He was holding in the unprecedented 'darling' and it was making him as warm and giddy as the pot. Then he let out the smoke and saw the baldly hetero claims of the rest of the remark. He said,

'And how would you know?' – wondering primly if Toby really had been to a tart's parlour. It was an image of him lurching up a narrow staircase.

Toby winked. 'Having a good time?'

'Yes, fantastic.' Nick looked around appreciatively, glossing over his inner vision of the night as a long stumbling journey, half chase, half flight, like one of his country-house dreams, his staircase dreams. 'What's happened to Sophie, by the way?'

'She had to go back to London. Yeah. She's got an audition on Monday.'

'Ah . . . right . . .' This was good news to Nick, and Toby himself, drunk, stoned, eyes glistening, seemed happy about it – he liked the adult note of responsibility in sending her home, and he liked being free of her too. He raised his voice and said,

'Oh, do shut up about fucking Goebbels!' But after a brief incredulous whirr Gareth's shock-proof mechanism rattled on.

Toby was king tonight, on his great big bed, and his friends for once were his subjects. He was acting the role with high spirits, in a childishly approximate way. Nick found it very touching and exciting. As the pot took its delayed effect, squeezing and freeing like some psychic massage, he reached back and took Toby's hand, and they lolled there like that for thirty or forty seconds of heaven. It was as if the room had been steeped in a mood of amorous hilarity as sweetly unignorable as 'Je Promets'. He recalled what Polly had said in the garden long before, and thought that maybe, at last, for once, Toby would actually be his.

There was a surrounding murmur of stoned gossip, heads nodding over rolling papers, the figures blurred but glowing in the lamplight. 'But did the Führer license the Final Solution?' Gareth asked himself; and it was clear that the arguments on this famous question were about to be passed in detailed review.

There was a giggling protest from Sam Zeman, curly-headed genius who'd gone straight into Kesslers on twenty thousand a year. 'You're in a house full of Jews here, can you shut up about the fucking Final Solution, it's a party . . .' – and he reached for his drink with the frown and snuffle of a subtle person obliged to be brusque.

'I can go on to Stalin . . .' said Gareth facetiously.

After a minute's reflection Roddy Shepton said robustly, 'Well, I'm not bloody Jewish.'

'Tobias is,' said his girlfriend, 'aren't you, darling?'

'For god's sake, Claire . . .' said Roddy.

Claire gazed at Toby with eyes of deepening conviction. 'Wasn't someone saying the Home Sectary's Jewish too . . . ?' she said.

'Calm down, Claire!' said Roddy furiously. It was his own conviction that his large placid girlfriend, who had never been known to raise her voice, was dangerously excitable. Perhaps it was his way of implying he had tamed a sexual volcano; which in turn perhaps helped him to explain why he was going out with a strictly middle-class girl, the daughter of his father's estate manager.

Claire looked round in pursuit of her new idea. 'You're Jewish, aren't you, Nat?'

'I am, darling,' said Nat, 'or half Jewish, anyway.'

'And the other half's a bloody Welshman,' said Roddy. He turned his head on her knee and squinted up at her. 'God, you're drunk,' he said.

This was the kind of insult that passed for wit at the Martyrs' Club, and was in fact one of the things most often said there. Toby had once taken Nick to the club's poky panelled dining room, where Christ Church toffs and Union hacks conformed deafeningly to type and boozed and plotted and howled unacceptable remarks at each other and at the harried staff. It was another world, defiantly impervious, in which it was a shock to find that Toby had a place.

'You are so fucking drunk, Shepton,' Toby said. He had pulled off his socks and rolled them into a ball and he threw them very hard and accurately at the fat peer's head.

'Fucking Christ, Fedden,' Roddy muttered, but left it at that.

Nick was explaining about the sea in Conrad's novels being a metaphor for both escape from the self and discovery of the self – a point which took on more and more revelatory force as he repeated it. He laughed at the beauty of it. He wasn't a strong smoker, and a second frowning toke, taken in the belief that the first one had had no effect, could leave him swimming and gabbling for hours. Nat Hanmer was sitting on the floor beside him, and his warm thigh was pressed against his own. There was something charmingly faggy about Nat tonight. He nodded and smiled into Nick's eyes as he was talking. Nick thought the pressure of the dope on his temples was as if his skull was being gently squeezed by Nat's big hands. Sam Zeman was nodding and smiling too and corrected, as if it really didn't matter, a plot detail in *Victory* that Nick had got wrong. Nick loved Sam because he was an economist but he'd read everything and played the viola and took a flattering interest in people less sub-limely omniscient than himself.

He wanted to lie back and listen and perhaps have a long deep snog with Nat Hanmer, whose lips were not so full and soft as Leo's, but who was (Nick hadn't seen it before) almost beautiful, as well of course as being a marquess. The two of them in their shirtsleeves. Nat said he was having a go at writ-ing a novel himself. He'd bought a computer, which he said was 'a really sexy machine'. In the warm explanatory light of the pot Nick saw what he meant. 'I'd love to read it,' he said. Across the room Gareth had switched wars and was describing the Battle of Jutland to a paralysed circle of young women. His big velvet bow tie was all donnish conceit. He was going to go on like this for forty-five years.

Nick heard himself saying how he missed his boyfriend, and then his heart speeded up. Sam smiled – he was purely and maturely straight, but he was cool with everything. Nat said broad-mindedly, 'Oh, you've got a . . . you've got a bloke?' and Nick said, 'Yeah . . .' and already he'd told them all about answering the advertisement, and their meeting and having sex in the garden and the funny episode with Geoffrey from two doors down. And how they were now going out together on a regular basis. Pot was a kind of truth drug for him – with a twist. He had an urge to tell, and show himself to them as a functioning sexual being, but as he did so he seemed to hear how odd and unseen his life was, and added easy touches to it, that made it more shapely and normal.

'I didn't know about all this,' said Toby, who was going round in his bare feet with a bottle of brandy. He was grinning, slightly scandalized, even hurt perhaps that Nick hadn't told him he was having an affair.

'Oh, yes . . .' said Nick, 'sorry . . . He's this really attractive black guy, called Leo.'

'You should have brought him tonight,' Toby said. 'Why didn't you say?'

'I know,' said Nick; but he could only imagine Leo here in his falling-down jeans and his sister's shirt, and the jarring of his irony against the loaded assumptions of the Oxford lot.

'May one ask why?' said Lord Shepton, who had lately been snoring but had now been tickled awake and had a blearily vengeful look. Nobody knew what he was talking about. 'We've already got bloody . . . Woggoo here,' and he struggled upright, with a grimace of pretended guilt, to see if Charlie Mwegu, the Worcester loose-head prop and the only black person at the party, was in the room. 'I mean, fucking hell,' he said. Shepton was a licensed buffoon, an indulged self-parody, and Nick merely raised his eyebrows and sighed; for a moment the old dreariness and wariness surfaced again through the newer romance of the pot.

Claire was looking tenderly at Nick, and said, 'I think black men can be so attractive . . . they have sweet little ears, don't they . . . sometimes . . . I don't know . . . It must be nice—'

'*Calm down, Claire!*' barked Roddy Shepton, as if his very

worst fears had been confirmed. He struggled towards his glass on the floor.

'No, I'm quite jealous actually,' said Claire, and gave Lord Shepton a playful poke in the stomach.

'Oh, you cow!' said Lord Shepton; his attention refocusing, slowly but greedily, on Wani Ouradi, who had just come into the room. 'Ah, Ouradi, there you are. I hope you're going to give me some of that white powder, you bloody Arab.'

'Oh, really!' said Claire, appealing hopelessly to the others.

But Wani ignored Shepton and stepped through the group towards the bed and Toby. He had changed into a green velvet smoking jacket. Nick had a moment of selfless but intensely curious immersion in his beauty. The forceful chin with its slight saving roundness, the deep-set eyes with their confounding softness, the cheekbones and the long nose, the little ears and springy curls, the cruel charming curve of his lips, made everything else in the house seem stale, over-artful, or beside the point. Nick longed to abandon handsome Nat and climb back on to the King's bed. He rolled his eyes in apology for Shepton, but Wani gave no answering sign of special recognition. And the group soon started talking about something else. Wani lay back on his elbow beside Toby for a minute, and took in the room through the filters of his lashes. Toby had picked up one of the girls' pink chiffon scarves, and was winding it into a turban with drunk perseverance. Wani said nothing about the turban, as if they were almost too familiar with each other to comment, as if they were figures of some other time and culture. Nick heard him say, 'Si tu veux . . .' before getting up and going into the bathroom. Toby sat a while longer, laughing artificially at the conversation, and then went off with a yawn and a stumble after him. Nick sat sunk in himself, jealous of both of them, shocked almost to the point of panic by what they were doing. When they came back, he watched them like a child curious for evidence of its parents' vices. He could see their tiny effort to muffle their excitement, the little mock solemnity that made them seem oddly less happy and smashed than the rest of the party. They had a gleam of secret knowledge about them.

A joint came round again, and Nick took a serious pull on it. Then he got up and went to the open window, to look out at the damp still night. The great beeches beyond the lawn showed in grey silhouette against the first vague paling of the sky. It was a beautiful effect, so much bigger than the party: the world turning, the bright practical phrases of the first birds. Though there were hours still, surely, before sunrise . . . He stiffened, grabbed at his wrist, and held his watch steady in front of him. It was 4.07. He turned and looked at the others in the room, in their stupor and animation, and his main heavy thought was just how little any of them cared – they could never begin to imagine a date with a waiter, or the disaster of missing one. He made the first steps towards the door, and slowed and stopped as the pot took his sense of direction away. Where, after all, was he going? Everything seemed to have petered into a silence, as if by agreement. Nick felt conspicuous standing there, smiling cautiously, like someone not on to a joke; but when he looked at the others they seemed equally stilled and bemused. It must be some amazingly strong stuff. Nick thought his way towards moving his left leg forward, he could coax his thought down through the knee to the foot, but it died there with no chance of becoming an action. It was slightly trying if he had to stand here for a long time. He looked more boldly round the others, not easy to name at the moment, some of them. Slow blinks, little twitches of smiles. 'Yah . . .' said Nat Hanmer, very measuredly, nodding his head, agreeing with some statement that only he had heard. 'I suppose . . .' said Nick, but stopped and looked around, because that was part of a conversation about Gerald and the BBC. No one had noticed, though. 'But you're thinking, wasn't that Bismarck's whole point?' Gareth said.

Nick wasn't sure how it started. Sam Zeman was laughing so much he lay back on the floor, but then choked and had to sit up. One of the girls pointed at him mockingly, but it wasn't mockery, she was laughing uncontrollably herself. Nat was red in the face, pinching the tears out of his eyes and pulling down the corners of his mouth to try to stop it. Nick could only stop giggling by glaring at the floor, and as soon as he looked up he was giggling again convulsively, it was like hiccups, it was hiccups, all mixed up together with the whooping, inexplicable funniness of the brandy bottle, the Renoir lady, the gilded plaster crown above the bed, all of them with their ideas and bow ties and plans and objections.

4

'"That's not a Hero's Life," said a critic of the first performance, "but rather a Dog's Life." Or rather a dog's breakfast, you
may well feel, after hearing that rendition of the battle music
by Rudolf Kothner and the Tallahassee Symphony.' It was
Saturday morning, in the kitchen at Kensington Park
Gardens, and a sharp young man was comparing recordings of
Ein Heldenleben on 'Building a Library'.

'Ha, ha,' said Gerald sourly, who had been slouching up
and down, conducting first with a biro, now with a tennis
racquet. He loved these domestic mornings, deferring to
Rachel, making lists, carrying out small invented duties in the
kitchen and the cellar. Today was even better, with his
favourite composer on the radio; he lingered and got in the
way, swinging his head from side to side, and not at all minding having a passage repeated again and again in ever louder
rival interpretations. He took great interest in the breakdown
of the Hero's adversaries into carpers (flutes), vituperators
(oboe), and whiners (cor anglais), and drove them all into the
pantry with a vigorous forehand when the Hero won.

'But let's move on to "The Hero's Works of Peace",' said the
reviewer, 'where Strauss self-glorifyingly recalls material from
his own earlier symphonic poems and songs.'

'I don't like this chap's tone,' said Gerald. 'Ah, now . . . !
Nick . . . ' as the music revelled and swelled enormously. 'You
must admit!'

Nick sat at the table, quick-witted after a mug of coffee, and ready to say all kinds of things. Today especially he was maddened by Strauss's bumptious self-confidence, which took no account of his own frustrations, the two tense weeks in which the dream of Leo as a possible future had faded on the air. But he contented himself with making a ghastly face. In their ongoing Strauss feud he was always cheerfully combative and found himself leaping to more and more dizzy positions – after which he had to take a few moments to reason his way to them over solid ground. Simply having opposition brought latent feelings to the surface and polarized views he might otherwise hardly have bothered to formulate. It became urgent for him to revile Richard Strauss, and he did it happily but a little hysterically, as if far more than questions of taste were involved. He could measure the strange zeal of the process by the degree to which he found himself denying his own ingenuous pleasure in some of Strauss's material and the magical things he did with it – this massive tune now, for instance, which would be running through his mind for days to come. He watched Gerald revelling and swelling too, and a vague embarrassment at the sight made it easier for him to say, 'No . . . no . . . it just won't do,' as the music was quickly faded out.

'Herbert von Karajan there, with the strings of the Berlin Philharmonic in superlative form.'

'Exactly, that's the one we've got, isn't it?' Gerald said. 'The Karajan, Nick?' – since it was Nick, over the summer months, who had been through the record cupboard and put all the discs in alphabetical order.

'Um – I think so . . .'

'But it's possible, isn't it,' the clever young man went on, 'to wonder if the sheer opulence of the sound and those very broad tempi don't push this reading over the edge, losing that essential drop of self-irony without which the piece can all too easily become an orgy of vulgarity. Let's hear Bernard Haitink and the Concertgebouw in the same passage.'

Gerald had the stern, pinched look of someone wounded in debate and measuring his response with awkward dignity. The orchestra rampaged all over again. 'I don't think I care for this one quite so much,' he said. And then a little later, 'I don't see what's vulgar about being glorious.'

Nick said, 'Oh, if you were worried about vulgarity then you'd never listen to Strauss at all.'

'Ooh . . . !' protested Gerald, suddenly cheerful again.

'Perhaps the early Symphony in F,' Nick said. 'But even that . . .'

'I'm going over to Russell's,' said Catherine, walking through the room with a hat on and her fingers in her ears – whether to block out the Hero's Deeds or her father's objections wasn't clear. In fact Gerald said,

'OK, Puss,' and stamped his foot exultantly at a blasting entry for the horns. It was a clear case of God-dammery, her word for all heavily scored Romantic music. She went out into the hall and they heard the slam of the front door.

What the problem was was this colossal redundancy, the squandering of brilliant technique on cheap material, the sense that the moral nerves had been cut, leaving the great bloated body to a life of valueless excess. And then there was the sheer bad taste of applying the high metaphysical language of Wagner to the banalities of bourgeois life, an absurdity Strauss seemed only intermittently aware of! But he couldn't say that, he would sound priggish, he would seem to care too much. Gerald would say it was only music. Nick tried to read the paper for a couple of minutes, but was oddly too excited to concentrate.

'And then the cor anglais, changed at last from whining adversary to pastoral pipe, introduces the poignant melody which announces the Hero's impending departure from the world. For how *not* to do it, let's go back to that mid-price disc from the Caracas Radio Orchestra, whose soloist seems not to have been told of this important transformation in character . . .'

'Gerald, did you manage to get hold of Norman?' Rachel asked, with an insistent tone, as if herself not quite sure of getting through. But a question or command from her had automatic priority, and he said,

'I did, my darling, yes' – going towards her to help her with a trug of long-stemmed yellow roses that she had brought in from the garden. She didn't need help, and the gallant little pantomime passed off almost unnoticed, as their common idiom. 'Penny's going to come over for a chat. Norman says she's far too high-minded to work for the Tories.'

'She'll be very glad of a job,' said Rachel. Norman Kent, whose temperamental portraits of Toby and Catherine hung in the drawing room and the second-floor landing respectively, was one of Rachel's 'left-wing' friends from her student days, whom she'd stayed stubbornly loyal to; Penny was his blushing blonde daughter, also just down from Oxford. There was a notion she might come and work for Gerald. 'Is Catherine up yet? Or down?' Rachel asked.

'Mm . . . ? No – she's neither up nor down, in fact she's out. She's gone to see the man with the Face.'

'Ah.' Rachel clipped expressively at the rose stems. 'Well, I hope she'll be back for lunch with your mother.'

'I'm not *sure* . . .' said Gerald, who doubtless thought lunch would be a good deal easier without her, especially since Toby and Sophie were coming. He listened through to the final recommendation on *Ein Heldenleben*, and pensively turned off the radio. He said, 'He's all right, this fellow, isn't he, Nick?'

'Who . . . Russell? I think he's all right.' Having given him a fervent testimonial two weeks ago, when he hadn't even met him, he was obliged to remain vaguely positive now that he had met him and knew that he couldn't stand him.

'Oh, good,' said Gerald, glad to have got that cleared up.

'I thought he was rather sinister,' Rachel said.

'I know what you mean,' said Nick.

'One thing we have learnt, Nick,' said Gerald, 'is that all her boyfriends are marvellous. Criticism from us is the last betrayal. The more unprepossessing the individual the more strenuously we admire him.'

'We *love* Russell,' said Rachel.

'He's not much to look at,' Nick quickly conceded, knowing that that was part of his glamour for Catherine, who described him as 'a blinding fuck'.

'Oh, come on, he's a thug,' said Rachel, with an unsparing smile. 'The photographs he took at Hawkeswood were purely malicious, making everyone look like fools.'

'An easy target,' said Gerald, clearly meaning something different. Catherine had passed round a selection of the pictures at dinner the week before. They were grainy, black and white, taken without a flash on long exposures which dragged people's features into leering masks. The photograph of Gerald and the Home Secretary being photographed for *Tatler* was a minor masterpiece. Not shown were those of guests fornicating, mooning, pissing in the fountain, and snorting cocaine. 'Is that what *The Face* is like?' said Gerald. 'Sort of satire . . .'

'Not really,' said Nick. 'It's more pop – and fashion.'

'I wouldn't mind seeing a copy,' said Rachel warily. And Nick found himself climbing up the four flights of stairs to search for one in Catherine's room. A sense of criminal intrusiveness, a nagging memory of what had almost happened there three weeks before, made him hurry back down. He glanced through the magazine as he passed by the door of his hosts' bedroom, just to make sure it wasn't too outrageous. He quite liked *The Face,* but there was a lot of it he didn't understand. The picture of a blanched and ringleted Boy George on the cover had been taken by Russell. As he came back into the kitchen Nick felt suddenly embarrassed, as if he'd brought down one of his four porn mags by mistake. He handed it over and they placed it on the table and looked through it together.

'Mm . . . perfectly harmless,' murmured Gerald.

'Yah – it's just a kids' thing,' said Nick, hovering to interpret and deflect. He wasn't much use as a guide to his own youth culture, but he knew it wasn't just a kids' thing. They paused at a fashion spread that showed some sexy half-naked models in a camp pretence of a pillow fight. Gerald frowned faintly, to deny any interest in the women, and Nick realized his paradigm for this inspection was some difficult encounter with his own parents, who would have blushed at the sexualized style of the whole magazine, and called it 'daft' or 'rubbish' because they couldn't mention the sex thing itself. Nick looked at the sprawling beautiful men and blushed appallingly too. He said, 'I always think the *typography*'s rather a nightmare.'

'Isn't it a nightmare?' said Rachel gratefully. 'One feels quite lost.' They all started reading an article which began, '"Get that motherfucker out of here!" says Daddy Mambo of Collision.'

'OK,' said Gerald, with a dismissive drawl, flicking through pages of advertisements for clubs and albums. He seemed vaguely distressed, not at the magazine itself, but that Rachel should have seen it. 'This doesn't have the young genius's work in it . . . ?'

'Um – yes, he did the cover on this one.'

'Ah . . .' Gerald peered at it in an affectedly donnish way. 'Oh yes, "photo Russell Swinburne-Stevenson".'

'I didn't know he had a surname,' said Rachel.

'Much less two,' said Gerald – as if perhaps he might not be such a bad sort.

They looked at Boy George's carmine smile and unusual hat. He wasn't at all sexy to Nick, but he carried a large sexual implication.

'Boy George is a man, isn't he?' said Rachel.

'Yes, he is,' said Nick.

'Not like George Eliot.'

'No, not at all.'

'Very fair question,' said Gerald.

The doorbell rang – it was a quick brassy rattle as much as a ping. 'Is that Judy already?' said Rachel, fairly crossly. Gerald went into the hall and they heard him pluck open the front door and boom 'Hello' in a peremptory and discouraging way he had. And then, in another timbre that made Nick's heart thump and the still air in the house shiver and gleam, Leo saying,

'Good morning, Mr Fedden, sir. I was wondering if young Nicholas was at home.'

'Um, yes, yes he is . . . Nick!' he called back – but Nick was already coming through, with a strange stilted walk, it seemed to himself, of embarrassment and pride. It was abrupt and confusing but he couldn't stop smiling. It was the first time in his life he'd had a lover call for him, and the fact had a scandalous dazzle to it. Gerald didn't ask Leo in, but stood back a little to let Nick pass and to see if there was going to be any kind of trouble.

'Hello, Nick,' said Leo.

'Leo!'

Nick shook his hand and kept holding it as he stepped out onto the shallow porch, between the gleaming Tuscan pillars.

'How's it going?' said Leo, giving his cynical little smile, but his eyes almost caressing, passing Nick a secret message, and then nodding him a sign that Gerald had withdrawn; though he must have been able to hear him saying, '. . . some pal of Nick's . . .' and a few moments later, 'No, black chappie.'

'I'm so pleased to see you,' Nick said, with a certain caution because he didn't want to look mad with excitement. And then, 'I've been thinking of you. And wondering what you were up to,' sounding a bit like his mother when she was fondly suppressing a critical note. He looked at Leo's head as if he had never seen anything like it before, his nose, his stubble, the slow sheepish smile that admitted his own vulnerability.

'Yeah, got your message,' Leo said. He gazed down the wide white street, and Nick remembered his authentic but mysterious phrase about how he'd been round the block a few times. 'Sorry I didn't get back to you.'

'Oh, that's all right,' said Nick, and he found the weeks of waiting and failure were already half forgotten.

'Yeah, I've been a bit off colour,' Leo said.

'Oh, no.' Nick poured himself into believing this, and felt the lovely new scope it gave him for sympathy and interference. 'I'm so sorry . . .'

'Chesty thing,' said Leo: 'couldn't seem to shake it off.'

'But you're better now . . .'

'Ooh, yeah!' said Leo, with a wink and a squirm; which made Nick think he could say,

'Too much outdoor sex, I expect.' Really he didn't know what was allowed, what was funny and what was inept. He feared his innocence showed.

'You're bad, you are,' said Leo appreciatively. 'You're a very bad boy.' He was wearing the same old jeans of their first date, which for Nick now had a touching anecdotal quality, he knew them and loved them; and a zipped-up tracksuit top which made him look ready for action, or for inaction, the rigours and hanging about of training. 'I haven't forgotten our little tangle in the bushes.'

'Nor have I,' said Nick, with giddy understatement, glancing over his shoulder.

'I thought, he's a shy one, a bit stuck-up, but there's something going on inside those corduroy trousers, I'll give him a go. And how right I was, Henry!'

Nick blushed with pleasure and wished there was a way to distinguish shy from stuck-up – the muddle had dogged him for years. He wanted pure compliments, just as he wanted unconditional love.

'Anyway, I was in the area, so I thought I'd try my luck.' Leo looked him up and down meaningfully, but then said, 'I've just got to drop in on old Pete, down the Portobello – I don't know if you want to come.'

'Sure!' said Nick, thinking that a visit to Leo's ex was hardly his ideal scenario for their second date.

'Just for a minute. He's not been well, old Pete.'

'Oh, I'm sorry . . . ' said Nick, though this time without the rush of possessive sympathy. He watched a black cab crawling towards them, a figure peering impatiently in the back; it stopped just in front of them, and the driver clawed round through his open window to release the rear door. When the passenger (who Nick knew was Lady Partridge) didn't emerge, a very rare thing happened and the cabbie got out of the cab and yanked the door open himself, standing aside with a flourish which she acknowledged drily as she stepped out.

'Now who's this old battleaxe?' said Leo. And there was certainly something combative in her sharp glance at the two figures on the front steps, and in her sharp blue dress and jacket, as if she'd come for dinner rather than a family lunch. Nick smiled broadly at her and called out, 'Hello, Lady Partridge!'

'Hul*lo*,' said Lady Partridge, with the minimal warmth, the hurrying good grace, of a famous person hailed by an unknown fan. Nick couldn't believe that she'd forgotten him, and went on with almost satirical courtesy,

'May I introduce my friend Leo Charles? Lady Partridge.'
Up close the old woman's jacket, heavily embroidered with
glinting black and silver thread, had a scaly texture, on which
finer fabrics might have snagged and laddered. She smiled and
said,

'*How* do you do?' in an extraordinarily cordial tone, in
which none the less something final was conveyed – the certainty that they would never speak again. Leo was saying hello
and offering his hand but she had already drifted past him and
in through the open front door. 'Gerald, Rachel darling!' she
called, edgy with the need for reassurance.

The Portobello Road was only two minutes' stroll from the
Feddens' green front door, and there was no time for a love
scene. Leo was walking his bike with one hand, and Nick
ambled beside him, possibly looking quite normal but feeling
giddily attentive, as if hovering above himself. It was that
experience of walking on air, perhaps, that people spoke of,
and which, like roller skating, you could master with practice,
but which on this first try had him teetering and lurching. He
had such an important question to ask that he found himself
saying something else instead. 'I see you know about Gerald,
then,' he said.

'Your splendid Mr Fedden,' said Leo, in his deadpan way,
almost as if he knew that *splendid* was one of Gerald's top
words. 'Well, I could tell there was something you didn't want
me to know, and that always gets me – I'm like that. And then
your friend Geoffrey in the garden was going on something
about parliament – I thought, I'll look into all this at work.
Electoral roll, *Who's Who*, we know all about you . . .'

'I see,' said Nick, flattered but taken aback by this first
glimpse of the professional Leo. Of course he'd done similar
researches himself when he'd fallen for Toby. There had been a
proxy thrill to it, Gerald's date of birth, pastimes, and various
directorships standing in somehow for the intimate details, the

kisses and more he had wanted from his son. He thought it probably wasn't like that for Leo.

'He's quite nice-looking for a Tory,' Leo said.

'Yes, everyone seems to fancy him except me,' said Nick.

Leo gave him a shrewd little smile. 'I don't say I fancy him exactly,' he said. 'He's like someone on the telly.'

'Well, soon I'm sure he will be someone on the telly. Actually of course there are monsters on both sides – looks-wise.'

'True enough.'

Nick hesitated. 'There is a sort of aesthetic poverty about conservatism, though, isn't there.'

'Yeah?'

'That blue's an impossible colour.'

Leo nodded thoughtfully. 'I wouldn't say that was their main problem,' he said.

The weekend crowds were pressing steadily along the lane from the station and down the steep hill into the market. Pete's establishment was in the curving row of shops on the left: PETER MAWSON in gold on black, like an old jeweller's, the windows covered in mesh though today the shop was open. Leo shouldered the door and the wired doormat, as he stood there manoeuvring the bike in, kept sounding a warning chime. Nick had peered into the shop before, on one of the dead weekdays, when it was all locked up, and the mail lay unattended across the floor. There was a pair of marble-topped Empire tables in the windows flanking the door, and beyond that a space that looked more like a half-empty warehouse than a shop.

Pete could be heard on the phone in a back room. Leo propped up his bike in a familiar way and wandered through, and Nick was left alone, blinking longingly at that last image of him, the slight bounce or dance in his step. He heard Pete ringing off, a murmur of kissing and hugging. 'Ooh, you know . . . ' said Pete. 'No, I'm a bit better.'

'I've brought my nice new friend Nick round to see you,' said Leo, in a silly cheerful voice which made Nick realize this might be an awkward half-hour for all of them. He was very sensitive to anything that might be said. As so often he felt he had the wrong kind of irony, the wrong knowledge, for gay life. He was still faintly shocked, among other emotions of interest and excitement, at the idea of a male couple. He and Leo had come together, in their odd transitory way, but the truth was they weren't yet a couple themselves.

'So what's all this?' Pete asked, following Leo back into the room.

'This is Pete, this is Nick,' said Leo, with a large smile and a mime of urging them together. The effort to charm and reassure was a side of him that Nick hadn't seen before; it seemed to make all sorts of other things possible, in the longer view. 'Pete's my best old friend,' he said, in his cockney voice of concessions. 'Aren't you, darlin'?' They shook hands, and Pete winced, as at the grip of something not quite welcome, and said,

'I see you've been hanging around the school gates again, you terrible old man.'

Leo raised an eyebrow and said, 'Well, I won't remind you how old I was when you snatched me from my pram.'

Nick laughed eagerly, though it was a kind of camp slapstick he didn't naturally find funny, and it was surprisingly painful to be given a glimpse of their past together. He found himself picturing and half believing the story of Leo in his pram. Being small and fresh-faced was usually an advantage, but he was anxious not to be thought a child. 'Actually, I'm twenty-one,' he said, in a mock-gruff tone.

'Hark at him!' Pete said.

'Nick lives just round the corner,' said Leo. 'Kensington Park Gardens.'

'Oh. Very nice.'

'Well, I'm just staying there for a while, with an old college friend.'

Leo tactfully didn't elaborate; he said, 'He knows about furniture. His old man's in the trade.'

Pete made a shrugging gesture that took in the sparse contents of the shop. 'Feel free . . .' he said; so Nick had politely to do that, while the old lovers fell back into quiet scoffing chatter, which he deliberately blocked out with tunes in his head, not wanting to learn anything, good or bad. He examined some knocked-about Louis Seize chairs, a marble head of a boy, a suspiciously brilliant ormolu-mounted cabinet, and the pair of tables in the window, which made him think of the ones turned into washstands at Hawkeswood. One wall was covered with a huge dreary tapestry showing a bacchanalian scene, with figures dancing and embracing under red and brown trees; it was too high for the space, and on its loosely rolled bottom edge a satyr with a grin seemed to slide forwards like a limbo dancer on to the floor.

The only real object of interest, the thing to acknowledge and be equal to, was Pete himself. He was perhaps in his midforties, with a bald patch in his sandy hair and a bit of grey in his thin beard. He was lean, an inch or two taller than Nick and Leo, but already slightly stooped. He wore tight old jeans and a denim shirt, and something else, which was an attitude, a wearily aggressive challenge – he seemed to come forward from an era of sexual defiance and fighting alliances and to cast a dismissive eye over a little chit like Nick, who had never fought for anything. Or so Nick explained his own sense of discomfort, the recurrent vague snobbery and timidity with which he peered into the world of actually existing gayness. Nick had pictured Pete as the fruity kind of antique-dealer, or even as a sexless figure like his own father, with a bow tie and a trim white beard. That Pete should be as he was threw such a novel light over Leo. He glanced at Leo now, with his sublime little bottom perched on the corner of Pete's desk, and saw him totally at home with a far from attractive middle-aged man – he had been his lover and done a hundred things with him that Nick still only dreamed of, time and time again. Nick didn't know how it had ended, or when; they seemed to share the steadiness of something both long established and over, and he envied them, although it wasn't quite what he wanted himself. It was part of Leo's game, or maybe just his style, to have told Nick almost nothing; but if Pete was Leo's kind of man it looked suddenly unlikely that Nick would be chosen to replace him.

'Have a look at that, Nick,' Pete called out, as if amiably try-ing to keep him occupied. 'You know what that is.'

'That's a nice little piece,' said Leo.

'It's a very nice little piece,' said Pete. 'Louis Quinze.'

Nick ran his eye over the slightly cockled boulle inlay. 'Well, it's an *encoignure*,' he said, and with a chance at charm: 'n'est-ce pas?'

'It's what we call a corner cupboard,' Pete said. 'Where did you get this one, babe?'

'Ooh . . . I just found him on the street,' said Leo, gazing quite sweetly at Nick and then giving him a wink. 'He looked a bit lost.'

'Hardly a mark on him,' said Pete.

'Not yet,' said Leo.

'So where's your father's shop, Nick?' said Pete.

'Oh, it's in Barwick – in Northamptonshire?'

'Don't they pronounce that Barrick?'

'Only frightfully grand people.'

Pete lit a cigarette, drew on it deeply, and then coughed and looked almost sick. 'Ah, that's better,' he said. 'Yes, Bar-wick. I know Barwick. It's what you'd call a funny old place, isn't it.'

'It has a very fine eighteenth-century market hall,' Nick said, to help him to remember it.

'I picked up a little Directoire bureau there once, bombé it was, you'll know what that means.'

'That probably wasn't from us. It was probably Gaston's. My father sells mainly English things.'

'Yeah? What's trade like up there these days?'

'Pretty slow, actually,' Nick said.

'It's at a fucking standstill here. It's going backwards. Another four years of Madam and we'll all be on the street.' Pete coughed again and flapped away Leo's attempt to take the cigarette off him. 'So how long have you been in London, Nick?'

'About . . . six weeks?'

'Six weeks . . . I see. You'll still be doing the rounds, then. Or are you just shopping local? You've done the Volunteer.'

Leo saw Nick hesitating, and said, 'I wouldn't want him going to that old flea-box. At least not till he's sixty, like everyone else in there.'

'I'm exploring a bit,' said Nick.

'I don't know, where do the young things go these days?'

'Well, there's the Shaftesbury,' Nick said, naming a pub that Polly Tompkins had described as the scene of frequent conquests.

'You're not so much of a pubber, though, are you?' Leo said.

'He wants to get down the Lift,' said Pete, 'if he's a bit of a chocoholic.'

Nick blushed and shook his head dumbly. 'I don't know really.' He was very embarrassed, in front of Leo, but undeniably fascinated to have his taste guessed at and defined. He felt he had only just guessed at it himself.

'When did you meet Miss Leontyne?'

That he knew exactly, but said, 'About three weeks ago,' feeling more foolish with his quick straight answers to chaffing questions. He didn't flinch at the girl's name for Leo, and he had sometimes laboured through whole conversations calling

Polly Tompkins 'she', but he'd never found it as necessary or hilarious as some people did.

'That's what I call her,' said Pete, 'Leontyne Price-tag. I hope you've got your chequebook ready.'

There was nothing to say to this, but Leo muttered dutifully, 'There's not much you don't know about price tags, is there, Pete.'

Nick tittered and watched the affronted look fade from Pete's drawn features as he smoked and gazed at the dreary tapestry. It could have been one of those items which never sell, which the dealer ends up almost giving away because they seem to bring bad luck on the whole shop. He remembered that Pete had been ill, though he didn't know in what way. 'I've got this fucking great bed,' Pete said. 'I can't shift it.' The phone rang, and he went off into the back room. 'Have a look at it.'

The bed had been taken apart and the fluted poles, the ornate square frame of the canopy and the head- and footboards inset with painted rococo scenes were leaning up against the wall. 'Let's have a look at this, then,' Leo said, wandering over and briefly stroking Nick's arm as he passed; he was being sweet to both of them, he surely didn't really want to look at the bed. They didn't want to move anything in case it all fell over. Nick peered at the faded gilt and the unpolished inner edges that would normally be hidden. All his life he'd looked at furniture from odd angles, and he still had his childhood sense of tables and sideboards as elaborate little wooden buildings that you could crawl into, their bosses and capitals and lion-heads at face height, their rough undersurfaces retaining a dim odour of the actual wood. This was a very grand bed, but there was worm in the frame and apparently it had no hangings with it. He felt the old impulse to put it together and get into it. Leo squatted down to look at the picture on the footboard. 'This is nice,' he said. 'What do you think?'

Nick, standing behind him, gazed down on him as he had on their first date, when he was fiddling with the bike. Then he looked away, almost guiltily, at the wide-skirted ladies and their lovers in doublets, plucking at lutes; the trees that were blue and silver. Then he looked down again, at where Leo's beltless jeans stood away from his waist. He had lived and lingered through that glimpse a hundred times since their first meeting, it was almost more powerful and emblematic than the sex that had followed: the swell of Leo's hardened buttocks, the provoking blue horizontal of his briefs. So to be offered a second look had a double force, like the confirmation of a promise, and Nick's hesitation was only the twitch of wariness he felt at any prospect of happiness. 'It's very nice,' he said.

Leo shifted slightly on his heels. 'Can you see?' he said.

Nick was grinning and sighing at the same time. 'Yes, I can see,' he said, in a murmur that shrank the conversation away from Pete into heady subterfuge.

'And what do you think?' asked Leo brightly.

'Oh . . . it's beautiful,' Nick whispered. He checked the open door to the back room before he stooped and slid his hand in and verified that this time there was no blue horizontal, there was only smooth, shaved, curving Leo. A second or two, and then Nick straightened up and put his hands gently round Leo's neck – who tipped back against his legs for support, and rolled his shoulder a couple of times against Nick's hard-on.

'Mm, you do like it,' he said.

'I love it,' said Nick.

When Pete came back in they were loafing round the room with their hands in their pockets. 'You won't believe this,' he said. 'I think I've sold the bed.'

'Oh yes?' said Leo. 'Nick was just saying what a nice piece it was. But he says it'll take quite a bit of work, don't you, Nick?'

Their final few minutes in the shop had an atmosphere of ridiculous oddity. It was hard to take in what the other two were saying – Nick felt radiantly selfish and inattentive, and left it to Leo to wind things up. The furniture and objects took on a richer lustre and at the same time seemed madly irrelevant. It must have been obvious to Pete that something was up, that the air was gleaming and trembling; and it wouldn't have been beyond him to make some tart comment about it. But he didn't. It struck Nick that perhaps Pete was really over Leo, realistic and resigned, and he noticed he regretted this slightly, because he wanted Pete to be jealous.

'Well, we must get our lunch,' Leo said. 'I'm hungry, aren't you, Nick?'

'Starving,' said Nick, in a kind of happy shout.

They all laughed and shook hands, and when Pete had hugged Leo he pushed him away with a quick pat.

So there they were, out in the street, being nudged and flooded round by the crowds, and heedlessly obstructive in their own slow walk, which unfurled down the hill to the faint silky ticking of Leo's bicycle wheels. It was all new to Nick, this being with another man, carried along on the smooth swelling current of mutual feeling – with its eddies sometimes into shop doorways or under the awnings of the bric-à-brac stalls. There was no more talk of lunch, which was a good sign. In fact they didn't say anything much, but now and then they shared glances which flowered into wonderful smirks. Lust prickled Nick's thighs and squeezed his stomach and throat, and made him almost groan between his smiles, as if it just wasn't fair to be promised so much. He fell behind a step or two and walked along shaking his head. He wanted to be Leo's jeans, in their casual rhythmical caress of his strolling legs, their momentary grip and letting go. His hands flickered against Leo time and again, to draw attention to things, a chair, a plate, a passing punk's head of blue spikes. He must have come first, out of all the men Leo had auditioned. He kept touching Leo on the bottom, in the simple pleasure of permission. Leo didn't reciprocate exactly, he had his own canny eye for the street, he even raised a sly eyebrow at the sexy shock of other boys going past, but it didn't matter because they were a kind of super-fluity, the glancing overspill of his brimming desire for Nick. As they dawdled through the crowd Nick saw himself rushing ahead through neglected years of his moral education. This was what it was like!

Under the fringed canopy of a stall he saw the down-turned profile of Sophie Tipper, studying a lot of old rings and bracelets pinned on a ramp of black velvet. His first thought was to ignore her or avoid her. He felt his old envy of her. But then Toby rolled into view behind her, leaning forward with a little pursed smile of vacant interest – very like a husband. He rested his chin on her shoulder for a moment, and she mur-mured something to him, so that Nick had the uncomfortable feeling of peering at their own heedless self-content. They made a necessarily beautiful couple, somehow luminous against the dark jumble of the market, like models in a subtle but artificial glare. Nick turned away and looked for something he could buy for Leo; he longed to do that. He saw all the reasons the impending social encounter might not be a success. 'Hey, Guest!' said Toby, loping round the stall, grabbing him and giving him a firm kiss on the cheek.

'Hi – Toby . . .' Their kissing was a new thing, since the party, somehow made possible and indemnified by the presence of Sophie. And it seemed almost a relief to Toby, as if it erased some old low-level embarrassment about their not kissing. To Nick himself it was lovely, all the warmth of Toby for a moment against him, but unignorably sad too, since it was clearly the limit of concessions, granted in the certainty that nothing more intimate would ever follow.

'Hello, Nick!' said Sophie, coming round and kissing him on both cheeks with beaming goodwill, which he put down to her being such an up-and-coming actress. He wanted to introduce Leo, but he thought something wrong might be said, based on his excited gabble at Hawkeswood, when he was stoned. It was one of those inevitable but still surprising moments when mere wishful thinking was held to account by the truth. He said,

'You're going to be late for lunch,' and thought he sounded rather rude.

'I know,' said Toby. 'Gran wants one of her sessions with Sophie. So we're keeping it as short as possible.'

'Well, I love your grandmother,' Sophie said, with mock petulance.

'No, she's a marvellous old girl,' said Toby; and it reminded Nick of second-hand things he used to say at Oxford, sagacious remarks about his parents' famous friends. He smiled vaguely at Leo. If Sophie hadn't been there, Nick thought, then he could have shown Toby off to Leo as a glamorous accessory to his own past, perhaps something more . . . But like this Toby was hopelessly claimed and placed.

Nick said, 'Sophie Tipper, Toby Fedden: Leo Charles,' and Leo said 'Leo' both times as he shook hands.

'Right,' said Toby, 'fantastic . . . We know all about you,' and he gave an encouraging grin.

'Oh, do you,' said Leo, drily doubtful at the return of his own phrase.

'Leo's Nick's new boyfriend,' Toby said to Sophie. 'Yah, it's really great.'

Nick only took a quick agonized peep at Leo, whose expression was scarily blank, as if to dramatize his unrelinquished power of choice. The welling confidence of a few minutes before looked a foolish thing. Nick said, 'Well, we don't want to jump the gun.'

'But that's wonderful,' said Sophie, as though Nick's welfare, his unhappy heart, had long been her concern. He saw her reaching wide to bless the double triumph of boyfriend and black.

'He's been keeping you very much to himself,' said Toby. 'But now we've caught you at it. So to speak!' And he blushed.

'We're just going for a little toddle,' said Leo.

'That's marvellous.' Toby seemed as thrilled as Sophie by what they imagined was happening, and Nick had a sad clear sighting of his deeper, perhaps even unconscious reason: that an obscure pressure, a sense of unvoiced expectations, might be lifted from him by the transference of Nick's adoration to another man. As Gerald might have said of something quite different, it was hugely to be encouraged. And maybe Sophie sensed that too. They'd probably even talked about it, before sleep, as a vague problem – just for a moment, before it shrank into irrelevance like shoes kicked off at the end of the bed . . .

'So you're not joining us for lunch?' Toby went on.

'Not invited,' said Leo, but with a cheerful shake of the head. Nick raced away from the mere idea of it, as a nexus of every snobbery and worry, scene of tortured intercessions between different departments of his own life: Leo – Gerald – Toby – Sophie – Lady Partridge . . .

'Well, another time,' said Toby. 'We must be going, Pips. But let's all meet up soon?'

'I knew we wouldn't find my ring,' said Sophie, with the crossness that hides a sweetness that hides a toughness.

'We'll come back after lunch. The girl's got to have a ring,' Toby explained, which Nick didn't like the sound of.

Leo had kept up an attitude of steady ironic contemplation of the young couple, but then he said, 'I know I've seen you,' and looked faintly embarrassed by his own gambit. Sophie's face was a lesson in hesitant delight.

'Oh . . .'

'I may be completely wrong,' said Leo. 'Weren't you in *English Rose*?'

Disappointed, she seemed to struggle to remember. 'Oh, no . . . Clever you, but no, I wasn't in that one.'

'That was Betsy Tilden,' said Nick.

'Right, oh yeah, Betsy . . . No, I know I've seen you . . .'

Nick wanted to say that she'd only been in two things, an episode of *Bergerac* and a student-made film of *The White Devil*, bankrolled by her father, which had had a single late-night screening at the Gate.

'I was in a film that was called *The White Devil*,' said Sophie, as though speaking to a child.

'That was it!' said Leo. 'Yes! That was a fantastic film. I love that film.'

'I'm so glad,' said Sophie. 'You are kind!'

Leo was smiling and staring, as if the scenes were spooling through his head again, miraculously matched by the woman in front of him. 'Yeah, when he poisons him, and . . . Did you see this film, Nick, *White Devil*. . ?'

'Stupidly, I missed it,' Nick said; though he had a clear recollection of undergraduates acting at being film-makers, bouncing round in jeeps wearing dark glasses at night; the Flamineo, Jamie Stallard, a drawling Martyrs' Club twit, was one of his favourite bêtes noires.

'I've got to tell you, that guy – Jamie, is it? – ooh-ooh . . .'

'I know,' said Sophie. 'I thought you'd like him.'

'You're not wrong, girl,' laughed Leo, so lit up with sassy excitement that Nick thought he might be teasing Sophie. 'But he's not, though – you'd better tell me – he's *not* . . . is he . . ?'

'Oh . . . ! I'm afraid he isn't, no. A lot of people ask that,' Sophie admitted.

Leo took it philosophically. 'Well, when it comes on again I'm definitely taking *him*,' he said, tutting as if they both thought cultivated, first-class Nick, still heavy-headed with exam knowledge, steeped to the chaps in revenge tragedy, was a bit of a slob.

'All right,' said Nick, seeing it at least as a couple of hours in the warm dark together, rather than behind a bush. 'And I can tell you all about Jamie Stallard,' he added.

But Leo's real interest was in Sophie. 'So what are you doing next?' he said. Nick raised his eyebrows apologetically to Toby, who shook his head kindly, as if to say that going out with a promising actress he was bound to find himself in an attendant role. Sophie herself looked slightly overexcited, partly at the praise but partly because she wasn't used to talking to anyone like Leo, and it seemed to be going really well. 'I'll let you know,' she was saying. 'I can get your number off Nick!'

Nick wished he could match Toby's confidence. He felt snubbed by Leo's attentions to Sophie, but perhaps it was only because he felt foolish, childish at having put it about that they were boyfriends. Toby said, 'Really, we must go, Pips,' and there was something so silly about this nickname that it helped Nick not to care.

But then, alone again in the street with Leo, neither of them saying anything, he had a sense of what an affair might actually be like, and the endless miraculous permission was only a part of it. His limbs were oddly stiff, his hands tingling as if he'd just come in from snowballing to stand by a blazing fire. He felt the moment echoing other occasions when he had just missed success through a failure of nerve, or a stupidly happy anticipation. All Leo's effusiveness with Pete and then with Sophie had ebbed away, and left just the two of them, in this horrible noise and crush. Nick glanced at him with a tight smile; at which Leo stretched his neck with a moody, uninvolved air. 'Well,' said Nick finally, 'where do you want to go?'

'I don't know, boyfriend,' Leo said.

Nick laughed ruefully, and something kept him back from a further lie. 'A caff?' he said. 'Indian? A sandwich?' – which was the most he could imagine managing.

'Well, I need something,' said Leo, in his tone of flat goading irony, looking at him sharply. 'And it isn't a sandwich.'

Nick didn't take a risk on what this might mean. 'Ah . . .' he said. Leo turned his head and scowled at a stall of cloudy green and brown glassware, which was taking its place in their crisis, and seemed to gleam with hints of a settled domestic life. Leo said,

'At least with old Pete we had his place, but where are me and you ever going to go?'

Could this be his only objection, the only obstacle . . . ? 'I know, we're homeless,' Nick said.

'Homeless love,' said Leo, shrugging and then cautiously nodding, as if weighing up a title for a song.

5

Nick chose a moment before dinner to pay the rent. It was always awkward. 'Oh ... my dear ...' said Rachel, as if the two ten-pound notes were a form of mild extravagance, like a box of chocolates, or like flowers brought by a dinner guest, which were also a bit of a nuisance. She looked for somewhere to put down her bowl of steeping apricots. 'If you're sure ...'

Nick shrugged and snuffled. 'Heavens,' he said. He had just spent five pounds on a taxi, he was doing all sorts of incautious things, and would have loved not to pay.

'Well, thank you!' Rachel took the money, and stood folding it appreciatively, not sure where to put it. Then Gerald and Badger Brogan came in from tennis – there was the flat chime of their feet on the iron stair from the garden, and then they were in the kitchen like two big hot boys. Just for a second Gerald noted the transaction that was taking place. The next second he said, 'Thrashed him!' and threw down his racquet on the bench.

'God, Fedden, you're a liar,' said Badger. 'It was 6–4, Rache, in the third set.'

Gerald shook his head in the savour of triumph. 'I let him have it hot.'

'I'm sure you were very well matched,' said Rachel prudently.

This wasn't quite acceptable to either player. 'I chose not to question some frankly fantastic line calls,' said Badger.

He roamed round by the table, picking up a spoon and putting it down, and then a garlic press, without noticing. Nick smiled as if amused by the drama of their game, though in fact he felt challenged by Badger's free and easy way here, by the mood of competition he stirred up in Gerald, and perhaps by its counterpart, his longer and deeper claim on Gerald's affection. 'Hello, Nick!' said Badger, in his probing, sarcastic tone.

'Hello, Badger,' said Nick, still self-conscious at teasing a virtual stranger about the yellow-grey stripe in his dark hair, at having to enrol in the family cult of Badger as a character, but finding it easier after all than the sober, the critical, the almost hostile-sounding 'Derek'.

Badger in turn was clearly puzzled by Nick's presence in his old friend's house and made facetious attempts at understanding him. It was a part of his general mischief – he lurched about all day, asked leading questions, rubbed up old scandals and scratched beadily for new ones. He said, 'So what have you been up to today, Nick?'

'Oh, just the usual,' said Nick. 'You know, morning in the library, waiting for books to come up from the stacks; bibliography class in the afternoon, "How to describe textual variants".' He made himself as dull as he could for Badger, like a brown old binding, though to his own eye 'textual variants' glinted with hints at what he'd actually done, which was to cut the class and have two hours of sex with Leo on Hampstead Heath. That would have been more scandal than Badger could manage. On the first night of his stay he had described an Oxford friend of theirs as the most ghastly shirtlifter.

'LBW, Badge?' said Gerald.

'Thanks, Banger,' said Badger, using an interesting old nickname that Nick couldn't see himself making free with, and which Gerald was wise enough not to object to. The two men stood there, in their tennis whites, drinking their tall glasses of lemon barley water, gasping and grinning between swigs. Gerald's legs were still brown, and his confusingly firm buttocks were set off by his tight Fred Perry shorts. Badger was leaner and seedier, and his Aertex shirt was sweatier and pulled askew by being used to mop his face. He was wearing scruffy old plimsolls, whereas Gerald seemed to bounce or levitate slightly in the new thick-soled 'trainers'.

Elena hurried in from the pantry with the joint, or limb, of venison, plastered up in a blood-stained paste of flour and water. The whole business of the deer, culled at Hawkeswood each September and sent to hang for a fortnight in the Feddens' utility room, was an ordeal for Elena, and an easy triumph for Gerald, who always fixed a series of dinner parties to advertise it and eat it. Elena set the heavy dish on the table just as Catherine came down from her room, with her hands held up like blinkers to avoid the sight. 'Mm – look at that, Cat!' said Badger.

'Fortunately I won't even have to look at you eating it,' said Catherine; though she did quickly peer at it with a kind of relish of revulsion.

'Are you going out, then, old Puss?' said Gerald, his eagerness damped at once by a wounded frown.

'You'll have a drink with us, darling?' said Rachel.

'I might do if there's time,' said Catherine. 'Is it all MPs?'

'No,' said Gerald. 'Your grandmother's not an MP.'

'Thank Christ, actually,' said Catherine.

'And nor is Morden Lipscomb an MP.'

'There are two MPs coming,' said Rachel, and it wasn't clear if she thought this rather few or quite enough.

'Yup, Timms and Groom!' said Gerald, as if they were the jolliest company imaginable.

'The man who never says "hello"!'

'You're too absurd,' said Gerald. 'I'm sure I have heard him say it . . .'

'If Morden Lipscomb's coming I'm going to keep my coat on, he makes my blood run cold.'

'Morden's an important man,' said Gerald. 'He has the ear of the President.'

'Will Nick be making up numbers, I suppose,' said Catherine.

Nick fluttered his eyelashes and Gerald said, 'Nick doesn't make up numbers, child, he's part of the . . . part of the household.'

Catherine looked at Nick, slightly mockingly, across the space that separates good and bad children. She said, 'He's the perfect little courtier, isn't he?'

'Oh, Elena,' said Rachel, 'Catherine's not dining, we'll be one fewer for dinner – yes, one less.' Elena went into the dining room to adjust the placings, and came back a moment later with an objection.

'Miz Fed, you know is thirteen.'

'Ah . . .' said Rachel, and then gave an apologetic shrug.

'Yes, well I don't think any of us are triskaidekaphobes here, are we?' said Gerald. They were all very up on the names of phobias, since at various times Catherine had suffered from aichmo, dromo, keno, and nyctophobia, among a number of more commonplace ones – it was a bit of a game with them, but it cut no ice with Elena, who stood there biting her lip.

'You see, you'll have to stay,' said Badger, reaching out clumsily to hold Catherine. 'How can you resist that *beautiful* venison?'

'Hmm,' said Catherine. 'It looks like something out of a field hospital.' And she shot a tiny forbidding glance at Nick, who saw that it was probably the aichmophobia, the horror of sharp objects, that made the serving and carving of a haunch of venison impossible for her. The family knew about her trouble in the past, but had happily forgotten it when it seemed not to recur. It was only Nick who knew about the recent challenge of the carving knives. He said,

'I don't mind dropping out too if I'm going to spoil the seating.' He enjoyed the well-oiled pomp of the dinners here, but he knew he was too much in love to do more than smile in the candlelight and dream of Leo. He would be quiet and inattentive. And already he felt a tingle in the air, the more-than-reality of the memory of being with his boyfriend.

'No, no,' murmured Rachel, with an impatient twitch of the head.

'Elena, we'll risk it!' Gerald pronounced. 'Sì . . . va bene . . . Nick, you'll just have to be the odd man . . . um . . .' Elena went back into the dining room with that look of unhappy subjection that no one but Nick ever noticed or worried about. 'We're not living in twelfth-century Calabria,' said Gerald, as the phone started ringing and he plucked it from the wall and grunted, 'Fedden,' in his new no-nonsense style. 'Yes . . . Hello . . . What? . . . Yes, yes he is . . . Yes, all right . . . Mm, and to you,' then holding the receiver out towards Nick: 'It's Leo.' Nick coloured as though his thoughts of a few moments before had been audible to all of them; the kitchen had accidentally fallen silent and Gerald gave him a look which Nick felt was stern and disappointed, but perhaps was merely abstracted, the frown of a broken train of thought.

Catherine said, 'If it's Leo, they'll be *hours*.' And Rachel nodded sympathetically and said, 'Yes, why don't you take it in the study.' Gerald looked at him again as if to say that the brute reality of gay life, of actual phone calls between shirt-lifters, was rather more than he had ever imagined being asked to deal with; but then nodded and said genially, 'By all means, it's the red phone.'

'Ah, hotline,' said Badger, whose scandal-sensors were warming to something awkward in the air. Though as Nick went down the hall what struck him was that Rachel knew what was going on, and was protecting him. Gerald never really noticed anything about other people, they were moving parts in a social process, they agreed with him or they thwarted him, his famous hospitality disguised an odd lack of particular, personal skills – all this came clear to Nick in a liberating rush as he pushed open the study door. After which it was beautifully surreal to stand and talk in sexy murmurs beside his desk, to hear Leo's voice in the one room in the house which expressed Gerald's own taste, which was a vacuum of taste, green leather armchairs, upholstered fender, brass lamps, the stage set for his own kind of male conspiracy.

'Well, that was very jolly,' said Leo, with a half-teasing, half-aspiring use of a Nick word. 'Very jolly indeed.'

'Did you enjoy it, darling?' said Nick.

'I didn't mind it,' said Leo.

Nick glowed and grinned. 'I thought it was bearable.'

'I expect you can bear it,' said Leo. 'You don't have to ride a bike.'

Nick looked around at the half-open door. 'Was it too much for you?' he said wonderingly, and with a sense that recurred and recurred these weeks – of enormous freedom claimed through tiny details, of everything he said being welcome.

'You're a very bad boy,' said Leo.

'Mm, so you keep saying.'

'So what are you doing?'

'Well . . .' said Nick. It was lovely to be talking to Leo, but he wasn't quite sure why he had rung, and as it was the first time he had ever done so it made Nick uneasily expectant; until it struck him that probably Leo himself was only claiming the simple pleasure of talking to his lover, of talking, as he said he loved to fuck, for the sake of it. 'I'm sitting behind Gerald's desk with a most tremendous hard-on,' said Nick.

There was a pause and Leo murmured, 'Now don't get me going. My old lady's here.'

It was shadowy already in the room, and Nick pulled the chain that switched on the desk lamp. Gerald, like an uxorious bigamist, had photos of both Rachel and the Prime Minister in silver frames. A large desk diary was open at the 'Notes' pages at the back, where Gerald had written, 'Barwick: Agent (Manning) – wife *Veronica* NOT Janet (Parker's wife).' With his breezily asking Parker how Veronica was and Manning how Janet was, he had got some very confused looks. Nick knew Janet Parker, of course, she was a manager at Rackhams and sang in the Operatic. 'So what are you doing later?' Leo wanted to know.

'Oh, we've got a big dinner party,' Nick said. He noticed that he hoped to impress Leo with their life at Kensington Park Gardens and at the same time was ready to repudiate it. 'It'll probably be very tedious – they only really ask me to make up the numbers.'

'Oh,' said Leo doubtfully.

'It'll be a lot of horrible old Tories,' Nick said, in an attempt at Leo's language and point of view, and sniggered.

'Oh, is Grandma coming, then?'

'She certainly is,' said Nick.

'Old bitch,' said Leo; the passing insult of their doorstep meeting, unregistered at the time, had risen later like a bruise. 'You ought to ask me over, to continue our fascinating conversation,' he said.

The theme of Leo's coming over had cropped up several times since their first date, and hung and faded. Nick said, 'Look, I'm sure I can get out of this.' And really it did seem as if the logic of the evening – the numbers, the etiquette, the superstition – was only an expression of a deeper natural force, a love logic, pulling him out of the house and back into Leo's arms. 'I'm sure I can get out of it,' he said again. Though as he did so he felt there was also a rightness in not seeing Leo, a romance in separation, while the fabulous shock of their afternoon together sank in. Days like these had their design, their upward and downward curves: it would be unshapely to change the plan.

'No, you enjoy yourself,' said Leo, wise perhaps with the same instinct. 'Have a glass of wine.'

'Yes, I expect I'll do that. Unless you've got a better idea . . .' Nick swivelled in the desk chair with a tensely mischievous smile – the red phone cord stretched and bounced. The chair was a high-backed scoop of black leather, a spaceship commander's.

'You're insatiable, you are,' said Leo.

'That's because I love you,' said Nick, singsong with the truth.

Leo took in this chance for an echoing avowal; it was a brief deep silence, as tactical as it was undiscussable. He said, 'That's what you tell all the boys' – a phrase of lustreless backchat that Nick could only bear as a form of shyness. He turned it inside out in his mind and found what he needed in it. He said quietly, 'No, only you.'

'Yeah,' said Leo, all relaxed-sounding, and gave a big fake yawn. 'Yeah, I'll probably pop down to old Pete's a bit later, see how he's getting on.'

'Right,' said Nick quickly. 'Well – give him my best!' It was a sting of worry – hidden, unexpected.

'Will do,' said Leo.

'How is old Pete?' said Nick.

'Well, he's a bit low. This illness has taken all the life out of him.'

'Oh dear,' said Nick, but felt he couldn't enquire any further, out of delicacy for his own feelings. He looked about on the desk, to focus his thoughts on where he was rather than on imagined intimacies at Pete's flat. There was a thick typescript with a printed card, 'From the Desk of Morden Lipscomb', on 'National Security in a Nuclear Age', which Gerald had marked with ticks and underlinings on the first two pages. 'NB: nuclear threat', he had written.

'OK, babe,' Leo said quietly. 'Well, I'll see you soon. We'll get it together at the weekend, yeah? I've got to go – my mum wants the phone.'

'I'll ring you tomorrow . . .'

'Yeah, well, lovely to chat.'

And in the silence of the room afterwards, shaken, tight-lipped, Nick clutched at that cosy but cynical cockney *lovely*. Of course Leo was inhibited by being at home, he wanted to say more. Just think of this afternoon. It was terribly sweet that he'd rung at all. The chat was a romantic bonus, but nothing was certain when it came to words, there were nettles among the poppies. For a minute or two Nick felt their separation like a tragedy, a drama of the thickening dusk – he saw Leo at large on his bike while he stood in this awful office with its filing cabinets, its decanters, and the enlarged photograph, just back from the framers, of the hundred and one new Tory MPs.

In the kitchen he found that people had dispersed to bath and change, and these further unstoppable rhythms made him feel like a ghost. Rachel was sitting at the table writing place cards with her italic fountain pen. She glanced up at him, and there was a slight tension in her manner as well as obvious solicitude, a desire not to offend in a moment of kindness. She said, 'All well?'

'Yes, thank you – fine . . .' said Nick, shaking himself into seeing that of course life was pretty wonderful, it was just that there was more to it than he expected – and less as well.

'Now should I put Badger or Derek, do you think? I think I'll put Derek, just to put him in his place.'

'Well, they are place cards,' said Nick.

'Exactly!' said Rachel, and blew on the ink. She looked up at him again briefly. 'You know, my dear, you can always bring friends here if you want to.'

'Oh, yes . . . thank you . . .'

'I mean we would absolutely hate it if you were to feel you couldn't do that. This is your home for however long you are with us.' And it was the 'we', the general benevolence, that struck him and upset him; and then the practical acknowledgement that he wouldn't be there for ever.

'I know, you're very kind. I will, of course.'

'I don't know . . . Catherine says you have a . . . a special new friend,' and she was stern for a second, magnanimous but at a disadvantage: what should she call such a person? 'I just want you to know he'd be very welcome here.'

'Thank you,' said Nick again, and smiled through a blush at the thing being out. It was confusingly straightforward. He felt relieved and cheated. He wasn't sure he could rise to the freedom being offered – he saw himself bringing home some nice white graduate from the college instead, for a pointless tea, or convivial evening bleak with his own cowardice.

'We're such broody old things,' Rachel said, 'now that Toby's moved out. So do it just for our sake!' This was a charming exaggeration, in a woman of forty-seven, with thirteen for dinner, but it acknowledged a truth too: it didn't quite say she thought of him as a son – it didn't elevate or condescend – but it admitted a habit, a need for a young man and his friends about the house. She tapped the cards together and came across the room and Nick gave her a kiss, which she seemed to find quite right.

In fact Toby and Sophie were there that night. They came early and Nick had a gin-and-tonic with them in the drawing room. They seemed to bring along their own complacent atmosphere, the mood of their life together in the Chelsea flat, and of some larger future when they might curl up a leg on the sofa or stand with an elbow on the mantelpiece in a room as enormous as this. Toby played the lightly chivvied 'husband' very sweetly, and Sophie claimed him in the childish ways of someone experimenting with her power, with little exasperations and innuendos. She did a performance about how Toby ground his teeth in his sleep. Nick tittered warily at this glimpse of the bedroom, but found her lack of subtlety oddly reassuring. She'd got Toby, snoring and twitching, but the romantic reach of Nick's feelings for him, the web of sacrifice and nonsense and scented Oxford nights, survived untouched. Toby was very sweet to Nick too. He left his position by the fireplace and came and sprawled on the rug by his chair, so that Nick could have reached out and stroked the back of his neck. For a moment Sophie looked disconcerted, but then she took possession of that situation as well. 'Ah – you two should see more of each other,' she said. 'It's good to see you together.' A minute later, looking vaguely self-conscious, Toby got up and pretended to search for a book.

'And what about your lovely friend . . . ?' Sophie wanted to know.

'Oh . . . Leo, do you mean?'

'*Leo*,' said Sophie.

'Oh, he's – lovely!' Here was the subject again – Nick just hadn't got used to it yet, to the idea of anything so secret, so steeped in his own fears and fantasies, being cheerfully enquired after by other people. Toby too looked round from the bookcase with his encouraging grin.

'Such a . . . *lovely* man,' said Sophie, whose conversation tended not to develop, but to settle, snugly or naggingly, in one place.

Nick was glad of the praise, and mistrusted it at the same time. 'Well, he loved meeting you,' he said.

'Aah . . .' Sophie purred, as if to say that people usually did enjoy that.

'He's a great fan of your work, Pips,' said Toby.

'I know,' said Sophie, and sat looking down modestly. Her dark-blonde hair, worn long at Oxford, had been cut and backcombed, Diana-style, and quivered when she shook her head. She was wearing a red strapless number that didn't really suit her.

'You know she's got a part in a play,' said Toby.

'Oh, shoosh . . .' said Sophie.

'No, we've all got to go and see her. Nick – come to the first night, we'll go together.'

'Absolutely,' said Nick. 'What are you doing?'

Sophie quivered and said, 'Well, you might as well know,' as if being hurried into announcing a different kind of engagement. 'I'm doing *Lady Windermere* . . .'

'Fantastic. I think you'll be very good at that.' It was a surprisingly big part, but Nick could see her as the self-righteous young wife clipping rose stems in her Westminster drawing room; and delivering those awful soliloquies she has—

'I don't know what it will be like. It's one of these very way-out directors. He's . . . he's gay, actually, too. He says it's going to be a deconstructionist reading of the play. That doesn't worry me, of course, because I've done deconstruction; but Mummy and Daddy may not like it.'

'You can't go worrying about what your parents will think,' said Nick.

'That's right,' said Toby. 'Anyway, your ma's very with-it. She's always going to way-out concerts and things.'

'No, she'll be fine.'

Toby chuckled. 'Of course your father's most famous remark is that he wished Shakespeare had never been born.'

'I don't know that that's his *most* famous remark,' said Sophie, with a hint of pique. In fact if Maurice Tipper had made a famous remark at all it would probably have been something about profit margins and good returns for shareholders. 'He only said it after getting bitten to death by mosquitoes watching *Pericles* in Worcester College gardens.'

'Ah . . .' murmured Nick, whose own memory was of Toby's bashful swagger as a Lord of Tyre, when Sophie had been the Marina.

'You're too horrid about my poor papa,' said Sophie in a highly affected way, as if in her mind she was already on stage.

Catherine came in, dressed for her night out in a tiny spangled frock, over which she was wearing an unbuttoned light-grey raincoat. She wore high-heeled black shoes and stockings with a whitish sheen to them.

'Goodness!' said Toby.

'Hello, darling,' said Catherine confidentially to Sophie, stooping to give her a kiss. Sophie clearly found Catherine the most challenging aspect of an affair with Toby, and Catherine knew this, and treated her with the kind of clucking condescension that Sophie would otherwise have lavished on her. 'Love your clever frock,' she said.

'Oh . . . thank you,' said Sophie, smiling and blinking.

'Are you going out, then, sis?' said Toby.

Catherine headed towards the drinks table. 'I'm going *out* tonight,' she said. 'Russell's taking me to an opening in Stoke Newington.'

'And where might that be?' said Toby.

'It's a well-known area of London,' Catherine said. 'It's very fashionable, isn't it, Soph?'

'Yes, of course – darling, you've heard of it,' said Sophie.

'I was joking,' said Toby; and Nick thought it was true, you never expected him to; and when he did you couldn't always be sure that he had. And then the idea of a party, not this one, but a noisy party with cans of beer and trails of pot smoke, through which he moved with his lover, as his lover, came over him like a pang and he envied

Catherine. It was an image of an Oxford party, but blended with something known only from television, a house full of black people.

Toby said, 'I'm just going upstairs to see if I can find those trousers. Are you going to Nat's bash, Nick?'

'What is it?' said Nick, with another dimmer pang at the thought of another kind of party, a posh white hetero one, at which his presence was not thought necessary.

'Oh, he's having this Seventies party . . .' said Toby hopelessly.

'No, I'm not invited,' said Nick, with a superior smile, thinking of the loving closeness he had felt with Nat at Hawkeswood, when they were both stoned and sitting on the floor. 'Is it in London?'

'That's the thing. It's up at the blasted castle,' said Toby.

'Yes . . . It's absurdly soon, isn't it, for a Seventies party?' said Nick. 'I mean, the Seventies were so ghastly, why would any-one want to go back to them?' He'd been longing for a chance to see the castle – a marcher fortress with Wyatt interiors.

'Well, public schoolboys love reliving their puberty, don't they Soph,' said Catherine, coming back with a very tall drink.

'I *know*,' said Sophie crossly.

'Some of them spend their whole lives doing it,' Catherine said. She stood in front of the fireplace, with a hand on her hip, and seemed already to be moving to the music of a future very remote from any such nonsense.

Toby shrugged apologetically and said, 'I just hope I've still got those disco pants!'

Nick almost said, 'Oh . . . the purple ones . . . ?' – since he knew just where they were, having been through everything in Toby's room, read his schoolboy diary, sniffed the gauzy lining of his outgrown swimming trunks, and even tried on the flared purple trousers (standing foolishly on the long legs). But he merely nodded, and knocked back the rest of his g-and-t.

Gerald came down in a dark suit with characteristic pink shirt, white collar, and blue tie. He seemed to recognize, with a forgiving smile, that he had set a sartorial standard the others were unlikely to match. He kept on smiling as he crossed the room, as a sign of his decision that he would not react to Catherine's appearance. The mac worn over the micro-frock made her look almost naked. When Badger came in he was less circumspect. 'My god, girl!' he said.

'No, your god-daughter actually, Uncle Badger,' said Catherine, with the forced pertness of a much younger child.

Badger frowned and hummed. 'Well, exactly,' he said. 'Didn't I promise to safeguard your morals, or something?' He rubbed his hands together and had a good look at her.

'I'm not sure anyone thinks you'd be the best person for that,' Catherine said, sipping her gin and sitting down side-ways on a low armchair.

'You're going easy on that stuff, aren't you, Puss?' said Gerald.

'It's my first one, Daddy,' Catherine said; but Nick could see why Gerald was anxious, she was high on her own defiance tonight. He watched Badger watching her, his grey-striped peak slicked back after his shower, something disreputable and unattached about him; in parts of Africa, according to Toby, he was known not as Badger but by one of a number of words for hyena. Certainly he circled, and was hungry for something. His lecherous teasing of his god-daughter was allowed because it was of course impossible, a clownish joke.

Catherine stayed long enough to meet everyone and to test her claim that Barry Groom never said hello. Gerald played along and said, '*Hello*, Barry,' and not only seized his hand but covered it confirmingly with his other hand, as if he was can-vassing: at which Barry, looking round the room with a sus-picious smile, said, 'Gerald, I'm surprised at you' – holding him there long enough to make him uneasy – 'a *green front door*: that's hardly sending the right signal.' He got a laugh, which was warmer and more complex than he expected – there was a second or two while he grew into it, squared his shoulders. He followed Gerald across the room, nodding in a vain, critical way as he was introduced, but not saying hello. When Catherine shook his hand, he said, 'Aha! Beautiful creature!' with a vaguely menacing presumption of charm. Catherine asked him where his wife was and he said she was still parking the car.

It was good that Catherine should want to be present, to be presented, to help entertain the guests, but to the family it was also a little sinister. She put everyone on edge by having her coat on indoors, and seemed to be playing with her father's hopes that at any moment she might leave. He glanced at her distractedly from time to time, as if he would have liked to say something but had made the calculation that the oddity of the coat was preferable to the naked flesh beneath it. He introduced her to Morden Lipscomb with visible reluctance. The grey old American, with his tiny granite-like sparkle of charm, shook her hand and smiled mockingly, as if being confronted with an ancient indiscretion he meant entirely to deny. Toby and Nick were both watching her and Toby said, 'God, my sis looks like, you know, one of those girls who try and lure you into striptease parlours.'

'She looks like a strippergram,' Sophie said.

Lady Partridge came in with that air of social vexation Nick had seen in her before: she wanted to appear totally at home here and she also wanted her arrival to be an event; her deafness added a querulous uncertainty as to which effect she was having. Badger got her a drink and flirted with her, and she allowed herself to be flirted with. She liked Badger, having known him since he was a boy, and nursed him through mumps once, when he was staying in the holidays – an episode that was still referred to as a touchstone of their friendship, and in a vaguely risqué way, since apparently Badger's balls had been the size of grapefruit. Nick had heard them joke about it earlier in the week, and it had sounded like jokes he had with his own parents, that were ribald little reference points in a past before everything changed and became indescribable.

All the time Nick was thinking about Leo, so that Leo seemed to be the element, the invisible context, in which these daunting disparate people were meeting and sparring and congratulating each other. They didn't know it, which made it all the funnier and more beautiful. He mixed himself a fresh gin-and-tonic, Gerald-style, quinine lost in juniper, and drifted round not minding if he wasn't spoken to. He looked at the pictures with a new keenness, as though explaining them to Leo, his grateful pupil. The other MP and his wife, John and Greta Timms, were standing in front of the Guardi with the look of people who had come to the wrong party, who wanted more of a challenge, he in a grey suit, she in the helpless boldness of a blue maternity dress with a white bow at the neck: it was as if the PM herself were pregnant. John Timms was a junior minister in the Home Office; he must have been several years younger than Gerald, but he had precocious gravitas and unflappable self-importance. If Barry Groom never said hello, John Timms seemed at first not to blink. His gaze was fixed and almost sensual, and his speech had a hypnotic steadiness of pace and tone, irrespective of meaning: he was inspired, he seemed constantly to admit, but he wasn't in any dubious way excitable. They were talking about the Falklands War and the need to commemorate it with a monument and to celebrate it with an annual public holiday. 'A Trafalgar Day for our times,' said Timms, and his wife, in whom his certainty produced a more vibrant kind of urgency, said, 'Why not revive Trafalgar Day itself? Trafalgar Day itself must be revived! Our children are forgetting the War Against the French . . .' John Timms gazed out into the room as though flattered by his wife's zeal and loving her for it, but not himself being ready to go so far. He hadn't been introduced to Nick (indeed the Timmses were really speaking to each other), and his gaze played on him for a moment, seemed to feel him and test him and doubt him. 'You'd like to see a permanent Falklands memorial, wouldn't you,' he said.

'Mm, I wonder . . .' said Nick, not disrespectfully, and marvelled at just how unavailable his thoughts on the subject were. The doubtlessness of Timms was a wonder in itself. He imagined Leo being here beside him, and having one salient fact or objection to produce, of the kind Nick could never remember. Catherine came past, sampling each of the little power-centres in the room. 'We were talking about the Falklands,' said Nick.

'I understand the Prime Minister favours an annual parade,' said John Timms, 'as well as a prominent memorial. It was truly her triumph.'

'And the men's,' said Greta Timms, with her rich hormonal flush. 'The men were staunch.'

'They were certainly staunch, my darling,' said John Timms. 'They were dauntless.'

'No,' said Catherine, covering her ears and grinning, 'it's no good, I just can't bear words with that *au* sound in. Do you know what I mean?'

'Oh . . .' said Greta Timms. 'I think I've always found them rather splendid words!'

'Right, I'm off!' said Catherine, turning to the room with the big smile which perhaps all her life would seem unguarded and vulnerable. A rough chorus of 'Byes', a chuckling 'Oh, is she off?', and she was gazed at with relief, the suddenly conjured good humour that sends a child up to its early bed. 'Bye, Gran!' she said, specially loudly, kissing Lady Partridge in the middle of the room. 'See you in the morning, Dad.' And picking up her bag she stalked out on her tall heels. Lady Partridge peeped at Morden Lipscomb to gauge his surprise; if he seemed amused by this vision of a sex-club door-girl she was ready to take some droll credit as her grandmother. But Lipscomb was looking disappointedly at Gerald.

Lady Partridge was taken in to dinner by Lipscomb. They didn't really 'take people in' at the Feddens', but the procession from the drawing room, down the stone stairs, and into the candlelight, awoke a memory sometimes, or an anxiety, in guests. Lipscomb, with ponderous New World formality, presented his elbow to the senior lady, and Gerald's mother, who had a hurtling look to her after two gin-and-tonics, pressed against him like an old flame. In the dining room Lipscomb peered around with guarded curiosity as people found their places. 'Yes, I always think what a splendid room,' Lady Partridge said, trailing away towards her chair.

'And are these your forebears, Lady Partridge?' Lipscomb asked.

'Yes . . . yes . . .' said Lady Partridge, in a daze of graciousness.

'No, they are *not* her forebears,' said Rachel, quietly but firmly. 'They're my grandfather and my great-aunt.'

Nick was placed in the middle of the table, with Penny Kent on his right and Jenny Groom on his left – the dullest place of all, but he didn't mind because he had company of his own. He tucked into his crab cake as if sharing a joke. 'How do you fit in?' Jenny Groom wanted to know, with the air of someone steeled to unpleasant surprises.

'Oddly but snugly,' said Nick; and since she didn't like this, 'No, I'm an old friend of Toby's.'

'Oh, Gerald's son, you mean . . . And I hear *he's* working for the *Guardian!*' The scandal of Toby's having a traineeship at the *Guardian* seemed to Nick to eclipse his own dissidence, to be enough scandal for one household.

'Well, you can ask him. He's sitting just over there,' said Nick, loud enough to intrude on Toby as he listened to Greta Timms extolling the virtues of the Family: Toby gave a half-secret smile of acknowledgement but said, 'Yes, I see,' to Greta to show she still had his attention.

'Oh, of course. He's got his father's looks,' said Jenny with a frown. 'So what do you do?'

'I'm doing a doctorate at UCL – on ... on Henry James,' said Nick, seeing the style question might lose her completely.

'Oh ...' said Jenny warily, getting a hook on it. 'Yes. I've never got round to Henry James.'

'Well ...' said Nick, not caring if she had or not.

'Or hang on, did I read one? *Dr Johnson* or something.'

'No ... I don't think so ...'

'No, not *Dr Johnson*, obviously ...!'

'I mean there's the Boswell.'

'It was set in Africa ... I know: *Mr Johnson*.'

'Oh, *Mister Johnson* is a novel by Joyce Cary.'

'Exactly, I knew I'd read something by him.'

When the venison came in Gerald yapped, 'Don't touch the plates! Don't touch the plates!' so that it sounded as though something had gone wrong. 'They have to be white hot for the venison.' The fact was that the fat congealed revoltingly if the plates were less than scorching. 'Yes, my brother-in-law has a deer park,' he explained to Morden Lipscomb. 'A rare enough amenity these days.' The guests looked humbly at their help-ings. 'No,' Gerald went on, in his bristling way of answering questions he wished someone had asked, 'this is buck veni-son ... comes into season before the doe, and very much superior.' He went round with the burgundy himself. 'I think you'll like this,' he said to Barry Groom, and Barry sniffed at it testily, as if he knew he was thought to have more money than taste.

Nick shared a brief smile down the table with Rachel. It seemed subtly to mock not only Barry but Gerald himself. Nick took his first sip of the burgundy with a frisson at their shared understanding, like the liberty allowed to a child by a confident mother – the pretended conspiracy against the father. He wondered if Gerald and Rachel ever rowed. If anything happened, then it was in the white secrecy of the bedroom, which, with its little vestibule, was removed from hearing behind two heavy doors; it became somehow sexual.

When he thought of Leo after not thinking of him for a minute or two he heard a big orchestral sound in his head. He saw Leo lying on his coat under a bush, his shirt and jersey pushed up under his armpits, his jeans and pants round his knees, small dead leaves sticking to his thighs – and he heard the astonishing chord. It was high and low at once, an abysmal pizzicato, a pounce of the darkest brass, and above it a hair-raising sheen of strings. It seemed to knock him down and fling him up all in one unresisted gesture. He couldn't repeat it immediately, but after a while he would see Leo rising to kiss him, and the love-chord would shiver his skin again. It startled him while Penny was describing the enormous interest of working for Gerald, and he jumped, and smiled at his invisible friend, so that Penny worried that she'd been funny. He wondered if it came from something he knew, or if he'd written it himself. It certainly wasn't the *Tristan* chord, with its germ of catastrophe. The horrible thought came to him that if it existed, it had probably been written by Richard Strauss, to illustrate some axe-murder or beheading, some vulgar atrocity. Whereas to Nick, though it was frightening, it was also indescribably happy.

'So how are you getting on at UCL?' said Penny kindly, as

if it must be a sorry comedown after Oxford. Nick and Penny
had never met as students, the word Oxford meant different
things to them, but Penny relied on it as a thing they had in
common.

'Oh, fine . . . !' said Nick; and went on obligingly, 'It's not
at all like Oxford, you know. The place itself is fairly grim. I've
just found out that the English department used to be a mattress factory.'

'Really!' said Penny.

'It is a bit depressing. I suppose it's no wonder half the
staff are alcoholics.' Penny laughed, oddly titillated, and
Nick felt rather treacherous. In fact he revered Professor
Ettrick, who had taken to him with immediate subtle
confidence, and seen possibilities in his thesis topic that he
himself hadn't dreamt of. But nothing much was being done,
and through most of Nick's library days his eyes wandered just
beyond the page in a deep monotonous reverie about Leo: the
great unfolding sentences of Meredith or James would slow and
fade into subliminal parentheses, half-hour subordinate clauses
of remembered sex. And he felt guilty, because he wanted to
deserve the professor's trust and be as clever and committed as
he was meant to be. Penny said, 'Was it Henry James you're
working on?'

'Er . . . yes,' said Nick.

She seemed to settle comfortably on that, but only said, 'My
father's got tons of Henry James. I think he calls him the
Master.'

'Some of us do,' said Nick. He blinked with the
exalted humility of a devotee and sawed off a square of brown
meat.

'Art makes life: wasn't that his motto? My father often
quotes that.'

'It is art that *makes* life, makes interest, makes importance,
for our consideration and application of these things, and I

know of no substitute whatever for the force and beauty of its process,' said Nick.

'Something like that,' said Penny. She smiled contentedly into the candlelight. 'What would Henry James have made of us, I wonder?' she went on.

'Well . . .' Nick chewed it over. He thought she was rather like a high-minded aunt, proposing questions with virginal firmness and ignorance. He wondered condescendingly what her sexual prospects were. A certain kind of man might like to raise the colour in that plump white neck. He said, 'He'd have been very kind to us, he'd have said how wonderful we were and how beautiful we were, he'd have given us incredibly subtle things to say, and we wouldn't have realized until just before the end that he'd seen right through us.'

'Because he did write about high society, didn't he?' said Penny, clearly thinking that was where she was, and also perhaps that it was proof against being seen through.

'Quite a lot,' said Nick; and remembering his chat with Lord Kessler in the summer and really giving a long-pondered answer to him, 'People say he didn't understand about money, but he certainly knew all about the effects of money, and the ways having money made people think.' He looked fondly across at Toby, who out of sheer niceness tried now and then not to think like a rich person, but could never really get the hang of it. 'He hated vulgarity,' he added. 'But he also said that to call something vulgar was to fail to give a proper account of it.'

Penny seemed to be puzzling this over, but in fact she was listening to what Badger was suggesting in her other ear: her sudden blush and giggle showed Nick that this was one of Badger's little sexual challenges to him – it was almost a way of calling him a fag.

Toby was listening to Greta Timms, but leaning past her to keep an eye on Sophie, who was being drily examined by

Morden Lipscomb. 'No,' said Sophie reluctantly, 'I've only been in one sort of *major* film.'

'And what of the stage?' said Lipscomb, with an odd mixture of persistence and indifference.

'Well, I am about to be in something. It's . . . I'm afraid it's going to be rather a *trendy* production . . . it's *Lady Windermere's Fan*.'

Jenny Groom started asking something about Catherine, was she as mad as they said, and Nick's hesitations as he answered only half allowed him to hear the truth that Lipscomb dragged out of Sophie, that she wasn't playing Lady Windermere herself, but 'Oh, just a minor part . . . No! Not *too* much to learn . . . Oh no, not her, that's a wonderful part . . . Anyway it will probably all be *ruined* by the director . . .' and that in fact she'd been cast as Lady Agatha, a role which famously contained nothing but the two words 'Yes, mamma.' Nick thought this was very funny, and then felt almost sorry for her.

Rachel said, 'My dear, what fun, we shall all come to your first night,' apparently sincerely, so that a further alliance, of efficient, almost impersonal solidarity, was seen to be in place between the mother and her possible daughter-in-law.

Lady Partridge, jealous of Lipscomb's attention, went off on the unobvious tangent of her hip replacement. 'Oh, I had it at the Dorset . . . Well, yes, I always go there, I find them marvellous . . . charming girls . . . The nurses, yes . . . One or two of the doctors *are* coloured, but there's absolutely no need to have anything to do with them . . . Not that I'm much of a one for hospital!' she reassured him. 'My late husband was there a good deal.'

'Ah . . .' said Lipscomb, measuring the distance to a condolence.

She lifted her glass, with a worldly sigh. 'Well, I've outlived two husbands, and that's probably enough,' she said, as if still leaving a tiny loophole for further proposals. She looked at Lipscomb, perhaps wondering if he had said something, and went on, 'Actually they were both called Jack! They couldn't have been more different, as it happens . . . chalk and cheese . . . I don't think they'd have got on for a *moment* – had they ever met!' Nick thought she might almost have been on the phone, hearing answers and questions from far away. 'Jack Fedden, of course, Gerald's father, a funny sort of man, in a way . . . He was in the law, very much a law man . . . very, *very* handsome . . . and Jack Partridge, Sir Jack, of course . . . No, not a law man . . . Not at all . . . He was a practical man, a builder, he built some of the new motorways, as you may know . . . Yes, some of the Ms . . . the M, um . . . He did marvellous work . . .'

At the head of the table Gerald was perceptibly distracted by his mother's talk. Nick knew that Jack Partridge had gone bust not long after getting his knighthood, in one of the funny reversals of these recent years; it was a subject which might seem to tarnish his stepson by association. Gerald made a firm intervention and said, 'So, Morden, I was absolutely gripped by your paper on SDI.'

'Ah . . .' said Lipscomb, with a smile that showed he wasn't so easily flattered. 'I wasn't sure that you'd agree with my conclusions.'

'Oh, *absolutely*,' said Gerald, with a surprising mocking smile which confirmed to Nick that he hadn't read beyond those first few pages. 'How could one not!'

'Well . . . you'd be surprised,' said Lipscomb.

'Is this the telephones?' said Lady Partridge.

'It's missile defence, Ma,' said Gerald loudly.

'You know, Gran, Star Wars,' said Toby.

'You're thinking of STD, Judy,' said Badger.

'Ah,' said Lady Partridge, and chuckled, not in embarrassment but at the attention she'd won for herself.

'The President announced the Strategic Defence Initiative six months ago,' said Morden Lipscomb, gravely but a little impatiently. 'It aims to protect the United States from any attack by guided missile systems. In effect a defensive shield will be created to repel and destroy nuclear weapons before they can reach us.'

'Delightful idea,' said Lady Partridge. This sounded satirical, and the plan had indeed been greeted with derision as well as dismay; but then Nick thought, no, the old lady would take pleasure in weaponry, and arms budgets generally.

'It is, I believe, an irresistible one,' said Lipscomb, laying his left hand commandingly on the table. He wore a signet ring on his little finger, but no wedding ring. Of course that didn't mean much; Nick's own father and his father's male friends didn't wear wedding rings, they were thought, for all their symbolism, to be vaguely effeminate. He thought of the card, 'From the Desk of Morden Lipscomb' – it made one wonder where else it might have come from: 'the Back-burner', 'the Rest-room', 'From the Closet of Morden Lipscomb' . . . well, it was an idea. He was clearly a man with his own defensive systems.

After pudding the ladies withdrew. Nick's thoughts went with them as they climbed the stairs; he stood with one knee on his chair, hoping he might somehow be allowed to join them. 'Slide along, Nick,' said Gerald. The men all closed up together at Gerald's end of the table, in a grimly convivial movement, occupying the absent women's places. Nick handed Lady Partridge's lipstick-daubed napkin to Elena, who had come through to sort them out. There were many all-male occasions that he liked, but now he missed the buffer of a female, even Jenny Groom, whose general impatience he'd decided was a sad flower of her hatred of her husband. Now Barry Groom was sitting down opposite him with a scowl, as if familiar to the point of weariness with the etiquette of such occasions. Nick looked across to Toby for help, but he was laying out a box of cigars and the cigar cutter; Gerald was setting the decanters off on their circuit. Nick pictured Leo, as he had left him today, walking his bike away, and the love-chord sounded, warily now – he didn't want the others to hear it. How could he describe it, even to himself, Leo's step, his bounce, his beautiful half-knowing, half-unconscious deployment of his own effects? 'I'll give you one piece of advice,' said Barry Groom, choosing imperiously between the unmarked port and claret decanters.

'Oh, yes,' said Nick, and felt his erection begin to subside. 'Never speculate with more than twelve per cent of your capital.'

'Oh . . .' Nick gasped humorously, but seeing Barry Groom was almost angrily in earnest he went on, '*Twelve* per cent. Right . . . I'll try and remember that. No, that sounds like good advice.'

'Twelve per cent,' said Barry Groom: 'it's the best advice I can give you.' He slid the decanters over to him, since they formed the bridge, furthest from Gerald. Nick took some port and passed it on to Morden Lipscomb, with a little show of promptness and charm. Lipscomb was just clipping a cigar, and his thin mouth, turned down in concentration, seemed to brood on some disdain, not of the cigar, but of the company he found himself in. This was presumably the moment when he should be made way for, in the solemn but disinhibiting absence of the women, but he was cagey, or sulky. Nick felt sorry for Gerald, but didn't see how he could help. His own way of getting on terms with people was through the sudden intimacy of talk about art and music, a show of sensibility; but he felt Lipscomb would rebuff him, as though refusing intimacy of another kind. He wondered again what Leo would have said and done: he had such clear, sarcastic opinions about things.

'So, Derek,' said Barry Groom, in his cuttingly casual tone, 'how long are you staying here?'

Badger puffed coaxingly for a second or two, and then let out a roguish cloud of smoke. 'As long as the old Banger'll have me,' he said, jerking his head towards Gerald.

'Ah, that's what you call him, is it?' said Barry, with a rivalrous twitch.

Badger grunted, took a quick suck on his cigar, and said, 'Oxford days . . .' knowing how easy Barry was to tease. 'No, I'm having a place done up at the moment, that's why I'm here.'

'Oh, really? Where is it?' said Barry suspiciously.

Badger was deaf to this question, so Barry repeated it and he said at length, as if conceding a clue to a slow guesser, 'Well, it's quite near your place of work, actually.' The secrecy was presumably a further tease, though it fitted with something seedily hush-hush about Badger. 'It's just a little flat – a little pied-à-terre.'

'A fuck-flat in other words,' said Barry, sharply, to make sure the illusionless phrase, and his offensiveness in using it, struck home. Even Badger looked slightly abashed. Gerald gave a disparaging gasp and plunged as if confidentially into new talk with John Timms and his old mentor about the genius of the Prime Minister. Nick glanced across at Toby, who half closed his eyes at him in general if unfocused solidarity.

'I had wondered whether the Prime Minister might be with us this evening,' said Lipscomb. 'But I see of course it's not that kind of party.'

'Oh . . .' said Gerald, looking slightly guilty. 'I'm so sorry. I'm afraid she wasn't free. But if you'd like me to bring you together . . .'

Lipscomb gave a rare smile. 'We're lunching on Tuesday, so it's not at all necessary.'

'Oh, you are?' said Gerald, and smiled too, in a genial little mask of envy.

And so it went on for ten or fifteen minutes, Nick perching at the corner of two conversations, the 'odd man', as Gerald had briskly predicted. He passed the decanters appreciatively, and sat smiling faintly at the reflections of the candelabra in the table top or at a disengaged space just above Barry Groom's head. He grunted noncommittally at some of Badger's jokes, Badger appearing in the candlelight and its mollifications as almost a friend among the other guests. He nodded thoughtfully, without following the thread, at one or two of Lipscomb's remarks that caused general pauses of respect. The cigar stench was the whole atmosphere, but the alcohol was a secret security. There was something so irksome about Barry Groom that he had a fascination: you longed for him to annoy you again. He was incredibly chippy, was that the thing? – all his longings came out as a kind of disdain for what he longed for. And yet he got on with Gerald, they were business partners, they saw a use for each other; and that perhaps was the imponderable truth behind this adult gathering.

Barry said, 'The way you Oxford fuckers go on about the Martyrs' Club,' and frowned sharply as he swallowed some claret. 'What were you martyrs to, that's what I'd like to know.'

'Ooh . . . hangovers,' said Badger.

'Yes, drink,' Toby put in, and nodded frankly.

'Overdrafts and class distinctions,' said Nick drolly.

Barry stared at him, 'What, were you a member?'

'No, no . . .' said Nick.

'I didn't think so!'

And then there was a rattle in the hall as the front door was opened and the bang of it slamming shut. Then immediately the bell rang, in three urgent bursts. There was a shout of vexation, the door was jerked open again, and Catherine, it must have been, was talking – from the dining room they heard only the hurried shape of her talk. Nick's eyes slid round the faces of the others at the table, who looked puzzled, displeased, or even lightly titillated. John Timms stared unblinking towards the closed door of the room; Badger sat back in a curl of smoke. '*All right!*' It was Catherine.

'That child would try the patience of an oyster,' said Gerald, with evident feeling but also a snuffle of amusement, a darting glance to judge the effect of his allusion.

Then the front door closed again, more thoughtfully, and a man's voice was heard – 'You need to be careful, girl . . .' Nick gave a little snigger, trying to commute it into Russell's voice, but Gerald had set down his cigar and stood up: 'Sorry . . .' he murmured, and walked towards the door with a dwindling smile. 'That's my sis,' said Toby. 'As I was saying . . .' said Morden Lipscomb. When Gerald opened the door, the man was going on quietly but urgently, 'You need to calm down, Cathy, I don't like it, I don't like seeing you like this at all . . .' and Nick's heart went out to the Caribbean accent, in instant sentimental allegiance – he felt himself float out towards it from the cigar-choked huddle at the table, the Oxonian burble and Barry's whine.

'Who are you?' said Gerald.

'Oh, Christ, Dad!' said Catherine, and it was clear she was crying, the last word broke as she raised her voice.

'And are you Cathy's father, then . . .'

Nick got up and went into the hall, with the feeling he must try to curb Gerald's unhelpful sharpness, and an anxious sense of the things Gerald didn't know, that might now have to be named and negotiated. He was half in the dark himself. If someone told you they were OK, was it wrong to believe them? She was standing at the foot of the stairs, gripping the gold chain of her bag in both hands and looking both angry and vulnerable: Nick almost laughed, as you do for a second at the latest catastrophe of a child, and seem to mock it when you mean to reassure it; though he was frightened too. There was quite a chance he'd have to do something. He peered at her, with the frank curiosity allowed in a crisis – it really was childlike, the quick fall; she had only gone out two hours ago. Her mouth quivered, as if with accusation. She was tiny in her high heels. Nick knew the man, he was the minicab driver she'd been friendly with, the one she'd had back to the house when Gerald and Rachel were away, fiftyish, grizzled at the temples, heavy-built, a sweet hint of ganja about him: well, all the Orbis drivers sold the stuff. He was completely and critically different from everything else in the house. Nick said, 'Hi!' under his breath, and rested a hand on his shoulder. 'What's happened, darling?' he said.

'Who is this man?' said Gerald.

'I'm called Brentford, since you're asking,' the man said slowly. 'I brought Cathy home.'

'That's really kind of you,' said Nick.

'How do you know my daughter?' said Gerald.

'She needs taking care of,' said Brentford. 'I can't help her tonight, I got a job.'

'He's the minicab driver,' said Nick.

'Does he need paying?' said Gerald.

'I don't charge her,' said Brentford. 'She call me when he dump her.'

'Is this true?' said Gerald.

'It's really kind of you,' said Nick.

Catherine made a little scream of disbelief, and came and took Brentford's arm, but he kept a wary dignity with her too and didn't hold her: he pushed her gently towards Nick, and she leaned against him, wailing but not holding on to him. She was in her own distress, she wasn't seeking solace from Nick, just somewhere to stand; still he put a cautious arm round her. 'Is it Russell?' he said. But she couldn't begin to answer.

'What is it, darling?' said Rachel, hurrying downstairs.

Gerald explained, 'That bloody little shit's dumped her,' clearly saying, through pretended indignation, what he most hoped had happened. 'Poor old Puss.'

Rachel looked at the three men, and there was a hint of fear in her face, as if Brentford had brought some threat much larger than Catherine's tantrum into the house. 'Come upstairs, darling,' she said.

Barry Groom had come out into the hall, staring and twitching his head, and so drunk suddenly that there were unconscious delays to his aggression. 'Look here, you!' he shouted at Brentford. 'I don't know who you are. You fucker!'

Gerald put a hand on his wrist. 'It's all right, Barry.'

'You keep your hands off her, you . . .'

'Oh, shut up . . . you arsehole!' said Nick, without planning to, and shaken by the sound of his own raised voice.

'Yes, shut up, you wanker!' said Catherine, through her tears.

'Now, now!' said Barry, and then something awful, a sly smile, slid on to his face.

'God, I'm really sorry . . .' said Nick to Brentford.

'Why are we all standing here?' said Gerald.

'Darling, come up,' said Rachel.

'Let's finish our port and cigars,' said Gerald, turning his back on Brentford. He had to show, for the sake of the party, that he took scenes like this with habitual good humour. 'Will you take her up, darling?' he said, as if there were really a chance he might do it himself.

Catherine moved away and started up the stairs, and Rachel tried to put an arm round her, but she shook it off. Nick took Brentford to the door. 'Are you sure we can't pay you?' he said, though he doubted he had the price of a fare from Stoke Newington himself. He wanted Brentford to know he wasn't guilty of the thing the whole house stood accused of.

'He's a bad man,' said Brentford, on the doorstep.

'Oh . . .' said Nick, 'yes . . .' He wasn't certain which man was being referred to, and Brentford's shake of the head and flap of the arm seemed to write them all off.

Nick stood on the pavement for a while after the Sierra had gone, and heard the laughter of the women from an open window above. It was good to be out of the house, in the night air. He was trembling a little from having shouted at someone he hated. He thought of Leo, and smiled, and hugged his hands under his armpits. He wondered what Leo was doing, the afternoon flared up again and warmed him with amazement; then the thought of Pete came over it like the chill of a cloud. He went in and slowed as he passed by the half-open door of the dining room: '. . . the beggar stank of pot!' Gerald was saying, to odd humourless laughter. Now perhaps he could really go upstairs, and taste the freedom of being the odd man. He didn't have a place in either of the two parties. It was bad form to go away, it admitted a prior desire to do so; but he couldn't go back and sit with Barry Groom. He thought Gerald might be angry with him too, but he would surely be glad of his taking an interest in Catherine. It couldn't be called a shirking of responsibility. Nick started to climb the stone stairs, and had hummed several bright anticipatory bars from Schumann's Fourth Symphony before he stopped himself.

6

'God, you're a twit,' said Leo. He looked fretfully at different parts of Nick, unable to place his dissatisfaction exactly. In the end he licked his thumb and rubbed his cheek, as if Nick was a child. This word *twit*, a tiny sting, had come up before, and signalled some complex of minor reproaches, class envy, or pity, the obvious frustrations of having a boy like Nick to teach. As always Nick searched for something else in it too, which was Leo's tutting indulgence of his pupil; he still longed for flawless tenderness, but he forgave Leo, who for once was nervous himself. They were on the Willesden pavement, ten yards from his front gate. 'You're so fucking preppy,' said Leo.

'I don't know what that means.'

Leo shook his head. 'What am I going to do with you?'

They had met after work, across the road from the Council offices, and Leo was wearing a dark grey suit with square shoulders and a white shirt and a wide but sober tie. It was the first time Nick had seen this beautiful everyday metamorphosis, and he couldn't help smiling. He was in love to the point of idolatry, but the smiles, the appreciative glances, seemed to strike Leo like a kind of sarcasm. 'You look so handsome,' Nick said.

'Yeah, and so do you,' said Leo. 'Right, we're going in. Now what did I tell you, don't take the name of the Lord in vain. Don't say, "Oh my god!" Don't even say, "Good Lord!" ' (Leo fluted these phrases in the way that was his puzzling imitation of Nick.) 'Don't say, "Jesus fucking bollocks." '

'I'll try not.'

Nick was always a favourite with mothers, he was known to be a nice young man, and he liked the unthreatening company of older people. He liked to be charming, and hardly noticed when he drifted excitedly into insincerity. But he also knew the state of suspense, the faked insouciance, of bringing friends home, the playful vigilance with which certain subjects had to be headed off even before they had arisen; you took only a distracted, irrelevant part in the conversation because you were thirty seconds, a minute, ten minutes ahead of it, detecting those magnetic embarrassments towards which it would always twitch and bend.

'My sister sort of knows,' said Leo. 'You want to watch her.'

'Rosemary.'

'She's pretty.'

Nick followed him up the short concrete path and said in his ear, 'Not as pretty as you, I bet,' one of his light flirty jokes that he watched swoop to earth under its own weight of adoration.

Mrs Charles and her son and daughter lived on the ground floor of a small red-brick terrace house; there were two front doors side by side in the shallow recess of the porch. Leo applied himself to the right-hand one, and it was one of those locks that require tender probings and tuggings, infinitesimal withdrawals, to get the key to turn. Nick reflected briefly on the coloured glass in the inset window and the old Palm Sunday cross pinned above the doorbell. He pictured Leo going through this routine every day; and he noted his own small effort of adjustment, his disguised shock at the sight of the street and the house – perhaps he was a twit after all. When he stepped inside he had a memory, as sharp as the cooking smell in the hall, of school afternoons of community service, going into the homes of the old and disabled, each charitable visit a lesson in life and also – to Nick at least – in the subtle snobbery of aesthetics.

He took in the tiny kitchen in a photographic glance, the wall units with sliding frosted-glass doors, the orange curtains, the church calendar with its floating Jesus, the evidence of little necessary systems, heaped papers, scary wiring, bowls stacked within bowls, and the stove with plates misted and beaded on the rack above a bubbling pan; and at the centre Leo's mother, fiftyish, petite, with hooded eyes and straightened hair and a charitable smile of her own. 'You're very welcome,' she said, and her voice had the warm West Indian colour that Leo kept only as a special effect or a temporary camouflage.

'Thank you,' said Nick. 'It's very good to meet you.' He was so used to living by hints and approximations that there had always been something erotic in meeting the family of a man he was in love with, as if he could get a further vicarious fix on him by checking genetic oddities, the shared curve of the nose or echoing laziness of step. In the rich air of Kensington Park Gardens he seemed to live in the constant diffused presence of Toby, among people who were living allusions to him and thus a torment as well as a kind of consolation. But of course he had never done more than hug Toby and kiss him on the cheek; he had twice had a peep at his penis at a college urinal. Here, in a tiny flat in unknown Willesden, he was talking to the mother of the man who called him not only a 'damn good fuck' but also a 'hot little cocksucker' with 'a first-class degree in arse-licking'. Which clearly was way beyond hugging and peeping. Nick gazed at her in a trance of revelation and gratitude.

And then there was Rosemary, coming in from work, home early, it seemed, to help her mother out with this under-explained guest they had. She was a doctor's receptionist, and wore a blouse and skirt under her belted mac. They had an awkward introduction, edging round Leo's bike in the hall. Perhaps it was shyness, but she seemed disdainful of Nick. He looked for her prettiness, and thought she was like a silky fluffy version of Leo, without the devastating detail of an ingrowing beard. Then brother and sister both went off to change. Nick couldn't work out the plan of the house, but there were subdivided rooms at the back, and a sense of carrying closeness that made the bike entirely necessary; it waited there, shuddered and jangled faintly as Nick bumped against it, as if conscious of its own trapped velocity.

'Ah, that bicycle,' said Mrs Charles, as if it was some profane innovation. 'I told him . . .'

They went into the front room, in which a heavy oak dining table and chairs, with bulbous Jacobean-style legs, were jammed in beside a three-piece suite that was covered in shiny ginger leather, or something like it. There was a gas fire with a beaten copper surround under a ledge crowded with religious souvenirs. Mrs Charles's church life clearly involved a good deal of paperwork, and half the table was stacked with box-files and a substantial print-run of the tract 'Welcoming Jesus In Today'. Nick sat down at the end of the sofa and peered politely at the pictures, a large framed 'mural' of a palm-fronded beach and a reproduction of Holman Hunt's *The Shadow of Death*. There were also studio photos of Leo and Rosemary as children, in which Nick felt himself taking an almost paedophiliac interest.

'Now, young sir,' said Mrs Charles, with a clarity of enunciation that sounded both anxious and arch, 'he tells me next to nothing, Leo, you know, at all. But I think you're the fellow who lives in the big white house, belongs to the MP?'

'Yes, I am,' Nick said, with a self-deprecating laugh which seemed to puzzle her. Leo must have been talking up these facts to impress her, though on other occasions they were the object of vague derision.

'And how do you like it?' Mrs Charles asked.

'Well, I'm very lucky,' Nick said. 'I'm only there because I was at university with one of their children.'

'So, you met *her*?'

Nick smiled back with a little pant of uncertainty. 'What, Mrs Fedden, you mean . . .'

'No . . . ! Mrs Fedden . . . I assume you met Mrs Fedden, if I'm saying her name correctly.' Nick blushed, and then smiled as he saw the way, simple but nimble, religious even, that she'd gone for the big question. 'No – *her*. The lady herself. Mrs T!'

'Oh . . . No. No, I haven't. Not yet . . .' He felt obliged to go on, rather indiscreetly, 'I know they'd love to have her round, he, um, Gerald Fedden, has tried to get her at least once. He's very ambitious.'

'Ah, you want to make sure and meet Mrs T.'

'Well, I'll certainly tell you if I do,' said Nick, looking round gratefully as Leo came into the room. He was wearing jeans and a sweatshirt and Nick had a vivid image of him ejaculating. Then he saw the heavy spit as it loitered and drooled down the taut ginger back of the sofa. He felt deliciously brainwashed by sex, when he closed his eyes phallus chased phallus like a wallpaper pattern across the dark, and at any moment the imagery of anal intercourse, his new triumph and skill, could gallop in surreal montage across the street or classroom or dining table.

'And can I be allowed to hope you are a regular church-attender?'

Nick crossed his legs to hide his excitement and said, 'I'm not really, I'm afraid. At the moment, anyway.'

Mrs Charles looked used to such disappointments, and almost cheerful, as if taking a very long view. 'And what about your father and mother?'

'Oh, they're *very* religious. My father's a churchwarden, and my mother often does the church flowers . . . for instance.' He hoped this compensated, rather than merely highlighting, his own delinquency.

'I'm very happy to hear it. And what *is* your father's occupation?' she demanded, pressing on in interview mode, which made Nick wonder if she did somehow know, however subconsciously, that he was trying to tie his life to her son's. He was a puzzle, Nick, in many contexts – he was often being interviewed obliquely, to see how he fitted in.

He said, 'He's an antiques dealer – old furniture and clocks, mostly, and china.'

Mrs Charles looked up at Leo. 'Well, isn't that the exact same thing as old Pete!'

'Yeah,' said Leo, whose whole manner was withdrawn and unhelpful. He dragged out one of the dining chairs and sat down at the table behind them. 'There's a lot of antique dealers about.'

'The exact same thing,' said Mrs Charles. 'You go on, look around. We got some good old antiques here. You don't know old Pete?'

'Yes, I do,' Nick said, glancing round the room and wondering what Pete had said about it all before him, and how Pete had been explained to her.

'It's a small little world,' she marvelled.

'Well, Leo introduced me to him . . .'

'Ah, he's a good man, old Pete. You know we always called him "old" Pete, though he can't be not more than fifty.'

'He's forty-four,' said Leo.

'He was a great help to my son. He helped him with getting through college, and with the job on the council. And he didn't stand to get nothing from it – leastways not in this world. I always say to Leo he's his fairy godfather.'

'Something like that,' said Leo, with the sourness of a child subjected to the astounding iterations of a parent's treasured phrases – treasured often because they put a bright gloss on some anxious denial. The clumsy unconscious joke in this one must have made it specially wearing.

'A proper decent father Leo didn't have,' said Mrs Charles candidly, and again with an almost cunning air of satisfaction that they had been so tested. 'But the Lord looks after his own. And now, don't you reckon he's a good boy?'

'Yes, he's . . . splendid!' said Nick.

'What's for tea?' said Leo.

'I'm hoping your sister is bringing it off now,' said Mrs Charles. 'We're giving our guest our special spicy chops and rice. In this country,' she observed to Nick, 'you don't fry the chops so much, you're always grilling them, isn't that right?'

'Um . . . I don't know. I think we do both.' He thought of his own mother, as an embodiment of any such supposed tradition; but went on charmingly, 'But if *you* fry them rather than grilling them, then that's also what we do in this country!'

'Ha . . .' said Mrs Charles, 'well that's certainly one way of looking at the matter.'

At table the movement of Nick's left arm was limited by the leaning tower of 'Welcoming Jesus In Today'. He came down on his food in a hesitant but predatory fashion. The meal was a bold combination of bland and garishly spicy, and he wondered if Rosemary had mockingly overdone the chillies to make fun of his good manners. He was full of round-eyed appreciation, which was also a cover for the surprise of having his evening meal at five forty-five; some absurd social reflex, the useful shock of class difference, a childish worry perhaps at a changed routine, all combined in a mood of interesting alienation. At Kensington Park Gardens they ate three hours later, and dinner was sauntered towards through a sequence of other diversions, chats and decantings, gardening and tennis, gramophone records, whisky and gin. In the Charles household there was no room for diversions, no garden to speak of, and no alcohol. The meal came on straight after work, a wide-ranging grace was declaimed, and then it was eaten and done with, and the whole long evening lay ahead. There were things Nick guessed about them, from the habits of his own family, which lay somewhere between the two; but there were others he would have to wait for and learn. He had never been in a black household before. He saw that first love had come with a bundle of other firsts, which he took hold of like a wonderful but worrying bouquet.

After a longish silence Leo said, 'So how's it going at college?' as if they hardly knew each other.

'Oh, it's all right,' said Nick, disconcerted but then touched by Leo's stiffness. Whenever Leo was cold or rough to him he felt it like a child – then he turned it round and found some thwarted love in it. He was in awe of Leo, but he saw through him too, and each time he followed this little process of indulgence he felt more in love. 'It hasn't been very exciting so far. I suppose it's just different from what I've been used to.' He always came away from the sunless back court where the English department was with two or three newly shaped anecdotes, which gave his days there a retrospective sparkle; but he found it hard to interest Leo in them and they often went to waste. Or they were stored up, with a shadowy sense of resentment.

'He was at Oxford University before,' said Leo.

'And now where is he?' Mrs Charles wondered.

'I'm at University College,' Nick said. 'I'm doing a doctorate now.'

Leo chewed and frowned. 'Yeah, what is it again?'

'Oh . . .' said Nick, with a disparaging wobble of the head, as if he couldn't quite get the words out. 'I'm just doing something on style in the – oh, in the English novel!'

'Aaaah yes,' said Mrs Charles, with a serene nod, as if to say that this was something infinitely superior but also of course fairly foolish.

Nick said, 'Umm . . .' – but then she broke out,

'He's crazy for studying! I'm wondering just how old he is.'

Nick chuckled awkwardly. 'I'm twenty-one.'

'And he doesn't look like no more than a little boy, does he, Rosemary?'

Rosemary didn't answer exactly, but she raised one eyebrow and seemed to cut her food up in a very ironical way. Nick was blushing red and it took him a moment to notice Leo's embarrassment, the mysterious black blush, frowningly denied. His secret was heavy in his face, and Nick suddenly understood that the difference in their ages mattered to Leo, and that even an innocent reference to it seemed to lay his fantasy bare. Old Pete was licensed by being old, an obscurely benign institution; it was much harder to account for his friendship with a studious little boy of twenty-one.

Nick had to go on, though he could hear that he was out of tune, 'Of course one misses one's friends – it takes a while to settle down – I expect it will all be marvellous in the end!' There was another rather critical pause, so he went on, 'The English department used to be a mattress factory. At least half the tutors seem to be alcoholics!'

Both these remarks had gone down rather well at Kensington Park Gardens, and had left Nick suppressing a smile at his own silliness. But all families are silly in their own way, and now he was left with a puzzled and possibly offended silence. Leo chewed slowly and gave him a completely neutral look. 'Mattresses, yeah?' he said.

Rosemary stared firmly at her plate and said, 'I should think they ought to get help.'

Nick gave an apologetic laugh. 'Oh . . . of course, they should. You're quite right. I wish they would!'

After a while Mrs Charles said, 'You know, all the men like that, that's got that sort of problems, each and every one of them got a great big hole right in the middle of their lives.'

'Ah . . .' Nick murmured, flinching with courteous apprehension.

'And they can fill that hole, if only they know how, with the Lord Jesus. That's what we pray, that's what we always pray. Isn't that so, Rosemary?'

'That's what we do,' said Rosemary, with a shake of the head to show there was no denying it.

'So what's your success rate?' said Leo, in a surprisingly sarcastic tone; which explained itself when Mrs Charles leant confidentially towards Nick. You couldn't stop a mother when she was on the track of her 'idea'.

'I pray for all those in darkness to find Jesus, and I pray for the two children I've brought into this world to get themselves hitched up. At the altar, that's to say.' And she laughed fondly, so that Nick couldn't tell what she really thought or knew.

Leo scratched his head and shivered with frustration, though there was a kind of fondness in him too, since he was going to disappoint her. Rosemary, who was clearly her mother's right hand, found herself linked with Leo, and protested flatly that she was ready, just as soon as the perfect man turned up. With her eyes half closed she had her mother's devout look. 'There's nothing keeping me from the altar except that one thing,' she said, and as the look fell on Leo she seemed to play with betrayal, and then once again to let it go.

When the fruit and ice cream had been brought in, Mrs Charles said to Nick, 'I see you been looking at my picture there, of the Lord Jesus in the carpenter's shop.'

'Oh . . . yes,' said Nick, who'd really been trying to avoid looking at it, but had none the less found himself gingerly dwelling on it, since it hung just above Leo's shoulder, straight in front of him.

'You know, that's a very famous old picture.'

'Yes, it is. You know, I saw the original of it quite recently – it's in Manchester.'

'Yeah, I knew that's not the original when I saw one just the same in the Church House.'

Nick smiled and blinked, not sure if he was being teased. 'The original's huge, it's life-size,' he said. 'It's by Holman Hunt, of course . . .'

'Aha,' Mrs Charles murmured and nodded, as if a vaguely unlikely attribution had been shown to her in a newly plausible light. It was just the sort of painting, doggedly literal and morbidly symbolic, that Nick liked least, and it was even worse life-size, when the literalism so cried out to be admired. 'I heard tell he's the same fellow as painted *The Light of the World*, with the Lord Jesus knocking on the door.'

'Oh yes, that's right,' said Nick, like a schoolteacher pleased by the mere fact of a child's interest, and leaving questions of taste for much later. 'Well, for that you only have to go to St Paul's Cathedral.'

Mrs Charles took this in. 'You hear that now, Rosemary? You and me's going out to St Paul's Cathedral any day now to look at that with our own naked eyes.' And Nick saw her, in shiny shoes and the small black hat like an air hostess's that was nesting on a chair in the corner, making her way there, with waits at a number of bus stops, and the nervous patience of a pilgrim – he saw her, as if from the air, climbing the steps and going into the stupendous church, which he felt he owned, all ironically and art-historically, more than her, a mere credulous Christian. 'Or else, of course, you and me can go . . . eh?' she said to Nick, somehow shyly not using his name.

'I'd love to do that,' Nick said quickly, taking the chance to be kind and likeable that had been denied him earlier on.

'We'll go together and have a good look at it,' said Mrs Charles.

'Excellent!' said Nick, and caught the hint of mockery in Leo's eyes.

Mrs Charles said, cocking her head on one side, 'You know, they always got something clever about them, these old pictures, don't they?'

'Often they do,' Nick agreed.

'And you know the clever thing about this one now . . .' She gave him the tolerant but crafty look of someone who holds the answer to a trick question.

To Nick the clever thing was perhaps the way that the Virgin, kneeling by the chest that holds the hoarded gifts of the Magi, and seeing the portent of the Crucifixion in her son's shadow cast on the rear wall of the room, has her face completely hidden from us, so that the painting's centre of consciousness, as Henry James might have thought of her, is effectively a blank; and that this was surely an anti-Catholic gesture. He said, 'Well, the detail is amazing – those wood shavings look almost real, everything about it's so accurate . . .'

'No, no . . .' said Mrs Charles, with amiable scorn. 'You see, the way the Lord Jesus is standing there, he's making a shadow on the wall that's just the exact same image of himself on the Cross!'

'Oh . . . yes,' said Nick, 'indeed . . . Isn't it called in fact—'

'And of course that all goes to show how the death of the Lord Jesus and his Resurrection is foretold in the Bible from ancient times.'

Nick said, 'Well, it certainly illustrates that view even if it doesn't prove it,' in a perhaps misjudged tone of equable deliberation. Leo shot him a wincing glance and created a diversion.

'Yeah, I like the way he's got him yawning,' he said; and he stretched his own arms out and up and tilted his head with a yawn that was just like the Lord Jesus except that he was holding an ice-cream-smeared dessert spoon in his left hand. It was

the kind of camp you see sometimes in observant children –
and Rosemary watched him with the smothered amazement
and mocking anticipation of a good girl whose brother has
been insolent and reckless. But she said,

'Mm, it makes me shiver when he does that.'

Leo tutted and grinned, as his own shadow, in the room's
less brilliant evening light, stretched and shrugged and faltered
across the wall above his chair.

When the meal finished Leo was checking his bike and they
were out in the street almost at once. Nick was relieved but
ashamed – he made a joke of being dragged away in the
middle of a sentence, as if Leo was a lively dog on the end of
a leash. But Mrs Charles seemed not to mind. 'Ah, you go on
now,' she said, as if she might be quite relieved herself. Or
perhaps, he thought, as he hurried along in silence beside Leo,
she had sensed his own relief, and been saddened by it for a
second, and then had hardened herself against him . . . Her
tone was nearly dismissive, and perhaps she thought he was
false . . . Well, he was condescending, in a way . . . These
anxieties flared dully through him. He began to resent Mrs
Charles for thinking he was condescending.

Leo was walking briskly, as if they'd agreed where they were
going, but he said nothing. Nick couldn't tell if he was sulky,
angry, ashamed, defiant . . . but he knew that all these
emotions could rise and rush and fizzle and mutate very
quickly, and that it was wiser to let him settle than to guess his
mood and risk the wrong opener. Nick's consciousness of
being wise was a small refuge when Leo was difficult or distant. He took in the after-sunset chill, the upswept trails of
dark cloud above the rooftops, and the presence of autumn,
light but penetrating, in the cold cobalt beyond. In their four
weeks together these evening walks, with the ticking bicycle
beside them or between them, had taken on a deepening

colour of romance. He worried that the silence itself was a kind of comment, and as they reached the end of the road he pulled Leo against him with a quick chafing hug and said, 'Mmm, thank you for that, darling.'

Leo snorted softly. 'What are you thanking me for?'

'Oh, just for taking me home. For introducing me to your family. It means a lot to me.' And he found his little avowal released a sentiment he hadn't quite felt before he made it. He was very touched.

'So, now you know what they're like,' said Leo, stopping and staring, with just his mother's narrowing of the gaze, across the major road beyond. The evening traffic was let slip from the lights and accelerated down the hill towards them and past them, then thinned, and then there was only a waiting emptiness again.

'They're wonderful,' Nick said, meaning only to be kind – though he heard the word hang, in the silence between the lights, as if in inverted commas, and underlined too: the wonderful of gush, of connoisseurship, of Kensington Park Gardens. Leo seemed to find it absurdly unexpected, and kept blinking, but then smiled and said with a dry laugh,

'If you say so . . . darling' – the darling, longed for by Nick, taking on a dubious ironic twang.

Nick had a large wild plan of his own for the night, but for now he let Leo take charge: they were going to go back to Notting Hill and catch the seven fifteen screening of *Scarface* at the Gate – it had just come out and Leo had all the facts on it, including its enormous length, 170 minutes, each one of which appeared to Nick like a shadowy unit of body heat, of contact and excitement. They would be pressed together in the warm darkness for three hours. Leo said what a great actor Al Pacino was, and spoke of him almost amorously, which Nick couldn't honestly do – to him Pacino wasn't that sort of idol. There was an interview with him in the new *Time Out*, which

Leo had probably read, since his ideas on film seemed to Nick to be drawn pretty closely from the capsule reviews in that magazine. Still, film was Leo's province, rather humourlessly patrolled against Nick's pretensions, it was one of the interests he'd originally advertised, and Nick conceded, 'No, he's a genius,' which was a word he could thrill them both with. They stood at the bus stop with that idea in their heads.

When the bus came Nick hopped on and sat looking out at the back at Leo, who was ages fiddling with his bike and then getting on it, dwindling away every second into the night-lit street. Then the bus pulled in at a further stop, and the bike came almost floating up, Leo rising from his forward crouch to glance in at Nick – he seemed to ride the air there for a second, and then he winked and stooped and with a click of the gears he slipped past. Nick was glad of the wink this time, he raised his hand and grinned, and then was left, in the public brightness of the bus, to be eyed by the people opposite with vague suspicion.

The bus threaded down at last across the Harrow Road and began its long descent of Ladbroke Grove. He pictured Leo whizzing ahead, and kept losing him in the gleams and shadows of the night traffic. Where was he now? Nick was still in the alien high reach of the road, with the canal and the council estates, and longing for the other end, his own end, the safety and aloofness of white stucco and private gardens. He wondered what Leo thought as he made the transition, which occurred at the dense middle part by the market and the station, under clangorous bridges, where people loitered and shouted . . . After that there was a stretch of uneasy gentility, before the Grove climbed, taking palpable advantage of the hill as a social metaphor, and touching into life the hint of an orchard or thicket in the very name of the street. He didn't fool himself that Leo was sensitive to these things – he was a figure of wrenching poetry to Nick, but was not himself poetic, and clearly found something daft and even creepy in Nick's aesthetic promptings and hesitations. Nick sometimes made the mistake of thinking that Leo didn't feel things strongly, and then the shock, when his love and need for him leapt out, angry at being doubted, took his breath away, and almost frightened him. He thought back over the meal, the visit, and saw that of course it had meant a lot to Leo as well, but that everything was squashed and denied by secrecy: if he had been a woman the occasion would have had a ritual meaning, and Leo's mother could have let herself dream of the altar steps at last. To Nick the bulging subject of the visit had been his love for Leo, which obsessed him just as much as Mrs Charles's love of Jesus did her; but she had given herself licence to express her fixation, had embraced a duty to do so, whilst his burned through only in blushes and secret stares. She had eclipsed him completely.

When he got to the cinema he found Leo near the head of the queue. 'You made it,' he said, looking round at the people behind and nodding – 'Yeah, it's the first night,' as if it was a bore, he was a martyr to first nights. And when they reached the window it turned out that the cinema was nearly full, and they wouldn't be able to sit together. Nick shrugged and said, 'Ah well . . .' backing into the couple behind them, who were trying to overhear. 'We can come at the weekend.'

But Leo said, 'Yeah, we'll have them – god, we're here now,' and gave him a look of friendly concern.

Nick said quietly, 'I just thought, if we can't sit together . . .' since the only reason for sitting through a super-violent three-hour gangster movie was to have Leo's weight and warmth against him and his hand in his open fly. They had touched each other like that, with cautious delirious slowness, in *Rumblefish*, under the dreamy aegis of Matt Dillon, and in Fellini's *And the Ship Sails On*, which had been Nick's hopeless choice of picture and a peculiar backdrop to an orgasm.

Otherwise, they had only made love in parks, or public lavatories, or once in the back of Pete's shop, which Leo had kept a key to, and which felt even more furtive than these cinema handjobs. The thing about the cinema was that they seemed to share in the long common history of happy snoggers and gropers, and Nick liked that.

But now he was alone again, he felt it very keenly, accepting the 'better' ticket, in the middle of the back row. The ads were already showing as he clambered along and in their patchy glare he loomed and ducked and apologized, and was a clumsy intruder in a world of snuggling coupledom. He squeezed in and even the space of his seat seemed half absorbed by the lovers' coats and bags and angled limbs. The 170 minutes stretched out ahead like a long-ago detention, some monstrous test. They stretched out, in fact, like a film he had no wish to see, and for a moment he was gripped by a tearful bolshiness that he himself thought astonishing in a grown man. He saw that he could get up and go home and come back at the end. But then he was frightened of what Leo would say. There was so much at stake. There was a Bacardi advertisement, and the brilliance of tropical sea and white sand lit up the auditorium. He stared at the left side, near the front, to try to spot Leo, but he couldn't find him. Then he did see the squared-off silhouette of his head, and for a moment his oddly distant and attentive profile, played over by the reflected light. Of course the scene of palm trees and surf was much the same as Mrs Charles's mural. Now superbly handsome heterosexuals romped across it.

Critics had already described *Scarface* as 'operatic', which perhaps was only their way of saying it was Latin, noisy and bombastic. It was set in a Miami so violent and so opulent, so glittering and soulless, that Nick found himself worrying about how people survived in it, and then about how he would survive in it. In his disaffected mood he kept wandering off from the film itself into paranoid doubts and objections. He saw that he was reacting like his mother, for whom any film on the telly with a sex scene or the word shit in it took on a nearly hostile presence, and was watched thereafter with warm mistrust. *Scarface* was all about cocaine, which alarmed him. He remembered tensely how Toby had taken it at Hawkeswood with Wani Ouradi. The film confirmed his worst suspicions. Nowhere in it was there a hint of the delicious pleasure that Toby had spoken of. The drug was money and power and addiction – a young blonde actress in the film snorted joyless volumes of it.

The couple on Nick's left were slumped in a slowly evolving embrace. He was aware of a hand on a thigh left bare by a very short skirt – and when it moved his glance twitched guiltily away. He had an unusual sense of the cinema as a room – a long narrow space with the dusty plaster mouldings of an old theatre. Instead of the proper oblivion of the filmgoer he felt a kind of foreboding. When the picture brightened his eyes yearned down across the shadowy ranks of heads, but Leo was little and so was he, and he never had that one clear view of him again. Because the film was Leo's choice, he imagined him enjoying it, taking it on, adjusting himself, as it went along, to its new standards of hardness. A film that was shocking quickly lowered the threshold, it made people unshockable. Nick felt that if he'd been sitting with Leo he might have tittered and groaned at the shootings and blood like everyone else. But now they were apart, as they might have been on occasion in this very cinema before they even knew of each other's existence, sitting separately in the near dark. It was irrational, perhaps, but the glaring unreality of the film seemed to throw a suspicion of unreality over everything else, and his affair with Leo, which was so odd, so new, so unrecognized, felt open to crude but penetrating doubt. He wondered if he would have noticed Leo a year ago, in the shuffling semi-patience of the exit line, or carried his image home to lie awake with. Well, probably not, since one of Leo's affectations was to sit through to the very last credits, the lenses, the insurers, the thanks to the mayor and police department of . . . oh, somewhere obscurely a solution and a puzzle at the same time.

And it wasn't in fact until all that was over that Leo came into the foyer, blinking and nodding and then genially puzzled at the troubled look on Nick's face. 'All right, babe,' he said quietly, and gripped his upper arm to steer him out. 'That's what I call snorting coke,' he went on, referring to a scene in the film's final hour where Pacino had torn open a huge plastic bag of cocaine on his desk and plunged his nose into it, the slave at last to his own instrument of power. It had struck Nick as completely ridiculous. 'Did you like that, then?'

Nick hummed and cleared his throat like an anxious bringer of bad news. 'Not much,' he said, and gave Leo a thin smile.

'It was quite a laugh,' said Leo. 'The ending was outrageous.'

'Yes . . . yes it was,' Nick agreed, hesitantly but firmly, recalling the comprehensive final bloodbath. As so often he had the feeling that an artistic disagreement, almost immaterial to the other person, was going to be the vehicle of something that mattered to him more than he could say.

But Leo said, 'Nah, sorry about that, babe, it was pretty crappy. And we never got our kiss and cuddle.'

'I know,' said Nick with an archness that covered and somehow dissolved three hours of regrets – in his relief he couldn't see where he was going and grabbed and rattled one of the cinema's already locked glass doors.

Leo went out and into the blocked-off side street where he'd left his bike, and when Nick followed he found him putting his arms round his neck and kissing him, chastely but tenderly, on the forehead; then he kept looking at him, lightly frowning and smiling at the same time, with humorous reproach.

'Nicholas Guest.'

'Mm . . .' – Nick colouring but holding Leo's gaze submissively.

'You worry too much. You know that?'

'I know . . .'

'Yeah? You do trust your Uncle Leo, don't you?'

'Of course I trust you,' Nick burst out quietly, as if he'd been asked a simpler question.

'Well, don't worry so much, then. Will you do that for me?' And again he was all cockney softness.

'Yes,' said Nick, glancing a little worriedly none the less to left and right, since Leo was holding him against the wall like a mugger as much as a lover – he worried what people would think. In the wake of his relief this short exchange raised a vague dissatisfaction.

'Don't ever forget it.'

'I won't,' Nick murmured, and Leo stood back. He wasn't sure what it was that he mustn't forget, he had a restless ear for syntax, but he smiled at the general drift of the little catechism of reassurance. It was lovely that Leo saw at once what was wrong, even if his avuncular tone didn't put it completely right. Nick found he was confident enough, despite his racing heartbeat, to mention his plan.

'You're sure they're not here, yeah?'

'Yes, I'm positive. Well, Catherine might be in.'

'Catherine, right, that's your sister, yeah?' And then Leo winked.

The heavy, sharp-edged key to the mortise locks had already cut a gash in Nick's trouser pocket, and the whole bunch was tangled in the torn threads and hanging against the top of his thigh. As he tugged at it a few of the new pound coins dropped ticklingly down his leg and rolled across the tiled floor of the porch. Leo jumped on them. 'That's right, throw it away,' he said.

A light always burned in the hall, and gave it tonight a somehow eerie vigilance. Nick locked the door behind them, and put the keys back in his pocket, and this time, after two steps, they had shaken their way down his leg and out on to the chequered marble. Leo, peeking in the hall mirror, raised an eyebrow but said nothing. On the console table were spare car keys, opera glasses, one of Gerald's grey fedoras, a letter 'By Hand' addressed to the Rt Hon Mr and the Hon Mrs Gerald Fedden – and together, as a careless still life, reflected in the mirror, they seemed to Nick both wonderful and embarrassing. He stood still for a moment and listened. The light, from a brass lantern hanging in the well of the stair, threw steep shadows down inside the threshold of the dining room, revealing only the black satin bodice of a nineteenth-century Kessler. The Hon and the Rt Hon were both in Barwick for the night on constituency business, and whilst he confirmed this to himself he was also rewording the sentence in which he would explain Leo to them if, after all, they came chattering in. He had a sense of their possessing the house and everything in it, calmly but defiantly, and of its stone staircase and climbing cornices reaching rather pitilessly up into the shadows. He gave Leo a passing kiss on the cheek, and drew him into the kitchen, where the under-unit lighting stammered and blinked into life. 'Do you want a whisky?'

And for once Leo said, 'I don't mind if I do! Yeah, that would be nice. Thanks very much, Nick.' He strolled round the room as if not really noticing it, and stood scanning the wall of photographs. One of the *Tatler* pictures from Toby's twenty-first had now been bought, blown up and framed: a wildly smiling family group in which the Home Secretary seemed to show some awareness of being an intruder. Just above them the student Gerald, in tails, was shaking hands with Harold Macmillan at the Oxford Union. Again Leo made no comment, but when Nick handed him the cold tumbler he saw in his eyes and in his very faint smile that he was noting and storing. Perhaps he was calculating the degree of affront represented by all this Toryness and money. Nick felt his own kudos as family friend, as keyholder, was a very uncertain quantity. 'Let's go upstairs,' he said.

He went up two at a time, in too much of a hurry, and when he looked back on the turn he saw Leo dawdling by the same factor that he was rushing; he went into the drawing room and pressed switches that brought on lamps on side tables and over pictures – so that when Leo sauntered in he saw the room as Nick had first seen it two years before, all shadows and reflections and the gleam of gilt. Nick stood in front of the fireplace, longing for it to be a triumph, but taking his cue from the suppressed curiosity in Leo's face.

'I'm not used to this,' Leo said.

'Oh . . .'

'I don't drink whisky.'

'Ah, no, well—'

'Who knows what it'll do to me? I might get dangerous.'

Nick grinned tightly and said, 'Is that a threat or a promise?' He reached out and touched Leo's hip – his hand lay there for a second or two. Normally, together, alone, they would have been snogging, holding each other very tightly; though sometimes, it was true, Leo laughed at Nick's urgency and said, 'Don't panic, babe! I'm not going anywhere! You've got me!' Leo rested his glass on the mantelpiece, and eyed Guardi's *Capriccio with S. Giorgio Maggiore*, which certainly seemed a rather pointless picture after *The Shadow of Death*. It was hard to imagine Rachel haranguing her guests about the clever something in it. Underneath it the invitations were propped, overlapping, making almost one long curlicued social sentence, Mr and Mrs Geoffrey – & Countess of Hexham – Lady

Carbury 'At Home' for – Michael and Jean – The Secretary of State . . . and those others, amazingly thick, with chamfered edges, The Lord Chamberlain is Commanded by Her Majesty to Request . . . which tended to stay there long after the events they referred to, and which gave Nick as well a lingering pompous thrill. Though he saw now, very quickly, that such a pleasure required willing complicity in Gerald's habit of show-ing off to himself. He turned away, pretending the invitations weren't there, and Leo said, with a derisive tut,

'God, the snobs.'

Nick laughed. 'They're not really snobs,' he said. 'Well, he is perhaps a bit. They're . . .' It was hard to explain, hard to know, in the dense compact of the marriage, who sanctioned what. They were each other's alibi. And Nick saw that Leo was using the word in a looser way, to mean rich people, who lived in nice places, to mean nobs. It struck him that he might be about to take the whole treat of coming to Kensington Park Gardens and making love in a bed as an elaborate but crushing rebuff. He watched him sip some more, deliberately, and then wander towards the front windows. He tried to act on his advice of fifteen minutes earlier, tried to trust his Uncle Leo. The room was devised and laid out for entertaining, on a generous scale, and for a second, as if a thick door had opened, he heard the roar of accumulated talk and laughter, the consensual social roar, instead of the clock's ticking and the fizz of silence.

'That's a nice bit of oyster,' Leo said, pointing at a walnut commode. 'And that's Sèvres, if I'm not wrong, with that blue.'

'Yes, I think it is,' Nick said, feeling that this nod at a com-mon interest also brought old Pete rather critically into the room. Old Pete would have had some smart gay backchat to deal with an awkward moment like this.

'No, they've got some nice pieces,' Leo said, flatly, and a little ponderously, and so perhaps shyly. He turned round, nodding. 'You've done well.'

'Darling, none of it's mine . . .'

'I know, I know.' Leo sat down at the piano, and after a moment's thought stood his glass on a book on the lid. 'What's this, then . . . Mozart, all right, that's not too bad,' checking the cover of the music on the stand, but letting it fall back to the eternally open Andante. 'So what key's this in?' – as if the key required some special tactics, like a golf-shot. 'F major . . .'

'It's a funny old piano,' said Nick. He felt that if Leo played the piano, especially if he played it badly, it would waken the unconscious demons of the house and bring them in yawning and protesting.

'Ah, that's all right,' Leo murmured courteously; and he started to play, with a distracted frown at the page. It was the great second movement of K533, spare, probing, Bach-like, that Nick had discovered, and tried to play, on the night when he'd lost his chance of meeting Leo – till Catherine had complained, and he'd apologized and doodled off into Waldorf music. To apologize for what you most wanted to do, to concede that it was obnoxious, boring, 'vulgar and unsafe' – that was the worst thing. And the music seemed to know this, to know the irresistible curve of hope, and its hollow inversion. Leo played it pretty steadily, and Nick stood behind him, willing it along, nudging it through those quickly corrected wrong notes and tense hesitations that are a torture of sight-reading and yet heighten the rewards when everything runs clear and good. When Leo suddenly went steeply wrong he gave a disparaging shout, struck a few random chords, then reached for his glass. 'Must be too pissed to play,' he said, not necessarily joking.

Nick sniggered. 'You're good. I can't play that. I didn't know you could play.' He felt very touched, and chastened, as if by a glimpse of his own unquestioned assumptions. It opened a new perspective, the sight of Leo in his jeans and sweatshirt and baseball boots raising Mozart out of the sonorous old Bösendorfer. And it seemed to have loosened him up, he was like a shy guest who makes a brilliant joke, its lustre heightened by delay and distillation, and who suddenly finds he's enjoying himself. Nick grabbed him from behind and squashed a kiss onto his cheek.

Leo chuckled and said, 'All right, babe . . .'

Nick said, 'I love you,' shaking him in a tight hug, and grunting at the hard muscular heat of him. Leo reached up with his free right hand and gripped his arm. After a while he said,

'That's a terrible picture.'

It was Norman Kent's portrait of Toby, aged sixteen, and it was the image – beyond the intimidating bronze bust of Liszt – on which the eyes of the doodling pianist tended to dwell. While Leo had been playing, it had lent its sickly colour to Nick's thoughts.

'I know . . . Poor Toby.'

'Cos he's quite tasty, in my opinion.'

'Oh yes.'

'You never told me if you had him, when you were all up at Oxford University.'

Nick had still not quite let on to Leo that before their tangle in the bushes he had never exactly 'had' anyone. He said, 'No, no, he's completely straight.'

'Yeah?' said Leo, sceptically. 'You must have had a go.'

'Not really,' Nick said. He stood back, with his hands still on Leo's shoulders, and smiled wanly at the pink-faced blazered boy. The old regret could always come alive again, and for a moment even Leo, warm under his hands, seemed cheap and provisional compared to the unattainable bloom of Toby.

'I just thought the way he kissed you and looked at you was a bit poofy.'

'Don't!' Nick murmured, and then laughed, pulling Leo to get him up, and get the real kisses from him, the ones that Toby would never give him.

But Leo held out a moment longer. 'So they're easy about having a bender in the house, are they, their lordships?'

'Of course,' said Nick. 'They're absolutely fine with it.' And in his mind he heard Catherine saying, 'As long as it's never mentioned.' He went on, with a degree of exaggeration, 'They've got lots of gay friends. In fact they asked me to bring you here, darling.'

'Oh,' said Leo, with a subtlety of register worthy of Rachel herself.

Nick lay naked on top of the duvet, in quick-pulsed amazement. Leo had rung his mother, told her he was staying over: it was a risk, a yielding, and therefore a commitment. Nick listened to the hiss of the shower in the bathroom across the landing. Then, since he could see himself in the wardrobe mirror, he got under the bedclothes. He lay there, with one hand behind his head, in an almost painful state of happiness and worry. Far down below, the front door was triple-locked, the lights were all out in the drawing room and kitchen, the one lantern cast its cold glare into the hall. Catherine's bedroom door was closed, but he was certain she was out. They had the house to themselves. The window was open a notch, and he could hear the throat-tearing runs and trills of a robin that had taken to singing in the garden at night, and which he had eagerly decided was a nightingale; an old lady standing listening on the gravel path had put him right. He had still, therefore, never heard a nightingale, but he couldn't imagine it bettering his robin. The question was what time would Gerald and Rachel get back. But actually, probably, not till late, it was Gerald's 'surgery' in the morning, then a two-hour drive. Nick smiled at their unconscious generosity.

The shower-noise had stopped, and the robin skirled on, with sulky pauses and implacable resumptions. Nick would have liked it even better if Leo had come to bed without showering, he loved the faint sourness of his skin, the sharpness of his armpits, the sweet staleness deep between his legs. Leo's smells were little lessons constantly re-learnt, little shocks of authenticity. But to Leo himself they were a source of annoyance and almost of shame. He had a terribly keen sense of smell, revealed in a queue or a crowded room by a snubbed upper lip and an aristocratic flinching of the nostrils. He insisted he liked Nick's smells, and Nick, who had never really thought of himself as having smells, was nervously unsure if this was truth or chivalry. Perhaps it was a loving mixture of the two.

There was a kind of magic in this – to be lying in bed, a single bed, with all that it implied, and playing gently with himself, and waiting for his lover to appear. It was the posture of a lifelong singleness, incessant imagining, the boy's supremacy in a world of dreams, where men kept turning up to do his bidding; and now, that rattle of the bathroom door, snap of the light cord, squeak of the landing floor, were the signals of an actual arrival, and within three seconds the door would open and Leo would come in—

How black he looked, in the white skirt of a bath towel pulled tight round his buttocks and over the curbed jut of his dick. He held his folded clothes in his hands, like a recruit, stripped and scrubbed and given his slops – he looked around, then put them down on the desk, by the blue library books. He was a trifle formal, he winked at Nick but he was clearly moved by the ordinariness and novelty of the moment. To Nick it darkened, it had the feeling of an elopement, of elated action haunted by the fears it had defied, of two lovers suddenly strangers to each other on their first night in a foreign hotel. But after all they had only eloped upstairs, it was absurd. He felt breathless pride at having Leo here. He threw back the duvet, and said, 'I'm sorry about the bed' – shifting a bit to make room.

'Eh . . . ?' said Leo.

'I don't think you'll get much sleep.'

Leo let his towel drop to the floor and stared at Nick without smiling. 'I'm not planning on getting any,' he said.

Nick accepted the challenge with a little moan. It was the first time he had seen Leo naked, and the first time he had seen the masking shadow of his face, lazily watchful, easily cynical, clever and obtuse by turns, melt into naked feeling. Leo breathed through his mouth, and his look was a wince of lust and also, it seemed to Nick, of self-accusation – that he had been so slow, so vain, so blind.

'TO WHOM DO YOU BEAUTIFULLY BELONG?'
(1986)

7

Nick went ahead on the path and held the gate open for Wani, so that for several seconds the outside world had a view of naked flesh before the gate, with its 'Men Only' sign, swung shut behind them. It was a small compound, a concrete yard, with benches round the walls under a narrow strip of roof. It was like a courtyard of the classical world reduced to pipes and corrugated iron. There was something distantly classical, too, in the protracted nakedness, and something English, school-like and comfortless in the concrete and tin and the pond-water smell. Nick crossed the open space, past the books and towels of one or two sunbathers, and he saw it take account of them, someone greeted him, conversations stretched and lulled, and he felt the gaze of the little crowd, like idle finger-tips, run over him and come to rest, more tenderly and curi-ously, on Wani. Wani, in ice-blue mirror shades, was a figure of novel beauty, and only Nick perhaps, sitting down and beckoning to him, saw the wariness in his half-smile.

'Mm, very primitive,' Wani said, as if the place confirmed a suspicion he had about Nick.

Nick said, 'I know,' and grinned – it was just what he loved about it.

'Where do we put our things?'

'Just leave them here, they'll be fine.'

But Wani flinched at this. He had the keys to the Mercedes in his jeans pocket, and his watch, as he had told Nick more than once, cost a thousand pounds. 'Yah, maybe I won't go in.' And maybe Nick, who had never owned anything, was guilty of failing to imagine the worries of a millionaire.

'Really, it'll be fine. Put your stuff in here,' he said, offering him the Tesco carrier bag which had held his towel and trunks.

'This watch cost a thousand pounds,' said Wani.

'Perhaps don't tell everyone about it,' Nick said.

There was an old man drying near them, squat and bandy and brown all over, and Nick remembered him from last year, an occupant of the place, of the compound and the jetty and the pond, and more especially of the screened inner yard where on a hot day men sunbathed naked, hip to hip. He was lined but handsome, and Nick felt that smoothed and uniformed, in vigilant half-profile, his picture could well have accompanied the obituary of a general or air vice-marshal. He nodded amiably at him, as a leathery embodiment of the spirit of the place, and the old man said, 'George has gone, then. Steve's just told me, went last night.'

'Oh,' said Nick, 'I'm sorry. No, I didn't know George,' but assuming that by 'gone' the old boy didn't mean gone on holiday. It was George who needed the obituary.

'You knew George.' He looked at Wani as well, who was undressing in a slow, abstracted way, with pauses for thought before each sock, each button. 'He was always here. He was only thirty-one.'

'I've never been here before,' Wani said, courteous but cold. The old man frowned back and nodded, accepting his mistake, but perhaps thinking less of them for not knowing George.

After a pause Nick said, 'How's the water?' and held his stomach in as he took his shirt off because he wanted the man to admire him. But he didn't reply, and perhaps he hadn't heard the question.

Out on the jetty Nick strode ahead again, in his blue Speedos, and opened his arms to meet the embrace of the view, the green and silver expanse of the pond, young willows and hawthorns all round it, and the Heath behind, glimpsed only as patches of sunlit hillside. Nick was pleased with his own body, and he preened in pardonable ways, stretching and flicking his feet up against his buttocks as he ran on the spot. Across the surface of the water moved the dotted heads of swimmers. There was something sociable and inquisitive about them. Out in the middle of the pond was the old wooden raft, the site of endless easy contacts, and the floating platform of some of Nick's steadiest fantasies. Half a dozen men were on it now, and soon he would be with them. He turned round and grinned to encourage Wani, who was dawdling by the curved downward rail of the ladder, and gazing at the distant heads of the swimmers as if wondering how they'd ever got there. It seemed swimming was a rare omission from the list of things he did beautifully. There was a mild and interesting cruelty in bringing him here, so far out of his element. 'You've got to jump in,' he said. 'You'll find it torture going in slowly.' He smiled at Wani's tight black trunks, the smoothness and delicacy of his pale brown body, and the usual provocation of his penis, now held upright over his balls like a bold exclamation mark. Then he jumped in himself, to show how easy it was, and felt the shock of the cold water just below the thin warmth of the surface. He hung there, kicking back and nodding at Wani, who stood stooped like a skier, but with one hand pinching his nose; and then flung himself into the pond. When he came up he was gasping and sploshing about and for a second he had a look of undisguised fear. His black curls were half unwound by the water, and hung over his eyes and ears. Nick bobbed beside him and felt his grip on his upper arm; he let his legs wander and slide consolingly between Wani's, and with his free hand he swept his hair back, and that seemed to steady Wani, who swam off in a hasty, upright breaststroke, as if nothing had happened.

For a few minutes they pushed along in a rough circle, following the white cords strung between floating rings which marked the boundary of the swimming area. Beyond it, Nick supposed, the water must lie too shallowly over the deep soft mud. Wani swam well enough, in fact, with head up and the facetious expression of someone forced to be a good sport; he stopped at one of the rings and clung to it for a rest, with a heavy-breathing grin, and a shake of the head that seemed to say 'I can do this' as well as 'I'll get you back for it'. Nick pulled up the goggles that were bobbing loosely round his throat, and duck-dived. Under the yellowish sparkle of the surface the water was muddy green, deepening into murky brown, a world of bottle-glass colours. He twisted round, deciding what trick to play on Wani. Bubbles, dazzles from the rippling surface, stirred-up specks of black leaves swung and fled around Wani's legs, which hung there, lazily chasséing, in a princely pretence that no underwater attack was expected. And perhaps it was too childish, with Wani all at his mercy – instead of a grab or a tickle he shot up bursting for breath and laughing in his face. He would have kissed him if a watchful old gent hadn't been cruising so very close by them.

When they set off again, Nick raced ahead and came back, triumphing over Wani, decorating his steady course with curlicues, and all the while looking out for who else was there. It was hard to tell from their sleeked heads in the water; but through the smear of the goggles each figure waiting on the jetty or clambering onto the raft had the gleam of a new possibility. Nick swam close to the raft once, and kicked round it on his back, while he and a couple who were standing on it wondered if they knew each other.

After an almost complete turn of the pond Wani had done enough, and they trod water for a minute and talked while Nick glanced to left and right with his naked eyes. He loved it here but he was disappointed, it was too early in the season perhaps, he matched the calm of today and the chill of the water against the swarming heatwave Sundays of last year, the raft mad with clutching and jumping, the toilets crowded and intent, the queens on the grass outside packed like a city in a dozen rivalrous districts.

There were shouts and splashes from the raft, where a new group had converged. Nick felt the tug of curiosity and saw the chance to show Wani off and to show off to him, which was a lovely double vanity. Wani shivered and Nick said, 'You need to keep moving,' and kicked away towards the middle of the pond. A couple of dark men in black trunks were standing up, clumsily repelling a big blond muscle-queen who was trying to climb onto the stiffly lurching deck. Two other men who were crouching on the edge fell in, they half threw themselves in, like kids, and then scrambled back to join the assault. Thirty seconds of struggle followed, which some took more seriously than others, or with more thought for how they looked. Nick followed it all with smiling intensity, looking for his place in it.

Now there was a kind of truce, and everyone got back on board, so that when Nick cruised past he had a view of dangling legs, pinched dicks at funny angles, streaked hair and glistening skin, a floating tableau of men against the sky. Sex made them half conscious, half forgetful of the picture they made; they were sportsmen resting in stunned camaraderie, but some of them wriggled and held hands and breathed lustfully in each other's faces. They kicked their feet in the water, indolent but purposeful. One of them who was standing behind leant forward, out of the sky and the trees, and Nick reached him a hand and shot up and hopped out streaming as two queens plumped apart to make room for him. He stood breathing and grinning in a loose but curious embrace with the men in the middle. He had a sense of something fleeting and harmonic, longed for and repeated – it was the circling trees, perhaps, and the silver water, the embrace of a solitary child-hood, and the need to be pulled up into a waiting circle of men.

'Don't I see you at Bang last week?' the man beside him said, who had put a steadying hand on Nick's shoulder and left it there.

'I think not,' said Nick, who in fact had never been there. But he carried some memory-print of this man, some unplaced excitement. It took him a moment to realize that he used to see him at the Y, last year perhaps, in the showers there; and a moment more to confirm that as Nick had grown slowly and unseriously heavier, the Spaniard, if that's what he was, black-haired and lean, with large rosy nipples, had grown perceptibly thinner, into an eerily beautiful, etched-out ver-sion of himself. He leant lightly on Nick now, and seemed almost to shrug off this undeniable fact, or perhaps to chal-lenge him to see it, but not himself to allude to it in any way, unless by a lingering, fearful glance. Nick twisted casually away from him, and what came back gleaming out of the blur of memory was his round bottom and the tiny black curls just showing when he bent over: an image which also reminded him of Wani. He scanned the water blandly, and thought that perhaps he had gone in – just then the fun began again, the Spaniard abruptly dive-bombed, everyone shouted, and the raft itself groaned and creaked. Nick hopped around, laughing and shouting something himself into the unavoidable drench after drench as people jumped in. And there, in the wallow, was Wani's face, almost tearful with concentration as he tried to avoid the reckless arms and legs of the other men and find a moment to clamber out.

'Hello, darling!' said Nick, and went down on one knee to help him heave himself up. Wani didn't answer and didn't smile.

A few minutes later it was almost calm again. They were sit-ting there beside a man of fifty with thick grey chest hair and a restlessly sociable manner. His much younger friend, a Malaysian perhaps, was swimming some way from the raft, cruising other men outrageously, and doing clever duck-dives which made his trunks come off. 'Oh, he gives me some trouble, that one,' the man said. 'Look at him.' Wani smiled politely and turned to Nick; he wasn't used to meeting people like this, in the near-naked free-for-all of a public place. 'Don't get me wrong, though – it's all good fun.' The man waved cheerfully as if the boy was paying him even the faintest attention, and said, 'He's devoted to me, you know. I don't know why, but he is.'

'What's his name, then?' said a rough-voiced man, who was squatting behind them.

'He's called Andy.'

'Andy, yeah?' said the man. 'Here, Andy,' he shouted, getting to his feet, 'show us your arse!'

'He will!' said his old protector. 'He will!'

The raft shook and on the other side of them a sleekly muscly man twisted up out of the water and landed with a promising thump on the boards. Nick saw Wani glance across at him from under his long lashes, as if assessing a new kind of problem or possibility; Nick himself had seen him here last year. He was balding and dark eyed, round faced, with a nice long nose and the lazy but focused expression of a man who thinks of nothing but sex. Nick remembered his idling gaze, the huge dark pupils that seemed to fill his eyes, and the curving weight of him in his black trunks. His stomach was a smooth curve outwards as he sat, and it seemed his destiny to be fat, but for now the fat was held in easy balance with the muscle.

Wani was sitting with his knees drawn up, his hair swept back in shiny waves but bunching and tightening again as it dried. He had got back some of his social poise, and with it an oblique deprecating manner, as though afraid he might be recognized or fancied. The older man talked across him to Nick. 'He's getting so particular,' he said.

'Aha . . .' said Nick.

'KY not good enough any more, apparently. We have to have some other substance called Melisma. Then Melisma's not good enough, apparently, either. We're moving on to Crest. But you have to be careful, don't you, with these awful rubber johnnies. I never thought the day would come . . . What do you use?'

'Should keep him nice and clean, anyway,' said the rough-voiced man, who was clearly taking quite an interest in Andy. 'Crest's a kind of toothpaste, mate,' and shortly afterwards he dived in and swam powerfully in his direction.

'I'm Leslie, by the way,' said the older man.

Wani turned his head and nodded. 'Hi. Antoine.'

'Now where would you be from, I wonder?'

'I'm Lebanese,' said Wani, with a quick dry smile, in his driest English accent. Nick watched his aquiline profile and smiled mischievously. He liked to see another man acknowledge Wani's glamour, it gave him a quick jealous shot of the passion he had felt for him since Oxford, which was lust enlarged and diffused by mystery. Now he was looking down again, his extraordinary eyelashes lowered. Nick remembered him sometimes, after a class, or after dinner on a rarer night when he was unclaimed by his other worlds, coming back to the room of some poor student, with its shelf of paperbacks and a Dylan poster, and talking a bit more about *Culture and Anarchy* or *North and South*, swapping notes over Nescafé, and making a sweetly respectful attempt to show that he shared the concerns of these other boys, and like visiting royalty was quite unconscious of their clumsiness and deference. Wani, who could really only bear fresh coffee, with a little jug of hot milk on the side. Some of the snobbier people in college, like Polly Tompkins, mocked his fanciness and said he was only the son of a grocer, an immigrant orange-and-lemon seller, 'a Levantine cockney tart' was Polly's phrase – he was a cute little Lebanese boy who'd been sent to Harrow and turned into a drawling English gentleman. Some of them thought he must have been turned into a poof as well, on no stronger grounds than his tight trousers and his bewildering good looks.

'So what do you do?' said Leslie.

'I've got my own film-production company,' Wani said.

'Oh . . .' said Leslie, crushed and intrigued at once. And then, in a rather roundabout response, 'Did you see *A Room with a View*? I wonder what you thought of that, if you're in the film world.'

'I didn't, I'm afraid,' said Wani, with another tiny but chilling smile.

'Didn't I see you in the Volunteer last week?' Leslie said after a bit – at which Wani looked quite blank, but the question was aimed at the dark-eyed man, who all this time had been lying back on his elbow, with one knee raised and his tackle slumped unignorably towards them. It was difficult to tell if his vague smile was a reaction to their conversation, or even if he was looking at them. His eyes seemed to work on some scene of imminent gratification, unfolding on a screen that hung between himself and the afternoon. There was something confidently patient about him, no lecherous effort or rush. But when he was spoken to it was as if they'd already been talking, and there was an understanding between them. Nick gazed at him, feeling he allowed and absorbed gazes, and at the glinting water beyond, with a twinge of sadness that when they stopped talking they would have to leave the little sun-struck oblong of the raft and swim back to the solid world. Wani was looking at the man again too, but also at the waiting ladder of the jetty, with the flicker of someone calculating his escape.

When they were getting dried and dressed in the compound

Wani nodded and said, 'There's our friend Ricky again.' Nick looked over his shoulder and saw the sexy man emerging round the fence of the nudist yard and pulling carelessly at the draw-string of his trunks.

'Oh, yes. I didn't know he was called Ricky,' Nick said.

'Well, he looks like a Ricky,' said Wani, while getting out of his trunks sitting down and wrapped in a towel.

'Have you got an erection or something?' said Nick.

'Don't be puerile,' Wani said. He gave Nick a look that was part challenge and part broody supplication. 'Why don't you ask him if he'd like to come home with us?'

'What, "Ricky"?'

'Isn't that what goes on at this sort of place? I didn't imagine we'd come here for the exercise.'

Nick sniggered. 'You don't have to go mad,' he said, 'the first time I take you out.'

Wani coloured a little but he held his gaze. 'It could be a lot of fun,' he said. 'I should have thought. He's very common.'

Nick glanced round again at Ricky, who was loitering amiably by the path to the toilets, and loitered too of course in his memory, as unexplored potential. At the same time he felt a little clutch of warning. Wani didn't know what he might be getting them into, and nor did Nick. When he looked back Wani was standing up in his underpants and tugging on his jeans. 'I'm sure it could be,' Nick said drily. At which Wani, with a twitch of his eyebrows and a sour compression of his lips, seemed to shrug the thing off. He took his watch from his pocket and put it on.

'If you don't ask him soon,' he said, 'we won't have time. I'm sorry, I thought you liked him.'

'Yes, he's hot,' said Nick, and found he was describing himself, in his unexpected anxiety. He hated to see Wani's beautiful mouth curl like that, and to feel his disdain, so amusing and exciting when applied to others, fall on him. He wanted only love, and today perhaps a kind of obedience, from Wani, who knew that the local tactics of argument and persuasion confused and upset him. 'All right, I'll go and get him,' he said, pretending that for him as well to ask was naturally to get, and knowing that he could never allow Wani to ask him himself.

'I mean I know he's not one of your nig-nogs.'

'Oh, fuck off,' Nick said, and marched away, in his jeans, but still shirtless, towards the toilet. He felt the disadvantage of the clothed among the naked; and the floor of the lavatory, when he entered it, was unpleasantly wet under his bare feet.

The door of one of the two cubicles was shut, and at the raised tin trough of the urinal the man was standing, his big sleek back and arse to the room, but turning his head, in his odd expressionless way, to see who had come in. And that look, and the smell of the place, piss and disinfectant, the atmosphere of permission, the rules all changed by keen but furtive consent, gripped Nick and melted him. He went over and stood beside the man and a few seconds later the spray from the excited fizz of the flush was coldly tickling the tips of their two erections. Nick slid his foreskin slowly backwards and forwards and gazed at the other man's blunt-headed shaft. Then he looked into his eyes, and it was like when they had chatted on the raft, totally expected, the reason they were here, as commonplace as it was deep. He seemed to swim in that dark gaze, with little flickers of conjecture. The man tilted his head towards the open cubicle, so that Nick wondered if he could do that, quickly or partially, before 'getting' him, or trying to get him, to come home with them, but there was the snap of the bolt, the other door opened halfway and little Andy, the Malaysian handful, slipped out, and crossed the room to wash his hands. In the mirror Nick saw the mischief in his eyes fade into blankness. Then as if by magic the flush sounded, the door opened wide, and a grey-haired man, who was not his friend Leslie and not his rough-voiced admirer either, emerged and made off with a preoccupied look.

Now they were alone, and Nick felt there was something almost romantic in their patience, and in the man's delayed grab at his penis, and his own half embrace of the man's waist, his hand between his buttocks. The man was breathing in his face and Nick muttered, 'Wait . . . wait . . . what's your name?'

'Ricky,' said the man, and tried to kiss him again.

Nick giggled as he pulled back his head. 'I just wondered if you wanted to come home with me and my friend? You know, have a bit of fun . . .'

'Well . . .' Ricky clearly thought it was a lot of bother when he had him here already. 'How far is it?'

'Only . . . Kensington!'

'Kensington? Fuck – I don't know, mate.' And he pressed against Nick with another impatient nod at the waiting lock-up. Nick hugged him clumsily, and grunted at how much he would like to have him right here; but it would be a scandal with Wani waiting round the corner. He said,

'We've got a fantastic car.'

'Yeah?' said Ricky. 'Which is he, anyway, your friend? Sort of dark curly hair?' He gently pinched and twisted Nick's nipple, and Nick gasped as he said,

'You saw him . . .'

Ricky pondered and nodded and let Nick free himself. They took a moment to make themselves decent. 'He's a bit stuck-up, is he, that one? Butter wouldn't melt in his arse?'

'I wouldn't say that . . . He's a bit shy,' said Nick.

'We'll see about that, then,' said Ricky.

As they went out Nick said, 'Can you do us a favour?'

'I bloody well hope so.'

Nick winced. 'Can you pretend you're married – or at least you've got a girlfriend . . .'

Ricky shrugged and shook his head. 'I have got a girlfriend.'

'Have you?' Nick stopped for a second with his chin tucked in, while Ricky stared at him and then winked.

'Quick on the uptake, aren't I?'

Nick tutted and blushed. 'I must say you're fucking quick,' he said, almost in Ricky's voice.

Outside on the path Wani hurried ahead with the preoccupied look of a famous person, while Nick and Ricky followed behind. Ricky clearly never hurried, he was his own lazy happening. He kept his eyes on the pretty back view of Wani, which made Nick proud and also apprehensive. He wondered just what they were going to do, and couldn't distinguish the nerves that are a part of excitement from a kind of resentment. Wani's nerves showed in his cool dissociating manner. They went along beside the wide grass bank, and one of the sunbathing men called out something to Ricky, who gave him a nod and a dirty smile back – Nick smiled too, as if he knew what was going on.

In the lane above, Wani, who was playing with the car keys, flipping the leather fob about, said, 'You can drive, Nick,' and threw them over to him. It was typical of Wani to dress up a command as a treat. Nick had often been the passenger in WHO 6, but he had only driven it once before, by himself, a short hop from the river back to Kensington that became a whole glittering evening of darting about, the Brompton Road, Queen's Gate, along by the Park, round and round, and with the curious feeling (with the roof down and the coldish air blustering in) of passing for Wani, of being WHO, that glamorous enigma. All of which rather withered as he slid back into the driving seat. The car was parked in close to the rustic fence, under the lime trees, and their sticky exudations had already stippled the windscreen. He held down the button to retract the roof and watched in the mirror as it lifted and folded away behind him and sunlight through the leaves fell in glancingly on the dials and knobs and amber walnut. The other two stood waiting for him to pull out, but not talking. Then Wani gestured Ricky into the back, where he sat with his knees wide apart, since there was very little legroom. 'You all right there?' said Nick, looking over at the squashed contour of his packet and feeling oddly apologetic about both the splendour and the inconvenience of the car.

'I'm all right,' said Ricky, as if he was driven about like this every day.

They started on the steep hill towards Highgate and Nick was amazed all over again by the power leaping up under the ball of his foot. They seemed to wolf up the lane, in four thoughtless growls. He caught Ricky's eye in the mirror and said, 'So what time's your girlfriend getting back?'

Ricky said, 'She won't be back till really late, actually,' more clearly than when he told the truth, and then added, 'She's gone round to see her Uncle Nigel,' with a tolerant cluck. This bit of business acted visibly on Wani, who cleared his throat and half-turned in his seat to say,

'That's good.' The absurdity of the situation, something quite uncomfortable, tied a sudden knot in Nick, and at the top of the lane, instead of turning right down the hill towards town he turned the other way and climbed again towards Highgate village. He probably didn't need to explain, since as far as Wani was concerned they could have been in Lincolnshire, and Ricky would sit there with his half-smile of anticipation wherever they went, but he said,

'There's something I want to have a quick look at.' At the top he made an abrupt left into the long shady row that he knew must be The Grove. He was fairly sure he'd never been here before, it was something he'd imagined doing, a piece of research, historical, emotional . . . but as he peered through the line of trees at the beautiful old brick houses behind high railings, the house where Coleridge had lived and died, and then, as they crept along, bigger Georgian houses with flights of steps and carriage yards, he had the ghostly impression that he had been here, had been brought here on some unlocatable evening for some irrecoverable event. 'This is where Coleridge lived,' he said, with a glow of piety intended to stir Wani too, and then protracted to defy his evident lack of interest.

'OK,' said Wani.

'I just want to see where the Feddens used to live. Some old friends of mine,' he explained to Ricky. 'I know it was number thirty-eight . . .'

'This is sixteen,' said Wani.

It was one of the Feddens' sentimental routines to refer to their 'Highgate days', and Gerald would evoke the house where they had first lived in a tone of nostalgia and self-ridicule, as if remembering student digs. Rachel usually said it was 'a darling house', it was where she had raised her children, and a snapshot of Toby and Catherine, aged ten and eight, sitting on the front steps, remained in a silver frame on her dressing table. To Nick the place had an obscure proxy romance, as the first home of his second family. When they got to it there was a skip outside piled high with splintered timber, and a blue Portaloo in the front garden.

'Hm,' said Wani. 'OK . . .' And he turned and gave Ricky an encouraging glance, in case he was getting bored. 'Not much left.'

The house was having a restoration so thorough it looked like demolition. The roof was like another house, made of scaffolding and sheeting. Most of the stucco had been hacked from the walls, and you could see the buried arcs of brick over each window. Through the front door you saw the garden at the back. On the surviving white-stucco pier by the side gate there was a painted black finger and the words TRADESMEN'S ENTRANCE; underneath which, in red spray-paint, a wit had written CUNTS ENTRANCE, with an arrow pointing the other way.

'So much for that,' said Wani. A workman in overalls and a blue helmet came out through the aperture of the front door and stared at them like a janitor, trying to decide if they mattered. They were one of a thousand car-loads of easy wealth that roared and fluttered round London, knocking things down and flinging things up. They might be due for deference or contempt, or for the sour mixture of the two aroused by young money. Nick nodded affably at the man as he pulled away. Mixed in with his unease, and the rueful lesson of the skip and the scaffolding, was a feeling that the builder knew just what they would be getting up to half an hour from now.

Though half an hour later they were creeping down Park Lane. The decisive plunge from the heights had slowed and stalled in the inexhaustible confusion of traffic and roadworks and construction. The wolfish bites had turned into thwarted snaps, the squeals of half a dozen near-collisions. Shuddering lorries squeezed them and dared them and flushed their reeking fumes through the coverless car, as four lanes funnelled into one outside the Hilton Hotel. Wani had whisked Nick up one night to the top-floor bar of the Hilton, perhaps not fully aware of its glassy vulgarity – it was a place his father liked to take guests to, and there was something touchingly studied in the paying for the cocktails and the lordly gaze out over the parks and the palace and the fur and diamonds of the London night. And now here they were, trapped, motionless, half asphyxiated on the roadway outside. Since Nick was driving he felt guilty and clumsy, as if it were his fault, as well as angry and slightly nauseous. Wani's face tightened and his lips were pursed with blame. Even Ricky was letting out puffing sighs. Wani reached over and put a hand on Ricky's thigh and Nick kept an eye on them in the mirror. He tried to make normal conversation, but Ricky had no views on any current topic, and was marvellously incurious about his new friends. He'd given up his job at a warehouse in favour of doing nothing, and now obviously he couldn't find a job even if he wanted to, with three and a quarter million out of work: he smiled at that. He didn't drink, he didn't smoke, and he never read books. 'Perhaps we'll put you in a film,' said Wani archly, and Ricky said, 'All right.' He seemed to have forgotten he had a girl-friend, until Nick asked another question about her. At last they rushed out into Hyde Park Corner, and jostled their way round into Knightsbridge. Wani said, 'What's your girlfriend's name?'

'Felicity,' said Ricky – which was written on the awning of Felicity Prior's flower shop just beside them. 'Yeah . . .'

Wani turned and said, in a painfully roguish tone, 'Felicity's a very lucky girl.'

'Yeah, she is, isn't she,' said Ricky.

When they reached Wani's place there was no one in the office, the boys had left, and they went straight upstairs to the flat, Ricky following Wani, and Nick coming close behind, unpleasantly jealous of the other two. It was like the tension of a first date, but with an extra player who was also a competitor and critic. He was squeamish at the thought of Wani's little predilections being exposed, and angry because he was the one who had been trusted with the secret of them. He didn't know if he could go through with that drama in the presence of Ricky, whom obviously, elsewhere, he would have loved to fuck. Or perhaps it wouldn't be like that, they would just fool about a bit. He went across the room and put the car keys down on the side table, and when he looked back Ricky and Wani were snogging, nothing had been said, there were sighs of consent, a moment's glitter of saliva before a shockingly tender second kiss. Nick gave a breathy laugh, and looked away, in the grip of a misery unfelt since childhood, and too fierce and shaming to be allowed to last.

He took down the leather-bound *Poems and Plays of Addison* and got out the hidden gram of coke – all that was left of last week's quarter-ounce. He knelt down by the glass coffee table to deal with it, polishing a clean spot. The new issue of *Harper's* was open at 'Jennifer's Diary', and he peered at the picture of Mr Antoine Ouradi and Miss Martine Ducros at the Duchess of Flintshire's May ball. The pale inverted reflection of the two men kissing floated on the glass beside the photographed couple. If this was one of Wani's films – not the ones he wanted to make but the ones he liked to watch – Nick would have to join them in a moment. Sometimes there was an unaccountably boring scene where one man knelt and sucked the dicks of the other two in turn, or even tried to get them both in his mouth, and Nick could see Wani needing to do that. He chopped and drew out the fine white fuses of pleasure and watched Ricky tug at the buckle of his lover's belt.

8

Wani's new centre of operations was an 1830s house in Abingdon Road which he had had converted by Parkes Perrett Bozoglu. On the ground floor was the glinting open-plan Ogee office, and on the two upper floors a flat that was full of eclectic features, lime-wood pediments, coloured glass, surprising apertures; the Gothic bedroom had an Egyptian bathroom. The high tech of the office, PPB seemed to say, was less the logic of the future than another style in their post-modern repertoire. The house had been featured in *The World of Interiors*, whose art director had moved the furniture around, hung a large abstract painting in the dining room, and introduced a number of ceramic lamps like colossal gourds. Wani said this didn't matter at all. He himself seemed elegantly and equally at home in the reflecting glass and steel of the office and among the random cultural allusions of the flat. He knew very little about art and design, and his pleasure in the place was above all that of having had something expensive done for him.

Nick smiled to himself at the flat's pretensions, but inhabited it with his old wistful keenness, as he did the Feddens' house, as a fantasy of prosperity that he could share, and as the habitat of a man he was in love with. He felt he took to it well, the comfort and convenience, the discreet glimpsed world of things that the rich had done for them. It was a system of minimized stress, of guaranteed flattery. Nick loved the huge understanding depth of the sofas and the peculiarly gilding light of the lamps that flanked the bathroom basin; he had never looked so well as he did when he shaved or cleaned his teeth there. Of course the house was vulgar, as almost everything postmodern was, but he found himself taking a surprising pleasure in it. The hallway, where the grey glass bells of the lampshades cast cloudy reflections in the ox-blood-marble walls, was like the lavatory of a restaurant, though evidently of a very smart and fashionable one.

He slept there from time to time, in the fantasy of the canopied bed, with its countless pillows. The ogee curve was repeated in the mirrors and pelmets and in the wardrobes, which looked like Gothick confessionals; but its grandest statement was in the canopy of the bed, made of two transecting ogees crowned by a boss like a huge wooden cabbage. It was as he lay beneath it, in uneasy post-coital vacancy, that the idea of calling Wani's outfit Ogee had come to him: it had a rightness to it, being both English and exotic, like so many things he loved. The ogee curve was pure expression, decorative not structural; a structure could be made from it, but it supported nothing more than a boss or the cross that topped an onion dome. Wani was distant after sex, as if assessing a slight to his dignity. He turned his head aside in thoughtful grievance. Nick looked for reassurance in remembering social triumphs he had had, clever things he had said. He expounded the ogee to an appreciative friend, who was briefly the Duchess, and then Catherine, and then a different lover from Wani. The double curve was Hogarth's 'line of beauty', the snakelike flicker of an instinct, of two compulsions held in one unfolding movement. He ran his hand down Wani's back. He didn't think Hogarth had illustrated this best example of it, the dip and swell – he had chosen harps and branches, bones rather than flesh. Really it was time for a new *Analysis of Beauty*.

On the floor below was the 'library', a homage to Lutyens neo-Georgian, with one black wall and pilastered bookcases. A glass bowl, some framed photos, and a model car took up space between the sparse clumps of books. There were big books on gardens and film stars, and some popular biographies, and books valued for being by people Wani knew, such as Ted Heath's *Sailing* and Nat Hanmer's 'really rather good' first novel *Pig-Sty*. The room had a proper Georgian desk, and sofas, a huge staring television and a VCR with high-speed rewind. It was here, a few days after the Ricky episode, with its large tacit adjustment to Nick's understanding of things, that Wani had sat down, plucked the top off his Mont Blanc and made out a cheque to Nicholas Guest for £5,000.

Nick had looked at the cheque, drawn on Coutts & Co. in the Strand, with a mixture of suspicion and glee. He handled it lightly, noncommittally, but he knew in a second or two that he was fiercely attached to it, and dreaded its being taken away from him. He said, 'What on earth's this?'

'What . . . ?' said Wani, as if he'd already forgotten it, but with a tremor of drama that he couldn't fully suppress. 'I'm just fed up with paying for you the whole fucking time.'

This was quite a witty remark, Nick could see, and he took the roughness of it as a covert tenderness. Still, there was a sense that he might have agreed to something, when he was drunk and high – that he'd forgotten his side of a bargain. 'It doesn't seem right,' he said, already seeing himself doing the paying, taking out Toby, or Nat perhaps, to Betty's or La Stupenda; having a credit card, therefore . . .

'Yah, just don't tell anyone,' said Wani, pressing a video into the slot of the player, and picking up the remote control, with which he poked and chivvied the machine from a frowning distance. 'And don't just blue it all in a week on charlie.'

'Of course not,' said Nick – though the idea, and the hidden calculation he made, brought him up against the limits of £5,000 fairly quickly. If he was going to have to pay for himself, it wasn't nearly enough. Seen in that light, it was rather mean of Wani, it was a bit of a tease. 'I'll invest it,' he said.

'Do that,' said Wani. 'You can pay me back when you've made your first five grand profit.' At which Nick sniggered, out of sheer ignorance. It was all a bit tougher than he thought, if he was going to have to pay it back. But he didn't want to whinge.

'Well, thank you, my dear,' he said, folding the cheque reflectively, and going towards him to give him a kiss. Wani reached up his cheek, like a thanked but busy parent, and as Nick went out of the room Wani's favourite scene from *Oversize Load* was already on the screen, and the man in black was performing his painful experiment on the excited little blond.

'Oh, baby . . . !' Wani chuckled, but Nick knew he wasn't being called back.

A couple of nights a week Wani spent uncomplainingly at his parents' house in Lowndes Square. Nick had been ironical about this at first, and piqued that he seemed to feel no regret at passing up a night they could have spent together. The family instinct was weak in him – or if it flared it involved some family other than his own. But he soon learned that to Wani it was as natural as sex and as irrefutable in its demands. On other nights of the week he might be in and out of the lavatories of smart restaurants with his wrap of coke, and roar home in WHO 6 for a punishing session of sexual make-believe; but on the family nights he went off to Knightsbridge in a mood of unquestioning compliance, almost of relief, to have dinner with his mother and father, any number of travelling relations, and, as a rule, his fiancée. Then Nick would go back jealously to Kensington Park Gardens and the hospitable Feddens, who all seemed to believe his story that on other nights he worked at his thesis on Wani's computer and used a 'put-me-up' at his flat. He had never been invited to Lowndes Square, and in his mind the house, the ruthless figure of Bertrand Ouradi, the exotic family protocols, the enormous monosyllable of the very word Lowndes, all combined in an impression of forbidding substance.

On one of his nights alone, Nick went to *Tannhäuser* and met Sam Zeman in the interval. They gossiped competitively about the edition being used, an awkward hybrid of the Paris and Dresden versions; Sam had the edge in relevant and precisely remembered fact. Nick said there was something he wanted to ask him, and they agreed to have lunch the following week. 'Come in early,' said Sam, 'and try out the new gym.' Kesslers had just rebuilt their City premises, with a steel and glass atrium and high-tech dealing-floors fitted in behind the old palazzo façade.

When the day came Nick turned up early at the bank and waited under a palm tree in the atrium. People hurried in, nodding to the commissionaire, who still wore a tailcoat and a top hat. On the exposed escalators the employees were carried up and down, looking both slavish and intensely important. Nick watched the motorbike messengers in their sweaty water-proofs and leathers, and heavy boots. He felt abashed and agitated by closeness to so many people at work, in costume, in character, in the know. The building itself had the glitter of confidence, and made and retained an unending and authentic noise out of air vents, the hubbub of voices and the impersonal trundling of the escalators. Nick craned upwards for a glimpse of the regions where Lord Kessler himself might be conducting business, at that level surely a matter of mere blinks and ironies, a matter of telepathy. He knew that the old panelled boardroom had been retained, and that Lionel had hung some remarkable pictures there. In fact he had said that Nick should call in one day and see the Kandinsky . . .

Sam took him through and down into a chlorine-smelling basement where the gym and lap-pool were. 'It's such a godsend, this place,' he said. Nick thought it was very small, and hardly compared with the Y; he saw that he came to a gym as a gay place, but that this one wasn't gay. An old man in a white jacket handed out towels and looked seasoned to the obscenities of the bankers. Nick did a perfunctory circuit, really just to oblige Sam, who was pedalling on a bike and filling in the *Times* crossword. He felt he didn't know Sam very well, and had a vague sensation of being patronized. Sam's friendly Oxford cleverness had hardened, he had a glint to him like the building itself, a watchful half-smile of secret knowledge. All around them other men were slamming weights up and down. Nick wasn't sure if they were working up their aggression or working it off. In the showers they shouted esoteric boasts from stall to stall.

Nick had seen their lunch taking place in a murmurous old City dining room with oak partitions and tailcoated waiters. The restaurant Sam took him to was so bright, noisy and enormous that he had to shout out the details of his £5,000. When Sam understood he flinched backwards for a second to show he'd thought it was going to be something important. 'Well, what fun,' he said.

It was nearly all men in the restaurant. Nick was glad he'd worn his best suit and almost wished he'd worn a tie. There were sharp-eyed older men, looking faintly harassed by the speed and noise, their dignity threatened by the ferocious youngsters who already had their hands on a new kind of success. Some of the young men were beautiful and exciting; a sort of ruthless sex-drive was the way Nick imagined their sense of their own power. Others were the uglies and misfits from the school playground who'd made money their best friend. It wasn't so much a public-school thing. As everyone had to shout there seemed to be one great rough syllable in the air, a sort of 'wow' or 'yow'. Sam was somewhat aloof from them but he didn't disown them. He said, 'I saw a marvellous *Frau ohne Schatten* in Frankfurt.'

'Ah yes . . . well, you know my feelings about Strauss,' said Nick.

Sam looked at him disappointedly. 'Oh, Strauss is good,' he said. 'He's very good on women.'

'That wouldn't in itself put me off!' said Nick.

Sam chuckled at the point, but went on, 'The orchestral music's all about men and the operas are all about women. The only interesting male parts he wrote are both trouser-roles, Octavian, of course, and the Composer in *Ariadne*.'

'Yes, quite,' said Nick, slightly pressured. 'He's not universal. He's not like Wagner, who understood everything.'

'He's not like Wagner at all,' said Sam. 'But he's still rather a genius.'

They didn't get round to Nick's money till the end of lunch. 'It's just a little inheritance,' said Nick. 'I thought it might be fun to see what could be made of it.'

'Mm,' said Sam. 'Well, property's the thing now.'

'I wouldn't get much for five thousand,' said Nick.

Sam gave a single laugh. 'I'd buy shares in Eastaugh. They're developing half the City. Share price like the north wall of the Eiger.'

'Going up fast, you mean.'

'Or there's Fedray, of course.'

'What, Gerald's company?'

'Amazing performance last quarter, actually.'

Nick felt stirred but on balance uneasy at this idea. 'How does one go about it?' he said, with a gasp at his own silliness, but a certain recklessness too, after four glasses of Chablis. 'I wondered if you'd look after it for me.'

Sam put his napkin on the table and gestured to the waiter. 'OK!' he said brightly, to show it was a game, a bit of silliness of his own. 'We'll go for maximum profits. We'll see how far we can go.'

Nick fumbled earnestly for his wallet but Sam put the lunch on expenses. 'Important investor from out of town,' he said. He had Kesslers' own platinum MasterCard. Nick watched the procedure with a bead of anticipation in his eye. Outside on the pavement, Sam said, 'All right, my dear, send me a cheque. I'm going this way,' as if Nick had made it clear he was going the other. Then they shook hands, and as they did so Sam said, 'Shall we say three per cent commission,' so that they seemed to have solemnized the arrangement. Nick flushed and grinned because he'd never thought of that: he minded terribly. It was only later that it came to seem a good, optimistic thing, with the proper stamp of business to it.

Wani was still 'building up his team' at Ogee, and Nick was silently amazed by both his confidence and his lack of urgency. A woman called Melanie, dressed for a Dallas cocktail party, came in to do the typing, and artfully protracted her few bits of filing and phoning through the afternoon. Whenever her mother rang her she said things were 'hectic'. Wani had a wonderful Talkman, which was a portable phone he could take with him in the car or even into a restaurant, and Melanie was encouraged to call him on it if he was in a meeting and give him some figures. Then there were the boys, Howard and Simon, not actually a couple, but always referred to together, and acting together in the comfortable way of schoolboy best chums. Howard was very tall and square-jawed and Simon was short and owlish and pretended not to mind being fat. If anyone took them for lovers Simon shrieked with laughter and

Howard explained tactfully that they were merely good friends. Nick liked nattering with them when he dropped into the office, and enjoyed their glancing hints that they both rather fancied him. 'Well, I swim and I work out a couple of times a week,' Nick would say, leaning back in his chair with the glow of shame that for him was still the cost of bragging; and Simon would say, 'Oh, I suppose I ought to try that.' They all carried on as if they'd never noticed Wani's beauty, and as if they took him entirely seriously. If his picture appeared in the social pages of *Tatler* or *Harper's and Queen* Melanie passed the magazine round like a validation of their whole enterprise.

Nick was confident that none of them knew he was sleeping with the boss, and with ten or more years of practice he could head off almost any train of talk that might end in a thought-provoking blush. Part of him longed for the scandalous acclaim, but Wani exacted total secrecy, and Nick enjoyed keeping secrets. He worked up his earlier adventures as a cover, and told Howard and Simon a different version of the Ricky incident, replacing Wani with a Frenchman he'd met at the Pond the previous summer.

'So was he handsome, this Ricky?' said Simon.

Handsomeness was neither here nor there with Ricky, it was his look of stupid certainty, the steady heat of him, the way you started in deep, as though the first kiss was an old kiss interrupted and picked up again at full intensity – Nick said, 'Oh, magnificent. Dark eyes, round face, nice big nose—'

'Mmm,' said Simon.

'Perhaps a trifle too punctually, though not yet quite lamentably, bald.'

There was a moment's thought before Simon said, 'That's one of your things, isn't it?'

'What . . . ?' said Nick, with a vaguely wounded look.

'A trifle too . . . how did it go?'

'I can't remember what I said . . . "a trifle too punctually, though not yet quite lamentably, bald"?'

Howard sat back, with the nod of someone submitting to an easy old trick, and said, 'So did he have a beard?'

'Far from it,' said Nick. 'No, no – he spoke, as to cheek and chin, of the joy of the matutinal steel.'

They all laughed contentedly. It was one of Nick's routines to slip these plums of periphrasis from Henry James's late works into unsuitable parts of his conversation, and the boys marvelled at them and tried feebly to remember them – really they just wanted Nick to say them, in his brisk but weighty way.

'So what's that from, then?'

'The baldness? It's from *The Outcry*, it's a novel by Henry James that no one's ever heard of.' This was taken philosophically by the boys, who hadn't really heard of any novels by Henry James. Nick felt he was prostituting the Master, but then there was an element of self-mockery in these turns of phrase – it was something he was looking at in his thesis. He was at the height of a youthful affair with his writer, in love with his rhythms, his ironies, and his idiosyncrasies, and loving his most idiosyncratic moments best of all.

'It sounds like Henry James called everyone beautiful and marvellous,' said Sam, a little sourly, 'from what you say.'

'Oh, beautiful, magnificent . . . *wonderful*. I suppose it's really more what the characters call each other, especially when they're being wicked. In the later books, you know, they do it more and more, when actually they're more and more ugly – in a moral sense.'

'Right . . .' said Simon.

'The worse they are the more they see beauty in each other.'

'Interesting,' said Howard drily.

Nick cast a fond glance at his little audience. 'There's a marvellous bit in his play *The High Bid*, when a man says to the butler in a country house, "I mean, to whom do you beautifully *belong*?" '

Simon grunted, and looked round to see if Melanie could hear. He said, 'So what was his knob like, then? . . . You know, Ricky?'

Well, it was certainly worth describing, and embellishing. Nick wondered for a moment how Henry would have got round it. If he had fingered so archly at beards and baldness, the fine paired saliences of his own appearance, what flirtings and flutterings might he not have performed to conjure up Ricky's solid eight inches? Nick said, 'Oh, it was . . . *of a dimension*,' and watched Simon work what excitement he could out of that.

So he prattled on, mixing up sex and scholarship, and enjoying his wanderings away from the strict truth. In fact that was really the fun of it. And it seemed to fit in with the air of fantasy in the Ogee office, the distant sense of an avoided issue.

Nick couldn't quite have defined his own role there, and he only learned what it was when he was suddenly invited to Lowndes Square for Sunday lunch. He'd been dancing at Heaven till three the night before, and was still struggling with the rubber mask, the wobbly legs, the trill and glare of a beer and brandy hangover when Bertrand Ouradi grasped his hand very hard and said, 'Ah, so you're Antoine's aesthete.'

'That's me!' said Nick, returning the handshake as firmly as he could, and grinning in the hope that even an aesthete might be a good thing to be if it was sanctioned by his beloved son.

'Ha ha!' said Bertrand, and turned away along the chequered marble floor of the hall. 'Well, we need our aesthetes.' He stretched out his arms in a graceful shrug, and seemed to gesture at the shiny paintings and Empire torchères as necessary trappings of his position. He had an aesthete of his own, he seemed to say, on a small retainer. Nick followed on, wincing at the high polish on everything. He had the feeling there was only one thing in the house he would ever want to see. 'I'll join you in a moment,' Bertrand said, with a tiny gesture of deterrence, as Nick found himself following him into the lavatory. The dark little woman who'd opened the door led him dutifully upstairs, and he followed her instead, smiling and doomed. So Wani himself must have called him his aesthete, that was how he'd explained him to his parents . . .

He was shown into the pink and gold confusion of a drawing room. Wani called out, 'Ah, Nick . . .' like an old man remembering, and came across to shake his hand. 'Now here's Martine, who's been longing to see you . . .' (Nick stopped by the sofa where she was sitting and shook her hand as well with an exaggerated bow) – 'and you haven't met my mother.' Nick was aware of himself advancing in the high mirror which hung over the fireplace, and at a slight tilt, so that the room seemed to climb into a luminous middle distance. He kept up a wide smile, in self-protection, and only caught his own eye for an unwise second. It was a dazzled smile, perhaps even the smile of someone about to make a sequence of witty remarks. Monique Ouradi said she had been to Mass at Westminster Cathedral, and smiled back, but seemed not quite ready yet for mere social communication. 'And this is my Uncle Emile, and my cousin, little Antoine,' said Wani, as two people came in unexpectedly behind him. Everything impinged on Nick, but he couldn't take it in. He shook hands with Uncle Emile, who said 'Enchanté' in a coughing sort of voice, and Nick said 'Enchanté' back. Wani rested his hand on his little cousin's head, and the boy looked up at him adoringly before also shaking hands with Nick. Nick felt a tear rise to his eye at the thought of the child's utter innocence of hangovers.

Nick had decided in the taxi that he would stick to water,

but when Bertrand came in saying, 'Now, drinks!' he at once saw the point of a bloody Mary. Bertrand moved towards a drinks tray on a far table and at just that moment an old man in a black jacket hurried in with a salver and took control of the business. Nick gazed at them with the patient surmise of the hung-over, a sense of mysterious displacement and slow revelation. Bertrand could make a mere gesture towards an action which would at once be performed by someone else – there was a signalled readiness and then a prompt, never-doubted relief! It explained everything.

Really it was best to prop oneself at a life-like angle in the corner of the sofa and let the family talk trail back and forth . . . At the tall front windows white net curtains rippled very gently into the room. Outside on the balcony there were two pointed trees in tubs, and beyond them the planes in the square, forest-height, filled the entire view. Nick's thoughts drifted out and perched there.

Little Antoine had a remote-controlled toy car, which Wani was encouraging him to crash into the legs of the repro Louis Quinze tables and chairs. It was a bright-red Ferrari with a whiplike antenna. Nick crouched forward to watch it haring round, and made histrionic groans when it banged into the skirting board or got stuck under the bureau. He was pre-tending to enjoy the game, and trying to attach himself to it, but the two boys seemed oblivious of him, Wani almost snatching the controls now and then to cause a top-speed col-lision. Bertrand was standing talking to Uncle Emile, and shuffled obligingly out of the way a couple of times, with a certain hardening of expression. In the tilting mirror Nick saw them all, as if from a privileged angle, like actors on a set.

The parents were fascinating, Bertrand short and handsome as an old-fashioned film star, and Monique too, very smart and austere, with a black bob and a diamond brooch, evincing foreignness like a time-shift, into the chic of twenty years before. There was a subdued shine to Bertrand's dark suit, which was double-breasted, square-shouldered, and worn with a crimson breast-pocket handkerchief; he seemed to resolve into a pattern of squares and lozenges, with his square jaw, tougher than Wani's, and the same long hawkish nose, all parts of the pattern. Along his full upper lip he wore a thin black moustache. The light, low-cut patent slippers he had on seemed to Nick an eastern note. Wani had several pairs himself, with ridged rubber soles, 'for walking on marble' as he explained. Bertrand's voice, strongly accented, casual but coercive, dominated the room.

Martine was sitting at the other end of Nick's sofa, in what felt like her 'place', adjacent to Wani's mother. They were speaking quietly in French, in a kind of listless female conspiracy, while the men boomed and frowned and crashed cars. Nick smiled at them undemandingly. Martine in her long engagement must have become a fixture, a passive poor relation, who was waiting and waiting to turn into a millionairess. She seemed shy of speaking to Nick, for reasons he could only guess at. Wani's claim that she was longing to see him had been wishful social prompting – he had a habit of languidly implanting his wishes. But Martine, in her mild unexpectant way, had always seemed to have her own mind. So it was a minute or two before she slid a dish of olives towards him on the low glass table and said, 'And how are you getting on?'

'Oh, fine!' said Nick, blinking and smirking. 'I'm feeling a bit delicate, actually' – and he waggled his glass. 'This is helping. It's a miracle how it does.' He thought what extraordinary things one said.

She was too delicate herself to take on the subject of his hangover. 'Work is all fine?' she said.

'Oh – yes . . . thank you. Well – I'm trying to finish my thesis this summer, and of course I'm very behind,' he said, as if she must be familiar with his weaknesses, they seemed to grin out of him as he sat there. 'I'm so terribly lazy and disorganized.'

'I hope not,' she said, as if he could only be joking. 'And what is it concerning, this thesis?'

'Oh . . . it's concerning – Henry James . . .' He'd developed a reluctance that was Jamesian in itself to say exactly what its subject was. There was a lot to do with hidden sexuality, which struck him as better avoided.

'But Antoine says you are working with him too, at the Ogee?'

'Oh, I don't really do very much.'

'You are not writing a film? That is what he says.'

'Well, I'd like to. In a way, yes . . . We have a few ideas.' He smiled politely beyond her to take Wani's mother as well into the conversation. Since it was all he had, he said, 'Actually, I've always rather wanted to make a film of *The Spoils of Poynton* . . .' Monique settled back with an appreciative nod at this, and Nick felt encouraged to go on, 'I think it *could* be rather marvellous, don't you. You know Ezra Pound said it was just a novel about furniture, meaning to dismiss it of course, but that was really what made me like the sound of it!'

Monique sipped at her gin-and-tonic and looked at him with vague concern, and then, as if searching for the point, glanced about at the tables and chairs. Of course she had no idea what he was talking about.

Martine said, 'So you want to make a *film* about furniture?'

Monique said, raising her voice as the Ferrari tore past her ankles, 'We saw the latest film, which was so nice, of *The Room with the View.*'

'Ah yes,' said Nick.

'Mainly it took place in Italy, which we love so much, it was delightful.'

Martine slightly surprised him by saying, 'I think it's so boring now, everything takes place in the past.'

'Oh . . . I see. You mean, all these costume dramas . . .'

'Costume dramas. All of this period stuff. Don't the English actors get fed up with it – they are all the time in evening dress.'

'It's true,' said Nick. 'Though actually everyone is in evening dress all the time these days, aren't they.' He was thinking really of Wani, who owned three dinner jackets and had gone to the Duchess's charity ball in white tie and tails. He saw he was under attack, since the *Poynton* project would naturally involve a lot of dressing up.

Monique Ouradi said, 'I'm sure my son will make a beautiful film, with your help' – so that Nick felt she was encouraging him in some larger sense, in the inscrutable way that mothers sometimes do.

'Yes, perhaps you don't know him all that well,' Martine agreed. 'You will need to push and shove him.'

'I'll remember that,' said Nick with a laugh, and amazing arousing images of Wani in bed glowed in front of him, so that Martine was like a person in the beam of a slide projector, half exposed, half coloured over, and a little ridiculous.

The Ferrari smacked into Bertrand's slipper once again, and little Antoine made it rev and whine as it tried to climb over it, until Bertrand bent down and picked the toy up and held it like a furious insect in the air. Antoine came round from behind the sofa, dawdling as he caught the moment of pure fury on his uncle's face and then gasping with laughter as the glare curled into a pantomime snarl. 'Enough Ferrari for today,' Bertrand said, and gave it back to the child with no fear of being disobeyed. Nick felt abruptly nervous at the thought of crossing Bertrand, and those same naked images of his son melted queasily away.

Wani said, 'You must be longing to see round the house.'

'Oh, yes,' said Nick, getting up with a flattered smile. He felt that Wani had almost overdone the coolness and dissimulation, he'd barely spoken to him, and even now, as he lifted Nick on a wave of secret intentions, his expression gave nothing away, not even the warmth that the family might have expected between two old college friends.

'Yes, take him round,' said Bertrand. 'Show him all the bloody pictures and bloody things we've got.'

'I'd love that,' said Nick, seeing the hidden advantage of the aesthete persona, even in a house where the good things had the glare of reproductions.

'Will I go too?' said little Antoine, who was clearly as fond of his cousin's touch and smile as Nick was; but Emile crossly made him stay.

'We'll begin at the top,' Wani announced as they left the room and started upstairs two at a time. On the second flight he said quietly, 'You didn't say where you were last night.'

'Oh, I went to Heaven,' said Nick, with mild apprehension at telling an innocent truth.

'I wondered,' said Wani, without looking round. 'Did you fuck anyone?'

'Of course I didn't fuck anyone. I was with Howard and Simon.'

'I suppose that follows,' said Wani, and then allowed Nick a tiny smile. 'What did you do, then?'

'Well, you have been to a nightclub, darling,' said Nick in a voice where sarcasm almost wished itself away. 'You've been photographed in several with your fiancée. We danced and danced and drank and drank.'

'Mm. Did you take your shirt off?'

'I think I'll leave that to your jealous imagination,' Nick said.

They went along the landing and into Wani's bedroom. Wani bustled through, with a just perceptible air of granting a concession, of counting on Nick not to look too closely at what the room contained, and went into a white bathroom beyond. Nick followed slowly. Everything in the bedroom interested him, it was dead and alive at once, group photographs, from Harrow, from Oxford, the Martyrs' Club in their pink coats, Toby and Roddy Shepton and the rest; and the books, the Arnold and the Arden Shakespeare and the cracked orange spines of the Penguin *Middlemarch* and *Tom Jones*, the familiar colours and lettering, the series and ideas of all that phase of their life, stranded and fading here as in a thousand outgrown bedrooms, never to be looked at again; and the young man's princely bed, almost a double; and the mirror, where Nick now timidly checked his own progress – he looked perfectly all right. The puzzlement of a hangover . . . the creeping hilarity of the new drink . . . He strolled on into the bathroom.

Wani had got his wallet out, and was crushing and chopping a generous spill of coke on the wide rim of the washbasin. 'A lot of funny old stuff in there,' he said.

'I know,' said Nick. 'It's a little early for that, isn't it?' It was a lovely slide they were on with the coke, but sometimes Wani was a bit serious, a bit premature with it.

'You looked as if you needed it.'

'Well, just a small line,' said Nick. He looked around this room as well, with tense insouciance. He didn't really want to go down to lunch in reckless unaccountable high spirits and make a different kind of fool of himself. But a line wasn't feasibly resisted. He loved the etiquette of the thing, the chopping with a credit card, the passing of the tightly rolled note, the procedure courteous and dry, 'all done with money', as Wani said – it was part of the larger beguilement, and once it had begun it squeezed him with its charm and promise. Being careful not to nudge him as he worked, he hugged Wani lightly from behind and slid a hand into his left trouser pocket.

'Oh fuck,' said Wani distantly. In about three seconds he was hard, and Nick too, pressing against him. Everything they did was clandestine, and therefore daring and therefore child-like, since it wasn't really daring at all. Nick didn't know how long it could go on – he didn't dream of it stopping, but it was silly and degrading at twenty-three to be sneaking sex like this, like a pickpocket as Wani said. But then again, on a hungover morning, moronic with lust, he saw a beauty in the slyness of it. There were several pound coins in the flannel depths of the pocket, and they tumbled round Nick's hand as he stroked Wani's dick.

Wani drew the powder into two long lines. 'You'd better close the door,' he said.

Nick lingeringly disengaged himself. 'Yeah, we've only got a minute.' He pushed the door to and came forward to take the rolled £20 note.

'Turn the key,' said Wani. 'That little boy follows me every-where.'

'Ah, who can blame him,' said Nick graciously.

Wani gave him a narrow look – he was often dissatisfied by praise. They stooped in turn and zipped up the powder, and then stood for a minute, sniffing and nodding, reading each other's faces for comparison and confirmation of the effect. Wani's features seemed to soften, there was a subtle but invol-untary smile that Nick loved to see at the moment of achieve-ment and surrender. He grinned back at him, and reached out to stroke his neck, and with his other hand rubbed playfully at Wani's oblique erection. They were on to such a good thing. He said, 'This is fucking good stuff.'

'God yes,' said Wani. 'Ronnie always comes through.'

'I hope you haven't given me too much,' Nick said; though over the next thirty seconds, holding Wani to him and kissing him lusciously, he knew that everything had become possible, and that the long demanding lunch would be a waltz and that he would play with Bertrand the tycoon and charm them all. He sighed and pulled Wani's left arm up to look at his famous watch. 'We'd better go down,' he said.

'OK.' Wani stepped back, and quickly undid his trousers.

'Darling, they're waiting for us . . .' But Wani's look was so fathomlessly interesting to him, command and surrender on another deeper level, the raw needs of so aloof a man, the silly sense of privilege in their romantic secret – Nick knelt anyway, and turned him round in his hands, and pulled his pants, the loose old-fashioned drawers that Wani wore, down between his thighs.

On the way downstairs they met little Antoine, who had been dying to look for them and was going into every room in a mime of happy exasperation. It had taken a couple of flushes to dispose of the rubber, and they had got out with thirty seconds to spare. The boy claimed them and then wanted to know what they were laughing about.

'I was showing Uncle Nick my old photographs,' Wani said.

'They were rather funny,' said Nick, pierced by the generous twist to his lie, and also, absurdly, by the missed opportunity of seeing the photos.

'Oh,' said little Antoine, perhaps with a similar regret.

'You'd better have a quick look in here,' Wani said, and pushed open the door of the room above the drawing room, which was his parents' bedroom. He swept a hand over the switches and all the lights came on, the curtains began to close automatically and 'Spring' from *The Four Seasons* was heard as if coming from a great distance. Little Antoine clearly loved this part, and asked to be allowed to do it all again whilst Nick glanced humorously around. Everything was luxurious and he feigned dismay at his own deep footprints in the carpet. The richness of the room was its mixture of shiny pomp, glazed swagged curtains, huge mirrors, onyx and glaring gilt, with older, rougher and better things, things perhaps they'd brought from Beirut, Persian rugs and fragments of Roman statuary. On top of a small chest of drawers there was a white marble head of Wani, presumably, done at about the same age as little Antoine was now, the wider, plumper face of a child. It was charming and Nick thought if he could have anything in the house, any object, it would be that. Bertrand and Monique had separate dressing rooms – each of them, in its order and abundance, like a department of a shop. 'You'd better look at this too,' Wani said, showing him a large yellow painting of Buckingham Palace that hung on the landing.

'It's a Zitt, I see,' said Nick, reading the signature dashed across the right-hand corner of the sky.

'He's rather buying into Zitt,' said Wani.

'Oh – well, it's absolutely ghastly,' said Nick.

'Is it?' said Wani. 'Well, try and break it to him gently.'

They went down into the dining room, with little Antoine going in before them, lolling his head from side to side and saying 'eb-solutely gharstly' over and over to himself. Wani caught him from behind and gave him an enjoyable strangle.

Nick was placed on Monique's right, beside little Antoine, with Uncle Emile opposite. Uncle Emile had the air of a less successful brother, baggy and gloomy rather than gleamingly triangular. But it turned out that in fact he was Monique's brother-in-law, on a visit of indefinite duration from Lyon, where he ran an ailing scrap-metal business. Nick took in this story and smiled along the table as if they were being told a simmeringly good joke; it was only Wani's tiny frown that made him suspect he might be looking too exhilarated by his tour of the house. It was the magic opposite, all this, of the jolted witless hangover state of half an hour earlier. All their secrets seemed to fuse and glow. Though for Wani himself, severely self-controlled, it seemed hardly worth having taken the drug. The little old couple were bringing in elaborately fanned slices of melon and orange. It was clear that citrus fruits were treated with special acclaim in the house; here as in the drawing room there was a daringly stacked obelisk of oranges and lemons on a side-table. The effect was both humble and proprietorial. Another Zitt, of the Stock Exchange and the Mansion House, done in mauve, hung between the windows.

'I see you're admiring my husband's new Zitt,' said Monique, with a hint of mischief, as if she would value a second opinion.

'Ah yes . . . !'

'He's really an Impressionist painter, you know.'

'Mm, and almost, somehow, an Expressionist one, too,' said Nick.

'He's extremely contemporary,' said Monique.

'He's a bold colourist,' said Nick. 'Very bold . . .'

'So, Nick,' said Bertrand, spreading his napkin, and steadying his swivelling array of knives on the glassy polish of the table top: 'how is our friend Gerald Fedden?' The 'our' might have referred to just the two of them, or to a friendship with the family, or to a vaguer sense that Gerald was on their side.

'Oh, he's absolutely fine,' said Nick. 'He's in great form. Wildly busy – as always . . . !' Bertrand's look was humorous but persistent, as if to show that they could be candid with each other; having ignored him for the first half-hour he was turning the beam of his confidence on him, with the instinct of a man who gets his way.

'You live in his house, no?'

'Yes, I do. I went to stay for a few weeks and I've ended up staying for nearly three years!'

Bertrand nodded and shrugged, as if this was quite a normal arrangement. Uncle Emile himself, perhaps, might turn out to be just such a visitor. 'I know where it is. We're invited to the concert, whatever it is, next week, which we'll be charmed to come to.'

'Oh, good,' said Nick. 'I think it should be quite fun. The pianist is a young star from Czechoslovakia.'

Bertrand frowned. 'I know they say he's a bloody good man.'

'No, actually . . . oh, Gerald, you mean – yes, absolutely!'

'He's going to go to the very top of the ladder. Or almost to the top. What's your opinion of that?'

'Oh – oh, I don't know,' said Nick. 'I don't know anything about politics.'

Bertrand twitched. 'I know you're the bloody aesthete . . .'

Nick was often pressed for insider views on Gerald's character and prospects, and as a rule he was wafflingly loyal. Now he said, 'I do know he's madly in love with the Prime Minister. But it's not quite clear if the passion is returned. She may be playing hard to get.' Little Antoine did the furtive double-take of a child who is not supposed to have heard something, and Bertrand's frown deepened over his melon. It occurred to Nick that he was in a household with a very serious view of sexual propriety. But it was Monique who said,

'Ah, they're all in love with her. She has blue eyes, and she hypnotizes them.' Her own dark gaze went feelingly down the table to her husband, and then to her son.

'It's only a sort of courtly love, isn't it,' said Nick.

'Yah . . .' said Wani with a nod and a short laugh.

'You've met the lady, I imagine,' Bertrand said.

'I never have,' said Nick, humbly but cheerfully.

Bertrand made a pinched plump expression with his lips and stared into an imaginary distance for a moment before saying, 'You know, of course, she's a good friend of mine.'

'Oh, yes, Wani told me you knew her.'

'Of course, she is a great figure of the age. But she is a very kind woman too.' He had the mawkish look of a brute who praises the kindness of another brute. 'She has always been very kind to me, hasn't she, my love? And of course I intend to return the compliment.'

'Aha . . .'

'I mean in a practical way, in a financial way. I saw her the other day, and . . .' he waved his left hand impatiently to show he wouldn't be going into what had been said; but then went on, with weird candour, 'I will make a significant donation to the party funds, and . . . who knows what then.' He stabbed and swallowed a slice of orange. 'I believe you have to pay back, my friend, if you have been given help' – and he stabbed the air with his empty fork.

'Oh, quite,' said Nick. 'No, I'm sure you do.' He felt he had inadvertently become the focus of some keen resentment of Bertrand's.

'You won't hear any complaints about the lady in this house.'

'Well, nor in mine, I assure you!'

Nick glanced around at the submissive faces of the others, and thought that actually, at Kensington Park Gardens, the worship of 'the lady', the state of mesmerized conjecture into which she threw Gerald, was offset at least by Catherine's monologues about homeless people and Rachel's wry allusions to 'the other woman' in her husband's life.

'So he's on the up-and-up, our friend Gerald,' Bertrand said more equably. 'What's his role actually?'

'He's a minister in the Home Office,' Nick said.

'That's good. He did that bloody quickly.'

'Well, he's ambitious. And he has the . . . the lady's eye.'

'I'll have a chat with him when I come to the house. I've met him, of course, but you can introduce us again.'

'I'd be happy to,' said Nick; 'by all means.' The black-jacketed man removed the plates, and just then Nick felt the steady power of the coke begin to fade, it was something else taken away, the elation grew patchy and dubious. In four or five minutes it would yield to a flatness bleaker than the one it had replaced. However, the wine was served soon after, so there was an amusing sense of relief and dependency. Bertrand himself, Nick noted, drank only Malvern water.

Nick tried for a while to talk to Emile about scrap metal, which tested his Cornelian French to the limits; but Bertrand, who had been looking on with an insincere smile and a palpable sense of neglect, broke in, 'Nick, Nick, I don't know what you two young men are getting up to, I don't like to ask too many questions . . .'

'Oh . . .'

'But I hope it's soon going to start bringing in some money.'

'It will, Papa,' said Wani quickly, while Nick blushed in horror at the chasm he'd just hopped over, and said,

'I'm the aesthete, remember! I don't know about the money side of things.' He tried to smile out through his blush, but he saw that Bertrand's little challenges were designed to show him up in a very passive light. Bertrand said,

'You're the writing man—' which again was something allowed for, an item in a budget, but under scrutiny and probably dispensable.

Nick felt writing men were important, and though he had nothing to show for it as yet he said again, 'That's me.' He realized belatedly, and rather sickeningly, that he would have to improvise, to answer to Wani's advantage, to give body to what his father must have thought were merely fantasies.

'You know I want to start this magazine, Papa,' Wani said.

'Ah – well,' Bertrand said, with a puff. 'Yes, a magazine can be good. But there is a whole world of difference, my son, running a magazine than having your bloody face in a magazine!'

'It wouldn't be like that,' Wani said, somehow both crossly and courteously.

'All right, but then probably it won't sell.'

'It's going to be an art magazine – very high quality photography – very high quality printing and paper – all extraordinary exotic things, buildings, weird Indian sculptures.' He searched mentally through the list Nick had made for him. 'Miniatures. Everything.' Nick felt that even with his hangover he could have made this speech better himself, but there was something touching and revealing in how Wani made his pitch.

'And who do you suppose is going to want to buy that?'

Wani shrugged and spread his hands. 'It will be beautiful.'

Nick put in the forgotten line. 'People will want to collect the magazine, just as they would want to collect the things that are pictured in it.'

Bertrand took a moment or two to see whether this was nonsense or not. Then he said, 'All this bloody top-quality stuff sounds like a lot of money. So you have to charge ten pounds, fifteen pounds for your magazine.' He took an irritable swig from his glass of water.

Wani said, 'Top-quality advertising. You know, Gucci, Cartier . . . *Mercedes*,' reaching for names far more lustrous than Watteau or Borromini. 'Luxury goods are what people want these days. That's where the money is.'

'So you've got a name for the bloody thing.'

'Yah, we're calling it *Ogee*, like the company,' Wani said, very straightforwardly.

Bertrand pursed his plump lips. 'I don't get it, what is it . . . ? "Oh Gee!",' is that it?' he said, bad-tempered but pleased to have made a joke. 'You'll have to tell me again because no one's ever heard of this bloody "ogee".'

'I thought he was saying "Orgy",' said Martine.

'Orgy?!' said Bertrand.

Wani looked across the table, and since this unheard-of name had originally been his idea Nick said, 'You know, it's a double curve, such as you see in a window or a dome.' He made the shape of half an hourglass with his hands raised in the air, just as Monique, in one of her occasional collusive gestures, did the same and smiled at him as if salaaming.

'It goes first one way, and then the other,' she said.

'Exactly. It originates in . . . well, in the Middle East, in fact, and then you see it in English architecture from about the fourteenth century onwards. It's like Hogarth's line of beauty,' Nick said, with a mounting sense of fatuity, 'except that there are two of them, of course . . . I suppose the line of beauty's a sort of animating principle, isn't it . . .' He looked around and swooped his hand suggestively in the air. It wasn't perhaps the animating principle here.

Bertrand set down his knife and fork, and gave a puncturing smile. He seemed to savour his irony in advance, as well as the uncertainty, the polite smiles of anticipation, on the faces of the others. He said, 'You know, um . . . *Nick*, I came to this country, twenty years ago nearly, 1967, not a bloody good time in Lebanon incidentally, just to see what the chances were in your famous swinging London. So I look around, you know the big thing then is the supermarkets are starting up, you know, self-service, help-yourself – you're used to it, you probably go to one every bloody other day: but *then* . . . !'

Nick simpered obediently at the notion of how accustomed he was. He wasn't sure if the *Ogee* talk was over, or being treated to some large cautionary digression. He said coolly, 'No, I can see what a . . . what a revolution there's been.'

Like other egotists Bertrand cast only a momentary, doubting glance at the possibility of irony aimed at himself, and stamped on it anyway. 'Of course it is! It's a bloody revolution.' He turned to gesture the old man to pour more wine for the others, and watched with an air of practised forbearance as the burgundy purled into the cut-glass goblets. 'You know, I had a fruit shop, up in Finchley, to start off with.' He waved his other arm fondly at that distant place and time. 'Bought it up, flew in the fresh citrus, which was our own product by the way, we grew all that, we didn't have to buy it off bloody nobody. Lebanon, a great place for growing fruit. You know, all that's come out of Lebanon in the last twenty years? Fruit and brains, fruit and talent. No one with any brains or any talent wants to stay in the bloody place.'

'Mm, the civil war, you mean.' He'd meant to mug up a bit on the past twenty years of Lebanese history, but Wani grew pained and evasive when he mentioned it, and now here it came. He didn't want to concur in his host's harsh judgement on his own country, it was itself a bit of a minefield.

Monique said, 'Our house was knocked down, you know, by a bomb,' as though not expecting to be heard.

'Oh, how terrible,' said Nick gratefully, since it was another voice in the room.

'Yes,' she said, 'it was very terrible.'

'As Antoine's mother says,' said Bertrand, 'our family house was virtually destroyed.'

'Was it an old house?' Nick asked her.

'Yes, it was quite old. Not as old as this, of course' – and she gave a little shiver, as if Lowndes Square dated from the Middle Ages. 'We have photographs, many . . .'

'Oh, I'd love to see them,' said Nick, 'I'm so interested in that kind of thing.'

'Anyway,' said Bertrand, '1969 I open the first Mira Mart, up in Finchley, up in Finchley, it's still there today, you can go and see it any time. You know what the secret of it is?'

'Um . . .'

'That's what I saw, that's what you got in London, back then – twenty years ago. You got the supermarkets and you got the old local shops, the corner shops going back hundreds of years. So what do I do, I put the two bloody things together, supermarket and corner shop, and I make the mini-mart – all the range of stuff you get in Tesco or whatever the bloody place, but still with the local feeling, corner-shop feeling.' He held up his glass and drank as if to his own ingenuity. 'And you know the other thing, of course?'

'Oh! – um . . .'

'The hours.'

'The hours, yes . . .'

'Open early and close up late, get people before work and get people after work, not just the dear bloody housewifes going out for a packet of ciggies and a chit-chat.'

Nick wasn't sure if this was Bertrand's special tone for talking to an idiot or if its simplicity reflected his own vision of affairs. He said, critically, 'Some of them aren't like that, though, are they? The one in Notting Hill, for instance, that we always go to. It's quite *grand*' – and he shrugged in dulled respect.

'Well, now you're talking about the Food Halls! It's two different bloody things: the Mira Marts and the Mira Food Halls . . . The latter, the Food Halls, being for the bloody rich, posh areas. We got that round here. You know where that comes from.'

'Harrods,' said Wani.

Bertrand gave him a quick frown. 'Of course it does. The mother of all bloody food halls in the whole world!'

'I love to go to Harrods Food Hall,' Monique said, 'and look at the big . . . *homards* . . .'

'The lobsters,' muttered Wani, without looking at her, as though it was his accepted function to interpret for his mother.

'Oh, I know!' said Martine, with a smile of faint-hearted rebellion. Nick saw them often doing it, days probably were spent in Harrods, just round the corner but another world of possibilities, something for everyone who could afford it.

Bertrand gave them a patient five seconds, like a strict but fair-minded schoolmaster, and then said, 'So now, you know, Nick, I got thirty-eight Mira Food Halls all round the country,

Harrogate I got one, Altrincham I just opened one; and more than eight hundred bloody Mira Marts.' He was suddenly very genial – he almost shrugged as well at the easy immensity of it. 'It's a great story, no?'

'Amazing,' said Nick. 'It's kind of you to tell me a story you must know so well' – making his face specially solemn. He saw the bright orange fascia of the Notting Hill Food Hall, where Gerald himself sometimes popped round late at night with a basket and a bashful look as though everyone recognized him, shopping for pâté and Swiss chocolates. And he saw the corner Mira Mart in Barwick, with its sadder produce in sloping racks, remote poor cousins of the Knightsbridge obelisks, and its dense stale smell of a low-ceilinged shop where everything is sold together. An orange, of course, topped by two green leaves, was an emblem of the chain. Then he looked at Wani, who was eating pickily (coke killed the appetite) and entirely without expression. His eyes were on his plate, or on the gleaming red veneer just beyond it; he might have been listening thoughtfully to his father, but Nick could tell he had slipped away into a world his father had never imagined. His submissiveness to Bertrand's tyranny was the price of his freedom. Uncle Emile, too, looked down, as if properly crushed by his brother-in-law's initiative and success; Nick himself quickly saw the charm of running off to Harrods with the ladies.

Then Bertrand actually said, 'All this one day will be yours, my son.'

'Ah, my poor boy!' Monique protested.

'I know, I know,' said Bertrand, nettled, and then smirking rather awfully. 'That day is doubtless a long way off. Let him have his magazines and his films. Let him learn his business.'

Wani said, 'Thank you, Papa,' but his smile was for his mother, and his look, briefly and eloquently, as the smile faded, for Nick. He was at home with his father's manner, his uncontradicted bragging, but to let a friend in on the act showed a special confidence in the friend. Wani rarely blushed, or showed embarrassment of any kind, beyond the murmured self-chastisement with which he offered a seat to a lady or confessed his ignorance of some trivial thing. Nick absorbed his glance, and the secret warmth of what it acknowledged.

'No, no,' said Bertrand, with a quick tuck of the chin as if he'd been unfairly criticized, 'Wani is in all things his own master. At the moment fruit and veggies don't seem to interest him. Fine.' He spread his hands. 'Just as getting married to his bloody lovely bride doesn't seem to interest him. But we sit back, and we wait on the fullness of time. Eh, Wani?' And he laughed by himself at his own frankness, as though to soften its effect, but in fact acknowledging and heightening it.

'We're going to make a lot of money first,' Wani said. 'You'll see.'

Bertrand looked conspiratorially at Nick. 'Now you know, Nick, the big simple thing about money? The really big thing—'

Nick placed his napkin gently on the table, and murmured, 'I'm terribly sorry . . . I must just . . .' – pushing back his chair and wondering if this was even worse manners in Beirut than it was here.

'Eh . . . ? Ah, weak bloody bladder,' said Bertrand, as if he'd expected it. 'Just like my son.' Nick was ready to take on any imputation that enabled him to leave the room; and Wani, with a bored, almost impatient look, got up too and said,

'I'll show you the way.'

9

The piano tuner came in the morning, and then the pianist herself, little Nina Something-over as Gerald called her, came from two to five to practise: it was a wearing day. The tuner was a cardiganed sadist who tutted at the state of the piano and took a dim view in general of its tone, the tiny delay and bell-like bloom that were its special charm. ('Oh,' said Rachel, 'I know Liszt enjoyed playing it . . .') From time to time he would break off his pitiless ascent of the keyboard to dash out juicy chords and arpeggios, with the air of a frustrated concert pianist, which was even worse than the tuning. Little Nina, too, drove them mad with her fragments of Chopin and Schubert, which went on long enough to catch and lull the heart before they dropped it again, over and over. She had a lot of temperament and a terrifying left hand. She played the beginning of Chopin's Scherzo No. 2 like a courier starting a motorbike. When she'd finished Nick helped Elena bring up and arrange the old gilt ballroom chairs from the *trou de gloire*. The sofas were trundled into new alignments, tall flower arrangements mounted the stairs on Elena's legs, and the room took on an unnerving appearance of readiness. Nick had one more task to do, which was to phone Ronnie, and he eyed the clock, in the run-up to six, as jumpily as if he was giving a recital himself.

He went out to a phone box on Ladbroke Grove, but it was back-to-back with another and he thought perhaps the man

who was in it would hear what he said; he seemed almost to
be expecting him, since he wasn't evidently talking, just leaning there. And it was still very close to home; it seemed to
implicate Gerald. He went on down the hill, into a street that
looked far more amenable to drug-dealing, where a man who
could well have been an addict was just coming out of the
phone box on the corner. Nick went in after him, and stood
in the stuffy half-silence, fiddling in his wallet for the paper
with the number on it, and wishing he'd already had a line of
coke, or at least a gin-and-tonic, to put him in charge. He
wished Wani could have done this, as usual, in the car, with
the Talkman. Having given Nick the money, Wani liked to set
him challenges, which were generally tasks he could more
easily have done himself. Wani claimed never to have used a
phone box, just as he had never been on a bus, which he said
must be a ghastly experience. So he had never breathed this
terrible air, black plastic, dead piss, old smoke, the compound
breath of the mouthpiece—

'Yep.'

'Oh, hello . . . is that Ronnie?'

'Yeah.'

'Oh, hi! It's Nick here,' said Nick, with an urgent smile at a
spot low down on the wall. It was like calling someone you'd
fancied at a party, but much more frightening. 'Do you
remember – I'm a friend of, um, Antony's . . .'

Ronnie thought for quite a while, while Nick panted
encouragingly into the phone. 'I don't know any Antony. No.
You don't mean Andy?'

Nick tittered. 'You know – sort of Lebanese guy, has a white
Mercedes . . . sometimes calls himself Wani . . .'

'All right, yeah – enough said! Yeah, *Ronnie* . . .' said
Ronnie, and chuckled affectionately, or with a hint of ridicule,
so that Nick didn't know for a moment what he thought of
Wani himself, any view of him seemed plausible. 'The man

with the portable telephone. He's Lebanese, is he? I didn't know he was Lebanese.'

'Wani? Well actually he was born in Beirut, but he went to school here, and in fact he's lived in London since he was ten,' said Nick, getting snagged as usual in a sub-clause to a more important sentence.

'. . . right . . .' said Ronnie after a bit. 'Well I expect you'll be wanting to see me then. About something.'

The great thing about Ronnie, as Wani said, was that he always came through. The stuff was tip-top, he dealt to some big names, and if the price, at one-twenty a gram, was a little steep, the mark-down at three-fifty for a quarter-ounce was a deal indeed. (A quarter-ounce, seven grams, was the only metric equivalent Nick had yet been able to memorize.) The downside of Ronnie was a strange delaying manner that would have seemed sleepy if it hadn't been also a kind of vigilance. He never rushed, he was never on time, and he had a puzzled porous memory. Nick had only met him once, when they'd driven round the block in his red Toyota and he'd watched the simple way the exchange was made. Ronnie was a cockneyfied Jamaican, with a tall shaved head and doleful eyes. He talked a lot about girlfriend troubles, perhaps just to make things clear. His voice was an intimate murmur, and since he was giving them something they wanted he had seemed to Nick both seductive and forgivable.

Today, it all felt much less happy. Ronnie asked him to ring back ten minutes later, when the routine of the first call was repeated almost verbatim, and again ten minutes after that, to check he was on his way. After each call Nick hung around the streets and felt glaringly criminal as well as vulnerable, with £350 rolled up tight in rubber bands in his pocket. The area seemed suddenly to be infested with police cars. For several minutes a helicopter hammered overhead. Nick wondered how he would explain the money to the police, then thought it was more likely they would wait until he got into the car before they made their move. He wondered if Gerald would be able to keep it out of the papers, if they'd be able to get Gerald into the papers, it was more than vulgar and unsafe, he could lose his seat if it came out that drugs were being taken in his house. How long would the sentence be? Ten years? For a first offence . . . And then, god, how would a pretty little poof with an Oxford accent survive in prison? They'd all be after his arse. He saw himself sobbing in a doorless lavatory. But perhaps a character reference from Professor Ettrick would help, or even someone at the Home Office – Gerald might not abandon him entirely! He was already at the place, the corner by the Chepstow Castle – a minute or two early. He perched at one of the picnic tables outside. The pub itself was shut, bleared light came out through plastic sheeting as work went on after hours, a new brewery had bought it, they were knocking the little old bars into one big room to make it more spacious and unwelcoming. Twelve minutes went past. It was very suspicious the way that man at the bus stop kept glancing at him and never got on a bus. Ronnie was getting careless, his phone was obviously tapped, it would be what they called a knock, when everyone in the street, the blind man, the pizza boy, the lady with the dog, were revealed in a second as plain-clothes officers. The car pulled up, Nick strolled over and got in and they cruised off round the block.

'How's it going, Rick?' Ronnie said, his mournful head not moving but his glance going from side to side and back to the rear-view mirror. Nick laughed and cleared his throat. 'Very well, thanks,' he said. They sat low in the Celica, Ronnie long-legged, arms on his knees, like a boy in a go-kart, long fingers turning the wheel by its crossbar rather than the rim. 'Yeah?' said Ronnie. 'Well, that's good. How's that Ronnie, then?'

Nick laughed nervously again. 'Oh, he's fine, he's very busy.' It was a wonderfully approximate world the real Ronnie lived in, and perhaps he liked it that way, his customers all nicknames and mishearings, it was tactful and safe. He looked in the mirror again, and at the same time his left hand went to his waistcoat pocket and then across to Nick, with the neat little thing held invisible under it. Nick was ready for that but he had to grope for the roll of notes in his pocket. Ronnie accelerated through an amber light, and it struck Nick he was breaking the law by not wearing a seat-belt. Ronnie wasn't wearing his either, that was the sort of world he was moving in, and he thought it might hurt his feelings if he belatedly buckled up. The journey must be nearly over, and the chances were they wouldn't have a prang. Awful, though, to get pulled over for a seatbelt violation, and then be questioned, and then *searched* . . . He nudged Ronnie's arm and he took the money and lost it, again without looking.

They pulled in behind the church at the crown of Ladbroke Grove, in the shadowy crescent of plane trees. 'Thanks very much,' said Nick. He really had to rush but he didn't want to seem unfriendly. Ronnie was looking out thoughtfully through the windscreen.

'This is an old church, Rick,' he said. 'This must be old.'

'Yeah – well, it's Victorian, I suppose, isn't it,' said Nick, who in fact knew all about it.

'Yeah?' said Ronnie, and nodded. 'God, there's some old stuff round here.'

Nick couldn't tell quite what he was getting at. He said, 'It's not that old – sort of 1840s?' He knew not everybody had a sense of history, a useful image, as he had, of the centuries like rooms in enfilade. For half a second he glimpsed what he knew about the church, that the reredos was designed by Aston Webb, that it was built on the site of the grandstand of a long-vanished racetrack. It was a knobbly Gothic oddity in a street of stucco.

'I'm telling you, I'm moving up here, too fucking right I am,' said Ronnie, in his protesting murmur.

'Mm, you should,' said Nick, unsure if he was humouring him or sharing a wry joke, but excited anyway at the thought of having him as a neighbour. He was sexy, Ronnie, in his haggard spectral way . . .

'Get away from that woman, I'm telling you' – he shook his head and laughed illusionlessly. 'I hope you're not having woman trouble, do you, Rick?'

'Oh . . . no . . . I don't,' said Nick. 'Still bad, is it?'

'I'm telling you,' said Ronnie.

Nick could see that Ronnie might be a bit of a handful, and that his line of work might make a certain kind of girl uneasy. He wanted to lean over and get out his probably long and beautiful penis and give him the consolation that a man so perfectly understands – right here, in the car, in the dappled shade across the windscreen. But Ronnie had to get on – he offered his hand, coming down at an angle from a high raised elbow.

Nick got out of the car and turned to walk the two hundred yards to the house. In the street the sense of danger squeezed about him again, and the people who passed him as they came home from work frowned and sneered as they saw that he held a tiny parcel, a crass mistake, a heavy sentence, gripped tight in his hand in his pocket, ready, at the dreaded moment, to be flung down a drain. But when he turned up the steps and looked to left and right he had a gathering rapturous feeling he had got away with it. Of course nobody knew, it was totally safe, nobody had seen, it was nothing but an unknown car that slipped past the end of the street in a second. And now a flood of pleasure was waiting to be released. He rushed through the hall, up the stone stairs, there were voices already in the drawing room, the moan and yap of the first guests' opening platitudes, up and up, up the familiar creaking attic stairs, and into his hot still room that was waiting for him with birdsong through the window and the bed reflected in the wardrobe mirror. He closed the door, locked the door, and over a smiling five minutes changed his shirt, put in cufflinks, tied a tie and pulled on his suit trousers, all intercut with tipping out, chopping and snorting a trial line of the new stuff, hiding the rest in his desk, unrolling the banknote and rolling it up backwards, wiping the desk with his finger and his finger on his gums. Then he shrugged on the jacket, tied his shoes, leapt downstairs and talked brilliantly to Sir Maurice Tipper about the test match.

Nick sat at the end of a row, like an usher. He could see out onto the first-floor landing, where little Nina Glaserova, with her long red hair in a braid down her back, was standing and staring, not into the room but at a clear point in the dark oak of the threshold. Her eyes seemed to work straight through it, into a space where Chopin, Schubert and Beethoven waited for justice to be done to them. She listened as Gerald told the story – father a notable dissident – imprisoned – travelling scholarship withheld – without seeming to recognize it as her own, or knowing of course that dissident wasn't generally a term of approval in Gerald's book; artistic freedom was unemphatically invoked, and there was a joke, which she didn't get, though it made her look up, into the room, at the rows of utterly unknown laughing people, people of great consequence perhaps, whom it was her mission to enthral. The clapping started, Nick gave her an encouraging nod, she paused for a second, then scuttled in through the audience, looking so much like a determined waif that a sigh of startled tenderness seemed to sound like an undertone of the applause. She gave a momentary bow, sat down and began immediately – it was almost funny as well as thrilling when the motorbike summons of the Chopin Scherzo rang out.

There were about fifty people in the room, a loose coalition of family, colleagues and friends. Nina Glaserova was an unknown quantity, and Gerald's claims for her were political as much as artistic. He hoped for a success but he wasn't making a great social effort. Beside Nick a thin-lipped man from the Cabinet Office groped for his programme sheet as if the music had come as a slightly unpleasant surprise – he made a little scuffle with his chair and the paper. One or two people snapped their glasses cases as they tried well-meaningly to catch up with the leaping flood of sound. It was all so sudden and serious, the piano was quivering, the sound throbbed through the floorboards, and there were hints on some faces that it could be thought rather bad form to make quite so much noise indoors.

Nick could see the far curve of the front row, with Lady Partridge at the end, next to Bertrand Ouradi and his wife, and then Wani, in steep profile against the raised piano lid. Catherine, just behind them, was leaning on her boyfriend Jasper's shoulder, and Polly Thompson was casually squashing against Jasper from the other side. Then there was Morgan, a steely young woman from Central Office whom Polly had brought along as if no one would be surprised. To see Nina herself Nick had to crane round the big white bonce of Norman Kent, who was as sensitive to music as he was to conservatives, and kept shifting in his seat. His frayed denim jacket collar made its own effect among a dozen grades of pinstripe. Penny was sitting beside him, and pressing against him to calm him and to thank him for coming. Nick wondered what he thought of Nina, he wondered what he thought of her himself, too assailed by the sound, by the astounding phenomenon of it, to know if she was really any good. Here came the opening again, the admonitory rumble, the reckless, accurate leap. She had clearly been ferociously schooled, she was like those implacable little gymnasts who sprang out from behind the Iron Curtain, curling and vaulting along the keyboard. As the sadly questioning middle section gathered weight, she put on a fearless turn of speed. She gestured very hard at her effects, and made you doubt she knew their cause. For the programme sheet Nick had rifled some old sleeve notes, to give a professional look to things, and he had put in Schumann's description of the B-flat minor Scherzo as 'overflowing with tenderness, boldness, love and contempt'. He played the words through to himself as he gazed across the rows at his lover's head.

When the Chopin had finished, Nina bowed and rushed out, and Nick saw her on the landing again, waiting in fact like someone about to jump, too young and high-minded to care very much for applause, or to know what to do with it. Gerald was clapping in the loud, steady, hollow way he had. One or two people stood up, the man from the Cabinet Office took in the next item on the agenda, and the lady behind Nick said, 'No, *sadly* we're at Badminton that weekend.'

It was a couple of Schubert Impromptus that followed, the C minor and the stream-like E-flat major, which requires such unfaltering evenness of touch. Nick had heard her play through the very beginning of it a dozen times, until he was screaming at her in his head to go on. Well, now she did, watching her own hands busying up and down the keyboard as if they were astonishing automata that she had wound up and set in motion, in perfect synchrony, to produce this silvery flow of sound. She made it seem a bit like an exercise, but you could tell, if you listened, that the piece was life itself, in its momentum and its evanescence. The modulations in it were like instants of dizziness. Nick felt she played the B minor middle section too abruptly, so that the visionary coherence of the thing was spoiled.

He found himself staring at Gerald's mother and Wani's father, who made a funny pair. Bertrand was sitting there in the lustrous housing of his suit, very still, in respect for the tedious protocol of the event, with only his thin black moustache to betray his impatience as he pursed and flexed his lips in unconscious little kisses. Beside him Lady Partridge, her head tilted up, her face a mask of blusher and brown powder, like someone just back from a skiing holiday, was also clearly elsewhere. From time to time she glanced sideways at her neighbour, and at his drably dressed wife. Nick knew it was upsetting for her to sit next to what she always called an A-rab, but something seemed to kindle in her too at the closeness of so much money.

They had decided before the concert that they would do without an interval, so after the Schubert Gerald stood up and said in his genial, penetrating tone, the tone of a commander among friends, that they would go straight into the final item, Beethoven's 'Farewell' Sonata, and then they could all have more to drink and some rather good salmon – an idea that was greeted with applause all of its own. Nina came back in looking slighted and doubly determined, Nick clapped her very vigorously, and when she played the first three descending notes, 'Le-be-wohl', a shiver ran up his back. The man beside him looked at him suspiciously. But for Nick, to listen to music, to great music, which was all necessity, and here in the house, where the floor trembled to the sudden resolve of the Allegro, and the piano shook on its locked brass wheels – well, it was a startling experience. He felt shaken and reassured all at once – the music expressed life and explained it and left you having to ask again. If he believed anything he believed that. Not everyone here, of course, felt the same: Lady Kimbolton, there, the tireless party fund-raiser, kept a careful frown as she looked discreetly through her appointments diary, then shook the bangles down her arm as she came to attention again – the grey attention, mere good behaviour, of the governing class; she might have been in church, at the memorial service of some unloved colleague, in a world of unmeant expressions, the opposite of Beethoven. Gerald, at the other end of Nick's row, loved music, and was nodding now and then, just off the beat, like someone catching on to an idea, but afterwards Nick knew he would say it had all been either 'glorious' or 'great fun' – even *Parsifal* he had described as 'great fun', when 'glorious' had seemed the more likely option. Others were clearly touched by what they heard: it was Beethoven, after all, and the piece told a story, of departure, absence and return, which no one could fail to follow or to feel.

It was the absence that was best, and little Nina, whom it was hard to think of without her 'little', seemed almost visibly to grow up as she played it. It was a proper *andante espressivo*, it moved and it moved along, she didn't ham up the emotion, in fact you saw her curbing some keen emotion of her own to the wisdom of Beethoven, so that the numbness of absence, the wistful solitude, the stifled climaxes of longing, came luminously through. Nick searched out Wani again, the sliver of profile, the dark curls crowding behind his ear – and wondered if he was touched, and if so in what way. He was watching his ear but he couldn't tell what he heard. In Wani, it was hard to distinguish complete attention from complete abstraction. Nick focused on him, so that everything else swam and Wani alone, or the bit of him he could see, throbbed minutely against the glossy double curve of the piano lid. He felt he floated forwards into another place, beautiful, speculative, even dangerous, a place created and held open by the music, but separate from it. It had the mood of a troubling dream, where nothing could be known for certain or offer a solid foothold to memory after one had woken. What really was his understanding with Wani? The pursuit of love seemed to need the cultivation of indifference. The deep connection between them was so secret that at times it was hard to believe it existed. He wondered if anyone knew – had even a flicker of a guess, an intuition blinked away by its own absurdity. How could anyone tell? He felt there must always be hints of a secret affair, some involuntary tenderness or respect, a particular way of not noticing each other . . . He wondered if it ever would be known, or if they would take the secret to the grave. For a minute he felt unable to move, as if he were hypnotized by Wani's image. It took a little shudder to break the charm.

There was a strange rough breath from Norman Kent, who was crying steadily – making rather a thing of it perhaps, pulling off his glasses and swiping his face with his hand. Nick admired the spirit of it, the defiant sensitivity, and also felt put out, since he often cried at music himself but on this occasion hadn't managed to do so. Penny rested her hand on her father's shoulder, and braved this familiar embarrassment. Nick saw she was blushing, which she easily did. Then the music turned on a sixpence, and the light-headed rush of the finale began. The marvellous marking, *Vivacissimamente*, was a red rag to Nina, and the music flashed by in delirious chirrups and stampings. Nick seemed to see Beethoven, or rather Nina herself, striding up and down some sonorous wooden-floored room in frenzied impatience for the joyful return. Norman made a grunt of rueful amusement, and Penny twisted round, as if freed by the optimistic turn of events, and looked gently, and still blushing, at Gerald, who caught her eye, lowered his gaze and coloured slightly also. Well, there was such an old tension between the two men, on stubborn matters of principle; for years it had been only Rachel's stubbornness that could make them forget their principles enough to meet, and nod at each other, and exchange doggish banter. Of course it was painful for Penny, and now perhaps she was making her own plea for reconciliation. Typing up Gerald's diary from the tape each day she must have a useful sense of his feelings.

The sonata finished and firm applause broke out, given a new edge of enthusiasm by the fact of its being the end – the whole experience was suddenly seen in a brighter light, it was time for a drink, they'd all done rather well. Norman Kent clapped with his hands above his head when Nina came back in, Catherine called out a hectic 'Bravo,' and Jasper imitated her and grinned as if he'd made a joke in class. For a second or two Nina stood there stiffly, then she sat down without a word and played Rachmaninov's Prelude in C-sharp minor. It was a piece the older members of the audience tended to know well, and though they didn't specially want to hear it, they indulged it and exchanged distracted smiles. After that there was very decisive applause, the piece had gone on for quite a while, one or two people looked round at the drinks table and the exit and started talking, and Nina came back in and played Bach's Toccata and Fugue in D minor, in the famous Busoni transcription. At this Lady Kimbolton looked at her watch as if she was virtually blind, holding her arm up to the light, and a number of people started fanning themselves with their programme sheets. This caught on as a form of mutiny, with the associated jiggling of bracelets. When Nina came back the next time Gerald had stood up and was saying, 'Um . . . aah,' as if amiably bringing a meeting to order, but she sat down anyway and played the Sabre Dance by Khachaturian. It all seemed quite natural to Nick, she must have been told to have three encores ready, but there was still a possibility that she had four, so at a sign from Gerald he went out after her and congratulated her and asked her to stop. She stood on the landing and gazed down the pompous curve of the stairs as the applause pattered quickly to a close and the greedy roar of the party began.

'Hello, Judy!'

'My dear.' Lady Partridge stood rigid while he kissed her rosy cheek – Nick never knew if she regarded a kiss as a homage or a liberty. He grinned at her, as if she was having as much fun as he was. 'You seem very cheerful,' she said.

Nick looked in the mirror where he did appear bright-eyed, sharing a rich secret with himself. 'Well, a successful recital, I thought.'

'Did you,' said Lady Partridge; and then, merely to be agreeable, 'I liked the last piece she played. I think I've heard it before.'

'Oh, the Khachaturian.'

She gave him a very dry look. 'Got a swing to it.'

'Mm, it certainly has' – Nick laughed quietly and delightedly, and after a second Lady Partridge smiled slyly too, as if she'd been cleverer than she knew.

A waitress came past and they both took new glasses of champagne. 'Extraordinary people . . .' Lady Partridge was saying. As a rule she was happy and busy in Gerald's political world, she treated his colleagues very graciously, and felt a fierce thrill when, amongst the drab shop talk that alas made up most of their social dealings, they gave her an undiluted fix of policy, the really unanswerable need to reduce manufacturing, curb immigration, rationalize 'mental health' (what abuse and waste there were there!), and get public services back into private hands. They were like rehearsals for the telly, and even more inspiring. They liquidated every doubt. Nick said,

'That's Lord Toft, isn't it . . . the man who builds all the roads.'

'Nothing extraordinary about Bernie Toft,' Lady Partridge said. Sir Jack himself of course had been in the construction business. 'I don't know why Gerald has to ask that awful *artist* man.'

'Oh, Norman, you mean? He's not very good, is he?'

'He's a red-hot socialist,' said Lady Partridge.

They both looked over to where Norman Kent was standing by the piano, holding on to it symbolically, and probably conscious of his portrait of Toby hanging behind him, as if it was an element in his own portrait. Most people dodged him with a preoccupied smile and pretended to be searching for someone else, but Catherine and Jasper were talking to him. His voice rose emotionally as he said, 'Of course you must, my dear girl, paint and paint and paint,' and shook Catherine by the shoulder.

'Do you happen to know who that young man is with my granddaughter?' Lady Partridge said.

'Yes, it's Jasper, he's her new boyfriend.'

'Ah . . .' Lady Partridge gave an illusionless nod or two; but said, 'He looks a cut above the last one, anyway.'

'Yes, he's all right . . .'

'He even appears to own shoes.'

'I know, amazing!' Nick's main feeling about Jasper, very clear to him at the moment, was that he needed to be tied up face down on a bed for an hour or two. 'He's an estate agent, actually.'

'Very good-looking,' said Lady Partridge, in her own odd lustful way. 'I imagine he sells masses of houses.'

Trudi Titchfield came past with a grimace, as if not expecting to be remembered. 'Lovely party,' she said. 'It's such a lovely room *for* a party. We sadly only have the garden flat. Well, one has the garden, but the rooms *are rather low*.'

'Yes,' said Lady Partridge.

Trudi lowered her voice. 'Not long of course before a very special party. The Silver Wedding . . . ? I hear the PM's coming.'

'I don't think the Queen's coming,' said Lady Partridge.

'No, not the Queen – *the PM*' – in a radiant whisper. 'The Queen! No, no . . .'

Lady Partridge blinked magnificently. 'All rather hush-hush,' she said.

Sam Zeman came past and said, 'You're making me a rich man, my dear!' which was charming and funny, but he didn't stop to expand. Perhaps it was just the code of business, but

Nick felt they'd used up their store of friendship in the gym
and the restaurant, and that they would never be close to each
other again.

In the crowd around the buffet (all chaffing courtesy and
furtive ruthlessness) little Nina was mixing with her audience,
who in general were nice enough to say 'Well done!' and ask her
where on earth she had learnt to play like that. She had simple
expressionless English, and the English people talked to her in
the same way, but louder. 'So your *father*, is in *prison*? You poor
thing!' Just in front of Nick, Lady Kimbolton was greeting the
Tippers. Lady Kimbolton's first name was Dolly, and even her
close friends found ways of avoiding the natural salutation.

'Good evening, Dolly,' said Sir Maurice, with a satirical
little bow.

'Hello!' said Sally Tipper. 'Well, that was very enjoyable.'

'I know, heartbreaking,' said Lady Kimbolton. 'I imagine
you saw the *Telegraph* this morning?'

'I did indeed,' said Sir Maurice. 'Congratulations!'

'I do like to hear music in the home,' Lady Tipper said, 'as
in the times of Beethoven and Schubert themselves.'

'I know . . .' said Lady Kimbolton, her square practical face
tilting this way and that to see what was on the table.

'Nigel must be chuffed,' Sir Maurice said.

'Maurice and I have been to a number of concerts at friends'
houses lately, it's an excellent move,' said Lady Tipper, who
was known to be artistic.

'I know, there seems to be an absolute mania for concerts,'
Lady Kimbolton said. 'This is the second one I've been to this
year.'

'I hear Lionel Kessler, you know . . . ? had the Medici
Quartet at Hawkeswood for a marvellous evening with
Giscard d'Estaing.'

'I think that's really what gave Gerald the idea,' said Nick,
joshing in between them as they got to the table.

'Oh, hello . . .'

'Hello, Dolly,' said Nick. He knew he could do quite a funny sketch about Gerald's growing preoccupation with the concert idea, which had come to a peak of competitive angst when Denis Beckwith, a handsome old saurian of the right enjoying fresh acclaim these days, had hired Kiri te Kanawa to sing Mozart and Strauss at his eighty-fifth birthday party. But something made him tread carefully. 'You know how competitive he is,' he said.

'We're all for competition!' said Dolly Kimbolton, claiming her plate of salmon from the waiter.

'Jolly good, jolly good . . .' said Gerald, weaving through behind them.

'Clever you to introduce us to a new artiste,' said Sally Tipper.

'I liked that last thing she played,' said Sir Maurice.

Gerald looked round to see where Nina was. 'We thought rather than going for a big name . . .'

The 'Badminton' lady was darting in for a bread roll. 'You're so right,' she said. 'I hear Michael's hiring *the Royal Philharmonic* for their summer party.'

'Michael . . . ?' said Gerald.

'Oh? . . . Heseltine? Yup . . . yup . . .' She hunched in fake apology as she backed away. 'Yup, the whole blinking RPO. What it must be costing. But they've had a good year,' she added, in a tenderly defiant tone.

'I thought we'd had a pretty good year,' Gerald muttered.

Nick had been avoiding Bertrand Ouradi, but as he turned from the table with his plate there Bertrand was. 'Aha, my friend the aesthete!' he said, and Nick was reminded of an annoying foreign waiter, perhaps, or taxi driver, for whom he was identified by a single joke. But he was able to say excitedly,

'How *are* you?'

Bertrand didn't answer – he seemed to suggest the question was both trivial and impertinent. He looked around the room, where people were grouping on the sofas and at little tables brought in by the staff and swiftly covered with white cloths. He didn't know where to settle, among these braying English snobs; his expression was proud and wary. 'Bloody hot, isn't it,' he said to Nick. 'Come and talk to me'; and he led him, again like a waiter, with half-impatient glances over his shoulder, among the dotted supper tables – not to the cool of the great rear balcony but to a window seat at the front, looking onto the street. Perching there, knee to knee, partly screened by the roped-back curtains, they had a worrying degree of privacy. 'Bloody hot,' said Bertrand again. 'Thank god that beast has got bloody air conditioning': he nodded at the maroon Rolls-Royce Silver Shadow parked at the kerb below.

'Ah,' said Nick, unable to rise to such a wretched brag. In the back window of the car shiny white cushions were neatly aligned; he couldn't see the number plate but the thought that it must be BO something made him smirk – he pressed the smirk a little harder into a ghastly smile of admiration. One of Catherine's neuroses was a horror of maroon; it outdid her phobia of the *au* sound, or augmented it perhaps, with some worse intimation. Nick saw what she meant.

Bertrand asked him a few questions about the recital, and paid attention to the answers as though at a useful professional briefing. 'Amazing technique,' he repeated. 'Still very young,' he said, and shook his head and dissected his salmon. High and capable though he was, Nick hesitated to play the aesthete very thoroughly, hesitated to be himself, in case his tone was too intimate and revealing. The influence of Bertrand was as strong in its way as the coke, and he found himself speaking gruffly to him. He wondered actually, despite the keenness of his feelings, if Nina had been much good. Reactions were skewed by her being so young. He pretended he was Dolly Kimbolton and said, 'The Beethoven was heartbreaking,' but it wasn't a phrase that Bertrand saw a use for. He looked at him narrowly and said, 'That last thing she played was bloody good.'

Nick glanced out into the room to find Wani, who was sitting at a table with his mother and a middle-aged woman who looked quite prickly and confused under his long-lashed gaze. It was almost a decoy of Wani's to let his gaze rest emptily but seductively on a woman. He still hadn't spoken to Nick since his arrival; there had been a turn and a nod, a sigh, as if to say, 'These crowds, these duties,' when they were taking their seats. If it made him uneasy to see his lover and his father tête-à-tête he was too clever to show it. Bertrand said, 'That son of mine, who's he flirting with now?'

Nick laughed easily and said, 'Oh, I don't know. Some MP's wife, I expect.'

'Flirting, flirting, that's all he bloody does!' said Bertrand, with a mocking flutter of his own eyelashes. Dapper and primped as he was, he became almost camp. Nick pictured the daily task of shaving above and below that line of moustache, the joy of the matutinal steel, and then the joy of the dressing room that was like a department of a shop. He said,

'He may flirt, but you know he never really looks at another woman,' and was thrilled by his own wickedness.

'I know, I know,' said Bertrand, as though cross at being taken seriously, but also perhaps reassured. 'So how's it going – at the office?'

'Oh fine, I think.'

'You still got all those pretty boys there?'

'Um . . .'

'I don't know why he has to have all these bloody pretty poofy boys.'

'Well, I think they're very good at their jobs,' Nick said, so horrified he sounded almost apologetic. 'Simon Jones is an excellent graphic designer, and Howard Wasserstein is a brilliant script editor.'

'So when does the bloody shooting start on the film?'

'Ah – you'd have to ask Wani that.'

Bertrand popped a new potato into his mouth and said, 'I already did – he never tells me nothing.' He flapped his napkin. 'What is the bloody film anyway?'

'Well, we're thinking about adapting *The Spoils of Poynton*, um . . .'

'Plenty of smooching, plenty of action,' Bertrand said.

Nick smiled thinly and thought rapidly and discovered that these were two elements entirely lacking from the novel. He said, 'Wani's hoping to get James Stallard to be in it.'

Bertrand gave him a wary look. 'Another pretty boy?'

'Well, he's generally agreed to be very good-looking. He's one of the rising young stars.'

'I read something about him . . .'

'Well, he recently got married to Sophie Tipper,' Nick said. 'Sir Maurice Tipper's daughter. It was in all the papers. Of course *she* used to go out with Toby – Gerald and Rachel's son.' He produced all this hetero stuff like a distracting proof; he hoped he wouldn't normally be so cravenly reassuring.

Bertrand smiled as if nothing would surprise him. 'I heard he let a big fish go.'

Nick blushed for some reason, and started talking about the magazine, with the brightness of a novice salesman, not yet committed and not yet cynical; he told him that he and Wani were going on a trip to research subjects for it – and that was the nearest he could get to stating the unspeakable fact of their affair. For a second he imagined telling Bertrand the truth, in all its mischievous beauty, imagined describing, like some praiseworthy business initiative, the skinhead rent boy they'd had in last week for a threesome. Just then he felt a kind of sadness – well, the shine went off things, as he'd known it would, his mood was petering into greyness, a grey restlessness. He felt condemned to this with Bertrand. It was just what had happened at Lowndes Square: the secret certainty faded after half an hour and gave way to a somehow enhanced state of doubt. The manageable joke of Bertrand became a penance. Nick was powerless, fidgety, sulkily appeasing, in the grip of a man who seemed to him in every way the opposite of himself, a tight little bundle of ego in a shiny suit. Something awful happened with a waitress, who was taking round a wine bottle. She was black, and Nick had noticed already the flickers of discomfort and mimes of broadmindedness as she moved through the room and gave everyone what they wanted. Bertrand held out his glass and she filled it with Chablis for him – he watched her as she did it, and as she smiled and turned interrogatively to Nick, Bertrand said, 'No, you bloody idiot, do you think I drink this? I want mineral water.' The girl recoiled for just a second at the smart of his tone, at the slap-down of service, and then apologized with steely insincerity. Nick said, 'Oh, I'm sure we can get you some water, we've got masses of water!' in a sweetly anxious way, as if to soften Bertrand's tone, to apologize for him himself, to give a breath of laughter to a rough moment; while Bertrand held the glass out stiffly towards her, expressionless save for a steady contemptuous blink. She held her dignity for a moment longer, while Nick's smile pleaded with her not to mind and with him to relent. But Bertrand said, 'Don't you know bloody nothing? – Take this away,' and glared at Nick as if to enlist or excite a similar outrage in him. Then when the girl had marched off, without saying a word, he looked down, sighed, and smiled ruefully, almost tenderly at Nick, as though to say that he would have liked to spare him such a scene, but that he himself was afraid of no one.

Nick knew he should move away, but he hadn't finished his main course; he took shameful refuge in it as a reason not to make a scene of his own. Other people must have heard. Tucked away in the window seat they must look like conspirators. Bertrand was talking about property now, and weighing the merits of WII against those of SW3; it seemed he too was thinking of moving to the neighbourhood. He looked at the room as if trying it on. 'Well, it's lovely here,' Nick said sadly, and gazed out of the window at the familiar street, at Bertrand's horrible maroon car, at the half-recognized evening life in the houses opposite, and at the big blond man who came up from the area of one of them, unlocked the big black motorbike that stood on the pavement outside, straddled it, pulled on and buckled his helmet, kicked the bike into eager life and three seconds later was gone. Only a buzz, a drone that faded as it rose, could be heard amid the high noise of talk in the room. It was as if the summons of the Chopin had been answered and the freedom seized by a lucky third person.

'Aah . . .' Gerald was saying, hovering like a waiter himself, the best of all waiters, 'I hope everything's all right.' He held a bottle of water in one hand and a freshly opened bottle of Taittinger in the other, as if hedging his bets.

'Marvellous!' said Bertrand, pretending not to notice these things, and then making a Gallic gesture of flattered surprise. 'You're very kind, to wait on me yourself.'

'These young girls don't always know what they're doing,' said Gerald.

Nick said, 'Gerald, obviously you've met . . . Mr Ouradi.'

'We haven't really met,' said Gerald, bowing and smiling secretively, 'but I'm absolutely delighted you're here.'

'Well, what a marvellous concert,' Bertrand said. 'The pianist had amazing technique. For one so young . . .'

'Amazing,' Gerald agreed. 'Well, you saw her here first!'

With an effect of creaking diplomatic machinery Dolly Kimbolton rolled into view, and Bertrand stood up, passing his plate with its toppling knife and fork to Nick. 'Hello!' she said.

'Have you met Lady Kimbolton? Mr Bertram Ouradi, one of our great supporters.'

They shook hands, Dolly leaning forward with the air of a busy headmistress rounding up stragglers for some huge collective effort. Bertrand said, in his tone of clear, childish self-importance, 'Yes, I'm making quite a contribution. Quite a big contribution to the party.'

'Splendid!' said Dolly, and gave him a smile in which political zeal managed almost entirely to disguise some older instinct about Middle Eastern shopkeepers.

'I don't know if we might all have a little chat . . . ?' said Gerald, raising the champagne bottle. 'And I think we might be needing this.' The suggestion obviously didn't include Nick, who as so often wasn't visible and certainly wasn't relevant, and who was left, when the other three went off, holding Bertrand's unfinished supper as well as his own.

He closed the door, locked the door, and reached out for Wani, who patted him and kissed him on the nose as he turned away.

'Where's the stuff?' said Wani.

Nick went over to the desk, unhappy but caught up too in the business of the coke, which if he was patient enough might make them both happy again. He got out the tin from the bottom drawer. Wani said, 'A tin is such an obvious place to hide it.'

'Darling, no one even knows I've got anything to hide.' He passed Wani the packet and smiled reproachfully. 'It's just like our wonderful secret love affair.'

Wani pulled out the chair and sat down at the desk, little clouds and gleams of possible rejoinders passing across his features. He peered at the stack of library books and selected *Henry James and the Question of Romance* by Mildred R. Pullman, which had a sleek Mylar sleeve protecting its dark jacket. 'This should do,' he said. He had never been in Nick's room before, and it was clear that it held no magic for him of the kind Nick had felt in Wani's room at Lowndes Square. Well, he wasn't one who noticed such things. He didn't thank Nick for meeting Ronnie or show any intuition of the scary drama it had been for him. Nick said, to remind him,

'I had such a sweet little chat with Ronnie. It seems he's hoping to move to this area.' Wani said nothing, tipping out a bit of the rough powder onto the book. 'He is very nice, isn't he?' Nick went on. 'It was quite a business – ringing him and waiting and ringing again . . . And of course he was late . . . !'

Wani said, 'You only like him because he's a wog. You probably fancy him.'

'Not particularly,' said Nick, whose wave of sexual feeling for him had been just a part of the criminal excitement, tension and relief at the same time, the feeling that Ronnie accepted not only his money but him; and then, to get it done, 'I wish you wouldn't use that word. I keep trying to believe you're not as irredeemable as your father.'

Wani weighed this up for a moment. 'So what was Papa talking to you about?' he said.

Nick sighed and paced across the room – where they both were again, in the subtly glamorized light and depth of the wardrobe mirror. He had imagined Wani's being here so often, for secret sleepovers and also, in some other dispensation, freely and openly, as his lover and partner. He said, 'Oh, he wants to move to this area too, apparently.' He gave a snuffly laugh. 'I ought to put him in touch with Jasper.'

'That Jasper's a sexy little slut,' said Wani, and it wasn't quite his usual tone.

'Yeah . . . ? All white boys look the same to me,' said Nick.

'Ha ha.' Wani studied his work. 'So – what else did he say?'

'Your old man? Oh, he was just pumping me again about you, and about the film. He has no idea what's going on, of course, but I think he's decided that I hold the key to the mystery. I did what I could to persuade him there wasn't a mystery.'

'Maybe you're the mystery,' said Wani. 'He doesn't know what to make of you.'

This was probably true, but also terribly unfair. Nick was longing to make a declaration, and now he felt violent towards Wani as well: his pulse was thumping in his neck as he stood behind him, then put his hands on his shoulders. All evening he'd needed to touch him, and the contact was convulsive when it came. Wani was working painstakingly and a little defensively with his gold card, making rapid hatching movements to and fro across the partially visible features of Henry James – not the great bald Master but the quick-eyed, tender, brilliant twenty-year-old, with an irrepressible kink in his dark hair. Nick squeezed Wani's neck with each clause: 'I wish we didn't have to carry on like this, I feel I've got to tell someone, I wish we could tell people.'

'If you tell one person you've told everybody,' Wani said. 'You might as well take a full-page ad in the *Telegraph*.'

'Well, I know you're very important, of course . . .'

'You don't think we'd be at a party like this if people knew what we did, do you?'

'Mm. I don't see why not.'

'You think you'd be hobnobbing with Dolly Kimbolton if she knew you were a pretty boy.'

'She does know I'm a – that's such an absurd phrase!'

'You think so?'

'And anyway hobnobbing, as you call it, with Dolly Kimbolton is hardly an indispensable part of my life. I've never pretended not to be gay, it's you that's doing that, my dear. This is 1986. Things have changed.'

'Yes. All the poofs are dropping like flies. Don't you think the mother and father of Antoine might worry a bit about that?'

'That's not really the point, is it?'

Wani made a little moue. 'It's part of the point,' he said. 'You know I have to be incredibly careful. You know the situation . . . There!' He raised his hands as if he'd balanced something. 'Now there's a line of beauty for you!' And he looked aside into the mirror, first at Nick and then at himself. 'I think we have a pretty good time,' he said, in a sudden weak appeal, but it was short of what Nick wanted.

Something happened when you looked in the mirror together. You asked it, as always, a question, and you asked each other something too; and the space, shadowy but glossy, the further room in which you found yourself, as if on a stage, vibrated with ironies and sentimental admissions. Or so it seemed to Nick. Now it was like a doorway into the past, into the moment he had thought 'Oh good' when Ouradi first appeared, having missed the start of term, in the Anglo-Saxon class, and was called on to translate a bit of King Alfred, which he did very decently – Nick had fixed on him already and expected him, as a latecomer and a foreigner, to look for a friend in this group of raw eighteen-year-olds. But he had vanished again at once, into some other world not quite discernible through the evening mist on Worcester College lake. And the 'Oh good,' the 'Yes!' of his arrival, the sight of his beautiful head and provoking little penis, were all Nick got, really, from Wani, in those Oxford years, when he himself was in disguise, behind books and beer glasses, 'out' as an aesthete, a bit of a poet, 'the man who likes Bruckner!' but fearful of himself. And now here he was with Wani, posing for this transient portrait, almost challenging him in the glass – and it was like the first week again: he was tensed for him to disappear.

He said, 'Do you ever sleep with Martine?' It hurt him to ask, and his face stiffened jealously for the answer.

Wani looked round for his wallet. 'What an extraordinary question.'

'Well, you're quite an extraordinary person, darling,' said Nick, thinking, with his horror of discord, that he'd been too abrupt, and pulling a hand through Wani's springy black curls.

'Here, have some of this and shut up,' said Wani, and grabbed him between the legs as he came round the chair, like boys in a playground, and perhaps with the same eagerness and confusion. Nick didn't resist. He snorted up his line, and stepped away. Then Wani too, re-rolling the note, bent his head and was about to swoop when they both heard the dim cracks of footsteps, very close, already on the turn of the top stairs; and a voice, under the breath, indistinguishable. Wani twitched round and glared at the lock of the door, and Nick with his heart racing ran through the memory of turning the key. Wani snorted his line, up one nostril, pocketed the note and the wrapper and turned over the book, all in a second or two. 'What are we doing?' he muttered.

Nick shook his head. 'What *are* we doing . . . ? Just talking about the script . . .'

Wani gave an absurd sigh, as if it might just do. Nick had never seen him so anxious; and somehow he knew, as he held his gaze, that Wani would punish him for having observed this moment of panic. It wasn't the drugs so much as the hint of a guilty intimacy. And now that it was done it was surely the locking of the door that was suspicious. 'No, just ten minutes, baby,' the same voice said, Nick smiled and closed his eyes, it was Jasper's phoney drawl, the familiar floorboard outside the bathroom creaked, a dress brushed the wall, and they heard the door of Catherine's room close, and almost at once the rattle of the key. Nick and Wani nodded slowly and smiles of relief and amusement and anticipation moved in sequence across their faces.

For Wani the first hit of coke was always an erotic rush, and for Nick too. They had kissed the first time they did coke together, their first kiss, Wani's mouth sour with wine, his tongue darting, his eyes timidly closed. Each time after that was a re-enactment of a thrilling beginning. Anything seemed possible – the world was not only doable, conquerable, but

lovable: it showed its weaknesses and you knew it would submit to you. You saw your own charm reflected in its eyes. Nick
stood and kissed Wani in the middle of the room – two or
three heavenly minutes that had been waiting to happen, a
glowing collision, a secret rift in the end of the day. They stood
there, in their suits, Wani's lightweight Italian 'grey', black
really, like one of his father's suits but made to hint and flow,
Nick, in the needle-fine pinstripe Wani had bought him, like
one of the keen young professionals of the age, the banker, the
dealer, the estate agent even . . .

Funny how sound travelled in an old house – through
blocked-off chimney spaces, along joists. A rhythm almost
inaudible to the cautious couple or unsuspecting soloist who
made it was relayed as a workmanlike thump through the ceiling below or, as in this case, a busy squeak in the room next
door. Stroking Wani's penis through his open fly, kissing his
neck so that his skin stood up in shivers, Nick laughed but he
was embarrassed too, almost shocked to hear them at it (which
he never had before) and at it so promptly and so fast. No
wasteful foreplay there – it made him wonder if Catherine was
liking it, if Jasper wasn't being a brute with her, when surely
she needed such careful handling. He felt Wani's grip tighten
on his shoulder, pressing him down, and he went down on one
knee, looking up at him sternly, and then on both knees and
pulled his cock into his mouth. Wani wasn't big but he was
very pretty, and his hard-ons, at least until the coke piled on
too deep, were boyishly steep and rigid.

Nick worked on him easily and steadily, his own dick still
buttoned away in a hard diagonal, something else waiting to
happen, and the squeak of the telltale floorboard coming in
rapid runs, like a manic mouse, and then with impressive
intermittence; Nick almost went with it, but it was a distraction too, like the voices on the stair, a kind of brake or warning. They must have moved the bed, or they were fucking on

the floor perhaps. He pictured them, Catherine vaguely and anxiously, Jasper much more vividly.

Wani's hands stroked and clutched at Nick's hair, tugged on it unpleasantly hard. 'They're really going at it,' he murmured. 'The little sluts . . .' Nick glanced up and saw him smiling, in his erotic trance, not at him directly but at the two of them in the mirror; and also (Nick knew) staring through the mirror, and the wardrobe itself, into the room beyond, which he had never seen and which was just as readily the motel bedroom of some seedy flick. 'They're really going at it – the little sluts' – Nick heard how he loved saying it again, whispering it, and grunted as Wani's little thrusts against his face fell into the accelerating rhythm of the kids next door. He felt awkward, pulled in to service a fantasy he couldn't quite share – he tried again, he'd jerked off a few times about Jasper already, but Catherine was his sister, and on lithium, and, well . . . a girl. He heard her voice now, quick staccato wails . . . and Wani's breathing, slipping away from him just at the moment he had him. And then another idea came to him, a second resort, a silent, comical revenge on Wani while he brought him off – it was Ronnie he'd invited in, to solace him for his woman trouble, to give him ten minutes of real care, man to man. It took a little adjustment, of course, a little further twist on make-believe, since the Ronnie he'd imagined was twice the size of Wani – at least. But as Wani pulled out and Nick squeezed his eyes tight shut, it could almost have been Ronnie in front of him, instead of the man he loved.

Downstairs, a little later, in the drawing room, the coda of the party was unwinding, and Gerald opening new bottles of champagne as though he made no distinction between the boring drunks who 'sat', and the knowing few of the inner circle, gathered round the empty marble fireplace. The Timmses were there, and Barry Groom, with their different fanatical ways of talking, their shades of zeal and exasperation

– all alien to Nick more than ever in the lull after drugs and sex. He saw that Polly Tompkins was sitting with them, as if among equals, and already impatient for something superior. Gerald, it was clear, hadn't yet got round to the new paper on Third World debt. 'Have a look at it,' said Polly, and nodded at him like a genial don. The strange thing was that it was also Gerald's nod, just as his white collar was Gerald's collar. The mimicry was artful, slightly amorous, and since the love was hopeless, slightly mocking too. Really everything nice about Polly was a calculation.

Morgan, the woman Polly had brought, came to join Gerald's group, where they were going back over the scandal of Oxford refusing the PM an honorary degree. John Timms, with his intense belief in form, regarded the incident as an outrage, but Barry Groom, who hadn't bothered with Oxford, said, 'Fuck 'em's what I say,' in a sharp frank tone that made Morgan blush and then weigh in like a man herself. The only touching thing about her was her evident uncertainty as to when or why anything was funny. 'They seem to think the lady's not for learning,' Gerald said. She looked bewilderedly at their laughing faces.

From the balcony, in the late July evening, the gardens receded in depth beyond depth of green, like some mysterious Hodgkin, to a point where a faintly luminous couple reclined on the grass. The astonishing greenness of London in summer. The great pale height of the after-dusk sky, birds cheeping and falling silent, an invincible solitude stretching out from the past like the slowly darkening east. The darkness climbed the sky, and the colours surrendered, the green became a dozen greys and blacks, the distant couple faded and disappeared.

'Hallo there . . . !'

'Oh hi, Jasper.'

'How are you, then, darling?' – almost tweaking him in the ribs.

'Very well. How are you?'

'Ooh, not bad. A bit tired . . .'

'Hmm. What have you been up to?'

Young Jasper, no younger probably than Nick, but with his chancy just-out-of-school look, quick and lazy at the same time, his flirtiness, his assumption he knew you, as if by bedding, or flooring, Catherine he gained equal rights, an instant history, with her intimate old friend . . . Jasper couldn't have known they'd been overheard upstairs, but his little smirk coming and going invited you to guess he'd been up to something. He had the pink of sex about him still. He leant by Nick on the balustrade, and he was clearly fairly drunk.

'Is Catherine OK?'

'Yeah . . . She's a bit knackered, she's turned in. This isn't really her sort of scene.'

Nick stared at the compound presumption of this remark and said, 'Things going OK between you two?'

'Ooh yes,' said Jasper, with a momentary pout, a wincing frown, to say how very hot it was. 'No, she's a lovely lady.'

Nick couldn't rise to this. After a moment he said, as nicely as he could, 'You are looking after her, aren't you, Jasper?'

'Hark at Uncle Nick,' said Jasper, piqued and somehow furtive.

'I mean, she seems quite steady at the moment, but it would just be disastrous if she came off this medication again.'

'I think she's got it all sorted out,' said Jasper, after a pause, adjusting his tone, his whole accent. He stood back and pushed his right hand through his glossy chestnut forelock, which immediately fell forward again; then the hand went into his jacket pocket, with just the thumb hooked out: subtly annoying gestures meant perhaps to convey commitment and dash to the doubtful house-buyer. 'She thinks the world of *you*, Nick,' he said.

Polly Tompkins had come out onto the balcony, perhaps jealous at seeing Nick with the boy he had squashed unavailingly earlier. Nick introduced them in a thinly amused tone which made no great claims for either of them. 'I thought you were avoiding me,' he said.

Jasper was waiting casually to see what the terms were, and if this big fat double-breasted man, who could have been anything between twenty-five and fifty, was part of the gay conspiracy or the straight one. Polly said, 'You're such a social butterfly, I haven't been able to reach you with my net,' and looked at Jasper as if to say he could find a use for him, if Nick couldn't.

Nick said, 'Well, I was a social caterpillar for years.'

Polly smiled and took out a packet of fags. 'You seem to be very close with our friend Mr Ouradi. What were you talking to him about, I wonder?'

'Oh, you know . . . cinema . . . Beethoven . . . Henry James.'

'Mmm . . .' Polly looked at the Silk Cut – a quitter's ten – but didn't open them. 'Or Lord Ouradi, as I suppose we shall soon be saying.'

Nick struggled to look unsurprised as he ran through all the reasons that Polly might be pulling his leg. He said, 'I wouldn't be surprised – there's a sort of reverse social gravity these days, isn't there. People just plummet upstairs.'

'I think Bertrand's rather more deserving than that,' said Polly, successfully resisting and pocketing the cigarettes.

'Anyway, he's not British, is he?' Nick said airily, and rather proud of this objection. It was Polly, after all, who'd once called him a Levantine grocer.

'That's hardly an insuperable problem,' said Polly with a quick pitying smile. 'Well, we must be going. I just wanted to say goodbye. Morgan has an early start tomorrow. She has to fly up to Edinburgh.'

'Well, my dear,' said Nick, 'one never sees you these days. I've given up keeping your place warm for you at the Shaftesbury' – a kindness, a bit of a sentimental gesture at the sort of friendship they had never actually had.

And Polly did a small but extraordinary thing: he looked at Nick and said, 'Not that I remotely concur with what you've just said – about the peerage.' He didn't flush or frown or grimace, but his long fat face seemed to harden in a fixative of threat and denial.

He went in, and Jasper followed him, turning to give Nick a curt little nod, in his own unconscious impression of Polly, so that the mannerism seemed to spread, a note of contempt that was a sign of allegiance.

10

The service stairs were next to the main stairs, separated only by a wall, but what a difference there was between them: the narrow back stairs, dangerously unrailed, under the bleak gleam of a skylight, each step worn down to a steep hollow, turned tightly in a deep grey shaft; whereas the great main sweep, a miracle of cantilevers, dividing and joining again, was hung with the portraits of prince-bishops, and had ears of corn in its wrought-iron banisters that trembled to the tread. It was glory at last, an escalation of delight, from which small doors, flush with the panelling, moved by levers below the prince-bishops' high-heeled and rosetted shoes, gave access, at every turn, to the back stairs, and their treacherous gloom. How quickly, without noticing, one ran from one to the other, after the proud White Rabbit, a well-known Old Harrovian porn star with a sphincter that winked as bells rang, crowds murmured and pigeons flopped about the dormer window while Nick woke and turned in his own little room again, in the comfortable anticlimax of home.

On his back, in the curtained light, the inveterate habits of home took hold of him without a word... Wani, of course... yes, Wani... in the car... and that time with Ricky, the outrage of it... though home, historically, was a shrine of Toby-longing, almost extinct now, worked up only in moods of vicious nostalgia... still, it seemed possible... Toby of three years ago... at Hawkeswood... morning after the great party . . . calling him into the King's Room, sweaty with hangover under one roiled sheet . . . 'Fuck, what a night . . . !' and then he darted to the bathroom . . . only time he saw him naked . . . great innocent rower's arse . . . did that happen . . . did what happened next happen . . . and Wani that night . . . met him on the stairs . . . who would have dreamt . . . dark green velvet . . . oh god, Wani in the flat . . . tied to the posts of the ogee bed . . .

It must be Mrs Creeley with his mother in the drive. They were talking about the car, Nick's little Mazda, 'a nice little runaround' his father had called it, to minimize their evident anxiety as to how he had come by such a thing. NG 2485: Mrs Creeley was thrilled by the number plate, Mrs Guest perhaps not so sure. ('You must be doing very well, dear,' she had said, in just the tone she would use to say 'You don't look very well, dear.') Wood pigeons in the trees, in the thick spruces at the front, making their broody calls, reproachful, condoning – who knew? The two women moved away, in the slow trawl of gossip, over the gravel: talk about the sale of the field, syllables only, on the faint breeze through the open top window, over-laid by the pigeons, the talk beaded and chiming, rhythmic and nonsensical, the breeze lifting and dropping the curtain in one lazy breath, hushing the voices. The lie-in: time-honoured concession of school holidays, the rare weekend visits. His father would have gone to the shop – he might have woken to the familiar drag of garage door, thump of car door, and then wandered sideways again into staircase dreams. Mrs Creeley went, he didn't hear his mother come inside, she had probably got up in gardening trousers, an old blouse that didn't matter. They had Gerald descending tonight, and the house, inside and out, would be ready for an inspection . . . A little later came the leisurely clop of a horse, sounds as abstract and calm-ing as other people's exertions on the tennis courts at home – at his other home. He wasn't sure, but he thought it was right that no horse had equal tone or resonance in all four hooves, as it distanced it made an odd sauntering impression, a syncopation, until lastly only one hoof continued faintly to be heard.

Out on the edge of town was where they were, where they'd carefully and long-sightedly chosen to be, on Cherry Tree Lane, decent post-war houses with plenty of garden, and only a view of fields at the back, and horses leaning in from time to time to chomp at the delphiniums and the weeping willow. And now the dreaded thing had happened, Sidney Hayes had bought next door, and thus at last got access from the lane to the field where he kept his horses, and got planning permission too, exceedingly quickly, five houses to the acre. Everyone had objected to the plans, and Nick had even been made embarrassingly to bring it up with Gerald, as their MP, who said of course he'd put a stop it, but quickly lost interest since no conditions had been breached, in fact rather the reverse, there was a property boom, home ownership was within the grasp of all, and even with the new development on top of them the value of 'Linnells' was destined to soar. All this cast a muddling running shadow over Don and Dot Guest's lives. They were more comfortable than they'd ever been, business was better, and yet across their treasured view a long-held worry was about to materialize in bricks and slates.

Despite its long mute presence in his life Nick found it hard to care for the house, its pinkish walls and metal-framed windows; it lacked poetry. At Linnells, as Gerald had said of Hawkeswood, the contents were the thing: a ruck of furniture, crowded families of Staffordshire and Chelsea figures, three clocks ticking competitively in one room, where the real family sat, supervised and even a little oppressed by their own possessions. Which changed, unpredictably, when something came into the shop that Don wanted to live with, or when a buyer was suddenly found for something in the house. So the market squeezed on them, acceptably, amusingly, and they would let a chest or a grandfather clock go, which in Nick's young life had the status of an heirloom already. For years he had had a nice wide walnut bed, a snug double of imagined couplings – the whorls and fans in the grain of the walnut were the underwater blooms of adolescent thought, pale pond-life of a hundred lie-ins. But one Christmas, in fact the one after he had come out, he arrived home to find it had been sold from under him, and replaced by something plain, modern, single and inhibitingly squeaky. In the past year or so, as business boomed, Don had started asking 'London prices', which had always been family code for extortion. Meanwhile London prices themselves had climbed, so Guest's was still cheaper and worth a day trip from town. Yesterday, after the big uneasy surprise of the car, Nick had had his own surprise, the missing bureau. 'You'll never guess what I got for it,' his father said – with a look of unaccustomed and still embarrassed greed.

Nick came downstairs and glanced out coyly at the car. He liked to give himself that little prepared surprise, it was new enough for the thrill of its first arrival to flare up beautifully again each morning. Like a child's new present it lit up a dull day, and made it worth getting up and going out, just to sit in the simmer of London traffic and feel the throb of possession. If it had shocked his parents, then it had shocked him too, the colour, the grin of it, the number plate, all things he wouldn't have chosen for himself. But the burden of choice and discretion had been taken off him, it was what Wani wanted him to have, and he let himself go. The car was his lower nature, wrapped in a gift ribbon, and he came to a quick accommodation with it, and found it not so bad or so low after all. A first car was a big day for a boy, and he wished his parents could just have clapped their hands at the fun of it; but that wasn't their way. He explained, as he smiled anxiously, that it was all to do with work, it was a tax write-off, it was nonsense he didn't understand himself. He tried to entertain them with the mechanism of the roof, and opened the bonnet for his father to look at the cylinders and things, which he did with a nod and a hum; clocks, not engines, were his oily interest. Nick wondered why they couldn't share in his excitement; but had to admit, after ten minutes, that he'd somehow known they wouldn't – the hilarity of his arrival had been a self-delusion. He thought of an obscure childhood incident when he'd stolen ten shillings from his mother to buy her a present of a little china hen; he'd denied it through such storms of tears that he wasn't sure now if he'd stolen the money or not; he'd almost convinced himself of his innocence. The episode still darkened his mind as a failed, an obscurely guilty, attempt to please. It was the same with the car, they couldn't see where it came from, and they were right in a way, since they knew him so well: there was something very important he wasn't telling them. In Rachel's terms the Mazda was certainly vulgar and potentially unsafe; but for Don and Dot its shiny red snout in the drive was more than that, it was the shock of who Nick was, and the disappointment.

Gerald was in Barwick on various duties, first the Summer Fête, which he was opening at two o'clock, and later a dinner at the Crown to mark the retirement of the agent; in between he was due to look in at Cherry Tree Lane for a drink. It was the last weekend before their departure to France, and his usual bad temper about anything to do with Barwick was only soothed by the prospect of making speeches at at least two of these events. Rachel had stayed at home, and Penny had come up with Gerald to write down people's names on bits of paper and prevent those muddles which had caused some bad feeling in the past.

The Barwick Fête, which Nick hadn't been to since his schooldays, was held in Abbots' Field, a park near the middle of town. On a normal Saturday afternoon the field had two dim attractions, a fragment of the once great Augustinian abbey, and a Gents where the maniacal rejoinders and obliterations of the graffiti had come to interest Nick in his adolescence even more than the Curvilinear tracery of the monks' choir. He had never made contact in the Gents, never acted on the graffiti, but whenever he passed it on a walk with his mother and heard the busy unattended flush of the urinal, his look became tense and tactful, he felt the kinship of an unknown crowd. Today the field was ringed with stalls, there was a skittle alley hedged with straw bales, a traction engine let out shrill whistles, and the silver prize band warred euphoniously with a jangling old carousel. Nick wandered round feeling both distinguished and invisible. He stopped to talk to friends of his parents, who were genial but just perceptibly short with him, because of what they knew or guessed about him. The friendliness, a note of bright supportive pity, was really directed to his parents, not to him. It made him wonder for a moment how he was talked about; it must be hard for his mother to boast about him. Being sort of the art adviser on a non-existent magazine was as obscure and unsatisfactory as being gay. He scented a false respect, which perhaps was just good manners; a reluctance to be drawn into truth-telling talk. He saw Mr Leverton, his old English master, who had done *The Turn of the Screw* with him and sent him off to Oxford, and they had a chat about Nick's doctorate. Nick called him Stanley now, with a residual sense of transgression. He felt a kind of longing behind Mr Leverton's black-framed glasses for the larger field of speculation Nick was moving in, and for other things too. The old tone of crisp enthusiasm quavered with a new anxiety about keeping up. He said, 'Come back and see us! Come and talk to the A-level lot. We've had a very jolly Hopkins group this year.' Later Nick said hello to Miss Avison, who much earlier in his life had taught him ballroom dancing; his mother had said it would be something he'd always be grateful for. She remembered all the children she'd taught, and with no acknowledgement that they'd grown and changed and hadn't danced a waltz or a two-step for twenty years. Nick felt for a moment he was still a treasured and blissfully obedient little boy.

The tannoy crackled and whined. Nick was at the far end of the field, dawdling behind a group of local lads, and pretending to admire a stall of primitive local pottery. The mayoress made a very dull speech, but it rode on the goodwill of the audience, and on the expectation that it would be over much sooner than it was. Families rambled with a half-attentive air across the grass. Her chain could be seen, the glint of glasses, and her bright-blue, white-bowed prime-ministerial dress, on the low platform; and Gerald, standing behind, with beaming impatience. She said something unfortunate about not being able to get a celebrity to open the proceedings this summer, but at least the person they had got was on time – 'unlike a certain star of the airwaves last year!' After this Gerald leapt up to the mike as if seizing the controls of a bus from a drunk.

There was applause, not easy to measure, lost in the open air; as well as one or two shouts and klaxon-squawks to remind Gerald that though he had a large majority there were still constituents unsedated by council-house sales and tax cuts. 'I liked it when they had Derek Nimmo,' a woman said to Nick. Nick knew what she meant, he absorbed people's gibes about Gerald without protest, but still felt the old secret pride at knowing him. He gazed around, followed the Carter boy's amazing arse with his eyes, smiled loyally at Gerald's jokes, and sensed in them a mixture of piety and condescension rather like his own. He felt so decadent here. And how could you honestly expect Gerald, at the door of the Cabinet, in the Lady's favour, an amusing speaker from the floor of the House, to bother very much for an audience of squalling kids and deaf pensioners? Catherine said Gerald despised his constituents. 'If only you didn't have to be MP *for* somewhere,' she said, 'Gerald would be completely happy. You know he loathes Barwick, don't you.' Nick had laughed at this, but wondered if his 'dear ma and pa' were in fact exempt from the loathing. 'This is a classic English day,' Gerald was saying now, 'and a classic English scene.' And Nick appealed against Catherine's judgement. Surely something else is happening, beneath the cheerful imposture: it can't help mattering to him – as he speaks these platitudes he comes to think they're fine words after all, he's caught up on a wave of rhetoric and self-esteem. He told a joke about a Frenchman on a cycling holiday that went down well; and as he wound up, at just the right time, he managed to suggest that far from being a rich businessman who came down from London to loathe them he was in fact the spirit of Barwick, the Pickwick of Barwick, opening the fête to them as if it were his own house. He cut the tape, which demarcated nothing, in a decisive lunge: the sliding snap of the shears could be heard over the microphone.

After this Gerald was led off on a quasi-royal tour of the fête, his style hampered by the mayoress, who fell naturally into the role of consort. Nick wanted to keep an eye on who was going into the Gents, but felt the pull of the London party too, and strolled over to join Penny. 'That went well,' he said.

'Gerald was excellent, of course,' said Penny. 'We're not very pleased with the mayoress.' They watched the mayoress now, at the jam stall, looking at the prices as if they were trying to cheat her, and might need beating down; at which Gerald, who didn't know the shop price of anything except champagne and haircuts, impulsively bought two jars of marmalade for a fiver and posed with them for the local press. 'Hold them up a bit, sir!' – and Gerald, always reassured by the attendance of photographers, cupped them in front of him, almost lewdly, until Penny came forward, silent agent of a wish, and took them from him; he held on to them for a moment as he passed them over and murmured, 'Je dois me séparer de cette femme commune.'

At the tombola he bought ten tickets, and stood around waiting for the draw. The prizes were bottles, of all kinds, from HP Sauce to Johnnie Walker. He hadn't dressed for the country at all, and his keynote blue shirt with white collar and red tie, and his double-breasted pinstripe suit, stood out as a dash of Westminster among the shirtsleeves and jeans and cheap cotton frocks. He nodded and smiled at a woman beside him and said, 'Are you having a good day?'

'Mustn't grumble,' said the woman. 'I'm after that bottle of cherry brandy.'

'Jolly good – well, good luck. I don't suppose I'll win anything.'

'I don't suppose you need to, do you?'

'All right, Mr Fedden, sir!' said the tombola man.

'Hello! Nice to see you . . .' said Gerald, which was his politician's way of covering the possibility that they'd met before.

'Here we go, then! HP Sauce, I expect, for you, isn't it, sir?'

'You never know your luck,' said Gerald – and then, as the hexagonal drum was cranked round, 'Something for everybody! All shall have prizes!'

'Ah, we've heard that before,' said a man in gold-rimmed glasses who evidently fell into the category of 'smart-alec socialist', the sort who asked questions full of uncheckable statistics.

'Nice to see you too,' Gerald said, turning his attention to the numbers.

'Hah!' said the man.

The cherry-brandy lady won a half-bottle of Mira Mart gin, and laughed, and blushed violently, as if she'd already drunk it and disgraced herself. Lemonade, then Guinness, went next.

Then Gerald won a bottle of Lambrusco. 'Ah, splendid . . .' he said, and laughed facetiously.

'I understand you like a drop of wine, sir,' said the tombola man, handing it over.

'Absolutely!' said Gerald.

'Don't keep it,' whispered Penny, just beside him.

'Mmm . . . ?'

'One doesn't keep the prize. Doesn't look good . . .'

'Looks bloody awful,' Gerald muttered; then boomed considerately, 'I don't feel I should snatch victory from my own constituents.' Shy cheers were sounded. 'Barbara – can I persuade you . . . ?'

The lady mayor seemed to register at least three insults in this proposal: to her status, to her taste, and to her well-advertised abstinence. Nick had a hunch too that she wasn't called Barbara. Wasn't she *Brenda* Nelson? The bottle lay for a moment in Gerald's hands, as if tendered by a mocking sommelier. Then he passed it hastily back to the trestle table. 'Give someone else a treat,' he said, with a nod.

Still, the feeling that he ought to be allowed to win *something* had clearly taken hold of him. Seeing his chance, craning round as if he'd lost someone, he struck out by himself through the crowds. Penny trotted patiently after him, clutching the marmalade, and then Nick, some way behind the wake of laughter and agitation that followed Gerald's passage.

The sport of welly-whanging was unknown in the Surrey of Gerald's youth, as it was of course in contemporary Notting Hill; the only wellies he ever touched in middle life were the green ones unhoused from the basement passage for winter weekends with country friends. But at Barwick, which still had a regular livestock market and loose straw blowing in the street, the welly, black, leaden-soled, loose on the heel, was an unembarrassed fact, and whanging it a popular pastime. Gerald approached the flimsy archway made of two poles and a banner, beneath which a white chalk crease had been drawn. 'Put me in for a go!' he said. He had the expression of a good sport, since he was new to the game, but a glint of steel showed through.

'That's 25p a whang, sir, or five for a pound.'

'Ooh, give us a quid's worth,' said Gerald, in a special plummy voice he used for slang. He groped busily in his pockets, but he'd spent all his change already. He got out his wallet and was hesitantly offering a £20 note when Penny stepped forward and put a pound coin on the table. 'Ah, splendid . . .' said Gerald, observing a couple of teenage boys who weren't making an effort – the boot plonked to earth a few feet in front of them. 'OK . . . !'

He took the boot and weighed it in his hand. People gathered round, since it was something of an event, their MP, in his bespoke pinstripe and red tie, clutching an old wellington boot and about to hurl it through the air. 'Know how to whang it, then, Gerald?' said a local, perhaps kindly. Gerald frowned, as though to say that instruction could hardly be necessary. He'd seen the ineffectual lob of the boys. He took his first shot from the chest, in muddled imitation perhaps of a darts-player or shot-putter, the sole to the fore. But he had underestimated the weight of the thing, and it landed between the first two lines. 'You've got to really *whang* it,' said a sturdy but anxious-looking woman, 'you know . . .' – and she made a big arcing gesture. The boot was handed back to him by a little boy and he tried again, with a barely amused smile, as if to say that taking advice from working-class women in headscarves and curlers was all part of being their MP. He dutifully imitated her windmilling gesture, but perhaps because of the restriction imposed at the top of the arc by his tightly tailored jacket, he let go of the boot in a twirling spin – it turned over two or three times in the air before thudding to the grass. 'Now that's a bit better,' someone murmured. 'Now you're getting there!' Another man called out hectically, 'Up the Conservatives!' Nick realized with a soft shock that there was a lot of goodwill for Gerald among the crowd, as well as the common sense of delight at seeing a famous person perform even the simplest task; and Gerald seemed to draw on this for his third attempt. He unbuttoned his jacket, an action which itself was greeted with approval, and sent the welly in a vigorous underarm lob, still wastefully high, but landing beyond the twenty-yard mark. There was applause, and varied advice, as to where to hold the boot, at the top or halfway down or at the heel, and Gerald obligingly tried out the different grips. The fourth go was as wildly wrong as a return off the edge of the racket in tennis. There was some exasperation among the onlookers, again mixed in with a kind of solicitude, and a very ironic voice, which turned out to be that of the smart-alec socialist, said, 'That's all right, you have to be prepared to make a fool of yourself.' For his final shot, with a sharp snuffle as he let go, Gerald sent the missile in a long low arc, and it landed and bounced wobblingly aside in the uncalibrated zone beyond twenty-five yards. The boy ran in and stuck a blue golf tee at the point of contact. There was applause, and pictures were taken by the press and the public. 'I hope I've won a prize,' Gerald said.

'Ah, you won't know yet, Gerald,' said a helpful local. It was an extension perhaps of the bogus camaraderie of election time, the blind forging of friendships, that constituents felt free to call their MP by his Christian name, and in Gerald's face a momentary coldness was covered by a kind of bashfulness, bogus or not, at being a public property, the people's friend.

'Mr Trevor,' murmured Penny at his elbow. 'Septic tank.'

'Hullo, Trevor,' said Gerald, which made him sound like the gardener.

'Five o'clock,' Mr Trevor said. 'That's when we'll know: one that's thrown the farthest wins the pig.' And he pointed to a small pen, previously hidden by the crowd, in which a Gloucester Old Spot was nosing through a pile of cabbage stalks.

'Goodness . . .' said Gerald, laughing uneasily, as if he'd been shown a python in a tank.

'Breakfast, dinner and tea for a month!' said Mr Trevor.

'Yes, indeed . . . Though we don't actually eat pork,' Gerald said, and he was turning to move on when he saw the man in gold-rimmed glasses approaching the oche and weighing the gumboot knowingly in his hand.

'Ah, Cecil'll show you a thing or two!' shouted out the woman in curlers, who maybe wasn't Gerald's friend after all – you never knew with these people. Cecil was slight, but wiry and determined, and everything he did he did with a thin smile. Gerald waited to see what happened, and Nick and Penny closed in and tried to talk to him about something else. 'I bet he knows some trick,' said Gerald, 'what . . . ?'

Cecil's trick was to take a short run-up, and then with a complete revolution of the arm to send the welly flying as if to a waiting batsman – it was a dropper, the boot descending steeply to a spot a yard beyond Gerald's final mark; the boy ran out and pressed in a red golf tee. Then Cecil had another trick, which was to throw it underarm, lofting it not too high, and bringing it down short of the first shot, but still beyond the blue tee. He had a grasp of the weight and direction of the thing, the trajectory, no mid-air wavering or tumbling. He refined and varied these methods, and with his last go went a good three yards over his own record. Then, wiping his hands, his smile twitchily controlled, he walked over and stood not next to but near Gerald. 'Ah, shame, but there you are,' said Mr Trevor. 'Still, if you've no use for the animal –'

Gerald said breezily, 'Oh, damn the animal,' and looked

from Penny to Nick, and then to the bristlingly insouciant figure of Cecil. He began to remove his jacket, with tiny quick head-shakings, his colour rising, making a joke of his own temperament, frowning and smirking at once. 'I feel that can't be allowed to pass without a firm rejoinder,' he said, in his humorous but meaningful debating tone. There were cheers, and also a few whistles, as his jacket came off and blue braces, dark sweat-blooms, were revealed: a sense, depending on how you looked at it, that Gerald was being a terrific sport or that he was making a fool of himself, as Cecil had said. Penny, always vigilant, took his jacket with an eyebrow-flicker of caution, but enough of a smile to be publicly supportive. Then she had to search in her bag for another pound coin.

'So you've won a pig!' Nick's mother said, bringing Gerald through into the sitting room at Linnells. 'Goodness . . .'

'I know . . .' said Gerald. He still looked a bit flushed from the effort, in need of a shower perhaps, hair smeared back, a bit barmy still with adrenalin. 'It went to five rounds but I got him in the end. I won convincingly.' Dot Guest glanced about the densely furnished room, gestured at one seat after another, and seemed to feel that the house was too small altogether for Gerald. He kicked against things, he was untamed, it was almost as if the pig had come barging in after him. He went to the window at the back and said, 'What a charming view. You're virtually in the country here, aren't you.'

Courteously, and very timidly, clearing a space on a side table, Dot murmured, 'Yes . . . we are . . . as good as . . .' and then looked up gratefully as Don came in with gin-and-tonics on a silver tray. Gerald had entirely forgotten about the field.

'Well, what a day, who'd have thought it,' he said: 'welly-whanging: another string to my bow.' And he flung himself down in Don's armchair as if he lived there, just to put them at their ease. 'Thanks so much, Don' – reaching up for his drink. 'I feel I've earned this.'

'Where is the pig?' Nick's father said.

'Oh, I've given it to the hospital. One doesn't keep the prize, obviously, on these occasions. Good health!'

Nick watched them all take refuge in their first sip. He felt ashamed of the smallness of the drinks, and the way his father had made them in the kitchen and brought them in like a treat. His parents looked at Gerald proudly but nervously. They were so small and neat, almost childlike, and Gerald was so glowing and sprawling and larger than local life. Don was wearing a bright red bow tie. When he was little Nick had revered his father's bow ties, the conjuror's trick of their knotting, the aesthetic contrasts and implications of the different colours and patterns – he'd had keen favourites, and almost a horror of one or two, he had lived in the daily drama of those strips of paisley silk and spotted terylene, so superior to the kipper ties of other dads. But now he was made uneasy by the scarlet twist below the trim white beard; he thought his father looked a bit of a twit.

Dot said, 'We're lucky you had time to come and see us. I know you must be terribly busy. And you're about to go away, aren't you?' It was one of her 'professional' worries, all parts of the great worry of London itself, along with fainting Guardsmen and the tedium of being in *The Mousetrap*, as to how MPs coped with their massive workloads; it was something Nick had been asked to find out when he moved in. His conclusion, that Gerald didn't do the work at all, but relied on briefings by hard-working secretaries and assistants, was considered cynical and therefore untrue by his mother.

Gerald said, 'Yes, we're off on Monday,' and gave a great shrug of relief. Nick could see him, bored and suggestible, start brooding at once on the superior pleasures of the manoir.

'I wonder how you fit it all in,' Dot said, 'all the reading you must have to do. It worries me – Nick says I'm silly . . . You probably never sleep, do you, I don't see how you could! That's what they say about . . . the Lady, isn't it?'

Nick had inculcated his parents with Gerald's form *the Lady*, but was embarrassed to hear them use it in front of him. He seemed to take it as a tribute, however, both to her and to himself. 'What, four hours a night?' he said, with an admiring chuckle. 'Yes, but the PM's a phenomenon – *terrifying energy*! I'm a mere mortal, I need my beauty sleep, I'm not ashamed to say.'

'She looks beautiful without any sleep, then,' said Dot piously, and Don nodded his agreement, too shy, as yet, to ask the question that burned in them both: what was she like?

Gerald, knowing they wanted to ask that, showed he hadn't lost sight of the original question. 'But you're right, of course.' He took them into his confidence. 'The paperwork can be quite overwhelming at times. I'm lucky in that I'm a fast reader. And I've got a memory like an ostrich. I can gut the *Telegraph* in ten minutes and the *Mail* in four – you just get a knack for it.'

'Ah,' said Dot, and nodded slowly. 'And how is your daughter?' She was being attentive and courteous, and Nick saw that she would run through things that troubled her, and hope to get a better answer out of Gerald than she could out of him. 'I know you've been worried about her, haven't you?'

'Oh, she's fine,' said Gerald breezily; and then seeing some use in the idea of being worried, 'She's had her ups and downs, hasn't she, Nick – the old Puss? It's not easy being her. But you know, this thing called librium that she's on has been an absolute godsend. Sort of wonder drug . . .'

'Mm . . . lithium,' said Nick.

'Oh yes . . . ?' said Dot, looking uneasily from one to the other.

'She's just a much happier young pussycat. I think we've turned the corner.'

Nick said, 'She's doing some great work now, at St Martin's.'

'Yes, she's doing marvellous collages and things,' said Gerald.

'Ah, modern art, no doubt,' said Don, with a dreary ironic look at Nick.

'Don't pretend to be a philistine, Dad,' said Nick, and saw him unable to separate the praise from the reproach; the French pronunciation of *philistine* didn't help.

'It seems to work for her, anyway,' said Gerald, who liked the therapeutic excuse for Catherine's large abstract efforts. 'And she's got a super boyfriend, that we're all very happy about. Because we haven't always had good luck on that front.'

'Oh . . .' said Dot, and looked down at her drink as if to say that neither, indeed, had they.

'Mm, we're jolly proud of her, in fact,' said Gerald grandly, so that he seemed slightly ashamed. 'And we're all going to be together in France this year, which Rachel and I are delighted about. First time for some years. And Nick too, as you know, will be joining us . . . at least for a bit . . . long overdue . . .' and Gerald guzzled the rest of his gin-and-tonic.

'Oh,' said Dot, 'you didn't say, dear.'

'Oh, yes,' said Nick. 'Well, I'm going with Wani Ouradi, you know, who I'm working with on this magazine – we're going to Italy and Germany to look at things for that, and then we hope to drop in at . . . the manoir, for a few days on the way back.'

'That'll be a wonderful experience for you, old boy,' Don said. And Nick thought, really the poor old things, they do as well as they can; but for a minute he almost blamed them for not knowing he was going to Europe with Wani, and for making him tell them a plan so heavy with hidden meaning. It wasn't their fault that they didn't know – Nick couldn't tell them things, and so everything he said and did took on the nature of a surprise, big or little but somehow never wholly benign, since they were aftershocks of the original surprise, that he was, as his mother said, a whatsit.

'Because you normally have Nick to look after the house for you, don't you,' she said. 'When you're away.' She clung to this fact, as a proof of his trustworthiness to important others, who apparently didn't care about his being a whatsit one way or the other.

'Poor old Nick, he has got rather landed with that in the past. This year we'll have our housekeeper and her daughter move in, and they can do a massive clean-up of the house without us getting under their feet. It makes a bit of a holiday for them.' Gerald gestured liberally with his empty glass.

'That sounds like the sort of holiday I'm used to!' said Dot, who longed for the spoiling of a hotel, but was subjected to her sister-in-law's cottage at Holkham each September.

Don brought Gerald a refill, and had a tiny one himself; they tended not to go at quite that pace. He said, 'He's a good chap, is he, this Ouradi?'

'You haven't met him . . . no . . . Oh, he's a charmer, absolutely. My son Tobias and he were great friends at Oxford – well, you all were, weren't you, Nick.'

'I didn't get to know him well until a bit later,' Nick said carefully, remembering the bathroom of the Flintshires' Mayfair house, the way the coke numbed their lips as they kissed. It gave him a tingle now, the thought of the other world that was waiting for him.

'Someone in his position can't help but do well,' said Don.

'I have the feeling . . .' said Gerald, with a condescending twinkle. 'I know high hopes are riding on him. The father's quite a character, of course.'

'He's the supermarket chappie, isn't he.'

'Bertrand? Oh, a *great* man!' said Gerald, who used the word very freely, as if hoping it might stick as easily to himself. 'I mean, an outstanding businessman, obviously . . . Awfully sad, I didn't know till the other day, but you know, they lost their first son.'

'Oh, really . . .'

'Yup, he was knocked down by a lorry in the street, in Beirut of course. The child and his nanny or whatever they call them were both killed. Bertrand Ouradi was telling me about it only the other day.'

Nick had to pretend he already knew this, and nodded sombrely to confirm it to his parents, who murmured in sympathy but seemed not to care much, as if a death in Beirut were only to be expected. 'Yes, it was an awful thing,' Nick said. It was a total surprise. His first thought was that his smug reckonings of intimacy with Wani looked very foolish. It was the family mystery, hardly glimpsed, far stronger and darker than their little sexual conspiracy. And Wani was carrying that burden . . . He seemed instantly more touching, more glamorous and more forgivable.

'His fiancée looks a sweet little thing,' said Dot. 'I've seen her at the hairdresser's.'

'Really . . .'

'In the *Tatler*, I mean!'

'Ah, yes . . .'

'Of course Nick was in the *Tatler*, after that marvellous party of yours. We dined out on that for months.' This was one of his mother's favourite boasts, and strictly a figure of speech, since they only dined out about three times a year. 'Who's the other one we see? That great big fat one, that Nick knows? – Lord Shepton: he's always in.'

'What about this little runaround of Nick's?' said Don, with anxious enthusiasm.

'Mm, she's a lively little thing,' said Gerald.

'Did you say he'd *given* the car to you, dear, I didn't quite understand . . .'

'I told you, Mum,' Nick said, 'it's like a company car. I can drive it while I'm working for him.'

'He must think very highly of you,' Dot said doubtfully. 'Well, it's all another world, isn't it?' No one quite assented to this, and after a moment she went on, 'And how's your son?'

'Oh, he's in great shape. Set up his own little company now, we'll see how he gets on.'

'We used to see his name in the paper a lot!' said Don, as if Toby's back-half paragraphs on share prospects had been the highlight of their days.

'Mm, I think that was a bit of a wrong turning. He's an out-door sort of chap, you know, far too confined by office life . . . Well, it only lasted five minutes; and good on him for giving it a go.'

'Oh, absolutely . . .'

'It was a bit more than that,' said Nick.

'Mm? Nick's probably right,' said Gerald. 'What was it, six months on the *Guardian*, where I don't think he felt at *all* at home, and then a year or so on the *Telegraph*, on the City desk . . . yah.'

'Some of Nick's university friends seem to have made their fortunes already,' said Dot. 'Who was it, dear, you said had bought a castle or something?'

'Oh . . .' said Nick, regretting having bragged about this. 'Yes, one of them has. It's quite a small castle . . . ! But he's in reinsurance, you know.'

'Ah,' said Dot. Nick hoped she wouldn't ask him what reinsurance was. 'They go so fast these days, don't they!' she said, as if Gerald might be equally breathless at the thought.

'Lord Exmouth's son's doing jolly well,' said Don.

'Ah yes,' said Gerald. 'One of our local blue-bloods!' He had suddenly become a Barwick man at the mention of the indigenous aristocracy.

'That's right,' said Don. 'Well, I look after the clocks at Monksbury, so I've seen young Lord David on and off since he was a little boy.'

'Really . . . ?' Gerald gave him a narrow look over the rim of his glass. 'You don't go to the Noseleys, I suppose?'

'Not since the old lady died,' said Don. 'I did a lot of work out there, ooh, ten years ago now I suppose. Of course they had death-watch beetle at Noseley Abbey. They had a devil of a job getting rid of the little tinkers!'

Nick got up to pass round a dish of stuffed olives and made small waiterly noises to distract his father from saying what he knew was coming next. 'Thanks so much,' said Gerald.

'No, it's a pleasure doing things at these great houses,' Don said. 'Even if they're not very quick at settling their accounts.' He looked round fondly. 'We've got so many of them round here. Nick's tired of hearing this, but I've got two earls, one viscount, one baron and two baronets on my books!'

'Quite a tally,' said Gerald. 'We'll have to see if we can find you a duke.'

'Of course, the fabulous thing,' said Nick, in a rush of shame, 'is the quality of the furniture in all these houses. Things that have been there for centuries.'

'Quite so . . .' Gerald nodded, as if he took that point very seriously himself. He raised and lowered his eyebrows, in perplexity at his empty glass.

Don said, 'Nick tells me you have some lovely pieces at your London house.'

'Oh . . .'

'A fair bit of French work, I believe?'

'*Quite* a bit of French work, yes,' said Gerald, who didn't have a clue where most of it came from.

'And some lovely paintings too.'

Gerald gave them a look of thoughtful beneficence, just coloured with impatience, even a kind of disdain – or so it seemed to Nick, who felt for both parties, as though he were witnessing an argument with himself. 'You know you really should come and see us, shouldn't they, Nick? – or come even when we're away. Come when we're in France and make yourselves at home. Have the run of the place. You could have a look at all our stuff, while you're about it, and tell us what's what.'

'Well, that's immensely kind,' said Don, smiling at the seduction of the idea.

'Oh, I don't think we could,' said Dot, whose fear of liberties in general included even those that might be allowed to herself. 'I mean, it's awfully nice of you, of course . . .' She looked crushed by the offer, and bit her cheek as she peered at Don. Nick thought his mother sometimes obtuse and narrow-minded, he deplored her sillinesses, and at the same time he was so attuned to her moods, to the currents of implication between a mother and an only child, that he could trace the lines of her anxiety without effort. To come to Kensington Park Gardens, to stay in the house and rootle hesitantly around in it, would satisfy a curiosity; but it would also give unforgettable shape and detail to the world in which Nick lived, with its tolerance and its expenditure, its wine cellars and its housekeepers who hardly spoke English, and the Home Secretary ringing up just like that, which Nick said sometimes happened. It would be a flood of knowledge, and in general, as she said, she would rather not know anything more.

'Give it some thought, anyway,' said Gerald; and Nick knew, as his parents murmured and glowed, that it would never be mentioned again.

He drove into the Market Square and slowed down as they approached CLOCKS D. N. GUEST ANTIQUES: 'There's our shop!' – he raised an arm, as if showing him the Doge's Palace or some other great thing he was about to visit.

'Absolutely!' said Gerald. Nick could only glance at it, but it had a presence for him, like a surprise he had prepared for someone else who could never feel it as keenly as he did himself. That side of the square was in shadow now, though the sun still glared on the other side, on the white stucco front of the Crown Hotel. A cloudless sky above the roofs, the shops all shut, emptiness of a country town on a high summer evening; not quite empty, as weekenders strolled before dinner, peering into the locked shops, with a look of hoping to get the best from the place, and some lads, or 'louts', roamed about under the arches of the market hall. The market hall was the jewel of the town, a cage of glass and stone on a high arcade, still locally claimed, against all the evidence, as a work of Sir Christopher Wren. It had been the pride of Nick's childhood, he had done a project about it at school with measured plans and elevations, at the age of twelve it had ranked with the Taj Mahal and the Parliament Building in Ottawa in his private architectural heaven. The moment of accepting that it was not by Wren had been as bleak and excit- ing as puberty. Now he revved round it, the lads looked up, and he savoured the triumph of coming home in a throaty little runaround. It was as though the achievements of sex and equities and titles and drugs blew out in a long scarf behind him. No, it was real superiority, it was almost lonely, a world of pleasures and privileges these boys couldn't imagine, and thus beyond their envy. He pulled up in front of the Crown and Gerald sprang out, pushing a hand through his hair, torn between his sporty show-off self and a hint of compromised dignity, even of some worse anomaly in being seen in such a car with a young gay man. Penny was waiting, with her blush and her tight smile, her obedient strictness, and he went grate- fully towards her. 'Have fun!' said Nick, and roared off half round the square again, thinking just how much he would like to do so himself.

He pulled into a parking space in the middle, where the market was on a Thursday, and turned off the engine. He would have to go home in a minute for dinner, and a cautious post-mortem on Gerald's visit. There would be a sense, at dinner, of new avenues of worry opened up . . . the suspicion, now Gerald had gone, that they didn't quite trust him: for all their nerves and good manners they had a sharp ear for bombast, they were more sensitive than they admitted; they would have noticed that Gerald asked them nothing at all about themselves; and they would think about Nick's London life from now on with a degree or two less of reassurance. His eyes ran over the shop again, which looked very shut, empty but purposeful, everything shadowy beyond the chairs in the window. It seemed freshly strange to have his family name there on a shopfront, he felt his schoolboy pride and his Oxford snobbery pinch on it from both directions, on his very own name, N. GUEST, plumb in the middle. He watched a group of boys passing slowly behind him, and moved his head to follow them in the mirror, where they seemed to prance and linger in a tinted distance. There was the clatter of a kicked can, a belch that echoed across the square. He thought, what if he'd stayed here, so far from the essentials of Heaven, the Opera, Ronnie's deliveries . . . ? For a moment he laboured in the fiction of that alternative life – there were cultured people here, of course, with books and gramophones: when he tried to picture them they all took the form of his teachers at Barwick Grammar, Mr Leverton and his Hopkins group. There were one or two school friends he could probably count on. Statistically there ought to be five or six hundred homos in Barwick, hidden away, more or less, behind these shopfronts and unreadable upper windows. The Gents in Abbots' Field would become a wearisome magnet, an awful symbol.

Across the road, half-dazzled by the evening sun, couples were arriving at the Crown for the dinner, the women in long skirts, their hair done, the men in suits, greeting each other with little pats and after-yous, confusing attempts at social kissing (not between the men, of course), all of them excited to be hearing their MP later on, but calm too with the sense of accumulated rightness in being Conservatives. And fuck, there was Gary Carter, setting out on the scent of his own Saturday night, in a short denim jacket and stiffly tight new jeans and that terrible sexy haircut; he called across to a mate under the market hall, he showed himself off to him somehow, with the funny unchallengeable poofiness of a handsome straight boy in a country town. Though girls apparently loved boys' bums too – good judgement, though Nick wasn't sure what they wanted with them. Gary passed under the market hall and out the other side, and started to amble back along the pavement behind. It was time to go; Nick sensed the atmosphere of Linnells waiting, in all its stolid innocence of what it was taking him away from. Then he shook himself, shocked to be dragged under and back by these small-town dreams. One way or another the place had to be left; he felt his long adolescence, its boredom and lust and its aesthetic ecstasies, laid up in amber in the sun-thickened light of the evening square; how he always loved the place, and how he used to yearn for London across the imagined miles of wheat fields, piggeries, and industrial sidings. He thought he would just cruise out past Gary and stir his interest and fix a picture of him in his mind for later. He started the car, and craning round to reverse into the road he saw the folder with Gerald's speech in it lying on the back seat.

Penny was sure to have another copy for him, in the hotel, though probably one without these inked-in jokes, underlinings and reminders: the text was revealingly marked up for so confident a speaker. The names 'Archie' and 'Veronica' were ringed in red at the top of the first sheet. The thing to do was to find Penny and insinuate the speech back into Gerald's hands. Drinks would be under way now, and Nick pictured already one of the grimly decorous 'suites', used for low-grade business conferences and Rotary dinners, where the function would be taking place. He was only wearing crumpled linen trousers and a short-sleeved shirt, but he could dart in like a stagehand with a forgotten prop, he could be functionally invisible, and for the Barwick Conservatives disbelief could remain suspended.

In the crowded front hall he was still the driver, the messenger, and if any of the guests recognized him, members of the Operatic, men who had filled his teeth and fitted him for school blazers, they didn't show it. If it was a snub it was also a relief. He asked at reception, and the girl thought Gerald had gone out to the car park at the rear – she thought he wanted some air. Nick sidled out and went into the long corridor which turned and stepped up and stepped down through various awkward annexes towards the back of the building. Here hunting prints and old Speed maps of the county were hung against red-flock wallpaper; and the carpet was red, with an oppressive black swirl, like monstrous paisley. Couples came towards him, half-smiling, crisply reassuring each other about the locked car, the tidied hair, the tablets patted in a pocket. They seemed satisfied by this passageway, the sketchy historical sham of it, the beer smells and cooked lamb smells in the spaces between fire doors. And there was Gerald, at the next corner, glancing to left and right as if planning an escape, a last quick minute of his real life before the show started – Nick didn't shout out because of the people in between, but he saw him push open a door at the side and pop in.

The sign said 'Staff Only', so that Nick looked round too – it was probably a back way through to the Fairfax Suite. Inside there was a service passage, less glaringly lit, and he saw

Gerald's head through the small wired window in another swing door – and Penny's too, giggling: that was good, it meant things were under control. The door was still settling back in lazy wafts which was why perhaps the noise of Nick pushing it open didn't alert them – it was just a further rhythmic displacement of the stale air. He managed to make a kerfuffle, half turning back, trapping his leg and dropping the folder so that neither of them would know he had seen Penny's hand, like an amorous teenager's, tucked in the back pocket of Gerald's trousers.

However, he had seen it, and the shock of it, trite but enormous, made him distracted at dinner, when the anticipated crabwise conversation about Gerald took place. He agreed rather sourly with their jokey criticisms and spoke of him as if he'd never much cared for him. This made them even more uneasy. There was a summer repeat of *Sedley* on ITV, and they watched it after dinner in their excited ceremonious way, Dot saying (quite tipsy by now), 'My son knows him, you know! He's a great friend of Patrick Grayson!' and Nick thinking, why can't you see what a frightful old poof he is.

When they turned in, unbelievably early, the high summer twilight still beautiful outside, Nick called out 'Sleep well!' and closed his door with a bewildering sense of loss, as though Gerald and Rachel were really his parents, and not the undeviating old pair in their twin beds in the next room. Later he heard his father snoring through the wall, and the creak of his mother's bed – he pictured her pulling the blankets over her ears. Rachel had once admitted to Nick that Gerald snored too, though she'd done it in the way she sometimes pretended to a disadvantage, from polite awareness of her own good fortune ('I know, we can *never* get into Tante Claire'): 'He can make a bit of a rumpus,' she'd said. Nick drew and resisted various conclusions from what he had seen; he was greedy and then reluctant for unpleasant sensations. He thought perhaps he was being a bit of a prig. He thought of Gerald's regular visits to Barwick with Penny, almost always without Rachel. It was a system, a secret so routine it must have come to seem secure. And the steady disguise, of course, of the 'loathing' for Barwick, the chore of the surgery, the boredom of meetings with Archie Manning . . . And what about in London? Presumably they couldn't do it there, the risk of detection would be too great. Or didn't much actually go on? Could Penny possibly be the sort of girl for all that? There might be some other excuse for the glimpse he had had in the hotel. Impossible to think of one. He wondered if Gerald was snoring now, and the image of what he probably was doing rose alarmingly in Nick's sex-picturing mind. Or if he was snoring, then it seemed to his partner like a bearable penalty of an illicit affair . . . Nick stopped and drew back with distaste for his own imagining of the thing. A little later he woke and the house was silent again, and the shock of what was happening came over him, his grown-up scorn of its utter banality and his child's ache of despair. He saw it had already become a secret of his own, a thing to carry unwillingly, a sour confusion of duties. He lay awake listening to the silence, which was illusory, a cover to a register of other sounds . . . the sigh of a grey poplar, the late half-conscious toppings-up of the cistern overhead, and within his ears remote soft percussions, like doors closing in non-existent wings of the house.

II

(i)

Toby said, 'You get a glimpse of the château on your left,' and he slowed down as a gap in the trees appeared. They saw steep slate roofs, purple-black brick, plate glass, the special nineteenth-century hardness.

'Right . . .' said Wani. 'But you don't have that any longer?'

'My grandfather sold it after the war,' said Toby.

'So who lives there now?' said Nick, whose heart was always caught by a lodge-house on a side road or a pinnacle among trees, and by Gothic Revival more than Gothic itself. 'Can we go in?'

'It's a retirement home for old gendarmes,' Toby said. 'I have been in – it's pretty depressing'; and he pushed on along the potholed lane.

'Oh,' said Nick doubtfully.

'They don't give you any trouble?' Wani wanted to know.

'They can get a bit rowdy,' Toby said. 'Once or twice we've had to call the police' – and he looked in the mirror to see if Nick smiled at his joke. Oh, Toby's jokes! – they made Nick want to scrunch him up in a protesting hug.

'So the house we're going to . . . ?' said Wani.

'The manoir . . . was the original big house on the estate. It's jolly old, sort of sixteenth century I think – well, you'll see. It's not as big as the château, but it's much nicer. At least we all think so.'

'Right . . .' Wani drawled again, with a slight suggestion that he might have preferred the larger house, but was ready to muck in at the manoir. 'And this still belongs to Lionel?'

'Strictly speaking, yah,' said Toby.

Wani gazed out of the window as though he knew the value of everything. 'And so one day, old chap, it will all belong to you,' he said, with a mixture of rivalry and satisfaction.

'Well, me and my sis, of course.' This occupied a future that Nick couldn't easily imagine.

'So who's down here now?' asked Wani.

'Just us at the moment, I'm afraid,' said Toby: 'Ma and Pa, me and Catherine – oh, and Jasper.'

'Oh, is that her little boyfriend . . .'

'Yeah, have you met him, he's an estate agent.'

'I think I know who you mean,' said Wani.

'Jasper and Pa seem to have become best friends. I think he'll have the house on the market by the time we leave.'

Nick gave a snuffly laugh from the back seat, and thought what a terrible little operator Jasper was, oiling his way into the family with his forelock and his dodgy voice; and Wani too – how flawless he was, making his quick social reconnaissance, everything hidden from Toby, his old friend. He looked at the backs of their heads, Wani's black curls, Toby's cropped and sunburned nape, and felt for an eerie moment what strangers they were to him, and perhaps to each other. They were only boys, but the height and territorial presumption of the Range Rover threw them into relief as men of the world, Toby sporting and unimaginative, Wani languid, with the softness and vigilance of money about him. Perhaps being old friends didn't mean very much, they shared assumptions rather than lives.

Wani said, 'Oh, I bought the Clerkenwell building by the way.'

'Oh, you did,' said Toby, 'good.'

'Four hundred K. I thought, really . . .'

'Yah . . .' said Toby, setting his face, looking bored. There was something stiff but acceptably adult to them both about this, about saying so little. Wani hadn't even mentioned the deal to Nick. It was typical of his secrecy, both grand and petty, since he had given Nick the five thousand: he made him feel how that sum was eclipsed by the unnamed sublimities of his own transactions.

Nick said, 'Oh, that's great, I can't wait to see it.' He found he tried to keep up, as if to show that he had money, for the first time in his life; but having some money, and sitting in a car behind Toby and Wani, only made him realize how little money he had – he felt self-conscious with them now in a way that he never had when he was penniless.

'So no chance of Martine joining us?' Toby said.

'I don't think my mother can spare her,' said Wani, in a tone of imponderable irony.

'She'll have to one day,' said Toby, and gave a big laugh.

'I know . . .' said Wani; 'anyway, what about you, you fucker, are you seeing anyone?'

'Nah . . .' said Toby, with a sour grin of independence, and then gratefully, as if the joke could never fade, 'Ah! Here's our wrinkled retainer.' An old man was riding a bicycle towards them over the patchy road surface, his slowly rising and falling knees jutting out sideways – he stopped and tottered into the grass verge as Toby pulled up. 'Bonjour, Dédé . . . Et comment va Liliane aujourd'hui?'

The old man held on to the car and looked in at them cautiously and with a hint of cunning. 'Pas bien,' he said.

'Ah, je suis désolé,' said Toby – insincerely it seemed to Nick, but it was only the play-acting, the capable new persona that came with speaking in a foreign language. A longish conversation followed, Toby fluent but with little attempt at a French accent, a sense of heightened goodwill and simplicity between them, and the old man's laconic answers coming like stamps of authenticity to the new arrivals, trying to hear and follow what was being said. Wani of course was a native French-speaker, but for Nick there was a warm sense of success when he could make out Dédé's words. Jokes understood in a foreign language became amusing in a further, exemplary way: he was storing them already as the coinage, the argot, of their ten-day visit. He sat back, smiling tolerantly, loving the heat and the sunlight through the huge old roadside oaks and chestnuts, and the sense of a prepared surprise, of being led through screened back ways towards a view. There was that tingle in the air that you got in even modestly mountainous country, the imminence of a drop, of space instead of mass.

Toby wound up the conversation, they all nodded solicitously at Dédé, and the car crept on again. Nick said,

'I hope your grandmother's still coming down.'

'Don't worry,' said Toby, 'she's coming on Tuesday. And the Tippers are coming too, I'm sorry about that.'

'That's fine,' said Wani.

'It's bloody good to have you guys here,' Toby said, and looked affectionately for Nick again in the mirror.

'It's fabulous to be here,' said Nick, with just a shiver, as they turned in between urn-crowned gate-piers, of the old feeling, from the first day at Oxford, the first morning at Kensington Park Gardens, of innocence and longing.

A three-sided courtyard was made by the sombre entrance front of the house, creeper-covered and small-windowed, a lower wing to the left, and an old barn and stable on the right. The house itself hid the view, and it was only through the open front door and the shadowy hallway that Nick caught a hint of the dazzle beyond, a further small doorway of light. He picked his bags out from the car, and watched Wani gesturing belatedly as Toby plucked up his cases and strode indoors with them, his sandalled feet thwacking on the stone flags and his calf muscles square and brown. He seemed to tread there for a moment, framed and silhouetted, as he had at the Worcester lodge, all those years ago, in the archway that led from the outside world to the inner garden: Toby, who was born to use the gateway, the loggia, the stairs without looking at them or thinking about them. And something else came back, from that later first morning at Kensington Park Gardens: a sense that the house was not only an enhancement of Toby's interest but a compensation for his lack of it.

From the hall they caught a glimpse through a series of rooms curtained against the steep sunlight, but stabbed across by it here and there. There were china bowls, oak tables, books and newspapers, straw hats, the remotely threatening mood of holiday routines, of other people's leisure, of games to be inducted into, things the Feddens had already said and done lingering in the shadows among the squashy old armchairs. The rooms were tall, deep-raftered, stone-walled, so that you would have a sense of living in the depths of them, like rooms in a castle or an old school. But for now they were deserted, the party were all elsewhere.

Toby led them on up the wide shallow stairs. On the upper floor an ochre-tiled passageway ran the length of the house, with bedrooms opening off it like prettily appointed cells. Nick and Wani were at the far end. 'Mum's put you in opposite rooms,' said Toby, 'so I hope you're not fed up with each other.' Wani raised his eyebrows, puffed and shrugged like a Frenchman: they did their double act. It was hard for a moment to believe this wasn't the usual discreet arrangement for an unmarried couple, that Toby wasn't in on the secret, hadn't the first suspicion. Nick was used to deceiving adults but he felt sad about tricking Toby. He saw the wound it would be to his childish good nature if he found out. But Wani presumably was hardened against such anxieties. Nick looked at him, and had a brief cold intuition of their different shades of relief about the rooms – his own that they were close, and Wani's that they were apart. Wani was on the front, and Nick, as family perhaps, had the smaller, darker room looking out at the end of the house into the branches of an ancient plane tree. 'Fantastic!' he said. He got on with unpacking, and hung up the suits he had brought – always wary of what rich people meant by 'informal'. His laundry had all been done by the hotel in Munich, and was rustlingly interleaved with tissue paper. He noticed that a tap in his bathroom dripped and was leaving a rusty stain. By the bed there was a bookcase with old French novels, left-behind Frederick Forsyths, odd leather-bound volumes of history and memoirs with the coroneted Kessler bookplate. There was a pair of strange little paintings on glass in varnished pearwood frames. He took possession of the room, and talked himself out of a tiny sense of disappointment with it.

Toby was still chatting in Wani's doorway, his hands in his shorts pockets, the undeniable bulge above the waistband these days, something comfy about him, as well as something passive and perplexed. Nick loved him with that fondness of an old friendship that accepts a degree of boredom, and is soothed and even sustained by it. What he felt was distilled affection, undemanding but principled. 'Ah, he can tell us,' Toby said.

'Yah, what was the name of the brothel we went to in Venice?' said Wani. He was unpacking too, though as coyly and delayingly as he had undressed that day at the Highgate Ponds.

'Oh, the *ridotto*?' said Nick. 'Yes, it's this really exquisite little casino, I suppose it was a brothel, really. "Il ridotto della Procuratoressa Venier". It's just behind San Marco.'

'There you are,' said Wani.

'It's been done up by the American branch of Venice in Peril. You ring the bell and the lady shows it to you.'

'OK . . .' said Toby. 'So it's not a functioning brothel . . .'

Wani said, 'Anyone less like a madam than the lady from Venice in Peril it would be hard to imagine. I'm having a feature on the top brothels of the world in my first issue.'

'Your advertisers will love that,' said Toby.

'Don't you think?' said Wani. 'Well, beautiful brothels.' He looked at Nick, whose idea the feature had entirely been. 'You know – risottos.'

Toby said, 'You should have taken me with you. You can't expect poor old Guest to go sniffing round tarts' parlours.'

'No, you'd have been much more use,' Wani said, and gave him a level grin, so that Nick was jealous for a second and went on to wonder – it had never been clear – if Wani fancied Toby. Well, it was possible, but unlikely, for some large social reason, which perhaps boiled down to the fact that Toby couldn't be bought.

'Drinks at six,' Toby said. 'But come and have a swim first. Everyone's outside' – and he slapped off down the echoing hallway.

Then Nick strode across Wani's room, pushed open the loosely coupled shutters, and had his first look at the view: of wooded spurs, dropping from either side like interlaced fingers, and beyond them one bright curve of the Dronne with a rocky bluff above it, bright too in the late afternoon sun. There was the glare of France in high summer, the colours simplified, dry and drab, but twitching with light, and the shadows baffling, like deep grey gauze. Down below, three or four stony terraces dropped away from the house, linked by stairways – it was hard from here to work them out. 'Yeah, I'm going to change,' said Wani.

'Good idea,' said Nick, turning and smiling.

'Hmm. OK . . .' – with the frowning reluctance of a boy.

'Darling, I spent half last night with my tongue up your arse, I'm not going to be too shocked if you take your shirt off.'

Wani gave a dry little laugh and arranged his various pairs of slippers and moccasins on the floor of the wardrobe. 'It's what people might say,' he muttered.

'What, because I'm gay, you mean?' Nick said, with a flash of the eyebrows. 'Well, there's no one else in the house. And I'll just carry on looking out of the window . . . I'll *crane* out of the window': which he did, to see that directly below there was a white awning, covering, presumably, the table, the famous table evoked by Gerald – with apologies to Napoleon – as the first dining room of Europe. It was the table and the awning that made it *their* view – the one often referred to by Gerald as his own landscape, one of the few things, like the music of Strauss, on which he was all unembarrassed sensibility. Of course it wasn't quite what Nick had expected; again it took a minute for the reality to blot and erase the long-imagined, subtly finer view.

Beyond the awning, steps led down on the left through the shade of a sprawling fig tree towards a low-roofed further structure, which Nick thought must be the pool-house. And just then Catherine came up them, noiselessly barefoot, on tiptoe at the heat of the stones, a blue towel round her shoulders and her hair still wet. She looked very young, child-like, nipping across the terrace, peering about; and with a vague air of crisis to her, Nick felt, as if she'd been dressed like this in a London street. Toby came out from the house and she said, 'Are they here?' – in her way of not quite noticing him even though she was asking him a question. 'They'll be down in a minute,' Toby said, going on himself towards the steps to the pool. Catherine sat on her towel on the low terrace wall, pushed back her hair, and her eyes drifted slowly upwards across the front of the house until she saw Nick leaning out of the end window and grinning at her. 'Hello, darling!'

'Hello, darling!' Nick opened his arms to the view and then, with the sort of dumb camp she liked, pretended to throw flowers down at an adoring crowd. She beamed and raised her hands in noiseless applause.

'Come down at once!' she called.

'We're coming . . .'

Wani had put on his swimming trunks under his white linen trousers, and they showed as a provocative black shadow. Nick was a little exercised about the types of swimwear, and the different registers of poolside life. The knob-flaunting Speedos appropriate for an unsocial fifty lengths or a scientific hour of sunbathing might seem ill-judged for cocktails or ping-pong, when sexless bags might be preferred. But perhaps not; sun-worship was half the point of a home in France, and the Feddens might not feel, as Nick somehow did, that if the contours of his penis were visible, then the question of what he liked to do with it was at the forefront of everyone's mind.

Catherine kissed the two boys in very different ways: she butted her face against Wani's and brayed 'Hello!' and showed that she didn't really know him or expect much of him. She pulled Nick into the embrace of her towel, so that her thin body in its damp swimsuit pressed against him, and he wriggled away laughing as he hugged her. 'Thank god you're here at last,' she said.

'How are you, darling?'

'I'm fine. Gerald's having an affair, did you know?'

Nick blinked and recoiled offendedly, but then tried to keep smiling. 'Gerald?' His whole image of the coming ten days was changing; he would have to find out who knew, and how much Catherine knew, of course. He felt horribly guilty himself for knowing, and doing nothing, and his main wish, in this first instant, was to clear himself. 'You can't be serious,' he said, postponing for a further second or two the really irreversible question, with whom?

'No, it's true. He's having an affair with Jasper.'

Nick gasped. 'Darling! How outrageous!'

'I know, it's a scandal.'

'Has it been going on long?'

'The whole week. There's this hideous room called the *fumoir* and they go in there together and play chess and smoke cigars. Well, you'll see. No one else can bear to go in, so we don't know exactly what they get up to.'

'Let's hope the press don't get to hear about it,' Nick said, with a giddy feeling of reprieve mixed up with the real and re-awoken sense of risk.

'It's like being kissed by a lav.'

'Oh . . . the cigars . . . ?'

'Incidentally,' she said to Wani, 'we're on septic here, so nothing funny down the bog.'

'No . . . right . . .' said Wani, and chuckled and frowned. It was just comic brusqueness, an urge to ruffle this exquisite new arrival, and also clairvoyant, Nick felt, as though she knew that a closeted cokehead would always be in the WC. She led them down the stairs, under the wide leaves of the fig tree, and out onto the flagged surround of the swimming pool.

The pool occupied another long terrace, open to the south, so that the glitter of the water seemed to reach and hang against the distance. At the near end was the pool-house, a little cottage in itself, with shuttered windows and wet foot-prints going in and out at the door. Thick-cushioned loungers, turned towards the sun at different times, lay abandoned around the pool, but close by, under a huge red umbrella, Rachel was stretched out with her eyes closed, and the straps of her black swimsuit looped down over her upper arms. Her mouth was slightly open, she might have been asleep, or in the border-zone of voices where the sunned mind dallies with sleep for seconds at a time. She was more beautiful and vulner-able than Nick was prepared for; he had never seen her undressed – he thought it was a private view she might not want Wani to share. A few feet away, at an angle, Gerald was

lying, propped up, with the meltwater of a long drink in a
beaker beside him, dark glasses on, head bent over a book in
his lap, but unambiguously asleep, since the pages of the book
stood up in a quivering comb. Beyond them, Jasper sprawled
on his tummy on the blue-tiled ledge just below the surface of
the pool, looking away at the view, and giving an impression
of adolescent boredom. He was wearing huge multi-coloured
swimming-bags, and as he lazily kicked the water they glis-
tened and ballooned, deflated and clung, one buttock pink,
the other lime-green. Nick saw Wani looking at him. Then
Toby came marching out of the pool-house, and Catherine,
wanting to take the credit, shouted, 'Here they are!' and woke
them all up. 'You look such old wrecks lying there,' she said,
and cackled in the 'mad' style that she now allowed herself.
Gerald started speaking at once, Rachel wriggled as she
stretched and sat up, and the two boys bent down rivalrously
to kiss her. Jasper came sploshing across the pool. Nick hadn't
seen them for a while, of course, and finding them here, in the
nearly naked torpor of their private world, he saw everything
that was wonderful about them, and something else, like one
of Catherine's glittering intuitions, their unsuspecting readiness for pain.

At dinner under the awning Nick and Wani were given the
second stage of their welcome, which was to be made to feel
how dull and plotless life had been without them, and how
enjoyable it was going to be now they were here. They all
revealed their frustrations, and made bids on the new arrivals
to do the things they had been wanting to do themselves. After
a week of family deadlock, of interlocking boredoms, there
was going to be an outburst of activity, a high plateau of
achievement. Wani politely agreed to everything that was
proposed, though he looked a bit queasy at Toby's plan to dis-
cover an underground lake. Gerald said, 'We really must do

the Hautefort hike again, twenty kilometres, take all day if we need to.' Jasper squeezed Nick's knee under the table and said there was a little bar in Podier, which 'a man of discrimination such as yourself' should certainly visit; and Catherine, perhaps satirically, said she'd always wanted to do some hang-gliding. Then she said she was going to paint Nick's portrait, but everyone objected that it would take too much of his time. It was left to Rachel to say, with her ironic quiver, that she hoped Nick and Wani would feel free to do nothing at all.

'No, of course,' said Gerald insincerely. He was lazy, but he wasn't good at pure idleness, which he felt like a failure of self-assertion. He was obviously finding his annual poolside trek through one of the fatter Trollopes an irksomely passive exercise, though he said how splendid it was, and what great fun. 'I think they might enjoy the hike,' he said. 'We haven't done it since 83.' He poured himself a full glass of wine, and passed the bottle along the candlelit table.

'How did you get on in Venice?' Rachel said. She was looking at Nick, but Nick passed the question to Wani with a steady look.

'Fascinating!' he said. 'What a fascinating place.'

'I know . . . isn't it fascinating,' said Rachel. 'Had you never been before?'

'Do you know, I'd never been before.' Wani, who barely knew Gerald and Rachel, had immediately absorbed their echoing and affirmative style of chat.

'Where did you stay?'

'We stayed at the Gritti,' said Wani, with a shrug and a wince, as if to say they'd taken the path of least resistance.

'Goodness . . . ! Well . . . !' Rachel said, in dazzled surrender to the magnificence of this, but somehow agreeing that they could have made a subtler and more deeply informed choice.

'You must have stayed there yourself,' said Wani.

Rachel shook her head. 'I think perhaps once . . .'

'Mm, where was it we stayed, Puss?' said Gerald.

'I don't know,' said Catherine. After her breakdown last year she had gone with her parents to Venice for a tense attempt at recuperation, which she now claimed scarcely to remember.

'We had a marvellous time, I must say,' said Gerald, with jovial shortness of memory.

'Yeah, amazing place,' said Jasper, and smiled at him, with the candlelight in his eyes, as if recalling some intimate moment.

'Oh, when were you last there?' said Nick airily.

'Ooh, must be two . . . three years ago?' said Jasper, dropping his head and letting his forelock tumble.

'And where did *you* stay?' Wani asked, and watched for the answer as if himself imagining some intimacy – sweat-dampened sheets, discarded towels. Jasper appeared to consider several possible answers, very quickly, before saying,

'Some friends of ours have got a flat there, actually, yah.'

'Oh, well, you are lucky,' said Rachel smoothly, leaving a doubt as to whether she believed him.

'Near San Marco?' said Nick.

'Not far from there,' Jasper said, and made a business of passing the wine bottle back to Gerald, who emptied the last of it and said,

'We loved the Caravaggios.'

Nick said nothing, and couldn't decide if he wanted Wani to make a fool of himself. Wani was wary enough to say, 'I'm not sure . . .'. Rachel was blinking and saying, 'No, darling, aren't the Caravaggios—' and Catherine said, 'They're Carpaccios,' and slapped her hand on the table.

Gerald gave a wounded smile and said, 'You can remember those anyway.'

Wani, never ruffled, almost sinisterly charming, said, 'What made an enormous impression on me was the rococo architecture in Munich.'

This statement was left to resonate for a few moments, while they each forked over how to tackle it. Wani looked along the table with an absence of self-irony that was very like his father's – and in the upward glow of the candles the deep sculpture of his face was like his father's too. What touched Nick was partly his lover's conscienceless appropriation of anything useful he said, and partly Wani's evident feeling that in France, on the terrace of a beautiful old house, among Nick's own 'family', he could play the aesthete as confidently as Nick did at Lowndes Square. The actual history of their stays in both cities, the coke, the sex, the 'late starts', was their glamorous secret; the further story, of unseen treasures, wasted time and money, the dull dawn of the truth that Wani was rather a philistine, was Nick's secret alone. He said, 'Yes, you loved that stuff, didn't you.'

'You went to Munich, darling . . .' Rachel said to Gerald.

'Oh, yes,' said Gerald, with the fond, embarrassed look he had when recalling his humbler pre-Rachel life. 'Badger and I stopped off at Munich, didn't we, on our famous drive to Greece. Badger would seem, on reflection, to have kept me away from that city's more *rococo* . . . um . . .'

'There's one quite fabulous church,' said Nick.

Toby, who had been quiet since they'd moved on from potholing, said, 'What's the difference between baroque and rococo?'

'Oh,' said Wani, smiling tolerantly at his old friend, 'well, the baroque is more muscular, the rococo is lighter and more decorative. And asymmetrical,' he remembered, making a trailing gesture in the air with his left hand and batting his long lashes so that Nick thought he had absorbed far more from him than his capsule guides to style – it was extraordinary that they couldn't see at once what he was like. 'The rococo is the final deliquescence of the baroque,' he said, as if he really couldn't be plainer.

'Mm, extraordinary stuff,' said Gerald vaguely.

'Yuk,' said Catherine, 'I can't stand that kind of thing, it's all froth.'

'Well, we'd hardly expect you to like it, old girl, if we like it ourselves,' said Gerald.

'It's just make-believe for rich people,' said Catherine. 'It's like naughty lingerie.'

'Right . . .' said Toby, as if slowly getting the picture, but he blushed too.

Wani, not wanting controversy, said, 'It's really just a great subject for the magazine. Think luxury artwork!' And then, 'It was Nick's idea, actually.'

'Ah well, now it all makes sense,' said Toby.

'Oh, I hope it doesn't make that,' said Nick, and they all laughed at his droll murmur and the hint of a paradox.

He lay in the dark, as the smell of the burning mosquito coil spread through the room. The night was very still, the doors didn't quite reach the floor, and he could hear Wani moving about in his room across the landing. He wanted to be with him, as he had been, more or less, for the past ten days, in the thoughtless luxury of top-class hotels; but he felt the relief of being alone as well: the usual relief of a guest who has closed his door, and a deeper thing, the forgotten solitude which measures and verifies the strength of an affair, and which, being temporary, is a kind of pleasure. He heard Wani switch off his lamp, and his own darkness deepened a fraction, without the faint spill of his light under the door. He wondered if they were sharing this sense of ghostly proximity, if Wani was lying with his eyes open, thinking of him, listening for him, masturbating perhaps as Nick half consciously was – not even that, just a boyish solace and reflex of being alone, the blind friendship of the hand . . . Or had he plumped his pillow, tussled his head and shoulder into it with a sigh, drawn up his legs in the defensive position which made Nick want to curl in behind him and shelter him? It would be easy to go to him now, they both had wide beds, but he could hear already the echo of the door latches in the long corridor like triggers to Wani's sense of danger.

When he woke an hour later out of a Venice dream he stared in a sort of panic at the grey square of the window and the unrecognized mass of the chest of drawers. Then it came back to him, like going upstairs, the shocks and connections of the past twenty-four hours. He felt horribly hot, and kicked off the sheet and drank the dimly visible glass of water. In the dream Wani was drowning: he stood on the canal-side, knees bent in a tense crouch, looking back over his shoulder with an un-decided but accusing expression, then fell in with a dead splash.

It had been very hot all the trip, the hottest Nick had ever known; in Venice, for all its dazzlements, they had moved in a heatwave stink of decay; in Munich, in the glaring avenues, the temperature reached a hundred and four. The heat put a strain on them which they didn't acknowledge to each other. They went to the Asamkirche, which had Nick beaming and sighing with delight; Wani strolled about with an air of provi-sional goodwill, as if waiting for an explanation. Nick longed to share the beauty with him, to communicate with him through it, but Wani, out of shyness or pride, was lightly mocking of what Nick said. You could really only tell Wani one useful thing at a time – too much information was an affront to his self-esteem. Nick stayed on in the church, and the loneliness heightened his pleasure and his pride in his own responsiveness. At the Nymphenburg Palace, among surging coachloads, the pleasure was harder won, but he felt he took in these marvels of the rococo by right – they might have been make-believe for rich people when they were built, but now they were more than that, they were celebrations in and of themselves.

On their first afternoon there Nick went into a gay shop called Follow Me – something Wani did at last with a deprecating snigger. Surrounded by harnesses and startlingly juvenile pornography they bought the *Spartacus* gay guide to the world and a siege supply of rubbers, which Wani affected to have nothing to do with: he handled the book lightly, as if assessing its threat, the thick sleek india-paper weight of the thing, some heretical bible. They took a taxi to the English Garden, and had walked only a short distance under the trees when they realized that the people ahead of them were naked. There were families having picnics in their unembarrassable German way, and old men with peeling crowns standing by themselves like forgotten games masters, and then a zone that was mainly young men, sitting and sprawling in an air of casual tension as palpable as the dust and insects in the slanting sunlight. A wonderful cold stream, the Eisbach, chuckled past between steep banks, and Nick stripped off and clambered down into it – when he lifted his feet from the pebbly bottom he was swept along laughing and breathless, waving back to Wani, and then out of sight, racing past the lawns, the naked smiling figures on the bank, boys with guitars, games with rubber balls, in a rush of beautiful cold abandon towards a wood and a distant pagoda . . . until he saw that the boys were jeering and pointing and the people walking dogs were clothed and severely normal, as if they could have no connection with the happy nude species hidden round the bend in the river. So then he toiled back against the current, feet curled and aching on the slippery stones, until he could pull himself out and skulk back along the bank, giving quick furtive tugs to his embarrassingly shrivelled penis.

He woke again and took a long distracted moment to see that this hadn't happened. He'd been lying in the richly coloured recall of the minutes before sleep and the holiday story had slipped and run with its own fast current into an anecdote odder than the afternoon they had lived through, Wani's bright fixated attempt to pick up the boy who roamed through the gardens with a bucket shouting 'Pepsi!' – his astonishment that he couldn't be bought. Nick turned his pillow, and coughed and settled again. He sank through back-lit clouds, pink and grey, the landing at Bordeaux airport that morning. There had been a storm, but it was turning aside, and they saw suddenly how close the ground was, the sunlight passing in a crawling wink across ponds, glasshouses and canals, seams of gold flashing through the vapour in fiery collusion.

(ii)

On Monday morning Wani asked if he could make some phone calls. Rachel said, 'Absolutely!' and Gerald said, 'Please . . . my dear fellow!' with a gesture towards the cupboard-like room where the phone and the expectant new fax machine were.

'It's just these business things I've got to deal with,' Wani sighed, cleverly apologizing for what Gerald liked best about him. He went into the room and rather awkwardly, since everyone was watching him, closed the door. He had told them last night about the property he'd just bought in Clerkenwell, and had asked for Gerald's advice on aspects of the sale and the planned redevelopment: a wall had come down, and they'd suddenly seen how they might get on. When Wani emerged from the phone room he asked him if he could borrow the Range Rover to go into Périgueux, and this time it was vaguer magazine 'business' that he mentioned. Nick knew that frown of pretended vexation, the bold contempt for obstacles on the path to pleasure, and it made him nervous. But Gerald, clearing his throat and as it were waking up to his own kindness and reasonableness, said, 'Well yes . . . why not! – feel free . . .' And then added, 'Anything for business!'

'It's just that I can meet a very good photographer there, and after the fascinating things you were saying about the cathedral . . .'

'Oh, St Front,' said Gerald, warily flattered. 'Yes indeed . . .'

Nick almost said, 'Oh, but you know it's all a nineteenth-century rehash . . .'

'Will you be back for lunch?' said Rachel. Wani promised he would. He didn't suggest taking Nick, and Nick felt both jealous and relieved. They stood at the front door and watched the car disappear from the forecourt. It was the sort of moment when in London they would have begun a bold and funny family inquest into the absent person; but today that didn't feel right.

They went out onto the terrace, and Gerald nodded several times at Nick and said, 'Charming fellow, your friend.'

'He certainly is,' said Nick, seeing that Gerald wanted re-assurance, and noting that Wani was now properly his friend rather than Toby's.

'One doesn't quite know whether to mention the fiancée,' Gerald said.

'Oh, well I did,' said Rachel. 'And it's all right. He told me all about it. Apparently they're getting married next spring.'

'Ah, fine,' said Gerald, while Nick turned away with a pro-testing thump of the heart to look at the view.

The morning post brought several thick packets of papers for Gerald and he took them off to the end room, sighing petu-lantly. It was clear that without Penny he felt he couldn't tackle work, and clear too, presumably, that he couldn't invite Penny here. He had taken over the end room as an office; Nick wasn't sure what he did in it, but he always emerged with a watchful smile, even tiptoeing a little, like someone about to break a piece of news. The Penny question weighed on Nick, and then appeared so remote and unsubstantiated that he might have imagined it. Gerald was being thoroughly affectionate to Rachel, and when they lay side by side in the sun they seemed soaked in their own intimate history, as well as disconcertingly sexy and young. Even so there was something difficult and self-indulgent about Gerald, as if the holiday was both a licence and a penance.

Nick wandered off to explore the hidden corners of the little estate. He found the morning, and the freedom to use it, weighed rather heavily on him now Wani had gone. He went down the crumbling steps from terrace to terrace, like a descent into his own melancholy. The lower levels dropped more steeply, they were hidden from the house and had a neglected air: the parched stony soil showed through the thin grass. Clearly Dédé and his son hardly bothered with these bits – perhaps it was only guests, in their appreciative aimlessness, who ever climbed down here. There was a look of disused agricultural terraces as much as garden; a distant whine of farm machinery, and the scurry of lizards running over dead leaves. On each level there were walnut trees thick with half-hidden green fruit. Nick went through a gap in a hedge and found some old stone sheds, a grassy woodpile, a rusty tractor. He was doing what he always did, poking and memorizing, possessing the place by knowing it better than his hosts. If Rachel had said, 'If only we still had that pogo stick!' Nick could have cried, like a painfully eager child, 'But we do, it's in the old shed with the broken butter churn and the prize rosettes for onions nailed to the beams.' It struck him that a sign of real possession was a sort of negligence, was to have an old woodyard you'd virtually forgotten about.

He fetched his book and went down to the pool. The heat was climbing and a high-up lid of thin cloud had soon expired into the blue. Jasper and Catherine were already in the water, and Jasper looked pleased to be discovered struggling with her, almost fucking her; he winked at Nick as he went into the pool-house to change. The wink seemed to follow him in. There was a bare suggestive atmosphere in the pool-house, which always felt cool and secret after the dazzle of the pool-side, and seemed to carry some coded memory or promise of a meeting. Nick would have had Wani there last night if Gerald hadn't been hanging, even snooping about. There was the first room, with a sink and a fridge and bright plastic pool toys, lilos and rings, an old rowing machine standing on end; and the changing room beyond, with a slatted bench and clothes hooks, and the shower opening straight off it, behind a blue curtain. Only the rather smelly lavatory had a door that could be locked.

Nick came out in his new little Speedos and walked along the pool's edge. The water was the clear bright answer to the morning, a mesmerizing play of light and depth. A few dead leaves were floating on it, and others had sunk and patched the blue concrete bottom. Dragonflies paid darting visits. He crouched and stirred the surface with his hand. On the far side Jasper had lifted Catherine up to sit on the tiled shelf, with the water lapping between her legs, and him hanging on to her, looking as if he'd like to do the same. She made some quick remark about Nick's being there, and then called, 'Hello, darling!' Jasper turned and floated free and gave Nick his sure-fire smile, said nothing, but lazily trod water and kept looking at him. He had a tiny repertoire, a starter kit, of seducer's tricks, and got obvious satisfaction from deploying them, regardless of results. Nick found him embarrassing and resistible, which didn't preclude his figuring in some of his most punitive fantasies: in fact it made them all the more pointed. Jasper kicked across the pool towards him and it looked at first, in the welter of refractions, as if he was naked; then, when he sprang out streaming on to the poolside, he saw that he was wearing a little cut-away flesh-coloured item. 'What do you think of Jaz's thong?' said Catherine, obviously assuming that Nick fancied him.

'Yeah, I don't like to wear it when her mum's about,' said Jasper considerately. He posed for Nick, held in his brown stomach, and flashed him his number-two smile.

'What do you think?' said Catherine, grinning, a bit breathless, in her tone of sexual fixation.

'Hmm,' said Nick, peering at the sleek pouch in which Jaz's crown jewels, as he called them, were boyishly slumped. 'You'd have to say, darling, it leaves disappointingly little to the imagination.' He made a sorry moue and strolled off to the lounger at the far end of the pool, where he had left his book.

He was reading Henry James's memoir of his childhood, *A Small Boy and Others*, and feeling crazily horny, after three days without as much as a peck from Wani. It was a hopeless combination. The book showed James at his most elderly and elusive, and demanded a pure commitment unlikely in a reader who was worrying excitedly about his boyfriend and semi-spying, through dark glasses, on another boy who was showing off in front of him and clearly trying to excite him. From time to time the book tilted and wobbled in his lap, and the weight of the deckle-edged pages pressed on his erection through the sleek black nylon. He noted droll phrases for later use: 'an oblong farinaceous compound' was James's euphemism for a waffle – *compound* was sublime in its clinching vagueness. He wondered just what Wani was up to in Périgueux. He suspected he was picking up some charlie, which seemed a shame and a danger – he wished Wani wasn't so fond of it; then he felt frustratedly, after three days off that as well, how lovely and just right it would be to have a line. It was amazing, it went really to the heart of

Wani's mystique, that he knew how to find the stuff in any European city. In Munich Nick had waited in the taxi outside a bank, gazed tensely for ten minutes at the chamfered rustication of its walls and the massive swirling ironwork of its doors, while Wani was inside 'seeing a friend'. The photographer in Périgueux was probably another such friend. There were childish shrieks from the pool, as Jasper dive-bombed Catherine. Nick was delighted Wani had missed this airing, or drenching, of the thong; he would tease him about it later, over their first line. He longed to have a swim himself, but now the young couple were in a huddle, standing just within their depth, laughing and spluttering as they kissed: the pool was theirs, like a bedroom. They were mad with sex, in love with their own boldness; Nick felt Jasper might try to involve him too if he went in. His role was to be Uncle Nick, adult and sceptical, which seemed to make the baffled Jasper more and more provocative. He thought he could probably have him if he wanted, but he didn't want to give him that satisfaction. A minute later they got out, intently casual, Jasper's stocky hard-on sticking up at an angle, and went into the pool-house and closed the door. Edgar Allan Poe, James said, though a figure in his childhood, had not been 'personally present' – indeed, 'the extremity of personal absence had just overtaken him'. Minute after minute went by, now the hiss of the pool-house shower could be heard, and Nick lay and flicked a fly from his leg, and felt the morning's discontent rise into envy and impatience. 'The extremity of personal absence': at times the Master was so tactful he was almost brutal. He remembered what Rachel had said about Wani's wedding, and the image of him doing to Martine what Jasper was doing to Catherine filled him with a bitter jealousy – well, it was probably nonsense, probably waffle. The words slid and stuck meaninglessly in front of his eyes.

(iii)

Next day Toby was teaching Nick and Wani how to play boules: they were out on the dusty compacted square of the forecourt. Wani had been wet about the game until he turned out to be good at it, and now he was absorbed and unironical, tripping after the ball, yapping and grinning when he bombed the other boules away from the jack-ball, or *cochonnet*. 'Bien tiré!' said Toby, with a sweeter kind of happiness, at retouching an old friendship through a game, and with comic discuncertment, since he usually won games himself. Nick was applauded when he made a fluky good throw, but it was really a tussle between Wani and Toby. Now he'd got the drugs Wani had become more natural and more popular. 'Yup, seems to be settling in,' said Gerald, taking the credit himself, like the manager of a hotel renowned for its beneficial regime. 'I know . . .' said Rachel, who had borne the brunt of Wani's princely charm: 'he seems to be getting in the holiday mood.' A nod went round which admitted the reservations they'd had before, and a mood of solidarity was discovered, just in time, before the arrival of the Tippers and Lady Partridge. Nobody but Gerald wanted to see the Tippers, and Nick paced and stood about in the drive, bored by the game, but already sentimental about their little routines here, and his esoteric success, being deep in France, in a lovely old house, with his two beautiful boys.

Toby had just flung the *cochonnet* across the court when a big white Audi with Sir Maurice Tipper at the wheel swung in through the gate and ran over it. 'Fucking great,' said Toby, and waved and smiled resignedly. In the back were his grandmother and Lady Tipper, who had the passive air of women of all classes, nattering dutifully as they were driven they hardly knew where. Lady Partridge gestured in a general way at the house, as if to say she thought it was the right one. Nick ran over to open her door, and in the momentary release of chilled air the scent of leather and hairspray seemed to carry the story of the whole journey. 'I know,' said Lady Partridge, establishing her feet on the ground before pushing herself up, and looking for attention but not for help. 'I *have* always caught the train.'

'Good flight, Gran?' said Toby, kissing her cheek.

'It was perfectly all right,' said Lady Partridge, with her usual indifference to a kiss. 'It's quite a trek from the airport. Sally's been explaining to me all about operas' – and she gave the three boys a shrewd smile.

Sally Tipper said, 'The first-class seats were just the same as tourist class, you got proper china, that was all. Maurice is going to write to John about it.' She watched her husband, who came and shook hands with Toby, and said, 'Tobias,' in a coldly pitying tone.

'Welcome, welcome!' said Toby, in a weak flourish of good manners, avoiding the eye of the man who might have been his father-in-law, and going to the boot to take care of the bags. Nick got an inattentive hello from each of them, and the feeling, which he'd had in the past, of being an element they could neither accept nor ignore. Catherine came out of the house, as if to inspect some damage.

'Oh, how are you, Cathy?' said Sally Tipper.

'Still mad!' said Catherine.

Then Gerald and Rachel appeared. 'Good, good . . .' said Gerald. 'You found us . . .'

'We thought at first it was sure to be that splendid château up the road,' said Lady Tipper.

'Ah no,' said Gerald, 'we're not at the château any more, we muddle along down here.' There was a complicated double round of kisses, ending up with Sir Maurice facing Gerald and saying, 'Oh no, not even in France . . . !' and laughing thinly.

The Tippers were not natural holidayers. They came beautifully equipped, with four heavy steel-cornered suitcases, and numerous other little bags which had to be handled carefully, but something else, unnoticed by them, was missing. They muttered questions to each other, and gave an impression of covert anxiety or irritation. When they came down on their first afternoon Sir Maurice said a lot of faxes would be coming through for him, and could they be sure there was enough paper in the machine. He was clearly looking forward to the arrival of the faxes above all. Wani sucked up to him and said he was expecting some faxes too, meaning that he would keep an eye on the machine, but Sir Maurice gave him a sharp look and said he hoped they wouldn't impede his own faxes. It was only four thirty but Gerald was marking his guests' arrival with a Pimm's, and Lady Partridge, with her son as her licence, accompanied him in a gin and Dubonnet. The Tippers asked for tea, and sat under the awning, glancing mistrustfully at the view. When Liliane, slow, stoical, and clearly unwell, came out with the tray, Sally Tipper gave her instructions about different pillows she needed. Sir Maurice talked to Gerald about a takeover they were both interested in, though Gerald didn't look quite serious with a fruit-choked tumbler in his fist. Lady Tipper complained to Rachel about the smell of hot dogs in the Royal Festival Hall. Rachel said surely that would all change now they'd got rid of Red Ken, but Lady Tipper shook her head as if deaf to any such comfort. Nick tried naively to interest Maurice Tipper in local beauty spots which he hadn't yet seen himself. 'You're a fine one to talk!' said Sir Maurice – grinning quickly at Gerald and Toby to show he wasn't so easily taken in. He was used to total deference, and mere pleasantness aroused his suspicion. The democracy of house-party life wasn't going to come naturally to him. Nick looked at his smooth clerical face and gold-rimmed glasses in the light of a new idea, that the ownership of immense wealth might not be associated with pleasure – at least as pleasure was sought and unconsciously defined by the rest of them here.

Sally Tipper had a lot of blonde hair in expensive confusion, and a lot of clicking, rattling, sliding jewellery. She shook and nodded her head a good deal. It was virtually a twitch – of annoyance, or of almost more exasperated agreement. She had a smile that came all at once and went all at once, with no humorous gradations. She said before dinner she'd like to have drinks indoors, which, since the whole point and fetish of the manoir for the Feddens was to do everything possible outside, didn't promise well. They sat in the drawing room with all the overhead lights on, like a waiting room. Nick had seen the names 'Sir Maurice and Lady Tipper' in gold letters on the donors' board at Covent Garden, and had seen her there in person, sometimes with Sophie, but never with her husband. He thought they might have a theme for the week, and said quietly that the recent *Tannhäuser* hadn't been very good.

'*Very* good . . . I know . . . *I* thought . . .' said Lady Tipper, and shook her head in wounded defiance of all the carpers and whiners. 'Now, Judy, that you really should see,' she went on loudly. 'You'll know that one, the Pilgrims' Chorus.'

Lady Partridge, fortified by being *en famille* and half-tight, said, 'It's no use asking me, dear. I've never set foot in an opera house, except once, and that was thirty years ago, when . . . my son took me,' and she nodded abstrusely at Gerald.

'What did you see, Judy?' said Nick.

'I think it was *Salome*,' Lady Partridge said after a minute.

'How marvellous!' said Lady Tipper.

'I know, *ghastly*,' said Lady Partridge.

'Oh, Ma!' said Gerald, who was listening in with a distracted smile from a chat about shares with Sir Maurice.

'I applaud your taste, Judy,' said Nick, with the necessary emphasis to get through, and heard what a twit he sounded.

'Mm, I think it was by Stravinsky.'

'No, no,' said Nick, 'it's by the dreaded . . .: Richard Strauss. Oh, by the way, Gerald, I've found the most marvellous quote, by Stravinsky, in fact, about the dreaded.'

'Sorry, Maurice . . .' murmured Gerald.

'Robert Craft asks him, "Do you now admit any of the operas of Richard Strauss?" and Stravinsky says' – and Nick beat it out, conducted it, in the weird overexcitement of the Strauss feud – '"I would like to admit all Strauss operas to whichever purgatory punishes triumphant banality. Their musical substance is cheap and poor; it cannot interest a musician today." '

'What?' snorted Gerald.

'Well, I'd rather have Strauss than Stravinsky myself, any day! I'm afraid to say!' said Lady Tipper. Sir Maurice looked at Nick, in the flush of his arcane triumph, with baffled distaste.

At dinner Gerald was already pretty drunk. He seemed to have had an idea of taking Maurice Tipper with him, and making their first night a rush of high spirits, followed next morning by the rueful bond of a shared hangover. But Sir Maurice drank as suspiciously as he did business, covering his glass with a dwindling flicker of amusement each time Gerald leant over his shoulder with the bottle. Gerald's face leaning into the candlelight had a glow of obstinate merriment. He sat down and summarized for the second time the division of the Périgord into areas called green, white, black, and purple. 'And we're in the white,' said Maurice Tipper drily.

The talk came round, as it often did with the Feddens, to the Prime Minister. Nick saw Catherine clench in annoyance when her grandmother said, 'She's put this country on its feet!' – clearly forgetting, in her fervour, which country she was now in. 'She showed them in the Falklands, didn't she?'

'You mean she's a hideous old battleaxe,' muttered Catherine.

'She's certainly a manxome foe,' said Gerald. Sir Maurice looked blank. 'One wouldn't want to be on the wrong side of her.'

'Indeed,' said Sir Maurice.

Wani somehow got people to look at him, and said, 'People say that, but you know, I've always seen a very different side of her. An immensely kind woman . . .'; he let them see him searching a fund of heart-warming anecdote, but then said discreetly, 'She takes such extraordinary pains to help those she . . . cares about.'

Maurice Tipper expressed both respect and resentment in a dark throat-clearing, and Gerald said,

'Of course you know her as a family friend,' smiling resolutely as he conceded to Wani the thing, so clearly seen, that he hankered for himself.

'Well . . .' said Wani, 'yes . . . !'

'I love her!' exclaimed Sally Tipper, hoping perhaps they would take love to include friendship, as well as surpassing it.

'I know,' said Gerald. 'It's those blue eyes. Don't you just want to swim in them – what?'

Sir Maurice didn't seem ready to go quite that far, and Rachel said, 'Not everyone's as infatuated as my husband,' lightly but meaningly.

Nick looked out over their heads at the vast night landscape, where the lights of farms and roads invisible by day shone in mysterious prominence. He said very little, holding on to the ignored romance of the place and the hour, the soft gusts in the trees, the stars that peeped in the grey above the silhouetted woods. It turned out to be Wani who saved the evening. He clearly admired Maurice Tipper, and tried to amuse him as well as impress him, neither an easy task. He had a significant lavatory break after the main course, and for the next half-hour supplied a sense of purpose and fun that the others had been groping for. Even Catherine was laughing at his far-fetched imitation of Michael Foot, and Lady Partridge, who kept waking from brief sleeps with a cough and a furtive stare, laughed too.

In the morning, before it was too hot, the Tippers went down to the pool, she with a clutch of sunscreens and a huge hat, he with the new Dick Francis in one hand as a decoy for the briefcase in the other. It was the time when Nick liked to do his fifty lengths – at least he invented this tradition to focus his resentment of the newcomers. When he went down a bit later, Lady Partridge, a keen but almost unmoving swimmer, was halfway across the shallow end, apparently unaware that Sally Tipper, beside her in the water, was asking her about her hip replacement: she glanced at her from time to time with mild apprehension. Maurice Tipper had got a table and chair fixed up under an umbrella and sat in tight biscuit-coloured shorts reading and annotating a sheaf of faxes. His lips quivered and pinched with the sarcastic alertness that was his own brand of happiness. Nick, dispossessed, went off to his favourite corner on a lower terrace and read *A Small Boy and Others* in the company of a lizard.

At noon there were calls and voices up above as a party was assembled for lunch. Nick went to see them off. Toby had pulled up the spare seats in the back of the Range Rover and was checking they were safely bolted; he was taking the extra trouble that delays a departure and disguises the relief of the person left behind. 'We don't want you flying through the windscreen,' he said to Lady Tipper.

'I think you'll find this restaurant acceptable,' Gerald burbled facetiously, gesturing Maurice Tipper to the front seat beside him.

'He just can't have anything too rich,' said Sally. 'His wretched ulcers . . .' She twitched while she pulled a long face. 'I'm afraid last night's dinner rather did for him.'

'Oh, they'll look after you, they'll do anything for you,' said Rachel, with unflinching sweetness. Gerald, ruefully baffled by his new guests' failure to notice the beauties of the manoir, was taking them to Chez Claude in Périgueux, normally the last-night treat of the holidays, in the hope of cracking a word of praise out of them.

'See if you agree with us that it merits a third Michelin star,' he said.

'We're not big lunchers,' said Sally Tipper.

Catherine and Jasper came out last, and Wani squashed in with them excitedly in the third row. Toby closed the doors like a guard and off they went, with a soft superior roar, perched and crammed, for what Nick pictured as a little outing in hell – not the starry Chez Claude or the turret-crowned countryside, but the atmosphere they carried with them. Toby put his arm round Nick's shoulder and they went into the silent house – both of them lightly excited and self-conscious.

Toby made them sandwiches for lunch, in a deliberately enthusiastic way, heaping in cold chicken and lettuce and olives and tomato rings which the first bite would send squirting and dropping from the edges. It was a bit of a mess, a mishmash, lots of dressing was sploshed in – it was almost as though he was saying to Nick, who had once had a job in a sandwich shop, 'I'm not a poof, I haven't got style, I can't help it.' They took them down to the poolside and sat under an umbrella to eat them, with the dressing and tomatoes squirting out and the lettuce dropping into their laps.

'Mm, lovely and quiet, isn't it,' said Toby after a bit.

'I know,' said Nick, and grinned. They were both wearing dark glasses, and had to search for each other's gaze.

'Fancy a beer?' said Toby.

'Why not,' said Nick. Toby went into the pool-house, and came back with a couple of Stellas from the fridge. It seemed to signal a desire to talk, but he didn't know how to start. Nick said, 'So when are Maurice and Sally going?' though he knew the answer.

'Funny you should say that,' said Toby. 'I was just thinking the same thing.'

'I can cope with her, somehow.'

Toby looked at him almost reproachfully: 'You're being a hero with her. Of course, she's a great opera queen, isn't she.'

Nick tried to work out, through their two pairs of sunglasses, if this was a joke – but it seemed to have been said in equal innocence of queens and opera.

'He's a total philistine,' he said.

'Oh, he's a bastard,' said Toby, who, unlike his father, hardly ever swore.

Nick did it for him. 'He's a cunt.'

'No, he really is.'

'I mean, why are they here actually?'

'Oh, business, of course . . .' Toby looked uneasy at hearing himself criticize his father: 'You know, I think Dad thought we were going to be one big happy family; but then there was . . . *the Sophie thing*, but – anyway, he's carrying on as if nothing had gone wrong.'

'Business as usual,' said Nick, reluctant to get into *the Sophie thing* all over again. 'I suppose Tipper's very powerful, isn't he?'

'Obviously he's one of the biggest.'

'What is it, exactly?'

'Nick, really . . . ! You've heard of TipperCo, for Heaven's sake, it's a huge conglomerate.'

'No, of course . . .'

'It was a huge asset-stripping story in the 70s, he was very unpopular but he made millions.'

'Right . . .'

'Yeah, you were probably doing Chaucer that week.'

Nick got as always a tiny amorous frisson from being teased by Toby; he coloured and giggled acceptingly. Of course, Toby knew about all this stuff, but you forgot that he did. It was as wonderful in its way that he'd written articles in newspapers as that his father should have something to do with immigration policy, or who went to prison. 'I had a look at a few of his faxes, but they were in some foreign language.'

'Oh, I wonder what that was.'

'You know, numbers and things.'

'Ha! Yeah, I had a look too, actually. There's a lot of property stuff going on now, which I guess is what Dad's interested in.'

'Sam Zeman says Gerald's doing awfully well.'

'Yah, he's plotting something.'

'I suppose he's a plotter . . . ?'

'Oh, yes. Well, you know how bored he gets.'

'That's true, actually . . . '

'I mean, he's bored to death down here.'

'He always says how much he loves it.'

'He loves the idea of it. You know . . . ' This was an interesting idea itself, and came somehow formulated, like the sage things Toby used to say at Oxford, as if he'd got it off a family friend.

'He's probably missing London,' said Nick, just wondering if Toby had an inkling of what he meant.

'I think he misses work,' said Toby.

Nick gave a hesitant laugh, but said nothing else. He stood up, and pulled off his T-shirt.

'Good idea,' said Toby, and did the same, and stood stretching needlessly. There was a little rise, for Nick, in the sexual charge of the afternoon. Toby was still beautiful, even though he was letting himself go. His beauty was held in an eerie balance with its own neglect. He tucked his chin in, the corners of his mouth twitched down as he looked down his body. It was a shame, but it was also oddly comforting, even lightly arousing, how he grew plumper, while Wani, whose smooth sleekness had been part of his charm, seemed to Nick to grow leaner and ever more aquiline. Toby sat back down, looked at Nick, and took a couple of quick swigs from his bottle, shy about what he wanted to say. 'Yeah, you're in pretty good shape these days, Nick,' he said. 'I was noticing.'

Nick pushed his chest out, flattened his stomach. 'Yeah,' he said, and had a quick proud suck on his own bottle.

'You're not seeing anyone at the moment, are you?'

He was touched by these little steps into intimacy, the sense that talking frankly to a friend was a kind of experiment for Toby, a puzzling luxury. It was an echo of the Oxford days, when Nick had invented occasions, engineered conversations, and led Toby into solemn and slightly bewildered talk about his feelings and his family. It was a pity now to have to say, as carelessly as he could, 'No, not really.' He sighed. 'You're right, actually, why haven't I got someone! It's a scandal!' And then, incautiously, 'How about you, by the way? Have you got your sights set on someone new?'

'No,' said Toby, 'not yet.' He smiled grimly at Nick, and said, 'That bloody business with Sophie, you know . . .' He shook his head slowly, invoking the shock of it. 'I mean, what went wrong there, Nick? We were going to get married, and everything.'

'I know . . .' said Nick, 'I know . . .' scenting a chance to tell the truth, which was sometimes a questionable pleasure.

'I mean, to go off with one of my own best mates.'

'I think eventually,' said Nick, conscious of having said this to Toby four or five times already, 'you'll come to see it as a fortunate escape.'

'Bloody Jamie,' said Toby.

'Of course she was a fool,' said Nick, with brotherly recti-
tude and secret tenderness. 'But just imagine, having all your
summer holidays with Maurice and Sally.'

'Of course he blames me for not hanging on to her, Maurice
does. He thought it was a good match.'

'It was a good match, darling, for her: far too fucking good.'

'Mm, thanks, Nick.' Toby pulled on his beer and stared
across the water. Nick's language seemed to set off a train of
thought. He said, 'I suppose it wasn't all that great, you know,
the sexual side of things.' He looked bitter and guilty too to be
saying this.

'Oh . . .'

'You know, she called it "doings".'

'That's not very promising, I agree.'

'She was a bit . . . babyish. I don't think she liked it very
much, actually.'

Nick couldn't help saying, '*Surely* . . . ?'

Toby sighed. 'She used to say I hurt her, and . . . I don't
know.'

There were various possible explanations of this: that
Sophie, child of the chilly Tippers, was frigid herself; or of
course that Toby's knob was too big, or that he didn't know
what to do with it, or that he was just too big and heavy
altogether for a slender young woman. Nick said, 'Well, if the
sex was no good, that's another reason to think you had a
lucky escape.' It struck him that the man who'd been the focus
of his longings for three years or more, and performed un-
tiringly in his fantasies, was perhaps after all not much good at
sex, or not yet, was clumsy from inexperience or the choice of
the wrong partner. He'd been so lucky, himself, to be shown
the way by someone so practised and insatiably keen. And for
a second or two, in the meridional heat, the thrill of that first
London autumn touched him and shivered him.

Toby mulled the thing over, emptied his bottle, and then went to the pool-house to get a couple more.

Later they had a swim, never quite saying if they were racing or not. It pleased Nick to beat Toby in a race, and then made him feel sorry. He felt warmed and saddened by his drug secrets and his sex secrets, like an adulterous parent playing with an unsuspecting child. It struck him as a strange eventuality, when for years the idea of romping almost naked in the water with Toby would have been one of choking romance. He pulled himself up and sat on the half-submerged shelf, with the water slapping round his balls, and looked at the view, and then the other way, at the pool-house, the steps up under the fig tree, and the high end-wall of the manor house, the windows shuttered against the sun. Afternoon randiness, the mood of desertion, opportunity silent and wide – he watched Toby getting out with a magnificent jump and shake of his big unsuspecting backside.

They had another beer together, lying flat in the sun. 'I wonder how they're getting on,' said Toby.

'I'm so glad I'm not there,' said Nick. 'I mean, I'm sure it's a lovely place . . .'

'It's been great just to spend some time with you, old chap,' said Toby, as if they had really used the time. 'How are you getting on with Wani, by the way?'

'OK, actually,' said Nick. 'He's been very generous to me.'

'He told me he relies on you a lot.'

'Oh, did he . . . ? Yes . . . He's quite a particular person.'

'He always has been. But you'll get used to that in time. I know him inside out by now.'

'Yes, you're very old friends, aren't you?'

'God, yes,' said Toby.

Nick smeared on some sunscreen, and Toby did his back for him, rather anxiously, and describing all the time what he was doing. Then Toby lay face down on his lounger, and Nick for the first time ever squatted over him, and squirted the thin cream across his shoulder blades, and set to working it in, briskly but thoroughly. He had the premonitory tingle of a headache from the sun and the beer, he felt parched and heavy-lidded, and he had a highly inconvenient erection. His hands moved sleekly over Toby's upper body, in weird practical mimicry of a thousand fantasies. His heart started beating hard when he dealt with the curve of the lower back, he turned it into a bit of a massage, a bit of a method, as he moved towards the upward rise of his arse and the low loosish waistband of his trunks. And Toby just took it, leaving Nick with a haunting tumultuous sense of how he might have gone on. He finished, jumped away, and lay down quickly and uncomfortably on his front. For a few minutes the two boys said things, widely spaced, calling only for mumbled answers, like a couple in bed.

Nick woke to a strange tearing sound, like an engine that wouldn't start. Sharp vocalized breaths came in rhythm with it. He turned over, looked blearily round, and saw that Toby had brought out the rowing machine from the pool-house. It had a sliding seat and stirrups and a hand-bar that pulled out a coiled and fiercely retracting white cord. Nick lay on his side and watched, with a suspicion that Toby was showing off to him, shooting forwards and backwards with each tug and each letting go. He was very powerful. The sun beat down on his back and sweat trickled from his armpits. His stomach muscles clenched and relaxed, clenched and relaxed. His breaths were keen and humourless, lips funnelled into a rigid kiss. It was surreal to be rowing so hard on dry land, beside a sheet of still blue water. The machine made its noise, like distant sawing or planing, a rhythmic nag and lull. And Nick remembered an evening in Oxford, drifting out through the Meadows to the Isis, and along by the boathouses, the eights all in and stowed, but one or two rowers still about, as if held by the late light, the mood of freedom and discipline by the river. The wide gritty path was streaked and puddled where the dripping boats had been carried across it. He dawdled along, and then saw what he'd hoped to see, Toby out in a single scull, shirtless, glowing, moving with astonishing speed across the welling water.

Nick was reading under the awning when he heard the slam of car doors and then tired, unsocial voices. For thirty seconds he was gripped by his old reflex of possession, resenting the real owners as intruders. The great glass jar was shattered, and the warm afternoon was spilt for ever. Catherine came clattering out, bent forward in a mime of exhaustion and nausea.

'Good lunch?' said Nick.

'Oh! Nick! God . . .' She subsided into a mumble and groped for him, for the table edge.

'Sit down, darling, sit down.'

'The Tippers.' She dragged a chair over the flags and fell onto it. 'You wouldn't believe. They're as ignorant as shit. And as mean as . . . as . . .'

'Shit . . . ?'

'They're as mean as shit! He let Gerald pay for the whole of lunch. It was over £500, I worked it out, you know . . . And not a single word of thanks.'

'I don't think they really wanted to go.'

'Then when we went into Podier afterwards, we went into the church—'

'*Hello*, Sally!' said Nick, getting up and smiling delightedly to annul what she might have heard. 'Have you had fun?'

It seemed to come as an unexpected and even slightly offensive question, and she twitched her hair back several times as she confronted it. Then she said severely, 'I suppose we have. Yes. Yes, we have!'

'Oh good. I believe it's a marvellous restaurant, isn't it. Well, you're back in time for drinks. Toby's just making a jug of Pimm's. We thought we might have it outside this evening.'

'Mm. OK. And what have you done all day?' She looked at him with a touch of criticism. He knew he was giving off the mischievous contentment of someone left behind for an afternoon, sleepy hints that he might have got up to something but in fact had done the more enviable and inexplicable nothing.

'I'm afraid we were very lazy,' he said, as Toby, red from dozing in the sun, came out with the jug. He saw that this was what he wanted her to understand, his deep and idle togetherness with the son of the house.

Gerald and Rachel didn't appear for a while, and so the Tippers sat down with the youngsters for a drink. Toby gave Sir Maurice a glass so thick with fruit and vegetables that he left it untested on the table. Catherine blinked a lot and put her head on one side ponderingly. 'You're really very rich, aren't you, Sir Maurice,' she said after a while.

'Yes, I am,' he said, with a snuffle of frankness.

'How much money have you got?'

His expression was sharp, but not entirely displeased. 'It's hard to say exactly.'

Sally said, 'You can never say exactly, can you – it goes up so fast all the time . . . these days.'

'Well, roughly,' said Catherine.

'If I died tomorrow.'

Sally looked solemn, but interested. 'My dear man . . . !' she murmured.

'Say, a hundred and fifty million.'

'Yep . . .' said Sally, nodding illusionlessly.

Catherine was blank with concealed astonishment. 'A hundred and fifty million pounds.'

'Well, not lire, young lady, I can assure you. Or Bolivian bolivianos, either.'

There was a pause while Catherine allowed them to enjoy her confusion, and Toby said something smooth about the markets, which Sir Maurice merely shrugged at, to show he couldn't be expected to talk about such things at their level.

Catherine poked at a segmental log of cucumber in her drink and said, 'I noticed you gave some money to the appeal at Podier church.'

'Oh, we give to endless churches and appeals,' said Sally.

'How much did you give?'

'I don't recall exactly.'

'Probably quite a lot, knowing Maurice!' Sir Maurice had the super-complacent look of someone being criticized.

'You gave five francs,' said Catherine. 'Which is about fifty new pence. But you could have given' – she raised her glass and swept it across the vista of hills and the far glimpse of river – 'a million francs, without noticing really, and single-handedly saved the Romanesque narthex!'

These were two terms Maurice Tipper had never had to deal with singly, much less together. 'I don't know about not noticing,' he said, rather leniently.

'You simply can't give to everything,' said Sally. 'You know, we've got Covent Garden . . .'

'No, OK,' said Catherine, tactically, as if she'd been quite silly.

'What's all this . . . ?' said Gerald, coming out in shorts and espadrilles, with a towel over his shoulder.

'The young lady was giving me some criticism. Apparently I'm rather mean.'

'Not in so many words,' said Catherine.

'I'm afraid the fact is that some people just are very rich,' said Sally.

Gerald, clearly sick of his guests, and glancing tensely towards the steps to the pool, said, 'My daughter tends to think we should give everything we've worked for away.'

'Not everything, obviously. But it might be nice to help when you can.' She gave them a toothy smile.

'Well, did you put something in the box?' said Sir Maurice.

'I didn't have any money with me,' said Catherine.

Gerald went on, 'My daughter lives her life under the strange delusion that she's a pauper, rather than – well, what she is. I'm afraid she's impossible to argue with because she keeps saying the same thing.'

'It's not that,' said Catherine vaguely and irritably. 'I just don't see why, when you've got, say, forty million you absolutely have to turn it into eighty million.'

'Oh . . . !' said Sir Maurice, as if at an absurdly juvenile mistake.

'It sort of turns itself, actually,' said Toby.

'I mean who needs so much money? It's just like power, isn't it. Why do people want it? I mean, what's the point of having power?'

'The point of having power,' said Gerald, 'is that you can make the world a better place.'

'Quite so,' said Sir Maurice.

'So do you start off wanting to do particular things, or just to have the sensation of power, to know you can do things if you want to?'

'It's the chicken and the egg, isn't it,' said Sally with conviction.

'It's rather a good question,' said Toby, seeing that Maurice was getting fed up.

'If I had power,' said Catherine, 'which god forbid—'

'Amen to that,' murmured Gerald.

'I think I should stop people having a hundred and fifty million pounds.'

'There you are, then,' said Sir Maurice, 'you've answered your own question.' He laughed briefly. 'I must say, I hadn't expected to hear this kind of talk in a place like this.'

Gerald moved off, saying, 'It's art school, I'm afraid, Maurice,' but not looking sure that this routine disparagement would please his guest any more than the lunch at Chez Claude.

(iv)

During dinner that evening the phone rang. Everyone out on the terrace looked ready for a call, and a self-denying smirk spread along the table as they listened to Liliane answering it. Nick was expecting nothing himself, but he saw the Tippers being called home by some opportune disaster. Liliane came out into the edge of the candlelight and said it was for Madame. The conversation at table continued thinly and with a vague humorous concern for the odd phrases of Rachel's that could be made out; then she must have closed the phone-room door. A few minutes later Nick saw her bedroom light go on; her half-eaten grilled trout and untouched side plate of salad took on an air of crisis. When she came back out and said 'Yes, please,' with a gracious smile at Gerald's offer of more wine, she seemed both to encourage and prohibit questions. 'Not bad news, I hope,' said Sally Tipper. 'We always get bad news when we're on holiday.'

Rachel sighed and hesitated, and held Catherine's gaze, which was alert and apprehensive. 'Awfully sad, darling,' she said. 'It's godfather Pat. I'm afraid he died this morning.'

Catherine, with her knife and fork held unthinkingly in the air, forgot to chew as she stared at her mother and tears slipped down her cheeks.

'Oh, I'm so sorry,' said Nick, moved by her instant distress more than by the news itself, and feeling the AIDS question rear up, sudden and undeflectable, and somehow his responsibility, as the only recognized gay man present. Still, there was a communal effort by the rest of the family to veil the matter.

'Awfully sad,' said Gerald, and explained, 'Pat Grayson, you know, the TV actor . . . ? Old, old friend of Rachel's . . .' Nick saw something distancing already in this and remembered how Gerald had called Pat a 'film star' at Hawkeswood three years earlier, when he was successful and well. 'Who was it, darling, on the phone?'

'Oh, it was Terry,' said Rachel, so tactfully and privately she was almost inaudible.

'We see so little TV,' said Sally Tipper. 'We don't have the time! What with Maurice's work, and all our travelling . . . And really I don't think I miss it. What was he in, your friend?'

Toby, clearly moved, said, 'He starred in *Sedley*. He was bloody funny, actually.'

'Oh, sitcoms,' said Sally Tipper, with a twitch.

'Would you say, Nick?' said Gerald. 'Not a sitcom exactly . . .'

'It was sort of a comedy thriller,' said Nick, who wanted them to like Pat before they found out the truth. '*Sedley* was the charming rogue who always got away with it.'

'Mm, quite a lady-killer,' said Gerald.

Wani said, 'I thought he was so charming when I met him . . . at Lionel's house, it must have been . . . frightfully funny!'

'I know . . .' said Rachel distractedly, stroking Catherine's hand across the table, enabling and containing the little episode of grief. She had probably been crying herself in her room, and now drew a certain resolve from having her daughter to look after.

Gerald, with his frowning moping manner of comprehending the feelings of others while being quite untouched and even lightly repelled by them, made little sighs and rumbles from the head of the table. 'Poor old Puss,' he said. 'Uncle Pat was her godfather. Not her real uncle, obviously . . . !'

'Madly left-wing,' said Lady Partridge, but with a chuckle of posthumous indulgence, as though that had been something else rather roguish about him. 'She had two – a true-blue one and a red-hot socialist. Godfathers.'

'Well, he might have been a red-hot socialist when Mum first met him,' said Toby. 'But you should have heard him on the Lady.'

'What . . . ?' said Gerald.

'Loved the Lady!'

'Of course he did,' said Gerald warmly, not wanting to risk the old jokes about Rachel's left-wing pals in front of the Tippers. 'Her god*mother*, of course, is Sharon, um, Flintshire . . . you know, yup, the Duchess.'

'You and Pat were old friends,' said Wani, with his instinct for social connections. 'You were at Oxford together.'

'He was Benedick to my Beatrice,' said Rachel, with a beautiful smile which seemed conscious of the spotlight of sympathy, 'and indeed Hector Hushabye to my Hesione!'

'Mm, jolly good!' said Gerald, outshone and subtly embarrassed.

This was enough to rouse Maurice Tipper, who said, in the airy unsurprisable way of a suspicious person, 'So how did he die?'

Gerald made a sort of panting noise, and Rachel said quietly, 'It was pneumonia, I'm afraid. But he hadn't been well, poor old Pat.'

'Oh,' said Maurice Tipper.

Rachel peered into the distance beneath the glazed earthenware salad bowl. 'He picked up some extraordinary bug in the Far East last year. No one knew what it was. It's thought to be some incredibly rare thing. It's just frightfully bad luck.'

Nick felt a kind of relief that this sinister fiction was being maintained, and looked at ignorant little Jasper, who was nodding at it and not quite meeting his girlfriend's eye. Then he saw him wince in anticipation.

'Mum, for Christ's sake!' said Catherine. 'He had AIDS!' – with a phlegmy catch in her voice, which her anger fought with. 'He was gay . . . he liked anonymous sex . . . he liked . . .'

'Darling, you don't know that . . .' said Rachel. It wasn't clear how much of the story she hoped to throw doubt over.

'Of course he did,' said Catherine, whose view of gay sex was both tragic and cartoonlike. She grinned incredulously down the table. Nick felt himself included in her scorn.

'Anyway . . . !' said Gerald, with a smile and a deep breath, as if the nasty moment had passed, lifting and tilting the bottle enquiringly towards his mother.

'Oh, it's pathetic!' shouted Catherine, with the rush and stare of someone hurtled along by a strong new mix of emotions. 'I mean surely the least we can do is tell the truth about him?' – and she smacked the table hard, but still somehow childishly and comically; there were one or two nervous smiles. She jumped her chair back over the flags and hurried indoors.

'Um . . . should I . . . ?' said Jasper, and sniggered.

'No, no, I'll go,' said Rachel. 'In a minute or two.'

'Experience suggests to wait a bit,' said Gerald, as if explaining some other local custom to his guests.

'An emotional young lady,' said Maurice Tipper with a grin of displeasure.

'She's a very emotional young lady,' said Jasper, in a cowardly mixture of boasting and mockery.

'She's quite unbalanced,' Lady Partridge agreed confidentially.

Gerald hesitated, peering over his raised wine glass, but

took his daughter's part. 'I think I'd say she's just very soft-hearted,' he said; which it seemed to Nick was just what she wasn't.

Rachel said, with a hint of frost, 'Does Sophie ever get upset?'

Sir Maurice seemed to think the question impertinent. His wife said, 'If she does, she doesn't let it show. Unless she's on stage, of course. Then she's all passion.' Nick thought of her performance in *Lady Windermere's Fan*, where all she had had to say was 'Yes, mamma.'

After dinner the four boys were in the drawing room, though Jasper fidgeted and soon went upstairs to skulk around Catherine's door. Wani was reading Sir Maurice's *Financial Times*, and Toby was sitting in the puzzlement of bereavement, tilting a glass of cognac from side to side, and trying occasional rephrasings of the same idea to Nick: 'God it's awful, poor old Pat, I can't believe it.'

Nick lowered the book he had just started, smiled to suggest the book itself was a bore. 'I know,' he said. 'Isn't it awful. I'm so sorry.' He thought of the two of them down by the pool after lunch, and the lustful tenderness he felt for Toby seemed to glow and fill the room. He was excited by Toby's grief, and the boyish need he seemed to feel for Nick's comfort, and for something wise Nick might say. Nick himself was impressed by Pat's death, and had a distantly acknowledged feeling of guilt, that he'd done nothing for Pat – though Pat, in another sense, had done nothing for him; Nick hadn't liked his brand of cagey camp, and had been snotty and even priggish with him: so that, more shamefully still, he felt subtly disembarrassed by the death, since it erased the memory of his own bad grace. 'I wonder how Terry's coping,' he said, to focus Toby's thoughts.

'Yah, poor guy. God it's awful, this bloody plague.'

'I know.'

'You'd bloody well better not get the fucking thing,' said Toby.

'I'll be all right,' said Nick. 'I've been taking very good care since – well, since we knew about it.' He glanced across at Wani, who was screened above the knees by the raised pink broadsheet with its headlines about record share prices, record house prices. From time to time he smacked the page flat. 'You don't have to worry about me,' Nick said.

Toby looked a bit shame-faced. 'I didn't know Pat, you know, slept around.'

'Well . . .' said Nick. He knew very well, because Catherine was indiscreet, that Pat had liked very rough sex. 'Don't believe everything Catherine says. She lives in a world of her own hyperbole.'

'Yah, but she was pretty close to Pat, Nick – he took her out to dinner quite often. She stayed at Haslemere three or four times. If she says he liked anonymous sex—'

Nick saw that the Tippers had come in. They'd been up to their room and now they'd come down, tight-lipped and close together, as though they felt obliged to put in another half-hour. Maurice had clearly been very displeased by the scene at dinner, and a suspicion of deviancy seemed to hang for him now over the whole party. The boys all stood up, and Nick set his book, face down, on the arm of his chair. Sally Tipper peered at it, to deflect her discomfort on to a neutral object, and said, 'Ah, that's Maurice's book, I see.'

'Um . . . *oh*,' said Nick, sure of himself but confused as to her reasoning; it was a study of the poetry of John Berryman. 'I don't think . . .'

'Do you see that, darling?'

Maurice brought his gleaming lenses to bear on it. 'What? Oh yes,' he said. He went towards Wani, who was quickly refolding the *FT*.

'You're very welcome to read it,' Nick said, with a frank

little laugh, 'but it's actually mine – it was sent on to me this morning. I'm reviewing it for the *THES*.'

'Oh I see, no, no,' said Sally, with a coldly tactful smile. 'No, Maurice *owns* Pegasus – I just noticed they publish it.'

'I didn't know that.'

'I've bought it,' said Sir Maurice. 'I've bought the whole group. It's in the paper.' And he sat down and glared at the vase of thistles and dried honesty in the grate.

'I'm just going up to see if my sis is OK,' said Toby, as though all this had decided him.

Nick didn't feel he could go out after him. He sat down again, opposite Sally, but not quite in relation with her, like guests in a hotel lounge. He said, 'I'm afraid this news has rather spoilt the evening.'

'Yes,' said Sally, 'it's most unfortunate.'

'Awful losing an old friend,' said Nick.

'Mm,' said Sally, with a twitch, as if to say her meaning had been twisted. 'So you knew him too, did you, the man?'

'Pat – yes, a bit,' said Nick. 'He was a great charmer.' He smiled and the word seemed to linger and insist, like a piece of code.

Sally said, 'As I say, we never saw him.' She took up a copy of *Country Life*, and sat staring at the estate agents' advertisements. Her expression was tough, as if she was arguing the prices down; but also self-conscious, so that it seemed just possible she wanted to talk about what had happened. She looked up, and said with a great twitch, 'I mean, they must have seen it coming.'

'Oh . . .' said Nick, 'I see. I don't know. Perhaps. One always hopes that it won't be the case. And even if you know it's going to happen, it doesn't make it any less awful when it does.' It had become unclear to him whether she knew that he was gay; he'd always assumed it was the cause for her coldness, her way of not paying attention to him, but now he'd started

to suspect she was blind to it. He felt the large subject mass-
ing, with its logic and momentum. There would be the social
strain of coming out to such people in such a place, and the
wider matter of AIDS concerning them all, more or less. He
said, 'I think I heard you say your mother had a long final
illness.'

'That was utterly different,' Sir Maurice put in curtly.

'It was a blessed relief,' said Sally, 'when she finally went.'

'She hadn't brought it on herself,' said Sir Maurice.

'No, that's true,' Sally sighed. 'I mean, they're going to have
to learn, aren't they, the . . . homosexuals.'

'It's a hard way to have to learn,' said Nick, 'but yes, we are
learning to be safe.'

Sally Tipper stared at him. 'Right . . .' she said.

Sir Maurice seemed not to notice this, but in her there was
a little spectacle of ingestion. Nick tried to put it in her language, but couldn't think what the term would be. 'You know,
there are very simple things that need to be done. For instance,
people have got to use protection . . . you know, when
they're . . . when they're humping.'

'I see,' said Sally, with another shake of the head. He wasn't
sure she followed. Were such cheerful genteelisms any use? She
had an air of being ready to take things on, and simultaneously
an air of puzzled and frightened offence. 'That's what he'd
been doing, had he, I suppose, your friend the actor?
Humping?'

'Almost undoubtedly,' said Nick. Sir Maurice made a rough,
dyspeptic sound, as if chewing a mint. 'But as we all know,'
Nick went on flatteringly, and with a sort of weary zeal now
the moment had come, 'there are other things one can
do. I mean there's oral sex, which may be dangerous, but is
certainly less so.'

Sally received this stoically. 'Kissing, you mean.'

Sir Maurice looked at him sharply and said, 'I'm afraid what you're saying fills me with a physical revulsion,' and seemed to be laughing in his distaste. 'I just don't see why anyone's remotely surprised. The whole thing had got completely out of hand. They had it coming to them.'

Sally, enlightened for a minute by her unusual talk with Nick, said wildly, 'Oh, Maurice is medieval on this one, he's like Queen Victoria!' It was a little shot at freedom, her silliness of tone almost invited correction.

'I'm not ashamed of what I think,' said Sir Maurice.

'Of course you're not, darling,' said Sally.

'No, well nor am I, as a matter of fact,' said Nick.

'What do you think, Wani,' said Sally, 'as a younger person, you know, on the other side of the picture?'

Wani had been watching Nick with mischievous patience. 'I suppose Nick must be right, you know . . . everyone's going to have to be more careful. There's really no excuse for getting the thing now.' He smiled wisely. 'I think it's so sad with little children having it – babies born with it, even.'

'That is awfully sad,' said Sally.

'I'm probably just old-fashioned on these things, but actually I was brought up to believe in no sex before marriage.'

'My own view entirely,' said Sir Maurice, as fiercely as if he was contradicting him.

Nick, tingling with ironies and astonishment, said merely, 'But if we're never going to get married . . .'

'Sort of sex-mad, isn't it, the world we live in,' said Sally, as if that was their general conclusion.

'I know . . .' said Wani.

(v)

Next morning there was a brief bit of shouting between Gerald and Catherine, down by the pool. Nick couldn't quite hear what it was about. He was surprised by it, so soon after Pat's death, when Gerald might have bothered to tread carefully; but it seemed also to make a kind of sense, as an awkward after-shock of that event. Nothing more was said about it in the day.

When Nick went upstairs in the afternoon Catherine came too, a little behind him, so that it wasn't clear if she was follow-ing him; he glanced back in the long passageway and saw her plotting expression. He left his door open, and a few moments later she came wandering in. 'Hello, darling,' said Nick.

'Mm, hello again, darling,' said Catherine, looking quickly at him, and then peering mysteriously around the room.

'Are you OK?'

'Oh, yes . . . fine. I'm fine.'

Nick smiled tenderly, but she seemed almost irritated by the question, and he thought perhaps she'd got over Pat, with her odd emotional economy, of feelings fiercely inhabited and then discarded. She was wearing tight white shorts and a grey tank top of Jasper's, in which her small breasts moved alertly. No one had come to his room before, and it felt intimate, and pleasantly tense, like a first date. She sat on the bed and tested the springs.

'Poor old Nick, you always get the worst room.'

'I love my room,' said Nick, gazing to left and right.

'This used to be my room. It's where they put the children. God, I remember those creepy pictures.'

'They are a bit spooky, aren't they.' They were the little German paintings on glass: *Autumn*, where a woman with an aigrette filled a girl's apron with easily reached fruit, and *Winter*, where men in red coats shot and skated and a bird sang on a bare branch. It was hard to put your finger on it, but they had a sort of sinister geniality.

'Still, you're nice and near your friend.'

'I can hear old Ouradi snoring, yes,' said Nick, rather heartily, and sat down at the table.

'Actually I don't mind old Ouradi,' said Catherine.

'He's all right, isn't he.'

'I always thought he was just a spoilt little ponce, but there's a wee bit more to him than that. He can even be quite funny.'

'I know . . .' said Nick, who thought of himself as much funnier than Wani.

'I mean he's bloody moody. Sometimes he's just not there, he's like a shop dummy going *charming . . . duchess . . .* et cetera; and sometimes he's the life and soul.'

'I know what you mean,' said Nick, with a wary laugh at her mimicry. 'You get used to that.'

Catherine leaned back on her arms and swung her legs. 'I'm quite glad I'm not his fiancée, I must say.'

'I think she's probably used to that too.'

'She's certainly had time to get used to it . . .'

Nick looked down, realigned the books on his table, his notebooks, Henry James's memoirs covering the *Spartacus* gay guide to the world. He assumed Catherine had come here with a purpose. She glanced round, and then got up and closed the door, in the abstracted way of someone already working on the next thing.

'I must say I'm beginning to wonder about old Wani,' she said.

'How do you mean . . . ?'

'He's rather brilliant, actually.'

'Oh . . . ?'

'He's completely pulled the wool over your blue eyes.'

Nick smiled dimly, with anxiety and a vague sense of a compliment. 'Quite probably,' he said.

Catherine sat down and said, 'My little Jaz has got a theory.'

'Oh, yes?' said Nick. 'I wouldn't automatically credit a theory of little Jaz's.'

Catherine carried on as if she didn't mind him sounding like her father. 'Perhaps not, but . . . Jasper's very observant, you know, well, you probably don't believe me . . . anyway, he thinks he's a fag.'

'Oh!' Nick tutted disappointedly. 'Yeah, people are always saying that. It's just because he baths so often and wears see-through trousers.' The odd thing, Nick thought, was that people said it so rarely.

'Jasper says he follows him round all the time trying to get a look at his knob.'

'Mm . . . It sounds to me a bit like vanity, darling. Jasper's always following me round trying to *show* me his knob.' Perhaps this was too frank. 'You must admit, he can be a bit of a flirt.' Nick was surprised by his own presence of mind, but still he sniggered, and crossed his legs in complex discomfort.

'Wani hasn't said anything at all, then? About Jaz? I suppose he would be extra careful to keep it from you, wouldn't he – in case you got the wrong idea! Wouldn't do at all!' said Catherine, perhaps not convinced by her own theory.

Nick was blushing, but he looked at her levelly. 'I don't know, darling,' he said, and bit his lower lip. 'Aren't they alone together down at the pool right now? Who knows what might be happening?'

'At least he's not wearing his thong today,' said Catherine.

'No, quite . . .' Nick pushed on defensively with his rough joke. 'Though once they get into the pool-house together . . .'

Catherine gave him a bothered stare, and coloured a little herself. She knew of course that Nick knew that Jasper fucked her in the pool-house, it was a silent brag; but of course she didn't know that Nick had fucked Wani there last night, after the awful dinner, in a storm of pent-up anger. She said, 'Oh, god, don't mention the pool-house.'

'What . . . ?'

'Gerald was on to me about it this morning, and behaving broadly like an ape, I must say.'

343

'Oh, darling . . . I saw something was going on': and the image of Gerald standing by the pool, head down, shoulders rounded in accusing disappointment, was somehow ape-like, it was true.

'Apparently her ladyship found a rubber johnny floating in the lav. She was frightfully upset, as you can imagine. It quite ruined her early-morning bathe.'

'Hoorah!' said Nick, and grinned at her, while his mind raced round a series of right-angled bends.

'I thought he'd flushed it, but Gerald came snooping round, and we only escaped by a *hare's breath*.'

'I'm surprised she knew what it was.'

'It's too pathetic,' said Catherine, who of course had missed last night's sex-education class. 'We're all adults, for god's sake.'

'I know . . .'

'You can't do it in the house, because the noise carries.'

'That *can* be a problem.'

'Actually, god, fuck, that's really weird . . . !' Catherine stared at him in excited self-doubt, whilst Nick felt his disguise grow eerily thinner. He smiled, not knowing if he'd been recognized, or if, by sitting still, he could avoid detection. 'Because I'm sure we didn't use one yesterday.'

'You must always use a rubber,' said Nick. 'There's no point in sometimes using one and sometimes not. You don't know where he's been.'

'Oh, Nick, he's a total innocent. He's never been with anyone else.'

'No, well . . .'

Catherine gaped. 'So if it wasn't us.'

'It might have been there from the day before, I suppose,' said Nick, with doomed insouciance, watching Catherine as she went on an Agatha Christie-like tour of the possible and frankly impossible suspects. He thought that perhaps like Poirot she had known the answer before she came into the room; but when she stood up, walked to the window, and turned he saw the shock, the disgust even, of discovery in her face.

'God, I've been stupid,' she said.

Nick looked at her, and she looked at him. He felt the painful stupidity of detection himself, and also a kind of pride, lurking still, waiting for permission to smile. She couldn't deny the scale and class of the deception. He thought he saw her quick recovery, her feel for anything salacious. He said, 'Perhaps he is rather brilliant, yes.'

Catherine came and sat down again, as dignified as she could be. 'I don't think he's brilliant any more,' she said.

Nick said carefully, 'You mean he was brilliant when you thought he was tricking me, but not when it turns out he's tricking you.' He felt, without time to work it out, that there could be a brilliance of concealment, over something simple and even sordid; and there could be a simple, dumb concealment of something glitteringly unexpected. Caught up in it, inured to it, he didn't know which was more nearly the case with himself and Wani. 'Of course, it's all for him,' he said.

'I mean how can he bear it?'

'The secrecy, you mean? Or me?'

'Ha, ha.'

'Well, the secrecy . . .' Often in life Nick felt he hadn't mastered the arguments, and could hardly present his own case, let alone someone else's; but on this particular matter he was watertight, if only from the regular need to convince himself. He checked off the points on his fingers: 'He's a millionaire, he's Lebanese, he's the only child, he's engaged to be married, his father's a psychopath.'

'I mean how did it start?' said Catherine, finding these points either too obvious or too involved to take up. 'How long's it been going on? I mean – god, really, Nick!'

'Ooh, about six months.'

'Six months!' – and again Nick couldn't tell if this was too long or not long enough. She stared at him. 'I'm going to write that poor long-suffering French girl a letter!'

'You're to do nothing of the kind. A year from now that poor French girl will be blissfully married.'

'To a Lebanese poofter with a psychopath for a father . . .'

'No, darling, to a very beautiful and very rich young man, who will make her very happy and give her lots of beautiful rich children.' It was a tiringly ample prospect.

'And what about you?'

'Oh, I'll be all right.'

'You're not going to carry on bumshoving him when he's married to the poor little French girl, I hope?'

'Of course not,' said Nick, with a glassy smile at the one thing he didn't want to think about. 'No – I shall move on!'

Catherine shook her head at him, she had the moral she wanted: 'God, men!' she said. Nick laughed uneasily, as an object of both sympathy and attack.

'But really, swear not to say a word to anybody.'

She weighed this up, teasingly, and teasing meant more to her than to Nick. She was on the side of dissidence and sex, but she was still huffy with her discovery, with having been tricked and not trusted. In the pause that followed they heard the faint scratch of footsteps on the stairs and then the clip of hard-soled slippers, which Nick knew at once, along the tiled hallway. He bit his lip, winced, and curled his head forward as if he was praying, to enjoin silence. Wani was coming up to his room, to change probably, which he did more often than anyone else, as if strictly observing an etiquette the others had let slide. And for another reason too, so that his reappearance in pressed white linen trousers or bright silk shirt was a cover and almost an explanation for his new liveliness; as if he sprang back to noiseless applause. He went into his room, and they could see him hesitate, the shadow on the gleam of the tiles under Nick's door, which wasn't normally closed. Then he closed his own door, and seconds later the catch jumped and settled. The door catches here had a life of their own, and kicked and rattled with stored energy, in accusing jumps.

As they sat there, compromised, staring attentively, but not at each other, waiting for Wani to be done, Nick pictured him having a line, his air of cleverness and superiority, and almost hoped that they would hear him, and that that secret would come out too. To hear it, like a lovers' rendezvous, a rhythm, a ritual: evidence of the other great affair in Wani's life. But he was probably in his bathroom. A light aircraft droned and throbbed in the heights, a summer sound, that came and went on the mind.

When he'd gone downstairs again, Catherine said, 'Of course switchers are a nightmare. Everyone knows that.'

'I don't suppose everyone knows it,' said Nick.

'God, you remember Roger?'

'He was Drip-Dry, wasn't he?' Nick felt annoyed, slighted, but undeniably relieved that Catherine had decided to show him up with talk about her own boyfriends. 'Always something just a *little* bit funny about the sex – as if he wished you had a hairy chest . . . you know. And the feeling that you never had his absolutely undivided attention.'

'I'm not sure one wants that, does one,' said Nick, not quite meaning it, but seeing as he said it that it could be a helpful kind of wisdom, if you shared your lover with a woman as well as a drug.

'They say they love you, but there's more reason than usual to disbelieve them.' In fact Wani had never said that, and Nick had stopped saying it, because of the discomforting silence that followed when he did. 'I'm surprised, actually, I wouldn't have thought he was your type.'

'Oh!' said Nick, and gasped at the thought of him.

347

'I mean, he's not black, really, he's been to university.'

Nick smiled disparagingly at this sketch of his tastes. He felt embarrassed – not at sex talk, which was always an enjoyable surrender, a game of risked and relished blushes, but at the exposure of something more private than sex and weirdly chivalrous. He said, 'I just think he's the most beautiful man I've ever met.'

'*Darling*,' said Catherine, in a protesting murmur, as if he'd said something very childish and untenable. 'You can't really?' Nick looked at his desk and flinched irritably. 'I can sort of see what you mean,' Catherine said. 'He's like a parody of a good-looking person, isn't he.' She smiled. 'Give me your pen': and on the top of Nick's notepad she made a quick drawing, a few curves, cheekbones, lips, lashes, heavily inked squiggles of hair. 'There! No, I must sign it' – and she scrawled 'Wonnie by Cath' underneath. Nick saw how accurate it was, and said, 'He doesn't look like that at all.'

'Hmm?' said Catherine teasingly, feeling she'd made a point but not knowing where it had got her.

'All I can say is, when he comes into the room – like when he got back late for lunch the other day, when we'd been gossiping about him, and I was playing along with you, sort of agreeing, actually – when he came in, I just thought, yes, I'm in the right place, this is enough.'

Catherine said, 'I think that's awfully dangerous, Nick. Actually I think it's mad.'

'Well, you're an artist,' said Nick, 'surely?' Whenever he'd imagined telling someone this, the story, the idea, had met with a thrilled concurrence and a sense of revelation. He had never expected to be contested on every point of his own beliefs. He said, 'Well, I'm sorry, that's how I am, you should know that by now.'

'You'd fall in love with someone just because they were beautiful, as you call it.'

'Not anyone, obviously. That *would* be mad.' He resented her way, now she'd gained access to his fantasy, of belittling the view. It was like her attitude to the room they were sitting in. 'It's not something we can argue about, it's a fact of life.'

Catherine cast her mind back helpfully. 'I mean, no one could have called Denton beautiful, could they?'

'Denny had a beautiful bottom,' Nick said primly. 'That was what mattered at the time. I wasn't in love with him.'

'And what about little thing? Leo? He wasn't beautiful exactly, I wouldn't have thought. You were crazy about him.' She looked at him interestedly to see if she'd gone too far.

Nick said solemnly but feebly, 'Well, he was beautiful to me.'

'Exactly!' said Catherine. 'People are lovely because we love them, not the other way round.'

'Hmm.'

'Did you hear anything more from him, by the way?'

'No, not since spring of last year,' said Nick, and got up to go to the lavatory.

The bathroom window looked out across the forecourt and the lane at the other, unmentioned view, northwards: over rising pastures towards a white horizon – and beyond that, in the mind's distance, northern France, the Channel, England, London, lying in the same sunlight, the gate opening from the garden to the gravel walk, and the plane trees, and the groundsmen's compound with the barrow and the compost heap. It came to Nick in a flash of acute nostalgia, as though he could never visit that scene of happiness again. He waited a minute longer, in the heightened singleness of someone who has slipped out for a minute from a class, a meeting, ears still ringing, face still solemn, into another world of quiet corridors, the neutral gleam of the day. He couldn't unwind the line of beauty for Catherine, because it explained almost everything, and to her it would seem a trivial delusion, it would seem mad, as she said. He wouldn't be here in this room, in this country, if he hadn't seen Toby that morning in the college lodge, if Toby hadn't burnt in five seconds onto the eager blank of his mind. How he chased Toby, the covert pursuit, the unguessed courage, the laughable timidity (it seemed to him now), the inch or two gained by pressure on Toby's unsuspecting good nature, the sudden furlongs of dreamlike advance when Toby asked him up to town – he could never tell her that. Her own view was that Toby was a 'vacuous lump'.

When he went back into the room she had found the *Spartacus* guide, and was looking at it, and then over it at him, with a mocking gape, as if this was the silliest thing of all. 'It's too hysterical,' she said.

'Marvellous, isn't it,' said Nick, slightly prickly, but glad of the distraction.

'Hang on . . . Paris . . . I'm just looking up Paraquat. I don't *believe* this book.' She studied the page, in her illiterate excitable way.

'I shouldn't think there's much there,' said Nick, who had already looked it up and imagined with mingled longing and satire the one disco and the designated park.

'Well, there's a disco, darling. Wed to Sat, 11 to 3. L'An des Roys,' she said, in her plonking French accent. 'We must go! How *hilarious*.'

'I'm glad you find it so amusing.'

'We'll suggest it to Ouradi, and see what he says . . . God, there's everything in here.'

'Yes, it's very useful,' said Nick.

'Cruising areas, my god! Look at this, rue St Front – we went there with the Tippers yesterday. If only they'd known . . . What does AYOR mean?'

'AYOR? At Your Own Risk.'

'Oh . . . right . . . *Right* . . . And it's the whole world!'

'Look up Afghanistan,' said Nick, because there was a famous warning about the roughness of Afghan sex. But she carried on flicking through. Nick disguised his interest, the vague comical rakishness he seemed to admit by having the book, and went and sat on the bed.

'I'm just looking up Lebanon,' she said, after a minute.

'Oh yes . . .' said Nick.

'It sounds marvellous. Mediterranean climate, well we knew that, and it says homosexuality is a delight.'

'Really,' said Nick.

'It does. "L'homosexualité est un délit",' she read, sounding like General de Gaulle.

'Yes, *délit* is a crime, unfortunately.'

'Oh, is it?'

'Delight is *délice*, *délit* is a misdemeanour.'

'Well, it's bloody close . . .'

'Well, they often are,' said Nick, and felt rather pleased with himself.

Catherine was bored with the book. She held Nick's eye, and said, 'So what's he into, old Ouradi?'

'He's into me.'

'Well, yes,' said Catherine, as if she could see round this.

'OK, he likes to get fucked,' said Nick briskly, and got up as if that was really all she was going to get out of him.

'I always thought he must be into some pretty weird sort of gay stuff.'

'You didn't even know he was gay till ten minutes ago.'

'I knew deep down.'

Nick smiled reproachfully. Telling the story for the first time he saw its news value, already wearing off on Catherine, the quick fade of a shock, and felt the old requirement not to disappoint her. It was their original game of talking about men, boasting and mocking, and he knew its compulsion, the quickened pulse of rivalry and the risk of trust. There were phrases about Wani that he'd carried and polished for some occasion like this and he imagined saying them now, and the effect on himself as much as on her, mere reluctant admission melting into the relief of confession. There was nothing, exactly, to confess. The secrecy of the past six months was not to be mistaken for the squeeze of guilt. He thought, I won't tell her about the hotel porn. He sat down again, to mark a wary transition to frankness. 'Well, he's quite into threesomes,' he said.

'Mm, not my cup of tea,' said Catherine.

'OK, we won't ask you.'

She gave a tart smile. 'So who do you have threesomes with?'

'Oh, just with strangers. He gets me to pick people up for him. Or we get a rent boy in, you know. A *Stricher*.'

'A what?'

'That's what they call them in Munich.'

'I see,' said Catherine. 'Isn't that a bit risky, if he's so into secrecy?'

'Oh, I think the risk's quite the thing,' said Nick. 'He likes the danger. And he likes to submit. I don't quite understand it myself, but he likes having a witness. He likes everything that's the opposite of what he seems.'

'It all sounds rather pathetic, somehow,' said Catherine.

Nick went on, not knowing if it was evidence for the defence or the prosecution, 'He's quite a screamer, actually.'

'A screaming queen, you mean?'

'I mean he makes a lot of noise.' It would probably be better not to tell her about that morning in Munich. 'It was hilarious one morning in Munich,' he said. 'He made so much noise in the room, I don't think he noticed, but the chambermaids were all laughing about us in the corridor outside.'

Catherine snuffled. 'Russell always liked me to shout a lot,' she said.

Again Nick allowed the allusion; he smiled thinly through it, and thought and said with a wince, 'He's got this rather awful thing for porn, actually.'

'Oh . . . ?'

'I mean, nothing wrong with porn, but you sometimes feel it's the real deep template for his life.'

Catherine raised her eyebrows and gave a deep sigh. 'Oh dear . . .' she said.

Nick looked away, at the open window, and the closed door. 'It just got a bit out of hand, actually, in Germany. You know, there's endless porn on the hotel TV.'

'Oh . . .' said Catherine, to whom porn was a blankly masculine mystery.

'He lay there all evening watching it – straight stuff, of course, which he likes just as much, if not more. One night, I'm afraid, I had to go off to dinner by myself. He just wouldn't turn it off.'

Catherine laughed, and so did Nick, though the image was a sad one, was pathetic, as she said: of Wani with his pants round his ankles, too crammed with coke to get an erection, in slavish subjection to the orgy on screen, whilst Nick, in the sitting room of their stuffy little suite, made a bed for himself on the sofa. He could hear Wani, through the door, talking to the people in the film. Catherine said, 'He sounds a *nightmare*, actually, darling.'

'He's very exciting too, but . . .'

'I mean, I rather worry about you, if you're loving him so much as you say, and he's treating you like this. Actually, I wonder if you do really love him, you see.'

He saw this was her usual hyperbole, and her usual solicitous undermining of his affairs. 'No, no,' he said, with a disparaging chuckle. It wasn't that she'd shown him the truth of the matter, but that telling her these few amusing details he'd told himself something he couldn't now retract. He had a witness too. 'Anyway,' he said, 'I probably shouldn't have told you all this.'

(vi)

The Tippers left the following day. Secret smiles of relief admitted also a dim sense of guilt, and a resultant hardening and defiance. Gerald was gloomily preoccupied, and seemed to carry the blame round with him, not knowing where to put it down. Wani was the only one who expressed real regret and surprise; he'd felt at home with the Tippers, they were the sort of people he'd been brought up to respect. It was Rachel who tried hardest to be diplomatic; her supple good manners struggled to contain the awkward turn of events, which she minded entirely for Gerald's sake.

The departure was handled very briskly. Sir Maurice was offended, active, in a surprising way fulfilled – this was what he looked for, a clarified antipathy, a somehow reassuring trustlessness. 'We're not enjoying it much here,' he said; and his wife took her usual strange pleasure in his hardness and roughness; they were her animating cause, his feelings were as unanswerable as his ulcers . . . Toby loaded up the luggage, with the straight-faced satisfaction of a porter.

After they'd gone, Wani, watchful and charming, suggested a game of boules to Gerald, and they went out and started playing in the bald space where the Tippers' car had stood. The day for once was overcast, and Nick sat in the drawing room with his book. The tingle of freedom made it a little hard to concentrate: he felt aware of the pleasure, the primacy of reading, but the content seemed to glint from a distance, as if through mist. Then Lady Partridge tottered in in her sun-

dress, clearly pleased, repossessing the place, but also at a loose
end without the irritant of Sally at her ear. The Tippers had
been a subject for her, they'd annoyed her and they'd excited
her with the raw fascination of money. She sat down in an
armchair. She didn't say anything, but Nick knew that she was
jealous of his book. From outside, through the open front
door, came the cracks and clicks and yelps of the boules game.

'Mm, what are you reading?' said Lady Partridge.

'Oh . . .' said Nick, disowning the book with a shake of the
head, 'it's just something I'm reviewing.' She turned her ear
enquiringly. 'It's a study of John Berryman.'

'Ah . . . !' said Lady Partridge, sitting back with the mocking contentment of the non-reader. 'The poet . . . Funny
man.'

'Oh – um . . . !' Nick gasped. 'Yes, he was rather funny, I
suppose . . . in a way.'

'I always thought.'

Nick smiled at her narrowly, and went on, to test the
ground, 'It's a sad life, of course. He suffered from these
terrible depressions.'

Lady Partridge smacked her lips illusionlessly, and rolled her
eyes back – a more terrible effect than she realized. 'Like . . .
er, young madam,' she said.

'Well, quite,' said Nick, 'though we hope it won't end the
same way! He drank a tremendous lot, you know.'

'I wouldn't be at all surprised if he drank a lot,' said Lady
Partridge, with a hint of solidarity.

'And then, of course,' said Nick clinchingly, but with a sad
loll of the head, 'he jumped off a bridge into the Mississippi.'

Lady Partridge reflected on this, as if she thought it unlikely.
'I always rather liked him on the telly. Came over awfully well.
Perhaps you never saw those . . . He went to the seaside. Or,
you know, poking round old churches and what-not. Even

those weren't too bad. He had what I'd call an infectious laugh. I think I'm right in saying he became the Poet Laureate.'

'Ah . . . No,' said Nick. 'No, actually—'

'*Fuck!*' came a howl from the forecourt, hardly recognizable as Gerald's voice. Lady Partridge's gaze slid uncertainly away. Nick got up with a soft laugh and went out into the hall to see what had happened. Gerald was coming in from outside, his face in a spasm of emotion that might have been rage or glee, and veered away from Nick into the kitchen, where Toby was sitting having coffee with Rachel. Nick glanced out of the front door, and saw Wani collecting up the boules with a dutiful but unrepentant expression.

'Darling . . . ?' said Rachel, with a note of anger, but looking him over quickly, to see if he was hurt.

'*Dad,*' said Toby, and shook his head disappointedly.

Gerald stood staring at them, and then hunched and grinned. He said, 'I'm on holiday!'

'Yes, darling, you are,' said Rachel. 'You ought to calm down.' She was solicitous, but firm: her own calm was a reproof. Nick stood in the doorway and looked at them, bright-eyed. There was a collective sense that they could tame Gerald.

'Beaten at boules by a bloody A-rab!' said Gerald, and gasped at his own candour, and as if it might be a joke.

'For god's sake, Dad,' said Toby.

'What . . . ?' said Gerald.

'You'll be calling me a bloody Jew-boy next.'

'I would never do that,' said Gerald. 'Don't be monstrous.'

'Well, I hope not,' said Toby, and coloured at his own emotion. 'Wani's my friend,' he said, with an effect of simple decency, so that Gerald stared and thought and then went out of the room. They heard him calling out, 'Wani! Wani, my apologies! OK . . . ? Yup! So sorry . . .' with improper cheerfulness, and tailing off as he turned indoors, as if it was a mere routine. He came back into the kitchen with a twitch of a smile, since Wani hadn't heard the thing he should really have been apologizing for. He drifted absent-mindedly into the larder and emerged with a dusty bottle of claret.

'Why don't you go and have a swim, Gerald. Or find Jasper, and take him for a walk,' recommended Rachel.

'Jasper isn't a cocker spaniel, you know,' said Gerald, amusingly but with a bit of a snap.

'Well, no,' said Rachel.

Gerald turned the little wooden-handled corkscrew with furtive keenness. 'Well, roll on Sunday, and Lionel's visit!' he said, to please Rachel and cover the exuberant pop of the cork.

'It's a bit early for that, isn't it Gerald?' said Rachel.

'For god's sake, Dad,' said Toby again.

'He wants to let it breathe,' said Nick with an anxious laugh.

Gerald looked at them all, and there was an odd charge of unhappiness, a family instinct, communicated, not quite understood. 'I just feel like a fucking drink, OK?' he said, and went off to the end room with the bottle.

Just before lunch, in the shade of the awning, he was more cheerful, but also more freely in touch with his troubles. 'The fucking Tippers!' he said, counting carelessly on his mother's deafness. 'God knows what the consequences of this little episode will be – for the business, I mean.'

'I'm sure you can do brilliantly without him,' said Rachel. 'You've been doing brilliantly without him so far.'

'True,' said Gerald. 'True.' He looked wryly along the table that he ruled. 'I'm afraid they didn't fit in here, exactly, did they?'

'They didn't quite get the hang of it,' said Rachel.

'Yah, why did they go?' said Jasper.

'Oh, who knows!' said Rachel. 'Now, Judy, asparagus!'

Gerald snuffled and seemed to ponder the question, like some undecidable conflict of loyalties, some inescapable regret. Nick couldn't help noticing that his own remarks were received very coolly that day, and sometimes he was ignored and talked over.

At the end of lunch Gerald took up his grievances again; it was clear that he was in the grip of his own schemes, and living only half attentively, after a bottle and a half of wine, in the chatter and family teasing at the table. There was something rehearsed and implausible in his tone. He went on about work, and the 'important papers' he had to deal with. 'You don't know what it's like,' he said. 'It may be vacation for you, it may be the recess for me, but actually the work simply doesn't let up. Well, you've seen the number of faxes coming through. And I'm terribly behind with the diary.'

He waited, sighing but vigilant, till Rachel said, 'Well, why don't you have some help?'

Gerald puffed and slumped, as if to say that was hardly possible; but then said, 'I do rather wonder whether we won't *have* to send for Penny.'

'Not Penny Dreadful,' said Catherine. 'Anyway, she can't go in the sun.'

Rachel didn't contradict this, but gave her enabling shrug. 'If you really *need* Penny, darling, by all means ask her out.'

'Do you think . . . ?'

'I mean, she's perfectly pleasant company. If *she* didn't mind . . .'

'Oh, she's *not* pleasant company,' said Catherine. 'She's a humourless white bug.'

'Or what about Eileen?' said Toby. 'I'm sure she'd come just like that. You know how she adores Dad!'

Gerald gave a short distracted laugh at this absurd alternative. Nick looked at him with a tense smile, an awful feeling of collusion. He'd said nothing, he'd dissimulated much more cleverly than Gerald himself: he felt that he'd been, all passively and peace-lovingly, the real enabler.

'Yes, I'm not so sure about Eileen,' said Rachel.

'OK, then . . .' said Gerald, as though conceding to a general wish. There was a complicated shame-in-triumph which perhaps only Nick could see. The party pushed back their chairs, giving hazy thought to the matter of the afternoon, and Gerald went in to the phone room, with a look of tense reluctance, as if about to break bad news.

12

For their twenty-fifth wedding anniversary, Lionel Kessler gave Gerald and Rachel two presents. The first came round in the morning, on the back seat of his Bentley, and the chauffeur himself brought the stout wooden box into the kitchen.

'Darling old Lionel,' said Toby, before they knew what was in it.

'Silver, I expect,' said Gerald, getting a screwdriver, and sounding both greedy and slightly bored.

Inside, held in a metal brace by foam-rubber collars, was a rococo silver ewer. The body of the thing was in the form of a shell, and the spout was supported by a bearded triton. 'Goodness, Nick,' said Gerald, so that Nick fell into his role as interpreter – he said he thought it might be by one of the Huguenot silversmiths working in London in the mid-eighteenth century, perhaps by Paul de Lamerie, since the greatest name was also the only one he could think of, and with Lionel anything seemed possible. 'Marvellous,' said Gerald: 'a work of rare device.' He looked in the box to see if there was a note, like the watering instructions that come with some worrying plant, but there wasn't. Nick explained that the tiny scene in relief, of Eros playing with the sword of Justice, meant 'Omnia Vincit Amor'. 'Ah, thoroughly apt,' said Gerald, with shy pomp, putting his arm briefly round Rachel. He perhaps suspected that it was something Lionel had had knocking round at Hawkeswood anyway. Nick carried on smiling at it, half-conscious of how his father would have stooped and turned it, holding it with a cloth; remembering their long-ago visits to Monksbury, where the silver had a brassy iridescent colour, since the servants were forbidden to clean it and scratch it. 'We'll have to have that looked at for the insurance,' said Gerald.

Toby and Catherine's present was also a bit of silver, a scollop-edged Georgian salver, on which they had had 'Gerald and Rachel ~ 5 November 1986' engraved in a curly script. It couldn't help but look dull, and even vaguely satirical, beside the ewer, and Gerald gazed into it with a falsely modest expression, as though he was retiring, or had won a local golf tournament. 'It's perfectly lovely,' said Rachel. They both seemed gratified, but not excited, and clearly felt no one could actually want an object of this kind.

A little later they were having a glass of champagne when Nick looked down from the drawing-room window and saw the Bentley pulling up a second time. Now it was Lionel himself who climbed out of it, and who carried across the pavement the small flat packing case. He glanced up and made a shooshing sign, half frown, half kiss. Nick, his champagne working nicely with a first short line of charlie, smiled secretly back. The subtle bachelor sympathy between himself and the little bald peer brought a tear to the corner of his eye – he felt quite silly for a moment at being so 'in love' with the family, and with this member of it in particular. A minute later Lionel was shown into the room amid groans of gratitude. He kissed his sister and her children, and shook hands with Gerald and Nick, who felt for the fervour in his briskness. The ewer was on the mantelpiece, crowded today with white lilies and white mop-headed chrysanths. 'Well, you had to have silver,' Lionel said, 'but I wanted you to have this as well. It came up in Paris last week, and since we're all feeling a little light-headed . . .' Something called the Big Bang had just happened, Nick didn't fully understand what it meant, but everyone with money seemed highly exhilarated, and he had a suspicion he was going to benefit from it too. Here was Lord Kessler, with a box under his arm, to give it his own superior licence.

It was Rachel who took and opened the box, with Nick standing by as if it was his present, as if he was giving it and perhaps also receiving it – he felt generous and possessive all at once. He kept himself from exclaiming when she lifted out a small oil painting. He determinedly said nothing. 'My dear . . .' said Rachel, fascinated, hesitant, but controlled, as though to be surprised would be to have some vulgar advantage taken of her. She held it up, so that everyone could see it. 'It's perfectly lovely,' she said.

'Mm . . .' said Lionel, with the canny little smile of someone who has made a good decision.

Gerald said, 'You're too kind, really . . .' and stared earnestly at the picture, hoping someone would say what it was. It was a landscape, about nine inches wide by twelve high, painted entirely in vertical dabs of a fine brush, so that the birch trees and meadow seemed to quiver in the breeze and warmth of a spring morning. A black-and-white cow lay under a bank at the front; a white-shawled woman talked to a brown-hatted man on the path in the near distance. It was in a plain dull-gilt frame.

'Hah, jolly nice,' said Toby.

Catherine, looking comically from side to side as though detecting a trick, said, 'It's a Gauguin, isn't it,' and Nick, who after all couldn't bear not to say, said, 'It's a Gauguin' at the same time.

'It's a nice one, isn't it,' said Lionel. '*Le Matin aux Champs* – it's a study, or a little version, of the picture in Brussels. I snatched it from the teeth of the head of Sony. Actually, I think it was a bit small for him. Not quite the ideally expensive picture' – and he chuckled with Nick as if they both knew just what to expect from the head of Sony.

'Really . . . Lionel . . .' Gerald was saying, shaking his head slowly and blinking to disguise his calculations as another kind of wonder. 'That and the silver . . . um . . .'

Catherine shook her head too, and said, 'God . . . !' in simultaneous glee and scorn of her rich family.

The picture was handed round, and they each smiled and sighed, and turned it to the light, and passed it on with a little shudder, as if they'd been oblivious for a moment, in the spell of sheer physical possession. 'Where on earth shall we put it?' said Gerald, when it came back to him; Nick laughed to cover his graceless tone.

Just then the front door slammed and Rachel went to look over the banisters; it was a day of incessant arrivals. 'Oh, come up, dear,' she said. 'It's Penny.'

'Ah, she can give us her thoughts about the picture,' said Gerald, as if from a view of her general usefulness. He got rid of the picture by propping it against Liszt's nose on the piano.

'Penny!' said Catherine. 'Why? I mean, she wouldn't have a clue,' and then laughed submissively, since it wasn't her day.

'Well,' said Gerald, beaming and blustering, 'well, her father's a painter.' And he turned away to see to the champagne; he had a fresh glass in his hand when Penny came into the room.

'Hello, Penny,' said Rachel, in her coolly maternal way.

'Congratulations to you both,' said Penny, coming forward with her curious bossy diffidence, her air, that was almost maternal in itself, of putting her duty to forgetful, forgivable Gerald before any thought of her own pleasure. 'I really came to do the diary.'

'The diary can wait,' said Gerald, with a note of reckless permissiveness, passing her the glass. 'Have a look at what Lord Kessler's just given us.' It struck Nick that he was avoiding any chance of a kiss. 'It's by Gauguin,' said Gerald. '*Le Rencontre aux Champs*' – giving it already his own, more anecdotal title. They all peered at it politely again. 'I can't help thinking of our lovely walks in France,' Gerald said, looking round for agreement.

'Oh . . . I see,' said Rachel.

'It's nothing like that,' said Catherine.

'I don't know,' said Gerald. 'That could be your mother going down to Podier, and bumping into . . . ooh . . . Nick on the way.'

Nick, pleased to have been put in the picture, said, 'I seem to have borrowed Sally Tipper's hat.'

Catherine smiled impatiently. 'Yeah, but the point is, they're peasants, isn't it, Uncle Lionel. You know, this was when he went to Brittany, what was it called, to get as far away as possible from the city and the corruption of bourgeois life. It's about hardship and poverty.'

'You're absolutely right, darling,' said Lionel, who never stood for cant about money. 'Though I expect he sent it to bourgeois old Paris to be sold.'

'Exactly,' said Gerald.

'It's funny, it looks like a Hereford cow,' said Toby. 'Though I don't suppose it can be.'   .

'Probably a Charolais,' said Gerald.

'Charolais are a completely different colour,' said Toby.

'Anyway, it's very nice,' said Penny, for whom being the daughter of Norman Kent had worked as a perfect inoculation against art.

'We were wondering where to hang it,' said Rachel.

They spent five minutes trying the picture in different places, Toby holding it up while the others pursed their lips and said, 'You see, *I* think it needs to go there . . .' Toby became a boy again, in a family game, pulling faces and then clearly thinking about something else. 'Over 'ere, guv'nor?' he kept saying, in a hopeless cockney accent which he found funny. He took down one or two things and replaced them with the Gauguin. The trouble was that the shapes of the other pictures showed on the wallpaper behind. Rachel didn't seem to mind too much, but Gerald said, 'We can't have the Lady seeing that.'

'Oh . . .' said Rachel, with a little tut.

'No, I'm serious,' said Gerald. 'She's finally agreed to honour us with her company, and everything must be perfect.'

'I'd be highly surprised if the Lady noticed,' Lionel said candidly. But Gerald shot back,

'Believe me, she notices everything,' and gave a rather grim laugh.

'We'll decide later,' said Rachel. 'We just might be awfully selfish and have it in our bedroom.'

'Though he'll probably get the Lady in there,' said Catherine under her breath.

After lunch two men from Special Branch came, to check on matters of security for the PM's visit. They passed through the house like a pair of unusually discreet bailiffs, noting and evaluating. Nick heard them coming up the top stairs and sat smiling at his desk with his heart pounding and ten grams of coke in the top drawer while they peered out onto the leads. Their main concern was with the back gate and they told him a policeman would be on duty all night in the communal gardens. This made everything look a bit more risky, and when they'd gone down again he had a small line just to steady his nerves.

Later he went downstairs and when he looked out at the front of the house he saw Gerald and Geoffrey Titchfield talking on the pavement. They both had a look of contained exaltation, like marshals before some great ceremony, not admitting their own feelings, almost languid with unspoken nerves. Whenever someone walked past, Gerald gave them a nod and a smile, as if they knew who he was. He had made a very successful speech at Conference last month, since when he'd adopted a manner of approachable greatness.

Geoffrey was pointing at the front door, the eternally green front door, which Gerald had just had repainted a fierce Tory blue. It was the moment when Nick had first caught the pitch of Gerald's mania. Catherine, in a vein of wild but focused fantasy, had said that the PM would be shocked by a green door and that she'd read an article which said all Cabinet ministers had blue ones; even Geoffrey Titchfield, who was only the chairman of the local association, had a blue front door. Gerald scoffed at this, but a little later strolled out to the Mira Foodhall for some water biscuits and came back looking troubled. 'What do you think about this, Nick?' he said. 'The Titchfields have only got the garden flat, but their front door is unquestionably blue.' Nick said he doubted it mattered, as drolly as possible, and feeling his own nostalgic fervour for the grand dull green. But the following day Gerald came back to it. 'You know, I wonder if the Cat's right about that door,' he said. 'The Lady might very well think it's a bit off. She might think we're trying to save the fucking rainforest or something!' He laughed nervily. 'She might think she's been taken to Greenham Common, by mistake,' he went on, in a tone somewhere between lampoon and genuine derangement. At which point Nick knew, since the colour of the door had become a token of Gerald's success, that Mr Duke would be set to work with a can of conference-blue gloss.

Now Penny came out, with her briefcase of papers, and Nick watched from his window seat as she spoke to the two men. She had been typing up the diary which Gerald dictated each day onto tape, and which the family resented even more since her busy week with them in France, when she'd made it quite plain that none of them was in it:

it was strictly the record of his political life, a kind of 'archive', she said, 'an important historical resource'. Penny carried out the diary duty with a smug devotion which only added to their annoyance.

Catherine drifted into the drawing room, and came to sit with Nick behind the roped-back curtains. 'I hate it when we have everyone in,' she said. There was something invalidish, semi-secret, about the window seats, the houses of children's games, spying on the room and the street.

'I know, isn't it awful,' said Nick absent-mindedly.

'Look, there's Gerald showing off outside.'

'I think he's just having a chat with old Titch. You know it's his big day.'

'It's always his big day these days. He hardly has a small one. Anyway, it's also Ma's big day. And she's got to spend it with a whole lot of *empees*,' said Catherine, for whom the two syllables were now a mantra of tedium and absurdity. 'Plus she's got to play hostess to the Other Woman in her own house, to cap it all. You can tell he's longing to put up a big sign, "Tonight! Special Appearance!" '

' "One Night Only". . .'

'God I hope so. That Titch man worships Gerald. Have you noticed, every time he walks past the house he sort of smirks at it fondly, just in case someone's looking out.'

'Does he . . . ?' said Nick, not quite forgetting that he had once done the same. He said, 'I thought the party was originally going to be at Hawkeswood.'

'Oh, well that was Gerald's idea, you bet. But of course Uncle Lionel won't have the Other Woman there.'

'Right . . .'

'It's rather funny,' said Catherine coldly. 'He's had this dream of getting her there. It's almost what's kept him going. And it's the one thing which simply can't happen.'

'I don't quite see why Lionel . . .'

'Oh, it's all the vandalism she's done to everything. Anyway, that's why he's having this rewiring done, so that no one can get in the house.'

Nick laughed protestingly, because he knew Catherine's neat deep readings of the family narrative, but she said, 'Oh, god, yes – why do you think he gave them that painting.'

'I don't know. You mean, to make up for it,' said Nick, considering the idea, which did make sense of his earlier rough impression, that Gerald hadn't liked being given the Gauguin. Perhaps he saw it as the confirmation of a mysterious snub.

'God, that Miss Moneypenny's a pain,' said Catherine, for whom the lens of the drawing-room window seemed to focus a world of irritants. Penny was now taking some impromptu dictation from Gerald, while clutching her briefcase between her knees. 'I suppose she must be madly in love with him, mustn't she?'

'Oh, in the noblest, purest way,' said Nick.

'She'd have to be, darling, to type all that tripe.'

'Some people just live for their work. Norman's an obsessive worker, as we know all too well, and she's got it from him. They're happiest when they're hard at it.'

Catherine snorted. 'God, the idea . . .'

'Mm . . . ?'

'Well – Gerald and Penny hard at it.'

'Oh . . .' Nick tutted and coloured.

'Now I've shocked you,' Catherine said.

'Hardly,' said Nick.

'Actually, she's got herself a boyfriend, you know.'

'Really?' murmured Nick, with a dart of treacherous sympathy for Gerald, the doomed older man. 'Have you met him?'

'No, but she told me all about him.'

'Ah, I see . . .'

Geoffrey Titchfield moved off, and as Gerald called some friendly command to him he looked back and gave a half-serious salute. Penny and Gerald were left alone. It was a moment when Nick saw they might do something incautious – kiss, or touch in a light but revealing way that would give Catherine's scurrilous joke the chill of reality. It was another of the secrets of the house that he kept, like a sleepy conscience. Gerald looked up as he talked, from floor to floor, and Nick waved to show him they were being watched.

In the hours before the party the atmosphere thickened uncomfortably. The caterers had taken over the kitchen, and made faces behind Elena's back as she went stubbornly about her business; loud squawks and whines came out of the marquee in the garden, where the sound system was being tested; in the dining room the chairs were clustered knee to knee, waiting for orders. Gerald's manner became bright and fixed, and he mocked others for their nervousness. Catherine said she couldn't bear the sight of a cardboard box in a room, and went out to 'look at properties' with Jasper. Even Rachel, who delegated with aristocratic confidence, was biting her cheek as Gerald described to her where the Lady would sit, whom she would talk to, and how much she would have to drink. He almost let it seem that the climax of the evening would be when he danced with the Prime Minister. Rachel said, 'But you and I will lead off the dancing, won't we, Gerald,' so that he said to her, from a rapidly covered distance, 'But my love of course we will!' and gave her a blushing hug, and stumbled her through a few unexpected steps.

About six Nick slipped out for a walk. The evening was gloomy and damp. Wet leaves smeared the pavement. He was infected with the house nerves about the PM, wondering what to say to her, and already imagining tomorrow morning, when the party was over, and the enjoyable phase of remembering it and analysing it could begin. The shrieks and bangs of fireworks sounded from the neighbourhood gardens. Sometimes a rocket streaked up over the housetops and shed its stars into the low-hanging cloud. Duffel-coated children were hurried through the murk. Nick's route was an improvised zigzag, an intention glimpsed and disowned; no one watching him could have guessed it, and when he turned the corner and trotted down the steps into the station Gents he wore a frown as if the whole thing was a surprise and a nuisance even to himself.

Walking briskly back down Kensington Park Road he was frowning again, at having done something so vulgar and unsafe – it was suddenly late, the waiting and wondering and then the intent speechless action swallowed up time; his lateness accused him . . . Nothing 'unsafe' in the new sense, of course; but reckless and illegal. It would have made a bad start to the evening to be caught. Simon at the office had said 'Rudi' Nureyev used to cruise that particular lav, long ago no doubt, but the prospect of some starry pas de deux seemed to Nick to haunt and redeem the place, every time he went in. Now he was sour and practical, the warmth of a secret naughtiness faded in the November air. He went quickly upstairs, his haste was his apology, and the house had a brilliant quietness to it, a genuine brilliance, planned and paid for and brought to the point.

When he came down there was still a bit of time before the guests arrived. He went out into the dance tent and circled the creaky square of parquet, where suspended burners made pools of heat in the empty chill. The tent was a dream-like extension to the house-plan. He came back in, across the improvised bridge, through the garlanded and lanterned back passage, and wandered from room to room, among the lights and candles and smell of lilies, with a sense almost of being in church, or at least of the memory of a ceremony. In the hall mirror he was lustre and shadow in his new evening suit and shiny shoes. He greeted Rachel and Catherine in the drawing room, and they chatted as if they were all guests, happily denatured, transformed by silk and velvet, jewels and make-up, into drawing-room creatures. The bangs of fireworks made them skittish. From downstairs came repeated stifled explosions of champagne corks, as the waiters got ready. 'Shall I get us a drink?' said Nick.

'Yes, do. And you might find my husband,' said Rachel.

He looked into the dining room, crowded like a restaurant with separate tables, where Toby was standing with a card in his hand. He was silently rehearsing his speech. 'Keep it short, darling,' Nick said.

'Nick . . . Fuck . . . !' said Toby, with a worried grin. 'You know it's one thing making a speech to your aunts and uncles and, you know, your mates, but it's quite another making a speech to the fucking Prime Minister.'

'Don't panic,' said Nick. 'We'll all shout, "Hear, hear!" '

Toby laughed gloomily. 'You don't suppose she might have to go to a summit or something at the last moment?'

'This is the summit, I'm afraid. It certainly is for your papa.' Nick edged between the tables, each place with its mitred napkin and black-inked card. No titles, of course. He leant on the chair-to-be of Sharon Flintshire. 'I love these pictures of the happy couple.'

'I know,' said Toby. 'The Cat's done a bit of art.'

Catherine had propped up on the sideboard a thing like a school project, where blown-up photographs of Gerald and Rachel before they were married flanked a formal wedding photo, with later family pics below. It looked rather like the placards of the cast outside a long-running West End farce.

'Your mother was so beautiful,' Nick said.

'I know. And Dad.'

'They're so young.'

'Yeah, Dad's not that keen on it actually. He doesn't want the Lady seeing him in his hippy phase.' To judge from the photos Gerald's hippy phase had reached its counter-cultural extreme in a pair of mutton-chop whiskers and a floral tie.

'I can't work out how old they were.'

'Well, Dad'll be fifty next year, so he was . . . twenty-four; and Ma's a couple of years older, of course.'

'They're our age,' said Nick.

'They didn't waste any time,' said Toby with a sad little smile.

'They certainly didn't waste any time having you, dear,' Nick said, making the amusing calculation. 'You must have been conceived on the honeymoon.'

'I think I was,' said Toby, both proud and embarrassed. 'Somewhere in South Africa. Ma was a virgin when she was married, I know that, and three weeks later she was pregnant. No playing around there.'

'No, indeed,' said Nick, thinking of the years his parents had taken to have him, and with an inward smile at his own freedoms.

Toby looked at his speech again, and bit his lip. Nick watched him affectionately: unbuttoned jacket over crimson cummerbund, heavy black shoes, hair cut short so that he looked fatter-faced, like an embarrassed approximation of his father, but his father as he was now, not when he was twenty-four. On a slow impulse Nick said, 'I may have just what you need. If you'd like a little, er, chemical help.'

'Have you . . . ?' said Toby, startled but interested.

And Nick murmured to him that he'd managed to get hold of a bit of charlie.

'God, amazing, thanks a lot!' said Toby, and then smiled round guiltily.

They sent a waiter to the drawing room with champagne, and went on up, with a little flutter about 'rehearsing'. For

Nick the flutter was that of sharing the secret. They went into Toby's old bedroom, and locked the door. 'The place is crawling with fuzz,' Toby said.

'So what are you going to say in your speech?' said Nick, tipping out some powder on the bedside table. The room had a special mood of desertion, not the mute patience of a spare bedroom but the stillness of a place a boy has grown up in and abandoned, with everything settling into silence just as it was. There was a chest of drawers in mahogany and a gilt-framed mirror, very nice pieces, and Toby's school and team photos, a young unguarded class sense to everything; and the wardrobe of clothes Nick had once daringly dressed up in, which had lost their meaning, even to him.

'I thought I might make a joke about the Conference,' said Toby. 'You know, the Next Move Forward, and Mum and Dad going on for ever, like the Lady.'

'Mm.' Nick frowned over the busy credit card. 'I think the thing is, darling, you should make the speech just as if the Lady wasn't there. And everything you say should be about . . . your father and your mother. It's their day, not hers, and not just Gerald's.'

'Oh,' said Toby.

'You might even make it more about Rachel.'

'Right . . . God, I wish you'd write it.' Toby slouched anxiously about the room. From downstairs the doorbell was heard and the first guests arriving. 'I mean, what can you say about the old girl?'

'You could say what a lot she's had to put up with in Gerald,' said Nick, with a dark sense of her not knowing the half of it. 'Actually, don't say that,' he added prudently; 'just keep it short.' He pictured Toby standing and speaking, his anxiety grinning through to a crowd that would be warmed with drink into roughness as well as affection. 'Remember, everyone loves you,' he said, to help him overlook the various monsters who were coming.

Toby stooped and sniffed up his line and stood back; Nick waited and watched for the amorous dissolve, not knowing quite what colour it would take in him. 'Haven't done this for yonks,' Toby said, half protest, half apology. Then, 'Mm, that's very nice . . .' And a minute later, in beaming surrender, 'This is great stuff, Nick, I must say. Where the hell did you get it?'

Nick snorted briskly and wiped the table with the flat of his finger. 'Oh, I got it off Ouradi, actually.'

'Right,' said Toby. 'Yah, Ouradi always gets great stuff.'

'You used to do it with him in the old days.'

'I know, we did once or twice. I didn't know you ever did it, though.' Toby pranced towards him, and it was all Nick could do not to kiss him and feel for his dick, as he would have done with Wani himself. Instead he said,

'Here, why don't you take the rest of this.' It was about a third of a gram.

'God, no, I couldn't,' said Toby, with the gleam of possession at once in his face.

'Yeah, go on,' said Nick. 'I've had enough, but you might need some more.' He held out the tiny billet-doux, which as always with Ronnie was made from a page of a girlie mag; a magnified nipple covered it like a seal. Toby took it and put it, after a moment's thought, deep in his breast pocket. 'God, that's fantastic!' he said. 'Yah, I think tonight'll be all right, you know, I'm just going to keep it short,' and he went prattling on in the simple high spirits of a first hit of cocaine. On the way downstairs he said, 'Of course, darling, tell me if you want some more – I won't use all this.'

'I'll be fine,' said Nick.

They sashayed into the drawing room, where Lady Partridge was asking a man from the Treasury about muggers, and Badger Brogan was flirting gingerly with Greta Timms, pregnant with her seventh child. Nick circled through the room, smiling and almost immune to the anxiety he noticed in others, the booming joviality, the glancing inattentiveness, the sense of a lack that was waiting to be filled by the famous arrival. He looked round for a drink. The coke trickle in his throat made him doubly thirsty. Two waiters came in with laden trays, which made him laugh: they were just the answer to a double thirst. He chose, on grounds of beauty, the dark, full-lipped one, 'Thanks – oh, hello,' Nick said, over his raised glass, knowing the waiter before he knew who he was – just for a second, while everything was shining and suspended, their eyes engaged, the bubbles sailing upwards in a dozen tall glasses. 'I remember you,' he said then, rather drily, as if he were a waiter who had memorably dropped something.

'Oh . . . good evenin,' the waiter said, pleasantly, so that Nick felt forgiven; and then, 'Where do I see you before?' – so that he guessed he was in fact forgotten.

There was a commotion at the window, and Geoffrey Titchfield said, 'Ah, the Prime Minister's car has arrived,' like an old flunkey, steeped in the grandeur of his masters. He moved towards the door, too exalted by his own words to share in the fuss that they had triggered. Guests glanced into each other's faces for reassurance, one or two seemed already to give up, and withdrew into corners, and among the men there was some thinly amiable jostling. Nick followed through onto the landing, with the sense that the PM was beyond discretion, she'd be piqued if there wasn't a throng, a popular demonstration. He was pressed against the banister at the first turn of the stair, smiling down like an eye-catching unnamed attendant in a history painting. The door was standing open and the damp chill from outside gave an edge to the excitement. The women shivered with happy discomfort. The night was the fractious element they had triumphed against. The Mordant Analyst scurried in, almost tripped, amid laughs and tuts. Gerald was already in the street, in humble alignment with the Special Branch boys. Rachel stood just inside, haloed by the drizzly light and the diaphanous silver sheath of her dress. The well-known voice was heard, there was a funny intent silence of a second or two, and then there she was.

She came in at her gracious scuttle, with its hint of a long-suppressed embarrassment, of clumsiness transmuted into power. She looked ahead, into the unknown house, and everything she saw was a confirmation. The high hall mirror welcomed her, and in it the faces of the welcomers, some of whom, grand though they were, had a look beyond pride, a kind of rapture, that was bold and shy at once. She seemed pleased by the attention, and countered it cheerfully and practically, like modern royalty. She gave no sign of noticing the colour of the front door.

Upstairs, calm was re-established, but of a special kind, the engaged calm of progress once the overture has finished and the curtain has gone up. People recollected themselves. There was a sort of unplanned receiving line when the Lady came into the room (her husband, behind her, slipped modestly towards a drink and an old friend). Barry Groom, bouncing back from a low point with a call girl in the spring, dropped his head with horrible humility as the PM took his hand; it was later claimed that he had even said hello. Wani she greeted humorously, as someone she had seen recently elsewhere – he won the glow of recognition but surrendered the claim to need to speak to her so soon again; though he held on to her hand and it wasn't clear for a moment if he was going to kiss her. Gerald steered her jealously on, murmuring names. Nick watched with primitive interest as she approached; again she was beyond manners, however courtly and jewelled. Her hair was so perfect that he started to picture it wet and hanging over her face. She was wearing a long black skirt and a wide-shouldered white-and-gold jacket, amazingly embroidered, like a Ruritanian uniform, and cut low at the front to display a magnificent pearl necklace. Nick peered at the necklace, and the large square bosom, and the motherly fatness of the neck. 'Isn't she beautiful,' said Trudi Titchfield, in unselfconscious reverie. Nick was briskly presented, elided almost, in the rhythm of the long social sentence, but with a surprising detail, or fib, 'Nick Guest . . . a great friend of our children . . . a young don,' so that he saw himself enhanced and also compromised, since dons were not the PM's favourite people. He nodded and smiled and felt her blue eyes briefly but unconfidently focus on him before she seized the initiative and called out, 'John, hullo . . . !' to John Timms, who was suddenly right next to him. 'Prime Minister . . .' said John Timms, not shaking her hand but clasping her somehow with the fervour and humour of his tone. At the end of the row were the children themselves, a goggling unmatched pair, Toby still marvellously cheerful and Catherine, who could have sulked or asked an awkward question, shaking hands with a bright 'Hello!' and gazing at the PM like a child at a conjuror. 'Oh, and this is my boyfriend,' she said, producing Jasper but forgetting to name him. 'Hello,' said the Prime Minister, in a tone just dry enough to suggest that by now she deserved a drink: which Tristão, with his doe eyes and nerveless smile, was at hand to provide.

Nick trotted downstairs from a quick refresher and caught Wani coming out of Gerald and Rachel's bedroom. 'God, careful, darling,' he said.

'I was just using the lav,' said Wani.

'Mm,' said Nick. He was too drunk and high himself to take the danger at all seriously. 'Do use my lav if you need to.'

'The stairs,' said Wani.

Nick loved the way the coke took off the blur of champagne, claret, Sauternes, and more champagne. It totted up the points and carried them over as credit in a new account of pleasure. It brought clarity, like a cure – almost, at first, like sobriety. He put an arm round Wani's shoulders, and asked him if he was having a good time. 'We see so little of each other,' he said. They started to go downstairs and something caught Nick's eye at the third or fourth step, someone else moving in the great white bedroom that Wani had come out of. His instinct as guardian of the house, preventer of trouble, quickened. Jasper came out, businesslike, as if he had the keys and was showing the place to a buyer. He gave Nick a nod and a wink. 'Just going up to Cat's room,' he said.

'So,' said Nick, as he and Wani went on down, with a pensive hesitation each step or two, as though they might stop completely in the charm of a shared thought, 'you've been running the house tart up the hill . . .'

'It's got to be climbed, old chap, it's got to be climbed.'

'Yeah,' said Nick, with a sniff and a sour turning down of the mouth. He looked for guilt in Wani's oddly rosy face; he glimpsed, like shuffled cards, the two of them together in the bathroom, Wani's love of corruption, all the licence that went with the latest line. 'So it's not our secret any more,' he said. Wani gave him a look that was scornful but not aggressive. Nick might be in the clear, clever phase, but Wani was much further on, in the phase where high spirits reel and stall and blink at a barely recognized room or friend. Nick let him go, and the high heartbeat of the coke became a short sprint of panic. He smiled defensively, and the smile seemed to search and find a happier subject, in the opening bloom of the drug. It was hard to know what mattered. There was certainly no point in thinking about it now. Out in the marquee the music had started, and everything had the air of an escapade.

He found Catherine in a corner of the drawing room being chatted up by toothy old Jonty Stafford, the retired ambassador, who stooped over her like a convivial Jabberwock. 'No, I think you'd like Dubrovnik,' he was saying, with a suggestive hooding of the eyes. 'The Hotel Diocletian, *enormous* charm.'

'Oh,' said Catherine.

'They always gave us the bridal suite, you know . . . which has the most *enormous* bed. You could have had an orgy in there.'

'Not on your wedding night, presumably.'

'Hello, Sir Jonty.'

'Ah, now here's your handsome young beau, now I'm for it, now I'm done for!' said Sir Jonty, and lurched off after another passing female bottom, which happened to be that of the PM. He looked back for a moment with a shake of the head: 'Marvellous, you know . . . the Prime Minister . . .'

'I think you've just been propositioned by a very drunk old man,' said Nick.

'Well, it's nice to be noticed by someone,' said Catherine, dropping onto a sofa. 'Sit here. Do you know where Jaz is?'

'Haven't seen him,' said Nick.

The photographer was at large, and his flash gleamed in the mirrors. He slipped and lingered among the guests, approached with a smile, like a vaguely remembered bore, in his bow tie and dinner jacket, and then pouf! – he'd got them. Later he came back, he came around, because most shots catch a bleary blink or a turned shoulder, and got them again. Now they bunched and faced him, or they pretended they hadn't seen him and acted themselves with careless magnificence. Nick dropped onto the sofa beside Catherine, lounged with one leg curled under him and a grin on his face at his own elegance. He felt he could act himself all night. He felt fabulous, he loved these nights, and whilst it would have been good to top the thing off with sex it seemed hardly to matter if he didn't. It made the absolute best of not having sex.

'Mm, you smell nice,' said Catherine.

'Oh, it's just the old "Je Promets",' said Nick, and shook his cufflinks at her. 'Have you had your twelve seconds with the PM yet?'

'I was just about to, but Gerald put a stop to it.'

'I heard a bit of her talk at dinner. She does that Great Person thing of being very homely and self-indulgent.'

'Greedy,' said Catherine.

'They all love it, they breathe sighs of relief, they'd talk about marge versus butter all night, and then suddenly she's on them with the Common Agricultural Policy.'

'You've not given her your own thoughts on it.'

'Not yet . . .' said Nick. 'She's quite closely managed, isn't she? She's in charge, but she goes where she's told.'

'Well, she's not in charge here,' said Catherine, beckoning boldly to Tristão. 'What do you want to drink?'

'What *do* I want?' said Nick, matching Tristão's formal smile with a sly one, and running his eyes up the waiter's body. 'What would I like best?'

'Champagne, sir? Or something stronger?'

'Champagne for now,' Nick drawled, 'and something stronger later.' The view of pleasure deepened in front of him, the lovely teamwork of drugs and drink, the sense of risk nonsensically heightening the sense of security, the new conviction he could do what he wanted with Tristão, after all these years. Tristão himself merely nodded, but as he stooped to reach an empty glass he leant quickly and heavily on Nick's knee. Nick watched him going away through the crowded room and for several long seconds it was all one perspective, here and Hawkeswood, the gilt, the mirrors, room after room, the glimpsed coat-tails of a fugitive idea: which then came to you, by itself, and it was what you wanted. The pursuit was nothing but a restless way of waiting. All shall have prizes: Gerald was right. When Tristão came back and bowed the drinks on their tray towards them, Nick plucked up his glass in a toast that was both general and secret. 'To us,' he said.

'To us,' said Catherine. 'Do stop flirting with that waiter.'

A minute later she said, 'Fedden seems pretty lively tonight. Most unlike himself, I must say.' They looked across to where Toby was sprawled on the PM's sofa and telling some unimaginable joke. Just beside the PM the wide dented seat cushion was a reception zone on which supplicants perched for an audience of a minute or two before being amicably dislodged – though Toby, trading perhaps on the triumph of his speech after dinner, had been there rather longer.

'I wouldn't be surprised,' said Nick, 'if Wani hadn't given him a bit of laughing powder to get him through.'

'Oh, god,' said Catherine disparagingly, before smiling at the idea of it. 'You know what he's like, he'll offer her a poke or whatever it's called.'

'She's had a lot to drink, hasn't she. But it doesn't seem to have any effect.'

'It's so funny watching the men with her. They come up with their wives but you can see they're an embarrassment – look at that one now, yes, shakes hands, "Yes, Prime Minister, yes, yes," can't *quite* get round to introducing his wife . . . obviously longing for her to get lost so he can have a hot date with the Lady himself – now she's got to sit on the sofa, he's furious . . . but yes! she's got him – he's squatting down . . . he's kneeling on the carpet . . .'

'Maybe she'll make him kiss her, um . . .'

'Oh, surely not . . .'

'Her ring, darling!'

'Oh, maybe. It's a very big one.'

'Well, she's quite queenly, isn't she, in that outfit.'

'*Queenly?* . . . Darling, she looks like a country and western singer.'

Catherine gave a brief screech, so that people turned round with varying degrees of humour and irritation. She had a look of running on quite fast inside. She held her trembling glass in front of her face. 'These champagne flutes are simply enormous!' she said.

'I know, they're sort of champagne tubas, aren't they,' said Nick.

Some very loud fireworks started going off in the communal gardens, mortars and thunderclaps. The windows rattled and the bangs echoed off the houses. People shouted cheerfully and flinched, but the Prime Minister didn't flinch, she fortified her voice with a firm diapason as if rising to the challenge of a rowdy Chamber. Around her her courtiers started like pheasants.

'Actually what amazes me,' Nick said, 'is the fantastic queenery of the men. The heterosexual queenery.'

'I sort of expect that,' said Catherine. 'You know, having Gerald . . .'

'Darling, Gerald's like a navvy in overalls, he's a miner on a picket line compared to some of these people. Look at old, um, the Minister for . . . what is he the Minister for?'

'I don't know, he's the Monster for something. With the pink face. I've seen him on telly.'

It was one of the men standing directly behind the PM, like a showman, both protecting and exhibiting her. From time to time he cast covetous glances at her hair. His own grey curls were oiled back in deep crinkly waves, over which he passed a hand that barely touched. He was one of the few men who were wearing a white tuxedo, and his posture was a superb denial of a possible gaffe. The jacket had swooping lapels, with cream silk facings; a line of flashing blue dress studs climbed to a lolling, surely purple, velvet bow tie. His wing collar kept his head framed at a haughty angle, and a tight silk cummerbund kept him erect and deepened the dyspeptic flush on his face.

Catherine said, 'I can see no self-respecting homosexual would dress like that.'

'Oh, I wouldn't go that far,' said Nick, uncertain which of them was being more ironic. 'It's just the licensed vanity . . .'

'He's the Monster of Vanity, darling!' said Catherine with another whoop.

He went to the first-floor lavatory and had a quick line there. It seemed a bit unnecessary to go all furtively upstairs. He snorted with a thumb against each nostril in turn, and smirked back at Gerald shaking hands with Ronald Reagan. You never felt the old boy knew who Gerald was – he had that look of medium-level benevolence. From outside the music was thumping, it had been Big Band jazz and now it was earlyish rock 'n' roll, such as Rachel and Gerald might conceivably have danced to twenty-five years ago. Fireworks popped and screeched. Beyond the locked door the collective boom of the party could be heard, with its undertone of secret opportunities: there were two men here that he wanted. The door handle rattled, he tidied, checked, flushed, tweaked his bow tie in the mirror, and sauntered out, hardly seeing the policeman waiting.

The Duchess had taken his place next to Catherine, so he looked about. The crowded drawing room was his playground. He found himself lounging intently towards the PM's sofa. Toby came away like an actor into the wings, still smiling; he couldn't say what she'd said. Lady Partridge had been hovering, and bent and clasped the Prime Minister's hand. She seemed nearly as speechless as Nick would have been on meeting a revered writer. 'I love your work' was really all one could say. But in this case, as Lady Partridge was an old woman, a crinkle of wisdom and maternal pride could be seen beside the childlike awe and submission. Nick couldn't quite hear what she was saying . . . something about the litter problem? . . . and he was pretty sure that she herself couldn't hear the PM –

but it didn't matter, they hung on to each other's hands, in an act of homage or even of healing which for Judy was a thrilling novelty and for the PM a deeply familiar routine. They were both fairly sozzled, and might almost have been having an argument as they tugged their hands backwards and forwards and raised their voices. There was something in the PM that seemed to say she'd have preferred an argument, it was what she was best at, and as Judy withdrew, crouching blindly backwards, she picked up her empty whisky glass and banged it against the leg of the Monster of Vanity.

It was the simplest thing to do – Nick came forward and sat, half-kneeling, on the sofa's edge, like someone proposing in a play. He gazed delightedly at the Prime Minister's face, at her whole head, beaked and crowned, which he saw was a fine if improbable fusion of the Vorticist and the Baroque. She smiled back with a certain animal quickness, a bright blue challenge. There was the soft glare of the flash – twice – three times – a gleaming sense of occasion, the gleam floating in the eye as a blot of shadow, his heart running fast with no particular need of courage as he grinned and said, 'Prime Minister, would you like to dance?'

'You know, I'd like that *very much*,' said the PM, in her chest tones, the contralto of conviction. Around her the men sniggered and recoiled at an audacity that had been beyond them. Nick heard the whole episode already accruing its commentary, its history, as he went out with her among twitches of surprise, the sudden shifting of the centre of gravity, an effect that none of them could have caused and none could resist. He himself smiled down at an angle, ignoring them all, intimately held in what the PM was saying and the brilliant boldness of his replies. Others followed them down the stone stairs and through the lantern-lit passage, to watch, and to play their subsidiary parts. 'One's not often asked to dance,' said the PM, 'by a don.' And Nick saw that Gerald hadn't got it quite right: she moved in her own accelerated element, her own garlanded perspective, she didn't give a damn about squares on the wallpaper or blue front doors – she noticed nothing, and yet she remembered everything.

There was sparse but hectic activity on the parquet when they stepped on to it, to the thump of 'Get Off Of My Cloud'. Gerald was bopping with a tight-lipped Jenny Groom whilst Barry pushed Penny round the floor in a lurching embrace. Rachel, sedately jiving with Jonty Stafford, had a look of exhausted good manners. And then Gerald saw the PM, his idol, who had said before that she wouldn't dance, but who now, a couple of whiskies on, was getting down rather sexily with Nick. All Nick's training with Miss Avison came back, available as the twelve-times table, the nimble footwork, the light grasp of the upper arm; though with it there came a deeper liveliness, a sense he could caper all over the floor with the PM breathless in his grip. Anyway, Gerald put a stop to that.

They were up in Nick's bathroom, the three of them, Wani chewing and sniffing, almost shivering, like someone who is ill. He had a look of wide-eyed gloom, racing and lost. He said he was fine, never better. He concentrated on unfolding the square of *Forum* magazine, and then scraping the girl's dark pubic mound clear of powder. Nick sat on the edge of the bath, sat in the bath, crossways, with his legs hanging out, and watched Tristão taking a hugely protracted piss.

'Don't put that away,' said Wani, which was one of his little jokes.

Tristão clucked and said, 'He likes that.'

'I know,' said Nick.

'I know where I see you now,' Tristão said, putting it away none the less, and flushing the lavatory. He washed his hands and talked into the mirror. 'Is Mr Toby birthday party. In the big big house. Long time ago.'

'That's right,' said Nick, struggling up and taking off his jacket. Tristão took his tail-coat off too, as though it were agreed what they were going to do. The instinctive certainty made Nick smile.

'You come lookin for me, in the kitchen. I think you was very pissed.'

'Was I?' said Nick vaguely.

'Then I feel very bad because I say I meet you later, and I never come.'

'We know why,' said Wani.

'Don't worry,' said Nick. 'I'm sure I forgot too.'

Tristão put a hand on Nick's shoulder, and Nick understood and got out his wallet and gave him £20. Tristão tilted his face and stuck his long fat tongue into Nick's mouth, kissed him systematically for ten seconds, then pulled out and turned away. Wani hadn't noticed, busy with the hill of coke. Tristão went and peered over his shoulder. 'I get in big trouble for this,' he said.

'No trouble,' said Wani. 'Couldn't be safer. House under police guard.'

'Yeah, I mean with my boss. Just a short break, yeah?'

'See how you like it,' said Wani, groping back at the waiter's crotch without looking round.

'I mean, do you need more money?' said Nick.

'I've just given him fifty fucking quid,' said Wani in a loud drawl.

Tristão mooched about and looked in the mirror again. He said, 'So you no bring your wife with you to the party?'

'She's not my fucking wife, you slut,' said Wani cheerfully.

Tristão grinned at Nick. 'I see you dancin with the big lady tonight,' he said. 'Jumpin around. I think she likes you.'

Wani's head reared in a single laugh. 'I'm going to ask her just what she thinks of Nick the next time I see her.'

'You a good friend of hers then, are you?' said Tristão, and grinned at Nick again.

'A fucking good friend,' said Wani, tapping and peering at his work. 'An exceedingly good friend . . . There . . .' He turned and stared. 'No, don't you love her? Isn't she just beautiful?'

Tristão made a little moue. 'Yeah, she OK. OK for me, anyway. Lots of parties, lots of money. Lots of tips. Hundred pound. Two hundred pound . . .'

'God, you slut,' said Wani.

Nick went to the basin and drank two glasses of water. 'I need a li-ine,' he crooned. They were all wired up now and desperate to go on, with the great, almost numbing reassurance of having packets more stuff. It was beyond pleasure, it was its own motor, pure compulsion, though it gave them the delusion of choice, and of wit in making it.

Tristão bent to snort his line, and Wani felt his cock and Nick felt his arse. 'Is good stuff? So where you get this stuff?' he said, stepping back, escaping for a moment, sniffing sharply.

'I get it from Ronnie,' said Wani. 'That's his name. Ah, that's better' – pinching his nostrils. 'I love Ronnie. He's my best friend. He's really my only friend.'

'Apart from the Prime Minister,' said Nick.

Tristão had the big first smirk on his face. A dozen decisions were already being made for him. He said, 'I thought he's your best friend. Him, Nick. No?'

'Nick? He's just a slut,' said Wani. 'He takes my money.'

Nick looked round from the first half of his line. 'What he means is he's my employer,' he said, with necessary pedantry.

'Not that he does any fucking work,' said Wani.

'Actually that's one kind of work I do do,' said Nick pertly.

'What – *fuckin* work?' said Tristão, and laughed like an idiot.

'Anyway,' said Nick, 'he's a millionaire, so . . .'

'I'm a *multi*-millionaire,' said Wani, with a sort of airy scowl. 'I want you to do your trick now.'

'What is his trick?' said Nick.

'You'll see,' said Wani.

'I hope this drugs don't make my dicky go soft,' said Tristão.

'If your dicky go soft I'm having my fucking money back,' said Wani.

Tristão dropped his trousers and pants round his knees and sat on the edge of the little cane-seated chair. His dark heavy dick hung down. He put his hands up inside his shirt, pushed his shirt up over his ribs, and twisted his nipples. 'You want to help me?' he said.

Wani tutted and went to stand behind him, leaned over to watch as he pinched and coaxed the waiter's nipples between forefinger and thumb. Tristão sighed, smiled, and bit his parched lip. He looked down intently, as if it was always a marvel to him, as his cock stirred, and thickened, twitched its way languorously up across his thigh before floating free with a pink smile of its own as the skin slid back a little. 'That's what it's all about,' said Wani.

'Is that it?' said Nick.

'You like?' said Tristão, whose face seemed to Nick suddenly greedy and strange. Of course his penis was the latent idea of the night, of this strange little scene, an idea trailed and discounted and lifting at the end as a large stupid fact. Nick said,

'So you've seen this before?'

'Oh, he always want it,' said Tristão.

Wani was down on his knees, trying clumsily to do justice to the thing he always wanted. His pants were undone, but his own little penis, depressed by the blitz or blizzard of coke, was puckered up, almost in hiding. He was lost, beyond humiliation – it was what you paid for. He sniffed as he licked and sucked, and gleaming mucus, flecked with blood and undissolved powder, trailed out of his famous nose into the waiter's lap. Obviously the waiter never got like this himself, he'd learnt the danger from Wani's example. Now he was chatty, like someone among friends. He nodded down at Wani and said, 'That's when I see him first. Mr Toby party. He give me coke and I fuck him in the hass.'

'In the house . . . ? Oh, in the *arse*, I see.' Nick smiled with a funny mixture of coldness and hilarity, a certain respect for mischief, however painful. He watched him pushing his hands through his lover's black curls: which he did in a carefree, patient, familiar way, almost as if Wani wasn't sucking him off, as if he was some beautiful pampered child who'd run in among the adults, hungry for praise and confident of it. Tristão stroked his hair, and grinned and praised him. 'He always pay the best.'

'I'm sure!' said Nick, and took a condom out of his pocket.

'Here we go,' said Tristão.

Downstairs the Prime Minister was leaving. Gerald had danced with her for almost ten minutes. He had the glow of intimacy and lightness of success about him as he saw her to her car, careless of the rain. Late fireworks were still going off, like bombs and rifles, and they glanced upwards. Rachel stood in the doorway, with Penny behind her, whilst Gerald, usurping the secret policeman, leant forward and slammed the car door in a happy involuntary bow. The rain gleamed and needled in the street lamps as the Daimler pulled away with a noise like a brusque sigh.

THE END OF
THE STREET

(1987)

13

Nick went out to vote early, and took Catherine with him in the car. She had been up since six to catch Gerald on *Good Morning Britain*. In the long month of the election campaign she had refused to watch TV, but now that Gerald and Rachel had both gone up to Barwick she seemed able to do little else.

'How was he?' Nick said.

'He was only on for a minute. He said the Tories had brought down unemployment.'

'That is a bit rich.'

'It's like Lady Tipper saying the 80s are a marvellous decade for staff.'

'Well, it'll soon be over.'

'What? Oh, the election, yes.' Catherine stared out into the drizzle. 'The 80s are going on for ever.'

In the long tree-tunnel of Holland Park Avenue it was as if the dawn had been deferred, though it was high summer, and hours after sunrise. It was just the discouraging sort of weather that campaigners dreaded.

'Gerald's bound to get back in, isn't he?' said Nick. At Kensington Park Gardens no one had been able to put this simple question.

Catherine seemed to look up from the depths of her gloom at an impossible consolation. 'It would be just so wonderful if he didn't.'

At the polling station they gave in their cards and the woman smiled and blushed when she saw the name Fedden and the address. Nick felt she was being unduly confident. In '83 Catherine had fouled her paper, and this time she promised to vote for the Anti-Yuppie Visionary Vegetarian candidate. Nick stood in the plywood booth and turned the thick hexagonal stub of pencil in his fingers. Voting always gave him a heightened sense of irresponsibility. They were in the big classroom of a primary school, with children's drawings and a large and unusual alphabet (N was for Nanny, K for Kiwi-fruit) running round the walls. Today was an unearned holiday. Nick had a moment's glimpse of the hundred little rules and routines of the place, and a mood of truancy came over him. Besides, what happened in the booth was an eternal secret. His pencil twitched above the Labour and Alliance candidates, and then he made his cross very frowningly for the Green man. He knew the Conservative was bound to get back in.

There were doubts, though, in some quarters, and Labour was thought to have had a very good campaign. Nick himself found their press advertisements much wittier than the Tories'. 'In Britain the poor have got poorer and the rich have got . . . well, they've got the Conservatives' was one that even Gerald had laughed at. In general, Gerald's view was that campaigning was over-rated at the national level, and irksome, even counterproductive, in the constituencies. 'You know, the best thing I could have done on May 11, when the election was called, would have been to push off for a month's holiday somewhere,' he said to Catherine. 'Quite possibly on safari.' He got fed up with Catherine saying it was a 'TV election'. 'I don't know why you go on about it, Puss,' he said, looking in the hall mirror before a 'photo-opportunity' for the local news. 'All elections are TV elections. And a bloody good thing too. It means you don't have to go and talk to the voters yourself.

In fact if you do try and talk to them they're bored to death because they've heard it all already on TV.' ('Mm, that may be why,' said Catherine.)

He was surprised that he hadn't been asked to appear in more of the major broadcasts and televised press conferences, where the Lady herself had retained a tireless dominance. His personal highlight had been a *Question Time* on BBC1, where he stood in for the indisposed Home Secretary at the last moment but very much took his own line. He did a lot of smarmy joshing with Robin Day, whom he knew socially, and this irritated the Labour defence spokesman, who was fighting an uphill battle on nuclear disarmament. Nick and Rachel watched it at home. Caught on the TV screen in his own drawing room Gerald looked distinctly alien, fattened and sharpened by the studio lights. He played sulkily with his fountain pen while the other panellists were speaking. His breast-pocket handkerchief billowed upwards like the flame of a torch. He came out in favour of Europe, having as he said a house in France where he spent the summer. He said he believed there were tens of thousands of jobs available if only people would get out and look for them (cries, which he relished, of 'Shame'). Lively rudeness and childish antagonism were the point of the programme, and also its limitation. Rachel laughed in fond disparagement once or twice. Gerald's special mixture of laziness and ambition seemed to crystallize under the camera into brutal bumptiousness. A questioner from the floor, who looked like Cecil, the Barwick welly-whanger, accused him of being too rich to care about ordinary people; and while Gerald boomingly deplored the statement you could see it sinking and settling in his flushed features as a kind of acclaim.

When it came to canvassing in Barwick, Gerald felt there was less need than ever to put oneself out. He pooh-poohed the polls. All the Northamptonshire seats were Tory strongholds, even Corby, with its closed-down steelworks. 'Even the unemployed know they're better off with us,' Gerald said. 'Anyway, they've got a computer in the office up there now, and if they can find out how to work it they'll be able to pinpoint any dodgy waverers and bombard them with stuff.' 'What?' Catherine wanted to know. 'Well, pictures of me!' said Gerald. Nick wondered if his cavalier tone was a way of preparing for possible defeat. In the final week there was something called Wobbly Thursday, when everyone at Central Office panicked. The polls showed Labour barging ahead. Toby remarked that his father seemed very unconcerned. 'One has merely to cultivate,' replied Gerald, 'the quality that M. Mitterrand has attributed to the Prime Minister, and which he sees as the supreme political virtue.'

'Oh yes, what's that?' said Toby.

'Indifference,' said Gerald, almost inaudibly.

'Right . . .' said Toby; and then, with a certain canny persistence, 'But I thought she was climbing up the wall.'

'Climbing up the wall, nonsense.'

'It's like the adverb game,' said Catherine. 'Task: *Climb up the wall*. Manner: *Indifferently*.' At which Gerald went off with a pitying smile to correct his diary.

At the office Nick looked through the mail and dictated a couple of letters to Melanie. In Wani's absence he'd grown fond of dictating, and found himself able to improvise long supple sentences rich in suggestion and syntactic shock, rather as the older Henry James, pacing and declaiming to a typist, had produced his most difficult novels. Melanie, who was used to Wani's costive memos, and even to dressing up the gist of a letter in her own words, stuck out her tongue with concentration as she took down Nick's old-fashioned periods and perplexing semicolons. Today he was answering a couple of rich American queens who had a film-production company per-

haps as fanciful, as nominal, as Ogee was, and who were showing interest in the *Spoils of Poynton* project – though with certain strong reservations about the plot. They felt that it needed
an injection of sex – smooching and action as Lord Ouradi
had put it. The queens themselves sounded rather like porn
actors, being called Treat Rush and Brad Craft. 'Dear Treat and
Brad,' Nick began: 'It was with no small interest that we read
your newest proposals comma with their comma to us comma
so very open brackets indeed comma so startlingly close brackets novel vision of the open quotes sex-life close quotes of
italics capital S Spoils *semicolon*—'

A small commotion at the door, Simon looking up, going
over, Melanie setting down her pad. A crop-headed black girl,
like a busty little boy, and a skinny white woman with her . . .
it was usually a mistake, or they were market kids trotting
round cheap Walkmans, cheap CDs. No one much, sad to say,
arrived by design at the Ogee office. Melanie came back. 'Oh,
Nick, it's a, um, Rosemary Charles to see you. Sorry . . .'
Melanie twitched with her own snobbery, part apology, part
reproach – she stood in the way, box-shouldered, high-heeled,
so that Nick leant back in his chair to look round her, down
the length of the office, and with a view of the two words
Rosemary Charles bobbing on the air, weightless signifiers,
that took on, over several strange seconds, their own darkness
and gravity. He stood up and went towards her, her and the
other woman, who seemed to be here as a witness of his
confusion. It was a momentary vertigo, a railing withdrawn.
He gave them a smile that was welcoming and showed a
proper unfrivolous regard for the occasion, and well . . . he was
afraid he knew why they'd come, more or less. He felt something like guilt showed in his pretence that he didn't. He
grasped Rosemary's hand and looked at her with allowable
pleasure and curiosity – she was still coming clear to him, from
four years back, when she was pretty and fluffy and her eyes

were sly: and now she was beautiful, revealed, the drizzle silvering the fuzz of her crown, her jaw forward in the tense half-smile of surprise that her brother had had when he'd called for Nick one morning, unannounced, and changed his life.

'Yes, hello,' she said, with a hint of hostility, perhaps just the hard note of the resolve that had brought her here. Of course she was looking for him too, down this four-year tunnel: how he used to be and how he'd changed. 'This is Gemma.'

'Hi,' said Nick warmly. 'Nick.'

'I hope you don't mind,' said Rosemary. 'We went to your house. The woman there told us where you were.'

'It's wonderful to see you!' said Nick, and saw the phrase register with them like some expected annoyance. They had something dreadful about them, with their undeclared purpose and their look of supporting each other for some much bigger challenge than Nick was ever going to offer them. 'Come in, come in.'

Gemma peered round the room. 'Is there somewhere private where we could talk?' she said. She was Yorkshire, older, blue-eyed, hair dyed black, black T-shirt and black jeans and Doc Martens.

'Of course,' said Nick. 'Why don't you come upstairs.'

He took them out and in again and up to the flat, with a responsible smile that threatened to warp into a smirk, as if he was proud of this kitsch apartment and its possible effect on the two women. He saw it all with fresh eyes himself. They sat down in the 'Georgian-revival'-revival library.

'Look at all these books . . .' said Gemma.

On the low table all the papers were laid out, as in the reading room of a club. CHUCK HER OUT, begged the *Mirror*. THREE TIMES A LADY, bawled the *Sun*.

Rosemary said, 'It's about Leo.'

'Well, I thought . . .'

She looked down, she wasn't settled in the room, on the sofa's edge; then she stared at him for a second or two. She said, 'Well, you know, my brother died, three weeks ago.' Nick listened to the words, and heard how the West Indian colour and exactness in her tone claimed it as a private thing. It had been one of Leo's tones too: the cockney for defence, the Jamaican crackle and burn for pleasure, just sometimes, rare and beautiful like his black blush.

'Nearly four weeks now, pet,' said Gemma, with her own note of bleak solidarity. 'Yes, May the sixteenth.' She looked at Nick as though the extra days made him more culpable, or useless.

'I'm so sorry,' Nick said.

'We're trying to contact all his friends.'

'Well, because, you know . . .' said Gemma.

'All his lovers,' said Rosemary firmly. Nick remembered that she was, or had been, a doctors' receptionist; she was used to the facts. She unzipped her shoulder bag and delved into it. He found it screened them both, this angular attention to business – he was flinching at the frighteningly solemn thing she had just told him, and she twitched too at the power of her words, even if (as he thought he saw) they had a certain softness or drabness for her now from use, from their assertion of something that was shifting day by day from the new into the known. He said, with a sense of good manners that took him back to their long-ago meeting,

'How is your mother?'

'OK,' said Rosemary. 'OK . . .'

'She has her faith,' said Gemma.

'She's got the church,' said Nick; 'and she's also got you.'

'Well . . .' said Rosemary. 'Yes, she has.'

The first thing she passed him was a small cream-coloured envelope addressed to Leo in green capitals. He felt he knew it and he didn't know it, like a letter found in an old book. It had a postmark of August 2, 1983. She nodded, and he opened it, while they watched him; it was like learning a new game and having to be a good sport as he lost. He unfolded a little letter in his own best handwriting, and the photo slipped out into his lap. 'That's how we knew where to find you,' Rosemary said. He had sent it in the blank envelope to *Gay Times*, doubting how it could survive, how his own wish could take on form and direction, and someone there with a green biro had sent it on – he was seeing the history of his action, and seeing it as Leo himself had seen it, but distant and complete. He picked up the photo with the guarded curiosity he had for his earlier self. It was an Oxford picture, a passport-size square cut out from a larger group: the face of a boy at a party who somehow confides his secret to the camera. He only glanced at what he'd written, on the Feddens' embossed letter-head – the small size, meant for social thank-yous, because he hadn't had much to say. The writing itself looked quaint and studied, though he remembered Leo had praised it: 'Hello!' he'd begun, since of course he hadn't yet known Leo's name. The cross-stroke of the H curled back under the uprights like a dog's tail. He saw he'd mentioned Bruckner, Henry James, all his Interests – very artlessly, but it hadn't mattered, and indeed they had never been mentioned again, when the two of them were together. At the top there was Leo's annotation in pencil: *Pretty. Rich? Too young?* This had been struck through later by a firm red tick.

Nick folded it away and peeped at the two women. It was Gemma's presence, the stranger in the room, that brought it home to him; for a minute she seemed like the fact of the death itself. She didn't know him, but she knew about the letter, the affair, the tender young Nick of four years ago, and his shyness and resentment went for nothing in the new moral atmosphere, like that of a hospital, where everything was found out and fears were justified as diagnoses. He said, 'I wish I'd seen him again.'

'He didn't want people seeing him,' said Rosemary. 'Not later on.'

'Right . . .' said Nick.

'You know how vain he was!' – it was a little test for her grief, an indulgent gibe with a twist of true vexation, at Leo's troublesomeness, alive or dead.

'Yes,' said Nick, picturing him wearing her shirt. And wondering if the man's shirt she had on now was one of his.

'He always had to look his best.'

'He always looked beautiful,' said Nick, and the exaggeration released his feelings suddenly. He tried to smile but felt the corners of his mouth pulled downwards. He mastered himself with a rough sigh and said, 'Of course I hadn't seen him for a couple of years.'

'OK . . .' said Rosemary thoughtfully. 'You know we never knew who he was seeing.'

'No,' said Gemma.

'You and old Pete were the only ones who got asked to the house. Until Bradley, of course.'

'I don't know about Bradley,' said Nick.

'My brother shared a flat with him,' said Rosemary. 'You knew he moved out.'

'Well, I knew he wanted to. That was about the time he . . . I'm not sure what happened. We stopped seeing each other.' He couldn't say the usual accusing phrase *he dumped me*, it was petty and nearly meaningless in the face of his death. 'I think I thought he was seeing someone else.' Though this itself wasn't the whole truth: it was the painful story he'd told himself at the time, to screen a glimpse he'd had of a much worse story, that Leo was ill. But Bradley had been there. He sounded like a square-shouldered practical man, not a twit like Nick.

'Bradley's not well, is he?' said Gemma.

'You knew old Pete died . . .' said Rosemary.

'Yes, I did,' said Nick, and cleared his throat.

'Anyway, you're all right, pet,' said Gemma.

'Yes, I'm all right,' said Nick. 'I'm fine.' They looked at him like police officers awaiting a confession or change of heart. 'I was lucky. And then I was . . . careful.' He put the letter on the table, and stood up. 'Would you like some coffee? Can I get you anything?' Gemma and Rosemary pondered this and for a moment seemed reluctant to accept.

In the kitchen he gazed out of the window as the kettle boiled. The rain fell thin and silvery against the dark bushes of the garden and the brick backs of the houses in the next street. He gazed at the familiar but unknown windows. In a bright drawing room a maid was hoovering. At the edge of hearing an ambulance wailed. Then the kettle throbbed and clicked off.

He took the coffee tray through. 'This is so sad,' he said. He had always thought of this as a slight word, but its effect now was larger than mere tactful understatement. It seemed to surround the awful fact with a shadowing of foreknowledge and thus of acceptance.

Rosemary raised her eyebrows and pursed her lips. There was something stubborn about her, and Nick thought perhaps it was only a brave hard form of shyness, unlike his own shyness, which ran off into flattery and evasion. She said, 'So you met Leo through a lonely hearts?'

'Yes, that's right,' said Nick, since she obviously knew this. He had never been sure if it was a shameful or a witty way to meet someone. He didn't know what the women would think either (Gemma gave him a sighing smile). 'It was such a wonderful piece of luck he chose me,' he said.

'Right . . .' said Rosemary, with a look of sisterly sarcasm;

which maybe wasn't that, but a hint that he shouldn't keep boasting about his luck.

'I mean he had hundreds of replies.'

'Well, he had a lot.' She reached into her bag again, and brought out a bundle of letters, pinched in a thick rubber band.

'Oh,' said Nick.

She pulled off the rubber band and rolled it back over her hand. For a moment he was at the doctor's – or the doctor was visiting him, with the bundled case notes of all her calls. Both brother and sister were orderly and discreet. 'I thought some of them might mean something to you.'

'Oh, I don't know.'

'So that we can tell them.'

'What did he do?' said Gemma. 'He went out and tried them all?'

Rosemary sorted the letters into two piles. 'I don't want to go chasing people up if they're dead,' she said.

'That's the thing!' said Gemma.

'I don't expect I'll know anyone,' said Nick. 'It's very unlikely . . .' It was all too bleakly businesslike for him – he'd only just heard the news.

The funny thing was that all the envelopes were addressed in the same hand, in green or sometimes purple capitals. It was like one crazed adorer laying siege to Leo. The name came up at him relentlessly off the sheaf of letters. 'It must have looked odd, these arriving all the time,' he said. A lot of them had the special-issue army stamps of that summer.

'He told us it was all to do with some cycling thing, a cycling club,' said Rosemary.

'His bike was his first love,' said Nick, unsure if this was merely a quip or the painful truth. 'It was clever of him.'

'These ones I think he didn't see. They've got a cross on.'

'There's even a woman wrote to him,' said Gemma.

So Nick started going through the letters, knowing it was pointless, but trapped by the need to honour or humour Rosemary. He saw her as a stickler for procedure, however unwelcome. He didn't need to read them in detail, but the first two or three were eerily interesting – as the private efforts of his unknown rivals. He concealed his interest behind a dull pout of consideration, and slow shakes of the head. The terms of the ad were still clear to him, and the broad-minded age-range, '18 to 40'. 'Hi there!' wrote Sandy from Enfield, 'I'm early 40s, but saw that little old ad of yours and thought I'd write in anyway! I'm in the crazy world of stationery!' A snap of a solidly built man of fifty was attached to the page with a pink paper clip. Leo had written, *House/Car. Age?* And then, presumably after he'd seen him, *Too inexperienced.* Glenn, 'late 20s', from Barons Court, was a travel agent, and sent a Polaroid of himself in swimming trunks in his flat. He said, 'I love to party! And sexpecially in bed! (Or on the floor! Or half-way up a ladder!! Whoops – !)' *Too much?* wondered Leo, before making the discovery: *Invisible dick.* 'Dear Friend,' wrote serious-looking black Ambrose from Forest Hill, 'I like the sound of you. I think we have some love to share.' The exclamation marks, which gave the other letters their air of inane self-consciousness, were resisted by Ambrose until his final 'Peace!' Nick liked the look of him, but Leo had written, *Bottom. Boring.* Nick made a stealthy attempt to remember the address.

When he'd read a letter he passed it back to Rosemary, who put it face down on the table, by the coffee pot. The sense of a game ebbed very quickly with his lack of success. The fact was these were all men who'd wanted his boyfriend, who'd applied for what Nick had gone on to get. Some of them were pushy and explicit, but there was always the vulnerable note of courtship: they were asking an unknown man to like them, or want them, or find them equal to their self-descriptions. He recognized one of the men from his photo and murmured, 'Ah . . . !' but then let it go with a shrug and a throat-clearing. It was a Spanish guy who'd turned up everywhere, who'd been a nice dark thread in the pattern of Nick's early gym days and bar nights, almost an emblem of the scene for him, its routine and compulsion, and he knew he must be dead – he'd seen him a year ago at the Ponds, defying his own fear and others' fear of him. Javier, he was called. He was thirty-four. He worked for a building society, and lived in West Hampstead. The mere facts in his letter of seduction had the air of an obituary.

Nick stopped and drank some coffee. 'Was he ill for a long time?' he asked.

'He had pneumonia last November, he nearly died; but he came through it. Then things got, well, a lot worse in the spring. He was in hospital for about ten days at the end.'

'He went blind, didn't he,' said Gemma, in the way people clumsily handle and offer facts which they can neither accept nor forget.

'Poor Leo,' said Nick. Relief at not having witnessed this was mixed with regret at not having been called on to do so.

'Did you bring the photos?' said Gemma.

'If you want to see . . .' said Rosemary, after a pause.

'I don't know,' said Nick, embarrassed. It was a challenge; and then he felt powerless in the flow of the moment, as he had on his first date with Leo, he met it as something that was going to happen, and took the Kodak wallet. He looked at a couple of the pictures and then handed them back.

'You can have one if you like,' said Rosemary.

'No,' said Nick; 'thank you.'

He sat, rather hard-faced, over his coffee.

After a bit Gemma said, 'This is proper coffee, isn't it.'

'Oh . . . !' said Nick, 'do you like it. It's Kenyan Rich, medium roast . . . It comes from Myers' in Kensington

Church Street. They import their own. One pays more, but I think it's worth it.'

'Mm, it's lovely and rich,' said Gemma.

'I'd rather not look at the other letters now,' Nick said.

Rosemary nodded. 'OK,' she said, as if skimming forward for another appointment, a cancellation. 'I can leave them with you . . . ?'

'No, please don't,' said Nick. He felt he was being pressed very hard very fast, as in some experiment on his emotions.

Gemma went to the lavatory – she murmured the directions to herself as she tried the door, and then slipped in as if she'd met a friend. There was silence for a while between Nick and Rosemary. The extremity of events excused anything, of course, but her hardness towards him was another shock to get used to: it added puzzlingly to the misery of the day. She was his lover's sister, and he thought of her naturally as a friend, and with spontaneous fondness and fresh sympathy on top of mere politeness. But it seemed it didn't work the other way round. He smiled tentatively. There was such a physical likeness now that he might have been asking Leo himself to be nice to him, after some row. But she'd decided against the note of tenderness, even towards Leo himself.

'So you hadn't seen him for a year or two?' she said.

'That's right . . .'

She looked up at him warily, as though starting to concede his own, homosexual claim on her brother and wondering where such a shift might lead her. 'Did you miss him?' she said.

'Yes . . . I did. I certainly did.'

'Do you remember the last time you saw him?'

'Well, yes,' said Nick, and stared at the floor. The questions were sentimental, but the manner was detached, almost bored. 'It was all very difficult.'

She said, 'He hadn't made a will.'

'Oh, well . . . he was so young!' said Nick, frowning because he found himself on the edge of tears again, at the thought that she was going to offer him something of Leo's – of course she was cold because she found it all so difficult herself.

'We had him cremated,' Rosemary said. 'I think it's what he would have wanted, though we didn't ask him. We didn't like to.'

'Hm,' said Nick, and found he was crying anyway.

When Gemma came back she said, 'You must see the toilet.' Rosemary gave a loyal but repressive smile. 'Or is that trick photography?'

'Oh . . . !' said Nick. 'No . . . no, it's real, I'm afraid.' He was glad of the absurd change of subject.

'There's a picture of him dancing with Maggie!'

It was one of the photos from the Silver Wedding, Nick red-faced and staring, the Prime Minister with a look of caution he hadn't been aware of at the time. He wasn't sure Gemma would get the special self-irony of the lavatory gallery. It was something he'd learnt from his public-school friends. 'Do you know her, then?' she said.

'No, no,' said Nick, 'I just got drunk at a party . . .' as if it could happen to anyone.

'Go on, I bet you voted for her, didn't you?' Gemma wanted to know.

'I did not,' said Nick, quite sternly. Rosemary showed no interest in this, and he said, 'I remember I promised to tell your mother if I ever met her.'

'Oh . . . ?'

He smiled apprehensively. 'I mean, how has she coped with all this?'

'You remember what she's like,' said Rosemary.

'I'll write to her,' said Nick. 'Or I could drive over and see her.' He pictured her at home with her pamphlets and her hat on the chair. He had a sense of his charm not having worked on her years ago and was ready to do something now to make good. 'I'm sure she's been wonderful.'

Rosemary gave him a pinched look, and as she stood up and collected her things she seemed to decide to say, 'That's what you said before, wasn't it? When you came to see us?'

'What . . . ?'

'Leo told us, you said we were wonderful.'

'Did I?' said Nick, who remembered it painfully. 'Well, that's not such a bad thing to be.' He paused, unsure if he'd been accused of something. He felt there was a mood of imminent blame, for everything that had happened: they had hoped to pin it on him, and had failed, and were somehow more annoyed with him as a result. 'Of course, she didn't know, did she, that Leo was gay? She was talking about getting him to the altar.'

'Well, he's been to the altar now,' said Rosemary with a harsh little laugh, as though it was her mother's fault. 'Almost, anyway.'

'It's a terrible way to find out,' said Nick.

'She doesn't accept it.'

'She doesn't accept the death . . .'

'She doesn't accept he was gay. It's a *mortal sin*, you see,' said Rosemary, and now the Jamaican stress was satirical. 'And her son was no sinner.'

'Yes, I've never understood about sin,' said Nick, in a tone they didn't catch.

'Oh, the mortal ones are the worst,' said Gemma.

'So she doesn't think AIDS is a punishment, at least.'

'No, it can be,' said Rosemary. 'But Leo got it off a toilet seat at the office, which is full of godless socialists, of course.'

'Or a sandwich,' prompted Gemma.

There was something very unseemly in their mockery. Nick tried to imagine the house surprised by guilt and blame, the helpless harshness of the bereaved . . . he didn't know.

Rosemary said, 'She's got him back at the house.'

'How do you mean?'

'She's got the ashes in a jar, on the mantelpiece.'

'Oh!' Nick was so disturbed by this that he said, rather drolly, 'Yes, I remember, there's a shelf, isn't there, over the gas fire, with figures of Jesus and Mary and so on—'

'There's Jesus, and the Virgin Mary, and St Antony of Padua . . . and Leo.'

'Well, he's in very good company!' said Nick.

'I know,' said Gemma, shaking her head and laughing grimly. 'I can't stand it, I can't go in there!'

'She says she likes to feel he's still there.'

Nick shivered but said, 'I suppose you can't begrudge her her fantasies, can you, when she's lost her son.'

'They don't really help, though,' said Rosemary.

'Well, they don't help us, pet, do they?' said Gemma, and rubbed Rosemary's back vigorously.

Rosemary's eyes were hooded for a moment, just like her mother's, with the family stubbornness. She said, 'She won't accept it about him, and she won't accept it about us.' And then almost at once she shouldered her bag to go.

Nick blushed at his slowness, and then was mortified that they might think he was blushing about them.

When the women had gone, he went back upstairs, but in the remorseless glare of the news, so that the flat looked even more tawdry and pretentious. He was puzzled to think he had spent so much time in it so happily and conceitedly. The pelmets and mirrors, the spotlights and blinds, seemed rich in criticism. It was what you did if you had millions but no particular taste: you made your private space like a swanky hotel; just as such hotels flattered their customers by being vulgar simulacra of lavish private homes. A year ago it had at least the glamour of newness. Now it bore signs of occupation by a rich boy who had lost the knack of looking after himself. The piping on the sofa cushions was rubbed through where Wani had sprawled incessantly in front of the video. The crimson damask was blotted with his own and other boys' fluids. He wondered if Gemma had noticed as she sat there, making her inanely upsetting remarks. He wasn't letting her in here again, in her black boots. Nick felt furious with Wani for fucking up the cushions. The Georgian desk was marked with drink stains and razor etchings that even the optimistic Don Guest would have found it hard to disguise. 'That's beyond cosmetic repair, old boy,' Don would say. Nick fingered at the little abrasions and found himself gasping and whooping with grief.

He sat on the sofa and started reading the *Telegraph*, as if it was known to be a good thing to do. He was sick of the election, but excited to think it was happening today. There was something primitive and festive about it. He heard Rosemary saying, 'Well, he died, you know . . .' or 'Well, you know, he died . . .' in recurrent, almost overlapping runs and pounces – his heart thumped at the dull detonation of the phrase. He was horrified by the thought of his ashes in the house, and kept picturing them, in an unlikely rococo urn. The last photo she had shown him was terrible: a Leo with his life behind him. Nick remembered making jokes, early on, in the first unguarded liberty of a first affair, about their shared old age, Leo being sixty when Nick was fifty. And there he was already; or he'd been sixty for a week before he died. He was in bed, in a sky-blue hospital gown; his face was hard to read, since AIDS had taken it and written its message of terror and exhaustion on it; against which Leo seemed frailly to assert his own character in a doubtful half smile. His vanity had become a kind of fear, that he would frighten the people he smiled at. It was the loneliest thing Nick had ever seen.

He thought he should write a letter and sat down at the desk. He felt a need to console Leo's mother, or to put himself right with her. Some deep convolution of feelings about his own mother, as the one person who really suffered for his homosexuality, made him see Mrs Charles as a figure to be appeased as well as comforted. 'Dear Mrs Charles,' he wrote, 'I was so terribly sorry to learn about Leo's death': there, it existed, he'd hesitated, but written it, and it couldn't be unwritten. He had a feeling, an anxious refinement of tact, that he shouldn't actually mention the death. 'Your sad news,' 'recent sad events' . . . : 'Leo's death' was brutal. Then he worried that 'I was so terribly sorry' might sound like gush to her, like calling her wonderful. He knew his own forms of truth could look like insincerity to others. He was frightened of her, as a grieving woman, and uncertain what feelings to attribute to her. It seemed she had taken it all in her own way, perhaps even with a touch of zealous cheerfulness. He could see her being impressed by his educated form of words and best handwriting. Then he saw her looking mistrustfully at what he'd written. He felt the limits of his connoisseurship of tone. It was what he was working on, and yet . . . He stared out of the window, and after a minute found Henry James's phrase about the death of Poe peering back at him. What was it? *The extremity of personal absence had just overtaken him.* The words, which once sounded arch and even facetious, were suddenly terrible to him, capacious, wise, and hard. He understood for the first time that they'd been written by someone whose life had been walked through, time and again, by death. And then he saw himself, in six months' time perhaps, sitting down to write a similar letter to the denizens of Lowndes Square.

14

When he got back to Kensington Park Gardens he didn't tell Catherine about Leo straight away. To himself he seemed to gleam with his news, to be both the pale bereaved and the otherworldly messenger. He found himself lengthening his natural sighs and stares to provoke a question. But after ten minutes he accepted that she hadn't noticed. She was slumped in an armchair, with newspapers all around her, and half-empty glasses of water and mugs of tea on the table beside her. He looked down on her from behind, and she seemed as small and passive as a sick child. She looked up and said, with an effort at brightness, 'Oh, Nick, it's *Election Special* after the news,' as though it had taken great effort to find this out, as though it was itself a piece of good news.

'OK, darling,' said Nick. 'Great, we'll watch that.' He gazed round the room, feeling for the precedence, the protocol of their relative afflictions. 'Um . . . yes . . . OK!' It didn't seem right to land her with the news of a death. He felt that like all news it had its own momentum, and it would somehow go stale and unsayable if it was left too long.

He went up to his room with a slight mental stoop from the burden of Catherine's condition. It was hard work living with someone so helpless and negative, and much worse if you'd known them critical and funny. Well, sometimes, perhaps, it made your own problems look light; at others it amplified them, by a troubling sympathetic gloom. He had borrowed a book of Rachel's by Dr Edelman, who was treating Catherine, *A Path Through the Mountains: Clinical Responses to Manic Depression*. He had groaned over Dr Edelman's style, and corrected his grammar to protect himself from a superstitious fear that the book awoke in him: of finding the symptoms in himself, now he knew what they were. They certainly seemed to be present in all the more volatile, the more irascible, or oddly lethargic people he knew.

The book had helpful facts in it, but it left Nick with an imaginative uncertainty, as to where Catherine was when he looked at her and spoke to her: not in the black and shiny place of her old depressions, but in some other unfeatured place, policed by Dr Edelman's heavy new dosage of lithium. She lacked the energy and motivation to describe it herself. She said she couldn't concentrate on a book, or even an article. Sometimes she acted in her quick pert way, but it was a reflex: she observed it herself with bewilderment and a kind of longing. Mostly she sat and waited, but without any colour of expectation. Nick found himself talking with awful brightness of purpose, as if to someone old and deaf; and it was more awful because she didn't find it condescending.

There were various phone calls that evening. Nick's mother rang and talked excitedly about the election, which she seized on as a chance to share in Nick's London life. He was cool and humourless with her, and saw himself, as so often, almost blaming her for not knowing the important thing he was incapable of telling her. She had never heard of Leo, and he thought if he did try to tell her they would work each other up into a state of mutual resentment at the fact. She gave an account of Gerald's performance on the local radio, as if Nick needed to hear praise of him. 'He said we don't want these, you know, lesbian workshops,' she said, not unaware of her own bravery in using the word. Then Gerald himself was on the other line, and she rang off as if she'd been caught. 'All well?' said Gerald airily, obviously wanting to talk about himself. It was the long evening's wait for the results, when his confidence was the most stretched, and he was fishing for sympathy, almost as though he'd lost. 'How did your speech go?' said Nick. 'Went down like dinner,' Gerald said. 'Which is more than I can say for dinner itself – what? God these provincial hotels.' Nick felt a punitive urge to make Gerald listen to his problem, since he'd met Leo and had even been gingerly in favour of him; but he knew he wouldn't get his attention, it was the wrong moment, the wrong week, and actually the wrong death.

Elena had prepared some cannelloni, which Nick and Catherine ate in the kitchen, under the family gallery of photographs and cartoons; this had now spread over the pantry door and down the other side, where Marc's caricature of Gerald had pride of place. Gerald had still not received the accolade of a *Spitting Image* puppet in his likeness, but it was one of his main hopes for the new Parliament. Catherine stared at her food as she worked through it, like someone performing a meaningless task as a punishment, and Nick found himself contrasting her to her eager six-year-old self, with only half her big teeth, and a grin of excitement so intense it was almost painful; and to a feature from *Harper's* ten years later, where rich people's children modelled evening clothes, and white gloves covered the first scars on her arms. Really, though, it was Gerald's wall, and his wife and children appeared as decorative adjuncts to the hero's life, unfolding in a sequence of handshakes with the famous. The Gorbachev was the latest trophy, not a handshake, but a moment of conversation, the Soviet leader's smile just hinting at the tedium of hearing English puns explained by an interpreter. Nick said, 'Can you remember when that picture of you was taken?' and Catherine said, 'No, I can't. I can only remember the picture.' She glanced up over her shoulder with an apologetic cringe. It was as if all the pictures might come bashing down about her ears.

He said, 'Mum says there's a cartoon of Gerald in the *Northants Standard*; she's sending it down for possible inclusion.'

'Oh . . .' said Catherine. She looked at him steadily. 'I don't know about cartoons.'

'You love satire, darling, especially if it's of Gerald.'

'I know. Just imagine if people did look like that, though. Hydrocephalous is the word. Monstrous teeth of Gerald . . .' and her hand shook. She seemed startled to recall these words.

Afterwards they went up to the drawing room, and Nick, suddenly shaky too, poured himself a large Scotch. They sat side by side on the sofa, in the heavy but unselfconscious silence she generated. He remembered the one time Leo had come to this room, and surprised him, moved him, and slightly rattled him by playing Mozart on the piano. They'd both had a glass of whisky then, the only time he'd known Leo to drink. He caught the beautiful rawness of those days again, the life of instinct opening in front of him, the pleasure of the streets and London itself unfolding in the autumn chill; everything tingling with newness and risk, glitter of frost and glow of body heat, the shock of finding and holding what he wanted among millions of strangers. His sense of the scandalous originality of making love to a man had faded week by week into the commonplace triumph of a love affair. He saw Leo crossing this room, the scene brilliant and dwindling, as if watched in a convex mirror. It was the night he had stepped warily, with many ironic looks, into Nick's deeper fantasy of possession: his lover in his house, Nick owning them both by right of taste and longing.

Now the rain had stopped, and the sky brightened a little just as the dusk was falling. Pale neutral light stretched in through the front windows, seemed to search and fail and then probe again. Nick formulated the thing, 'I had some terribly sad news today, I heard that Leo's died, you remember . . .'; but it stayed shut in his head, like a difficult confession.

He listened to the birdsong from the gardens, with a more analytical ear than usual for the notes of warning and protest and ruffled submission. The long neutral light grew more tender and burning as it touched the gilt handles of the fire irons and the white-marble vines beneath the mantelpiece. Then it reached the turned legs of an old wooden chair and made them glow with new and unsuspected presence, like little people, skittle-people, with bellies and collars and Punchinello hats, shining fiercely and stoically with their one truth, that they would last for centuries longer than the young live people who were looking at them.

On the nine o'clock news they were talking already about a Tory landslide. Nick had another huge whisky, and felt a familiar relief begin to smooth down the bleak edges of the day. He felt he was missing the regard that was due to the bereaved, the indulgence, like a special sad prize, that was given to boys at school when the news came through. He even wondered for a while about a toot, but he knew he didn't want the irrelevant high spirits of coke. Drink showed more respect for the night, and seemed ready to mediate, for three or four hours, between the demands of grief and current affairs.

The election unrolled at its own unsatisfactory tempo. For ages the pundits sat in the studio, waiting for results to process and pronounce on. The tedium of the four long weeks of the election reached its purest form in their attempts to summarize and predict. Various old maxims and traditions were rehearsed, with a consoling effect of pantomime. Reporters were seen, perched in a dozen town halls with nothing as yet to report. Below them, out of focus, the tellers at their long tables were racing to finish, so that another game seemed to flourish on the back of the main contest. They were going to show the Barwick declaration later on, and for five seconds Nick saw the council room in the Market Hall and the not quite familiar figures at work; then there was a film clip showing the main candidates canvassing. Gerald's style was one of crisp confidence, striding through the square with glancing 'Good morning's, like a boss coming into an office, and not listening to anything that was being said. The inexperienced Alliance woman, by contrast, got snagged in well-meaning debate with Tracey Weeks, who she was slow to realize, and on camera was reluctant to acknowledge, wasn't all there. It was sad that the Barwick electorate should be exemplified to the nation by old Tracey; Nick distanced himself from his home town with a cagey laugh, though he was very curious to see it on TV. It had a steady provincial look to it, surprised but not overwhelmed to have been noticed by the outside world. It wasn't exactly the place he knew.

Later Nick was downstairs when Catherine called out, 'It's Polly Thing!' and he rushed back up and leant over the back of the sofa – the returning officer was already speaking. Polly Tompkins was standing for Pershore, traditionally Tory but with a strong SDP vote in '83; he couldn't be sure of getting in, and Gerald, who admired Polly, warned that his age might tell against him. Nick had read an article about young candidates – of the hundred and fifty or so under thirty the dry expectation was that half a dozen would get elected. Standing in the middle of the stage, fat and hot in a double-breasted suit, Polly could have passed for forty-five; he seemed camouflaged in his own elected future. Nick couldn't decide if he wanted him to win or not. It was a spectacle, and he looked at it with untroubled cruelty, like a boxing match. It would be good to see him smacked down. Nick supposed the candidates must know the result by now, since they'd been at the count; but perhaps not, if it was very close. Now Polly was staring out into the challenge of the lights, the invisible millions who suddenly had their eyes on him. The tiny Labour vote was announced, and he gave a heartless wince of commiseration. And now his own name was being said, 'Tompkins, Paul Frederick Gervase' – ('Conservative' in murmured parenthesis) – 'seventeen thousand, two hundred and thirty-eight votes': the word *votes* shouted over a roar of triumph so quick that Polly himself seemed not to have worked it out – there was a moment's blankness in his face, and then you saw him give in to the roar and grin like a boy and raise two fists in the air – he was monstrous, Catherine said 'God . . .' in her dullest tone, but Nick felt his grin turn wistful with unexpected pleasure as the returning officer fought on against the noise, 'And I therefore declare the said Paul Frederick Gervase Tompkins duly elected . . .' 'Paul Tompkins,' said the reporter briskly, showing in his equable tone that he hadn't known Polly as the nightmare queen of the Worcester MCR, 'only twenty-eight years old . . .' as Polly shook hands crushingly with the losers, and then stepped backwards, peered round with a kind of cunning confusion, using the crowd's indulgence, his first thrill of popularity, and stretched out an arm to call a woman forward from the back of the stage. She strode up to him, nudged against him, their fingers fumbled together, and then he jerked their hands upwards in the air. 'A great night for Paul Tompkins's wife, too,' said the commentator: 'only married last month – Morgan Stevens, one of the guiding lights at Conservative Central Office – I know she's been working tirelessly behind the scenes on this campaign . . .' Polly carried on shaking their awkwardly linked fists above their heads, his lapel dragged up against his jowls, and something he couldn't disguise in his face, something deeper than scorn, the madness of self-belief. It was already time for him to make a speech, but he milked the acclaim crudely – he looked a bit of a buffoon. He stepped forward, still loosely holding Morgan's hand, and then dodged back and kissed her, not wedding-style, but as one might kiss an aunt. He had hardly started to speak when the viewers were abruptly returned to the studio.

'Is Morgan really a woman?' said Catherine.

'Very fair question,' said Nick; 'but I think so.'

'She's got a man's name.'

'Well, there was Morgan Le Fay, wasn't there, the famous witch.'

'Was there?'

'Anyway, she's married to a man called Polly, so it's probably all right.'

Now the results were coming in too fast to be sure of individual notice. The talk of a landslide took shape in vertiginous diagrams. 'I thought it was a landslide last time,' said Catherine. 'We had that book about it.'

'Yes, it was,' said Nick.

She stared at the screen, where the famous swingometer was virtually at rest. 'But nothing's changing,' she said. 'I mean there's two more Labour seats. That's not a landslide.'

'Oh, I see,' said Nick.

'I mean a landslide's a disaster, it changes everything.'

'So you thought . . .' Nick thought he saw that Catherine, in her inattentive but literal way, had convinced herself it was a Labour landslide. 'It's a dead metaphor, darling. It just means a crushing victory.'

'Oh god,' said Catherine, almost tearfully.

'I mean, the land did slide once, as we all know. And it looks very much as though it's going to stay slidden.'

Barwick came up half an hour later. There was a buzz in the studio, as if they knew something was about to happen. Nick and Catherine sat forward on the sofa. 'Welcome to Barwick,' said the bearded young reporter: 'where we're in the splendid Market Hall built by Sir Christopher Wren.' ('No, you are *not*,' said Nick.) 'We're expecting the declaration in the next minute. Barwick of course held by Gerald Fedden since the last election – a minister in the Home Office – something of a maverick, but could be looking at a Cabinet post in the next government – he had a majority of over eight thousand in '83, but we're expecting to see a big increase in the Alliance vote here – Muriel Day, a very popular figure locally . . .' The camera found the two rivals, each in discussion with their people, Gerald chaffing as if nothing was going on, Muriel Day already rehearsing the smile of a good loser. The Labour man, perhaps under a delusion about the outcome, was running over a three-page speech.

Nick flopped back in the sofa with a laugh, to break the mood. Staring at the screen he felt awkwardly responsible, as if the place he'd come from, the very room that he'd measured and drawn as a schoolboy, was about to deliver its verdict on the room he was sitting in now. It was embarrassing, but there was nothing he could do. He watched the event quickly clarify, the intent activity was finished, the people redeployed themselves, officials were briefly in conference, and out of the toil of the day, metal boxes and rented tables, pure process without poetry, a kind of theatre emerged, so thick with precedent that it looked instinctual.

Old Arthur State was saying, extremely slowly, 'I, Arthur Henry State, being the returning officer for the parliamentary constituency of Barwick in the county of Northampton-shire . . .' and surely expanding his text with various quaint heraldic clauses, while Catherine eyed her father on the podium behind him. Nick glanced at her in profile. She had a look of exhaustion, as at an object constantly but inexplicably in her way; but a twitch of excitement too: she was powerless, but tonight there were other powers stirring. Something might happen. The Labour man was called Brown and so came first – he'd got eight thousand, three hundred and twenty-one votes ('that's more than three thousand up on last time'), and was cheered defiantly. Next was Muriel Day, and her vote too was well up on that of her predecessor, two and a half thousand up, at eleven thousand, five hundred and seven. She took the applause with a grateful but distracted smile, almost hushing her supporters to let them hear the rest – since Arthur always waited for total silence, and went back to the start of any sentence that was interrupted. It was a serious figure, and Gerald had a look Nick knew well, the condescending simper that covered a process of mental arithmetic. The suspense was made worse by the unignorable but somehow forgotten figure of Ethelred Egg ('Monster Raving Loony Party'), who'd only polled thirty-one votes but seemed to have a hall-full of supporters. He plucked off and waved his green top hat and capered about in his clown's suit. You couldn't help seeing some slight kinship between him and Gerald, whose white collar and pink tie were half hidden by a vast blue rosette with long tabs or streamers below and the breast-pocket handkerchief struggling above. 'Oh lose, lose . . .' muttered Catherine. 'Fedden,' said Arthur State, 'Gerald John' ('Conservative . . .'), and because there was a klaxon squawk he repeated it, the strange momentary levelling and exposure of the cited second name, 'eleven thousand, eight hundred and ninety-three' – so that Gerald grinned and coloured for a second, and perhaps thought he'd lost after all. The cheer that followed was a funny sound, because it had a loud 'Woo-oo' mixed in with it, at the luck of a man who had just got away with something.

Nick topped up his drink and went out onto the balcony. He rallied to the surprising chill out there. Gerald's close shave at the ballot box was a drama and an embarrassment, and it was going to be hard to know what to say when he got home. Congratulations might sound sarcastic or unduly blithe, even to Gerald. Anyway, he was in, and everything could go on as planned. His gleaming grin floated against the dark trees for a while, and then faded, as perishable as all news. Slowly the trees themselves took on shape and detail in the light from the houses and from the softly reflecting night clouds. Nick loved the gardens; when he strolled between the house and the gardens through the private gate he seemed to glance up at his own good luck, in the towering planes on one side and the white-stuccoed cliff on the other. It would be good to be out there now; but it was too dripping and cold. There were wonderful expanses of summer ahead, no need to panic.

He remembered taking Leo there, in a jitter of nerves and shadows, the night they'd finally met; and quite a few other men too, the summer before last, on the sand path behind the workmen's hut – it had been his trick, done confidently, dwindling a little in charm and danger. Something basic and unsocial about it, no giving them a drink or a shower: it was good. And perhaps it had been a secret tribute to Leo, a memory honoured and scuffed over in each careless encounter. Leo never knew how much Nick had imagined him, before he'd met him; or how the first kiss, the first feel of his body, had staggered a boy who till then had lived all in his mind. Leo wasn't imaginative: that was part of the point and the beauty of him. But he had a kind of genius, as far as Nick was concerned. That big red tick on his letter had bounced him into life.

He swilled round the whisky in his glass and shivered. There was a mood of homage and forgiveness: how could you begrudge the dead? And there was something else, a need to be forgiven himself, though he frowned the thought away. When Rosemary had asked him about the last time he'd seen her brother, he had blinked at her through the bleak little image of a parting on Oxford Street. The dense blind crowd, which could hide all kinds of intimacy in its rush, had this time made things impossible. Leo pushed away on his bike, crept through the red light and round the corner, without looking back. In fact the crowd almost hid the thing that Nick was remembering – the latest of several unhappy goodbyes not marked in

any way as the last of all. In the following weeks he'd had to
rescue that routine sequence of actions, and clarify it in the
light of what it had turned out to be. At the time it was just
an impatient escape into the traffic.

But then, far more recently, three or four months ago, on a
wet late February night, something else had happened, which
he hadn't quite thought of this morning. Wani must already
have been in Paris, and Nick had gone into the Shaftesbury on
a sudden urge to pick up, the glow in his chest and the ache in
his thighs. He went in through the little back bar, with its gas
fire and non-combatant atmosphere, where you got served
quicker. He noticed a couple of friends in his first half-sociable
push through the crowd, and took in, while he waited to be
served, the little black guy in a woolly hat, with his back to
him, talking to a middle-aged white man. He saw how his
beltless jeans stood away from his waist to give a glimpse of
blue underwear, and had a moment's sharp unexpected recall
of Leo, the double curve of his lower back and muscular
bottom. There was sadness in the likeness, but the image lay
quiet; it had more of the warmth of a blessing than the chill of
a loss. Nick was pleased at that. The pub was all potential – he
gazed busily over the counter into the main bar, which was
jostling with sexy self-regard. This little guy was much too
skinny, really, to excite him, and too odd: he had a beard that
was so bushy you could see it from behind, the black touched
with grey beside the ears. Still, Nick looked at the chap he was
talking to, caught his eye for a second, with a tiny smile of
collusion. Then instead of ordering the usual practical pint, he
asked for a rum and Coke.

He moved away with it, spoke to someone he knew, glancing off to check his own looks in one of the pub's many
mirrors, and saw the black man in profile, turning briefly,
unconsciously, to full face, and turning back again to answer
his friend. Even then, the nostalgic idea that he was like Leo

423

held off for a second or two the recognition that he was Leo. The greying beard hid the gauntness of his features, and the hat was rolled down to his eyebrows. Even after that Nick shunned the possibility, looked away, in case the man should meet his eye in the mirror with an answering slide into shock, and then glanced back, already hardened in the fiction that he hadn't recognized him. He pressed through into the other room. There was a party of French boys, there was a man he'd fancied at the Y, the whole bar was a fierce collective roar, and he edged and smiled politely through it like a sober late arrival at a wild party. His heart was thumping, and the expectant glow in his chest had become some neighbouring sensation, a clench of guilt and regret. It was simply an instinct, a reflex, that had made him turn away. A minute later he saw it could just as easily have thrown him towards Leo; but he was a coward. He was frightened of him – afraid of being rebuffed and full of grim doubts about what was happening to him. Perhaps he should go back in and check that it really was him – he was suddenly happy at the thought that it couldn't have been. He shouldered back through the crowd, sensing their vague annoyance at moving for him again; but stopped and got talking to the man from the Y, boldly but inattentively. He knew he had a bluebird tattooed on his left buttock, and he'd seen him with a sensible erection in the showers, but these cute memories seemed steadily more meaningless. He knocked back his drink in distracted gulps. Then he went downstairs to the Gents, and found, when he peeped sideways along the reeking trough, that the man had followed him; so they stood there for a bit, in a tense delay whilst other people came and went, until the man nodded towards the empty lock-up. Nick said it was too risky, felt almost annoyed that this was happening, yet curiously timid and grateful too. The man said he lived in Soho, they could go there, five minutes' walk, and Nick said OK. It was a kind of shield. Actually it was a brilliant quick success, a fantasy granted, but Nick couldn't feel it. 'We'll go out the side way,' said the man, who also gave his name, Joe. 'Oh, OK,' said Nick. They went through the back bar, Nick with his hand on Joe's broad shoulder, sticking cheerfully close to him and turning a blank gaze across the room to find the little woolly-hatted figure, utterly unknown to Joe, who had once been his lover.

15

'Oh my!' said Treat. 'Pansy salad!'

'It's really rather good,' said Nick.

Treat watched him, over his cocktail glass, to see if he was joking. 'Is it all pansies?'

'What's that?' said Brad.

'It's mostly rather butch lettuce,' said Nick. 'They just put one or two pansies on top.'

'Butch lettuce . . . !' said Treat, full of flirty reproach.

'They're token pansies,' said Nick.

'I'm going to have to try it,' said Treat.

'You should certainly have it once,' said Nick.

'What's that?' said Brad.

'Treat wants to try the pansy salad,' said Nick.

'Oh . . . oh, I see, "pansy salad": oh my!'

'I just said that,' said Treat.

Nick smiled round the restaurant, relieved to see two famous writers at one table, and a famous actress at another. Brad Craft and Treat Rush, till now mere muscular spondees of American suggestion, had turned out to be a socially hungry pair. Brad was indeed big and muscular, handsome and pleasant, if rather slow on the uptake. Treat was the talker, about Nick's height, with a shiny blond fringe that he kept in line with a pointed little finger. They had come over for Nat Hanmer's wedding, and were spending the whole of October in England ('Anything to escape the New England fall!' said

Treat). Today there was the film to talk about, but they were clearly working, with one eye always on the square beyond, at a thorough penetration of London, and were full of slapdash questions about people and titles. The point seemed to be to ask questions; they didn't bother much with the answers. They held out the threat of being easily bored. Nick hoped Gusto would amuse them. He saw Treat watching the kitchen through the blue glass wall, which turned the chef and his sweating minions into a faintly erotic cabaret of hard work.

'Do you know this guy Julius Money?' said Brad.

'Well, I've met him,' said Nick.

'Isn't that a great name? And kind of appropriate, I guess, right?'

'Oh yes,' said Nick. 'They have this huge Jacobean house in Norfolk, with a fabulous collection of paintings. Actually, I've always thought—'

'Oh, what about Pomona Brinkley!' said Treat. 'We met her. Now what's *she* all about?'

'I don't know her,' said Nick.

'She was great,' said Treat.

'Oh, yeah, we met this guy Lord John . . . *Fanshaw*?' said Brad. 'He knows all about you! He said you were the most charming man in London.'

'Yeah,' said Treat, and looked lingeringly at Nick again.

'I feel he must have been thinking of someone else,' said Nick coyly, and didn't come clean that he'd never heard of his lordship.

'You know Nat really well, right?' said Treat.

'Oh yes,' said Nick, with suaver confidence. 'We were at Oxford together. Though these days I suppose I see more of his mother than him. She's a great friend of my friend Rachel Fedden.' He watched the name make its frail bid for recognition.

'He's so sweet.'

'No, he's lovely. He's had, you know, he's had a lot of problems.'

'Yeah . . . ?' said Treat. 'It's such a shame he's not *family*.'

'Well . . .' said Nick. 'Where did you two meet him?'

'Oh, we met him at the Rosenheims' last fall, in East Hampton? Which of course is when we also met . . . Antoine.'

'And Martina,' said Brad.

'Yes, Martine,' said Nick.

'Yes, Brad loved Antoine,' said Treat. He put the straw to his lips and sucked pointedly at the reddish brown liquid.

Brad said, 'Yeah, what a lovely guy.'

'So you haven't seen him since?' Nick knew he should warn them, but didn't know how to start.

'So Nat's some kind of lord, right?' said Brad.

'Yes,' said Nick. 'He's a marquess.'

'Oh my god . . . !' said Treat under his breath.

'What, so he's Marquess . . . is it *Chirk*?'

'Chirk is the family name. His title is Marquess of Hanmer.'

'Brad . . . ? You see who's over there?'

'So what do we call his old man?' said Brad, shaking his head as he turned in his chair.

'His father's the Duke of Flintshire. I should just call him sir.'

'Treat, my god, you're right . . . it's Betsy!'

'I want *her* to be in my film,' said Treat. 'She's such a great British actress.'

'I don't know if you will meet the Duke,' Nick went on, uncertain how much pomp he was borrowing from mere use of the word. He aimed to speak of the aristocracy in a factual tone, because of his shame at his father's tally of earls. 'I've only met him once. He never leaves the Castle. You know he's a cripple.'

'You British . . .' said Treat, only half-relinquishing his childlike gaze at Betsy Tilden. She seemed to loom for him as a marvel and a dare, and Nick could see him going over to her. She was much too young for Mrs Gereth, and quite wrong for Fleda Vetch. 'You're so brutal!'

'Mm . . . ?' said Nick.

'You know, "he's a cripple" – really.'

'Oh . . .' said Nick, and blushed as if it was his lurking snobbery that had been criticized and not whatever this was. 'I'm sorry, but that's actually what the Duke calls himself. He hasn't walked since he was a boy.' He was slightly winded to be called on a point of delicacy – and one that impinged, obliquely but perceptibly, on their lunch. He cleared his throat and said, 'You know, there's something I should tell you . . . Ah, here we are.' He raised a hand as Wani appeared at the desk by the door, and as he got up he heard both Americans murmuring, 'Oh my god . . .'

He went over to him, smiling and capable but in a fluster of emotions – pity, defiance, a desire to support him, and a dread of people seeing him. The girl held his stick for him as she helped him off with his coat. 'Hello,' said Wani; he didn't seem to want Nick to kiss him. He took his stick again, which was an elegant black one with a silver handle, and tapped across the marble floor with it. He still wasn't quite convincing with the stick; he was like a student actor playing an old man. The stick itself seemed both to focus and repel attention. People looked and looked away.

The Americans stood up, Treat clutching his napkin to his chest. 'Hey, Antoine, great to see you!'

'How *are* you!' said Brad, in a sporting wheeze. He laid his hand for a moment on Wani's back, and Nick on his other side was doing the same, so that they seemed to congratulate him; though what they felt was the knobs of his spine through the wool of his suit. Wani sat down, smiling with distant courtesy, as if this was a weekly meeting, with a known format and outcome. There was a brief pause of silent adjustment. Nick smiled at Wani, but the shock was refreshed by the presence of their guests and a bubble rose in his throat.

'So what were you talking about?' said Wani. His voice was if anything more languid than before, though with a hint that it couldn't be forced.

'I was just explaining to Brad and Treat about the Chirks,' said Nick.

'Ah yes,' said Wani, as if this was a very old and silly story. 'It's only a nineteenth-century dukedom, of course.'

'Right . . .' said Brad, peeping at him and seeming to share, out of mere nerves and inattentiveness, the view that this was absurdly recent.

Treat laughed brightly and said, 'That's old enough for me. That'll do just fine.'

Nick said, 'It was really Sharon who saved the day – the Duchess . . .' and offered the story to Wani.

'Yes, a life-saving transfusion of vinegar,' said Wani; they all laughed loudly, as at the joke of a tyrant; and there did seem to be a trace of cruelty in the remark, against himself and thus obscurely against them. 'Shall we order straight away.' Wani turned and raised a hand to Fabio and as he did so Brad and Treat looked at each other with expressionless clarity for three or four seconds. Fabio was with them at once, and as always seemed to guess and applaud their decisions, to echo and confide to memory each item they mentioned; and perhaps it was only Nick who felt the new briskness in his tone and the quick decay of his laugh. Brad asked about the pansy salad and Fabio obliged with a noncommittal joke, and moved round the table holding the reclaimed menus flat against his chest. Nick said how well the restaurant was doing and smiled to insist on their part in its success, since Wani and he had been guests at its opening last year and had made it their local; and Fabio said, 'We can't complain . . . er, Nick, we can't complain,' just glancing at Wani on the second *complain* with something cold in his eyes, and then at the new arrivals at the door, who typically were the Stallards. Nick watched Fabio go to greet them and the coldness had gone – he heard the usual mutual primping of head waiter and fashionable customers. Well, Fabio must have been shaken to see Wani so changed; but there was something else in his reaction, fear and dis- pleasure, as if Wani's presence was no longer good for business.

Sophie and Jamie came over, Jamie slapping Wani on the shoulder and Sophie wrinkling her nose across the table rather than kissing him. Jamie had just played the romantic lead in a low-budget Hollywood comedy, and had been praised for his uncanny recreation of a dim but handsome Old Etonian with floppy hair. Sophie was pregnant, and thus resting, though thick packets that could well have been film scripts lay in the cradle-like basket she was carrying. Treat and Brad were thrilled to meet them, since Jamie was still a possible for Owen Gereth in *Spoils*; cards were exchanged, and social visits that were never going to happen were delightedly agreed on. Nothing was said about Wani's health, though Sophie, as they went off to their table, looked back with a finger-wave and a cringing smile of condolence.

'Wow, what a sweet guy,' said Brad.

Nick, taking praise for the introduction, said, 'Old Jamie . . . ? Yeah . . .'

'You guys go way back?'

'Yes – well, again we were all at Oxford together. He's really much more a friend of Wani's.'

But Wani seemed to disown any further intimacy. He sat very still, with his slender hands on the tablecloth. His square-shouldered jacket was buttoned but stood forward like a loose coat. He commanded attention now by pity and respect as he once had by beauty and charm. The claim to attention was constant, but it had turned fiercer and quieter. Nick thought he still looked wonderful in a way, though to admit it was to make an unbearable comparison. He was twenty-five years old. He said, 'Stallard has always been an absurd figure, and he's found the perfect partner in the lovely Miss Tipper.'

'Oh . . .' said Brad. 'Is she . . . er . . .'

'It was a good match for him. She's the daughter of the ninth richest man in Britain, and he's the son of a bishop.'

'Bishops don't make that much, I guess,' said Treat, and took another pull on his cocktail straw.

'Bishops make absolutely nothing,' said Wani; and after a second he flashed a smile round the table at the imbecility of bishops. Everyone else smiled too, in nervous collusion. Wani's face, gaunt and blotched, had taken on new possibilities of expression – the repertoire of someone not only older but quite different, someone passed unknown in the street, was unexpectedly his. He must have looked at himself in the mirror, winced and raised his eyebrows, and seen this unbearable stranger mugging back at him. Clearly he couldn't be held responsible for the latest ironies and startlements of his face, though there were moments when he seemed to exploit them. The cheekbones were delicate, the frontal bone heavy, even brutal – it was his father's look, brought out sometimes in the past by candlelight and now exposed to the light of day.

Nick said, 'You know Wani's father's been made a lord,' not sure whom he was pandering to.

'Oh wow,' said Brad. 'Does that mean you'll be a lord one day too?'

There were several seconds of silence till Wani said, 'It's not hereditary. What on earth are you drinking, by the way, Treat?'

'Don't ask . . . !' said Brad, eager with embarrassment.

'It's . . . what's he called? . . . Humphrey? Humphrey's latest invention. It's a Black Monday.'

Wani gave his grin again, bright and sarcastic in effect. 'That didn't take long,' he said. Humphrey was Gusto's venerable barman, keeper (up to a point) of long tabs and starlets' secrets. 'He trained on the *Queen Mary*. There's nothing he doesn't know about cocktails.'

'Well it's, what is it? It's dark rum, and cherry brandy, and sambuca. And loads of lemon juice. It tastes like a *really* old-fashioned laxative,' said Treat.

'I can't drink any more,' said Wani, 'but when I hear that, I don't mind.'

There was a brief pause. Treat ran his finger along his fringe, and Brad sighed and said, 'Yeah . . . I wanted to ask . . .' They both of them, nicely enough, seemed relieved the subject had been brought up.

Wani tucked in his chin. 'Oh, a disaster,' he said, frowning from one to the other. 'Quite unbelievable. One of my bloody companies lost two-thirds of its value between lunchtime and teatime.'

'Oh . . . oh, right,' said Brad, and gave an awkward laugh. 'Yeah, we had it real bad too.'

'Fifty billion wiped off the London stock exchange in one day.'

Treat looked at him levelly, to show he'd registered but wouldn't challenge this evasion, and said, 'Hey, the Dow was down five hundred points.'

'God, yes,' said Wani, 'well, it was all your fault.'

Brad didn't argue, but said job losses on Wall Street were terrible.

'Oh, fuck that,' said Wani. 'Anyway, it bounces back. It has already. It always recovers. It always recovers.'

'It's a worrying time for all of us,' said Nick responsibly.

Wani gave a mocking look and said, 'We'll all be absolutely fine.' And after that it was impossible to approach him on the subject of his fatal illness. Nick saw it was perplexing for the Americans, who had met him as a man about to get married. Now natural concern was mixed with furtive thinking back.

During lunch Brad, like Wani, drank only water, and Nick and Treat shared a bottle of Chablis. Treat touched Nick's arm a lot, and involved him in quiet side-chats about what they might do later. Nick tried to keep general conversation going. Wani's presiding coolness made them all hesitate. He seemed to play with their anxiety about him. Brad and Treat asked questions, and marvelled at their luck in having Wani to answer them. If Nick answered a question Wani listened to him and then gave a flat little codicil or correction. His technique was to hold a subject up and show his command of it, and then to throw it away in smiling contempt for their interest in it. He ate very little, and a sense of his disgust at the expensive food, and at himself for being unable to eat it, seeped into the conversation. He looked at the slivers of chicken and translucent courgettes as pitiful tokens of the world of pleasure, and clutched the table as though to resist a slow tug at the cloth that would sweep the whole vision away.

The question of the film was slow to come up, and Nick was shy to mention it, just because it was his own project. He'd spent months writing a script, and it was almost as if he'd written the book it was based on: all he wanted was praise. He often imagined watching the film, in the steep circle of the Curzon cinema – absorbing the grateful unanimous sigh of the audience at the exact enactment of what he'd written; in fact he seemed to have directed the film as well. He lay awake in the bliss of Philip French's review. Somehow another James film, *The Bostonians*, had come up, and the crazy thing that the actor who played Superman starred in it.

'One can imagine,' said Nick, 'only too well, the Master's irony, not to speak of his covert excitement, at *that* idea . . .'; though the others perhaps imagined it less vividly than he did.

'Oh, we loved your letters, by the way,' said Treat, with another squeeze of his arm: 'so *British*!'

'Well, I guess we should talk about ... *our* film,' said Brad. Just then the desserts, mere bonnes bouches in foot-wide puddles of pink coulis, were set in front of them. Wani looked at his plate as if it and the film were equally unlikely confections. 'Or we could talk about it next week ...'

'I don't mind,' said Nick, his heart thumping. He was suddenly incredulous that his beautiful plan, the best fruit of his passion for Henry James, depended on the cooperation of these two stupid people. He sensed already that it wasn't a question of changes, it was some larger defection from the plan.

'I mean we love what you've done, Nick.'

'Yeah, it's great,' said Treat.

Brad hesitated, peering at the grid of spun sugar that jutted from his loganberry parfait. 'You know, we've talked about this in the letter a certain amount. It's just the problem of the story where the guy doesn't get the girl, and then the stuff they're all fighting over – the Spoils, right? – goes up in flames. It kinda sucks.'

'Does it ... ?' said Nick; and, trying to be charming, 'It's just like life, though, isn't it – maybe too like life for a ... conventional movie. It's about someone who loves things more than people. And who ends up with nothing, of course. I know it's bleak, but then I think it's probably a very bleak book, even though it's essentially a comedy.'

'Yeah, I haven't read the book,' said Treat.

'Oh ...' said Nick, and coloured with proxy embarrassment, with the shame Treat should have been feeling. His loose idea of getting some time alone with him vanished in a sigh and a shrug.

'You've read the book, Antoine?' said Treat.

Wani was rose-lipped, popping in quarter-spoonfuls of ice cream, sucking them from the spoon and letting them slip down in luxurious spasms like a child with tonsillitis; he said, 'No, I haven't. I pay Nick to do that for me.'

'I don't know what you think,' said Brad, 'about the idea of including just a short love scene for Owen and . . . I'm sorry . . .'

'Fleda,' said Nick. 'Fleda Vetch.'

'*Fleda Vetch*!' said Treat, with a brief blare of a laugh. 'What sort of a name is that? Doesn't she sound like the ugliest girl in the school?'

'I think it's rather a touching name,' said Nick; and Brad looked reprovingly across the table.

'She sounds like a witch,' muttered Treat, as if agreeing to shut up; but then went on, 'I mean, can I imagine asking Meryl Streep, "Oh, Miss Streep, we've got this really great role for you, will you please, please play the lovely *Fleda Vetch*?" She'd think I'd just thrown up all over the phone.'

They all laughed except Wani, who said, very quiet and superior, as if she was someone else they would see at Nat Hanmer's wedding, 'Fleda Vetch is what she is called.'

'Yeah, I don't care overly what she's called,' said Brad. 'But . . . Owen and Fleda – we need to see them together more. We need some . . . passion!'

'We need him getting all hot,' said Treat, flicking his glance towards Jamie's table. Then he winked at Nick. 'Did he ever . . . you know . . .' lowering his voice and looking coyly away, 'at Oxford . . . like, with other guys – I'm sure I heard someone say—'

'He's straight,' said Wani.

'Oh, OK,' said Treat, with a wobble of the head, as if to say, who's talking about straight here? But there was something bleaker than impatience in Wani's tone. He was pale and motionless, gazing at the far rim of his plate but clearly caught by some unpostponable inner reckoning. He jerked his chair back a little, and his stick, swinging off from the back of it, fell on the marble with a ringing clatter: he groped round for it, bending down, and Brad jumped up to help him, and reclaimed the stick and managed to absorb the blame and reassure the restaurant with his friendly bulk. Wani's mouth was held shut and he had an intensely private expression of imminent surrender. It made Nick think for a second of the bedroom. He stood and went off at a hobbling lurch among the tables.

A few seconds later Nick followed, frowning down at the floor, giving a brisk nod to Fabio's cool 'Signore?' In the black marble lavatory there were two cubicles, and in one of them, with the door still ajar, Wani was stooping and vomiting. Nick came in behind him and stood there for a moment before laying a hand on his side. Wani flinched, whispered, 'Oh fuck . . .' and crouched and shuddered as he threw up again. There seemed to be far more coming out than the invalidish meal that had gone in. Nick touched him lightly, wanting to help him and discourage him at the same time. He looked over his shoulder into the bowl, with a certain resolve, and saw the bits of chicken and greens in the pool of the promptly regurgitated ice cream. He plucked out sheets of paper from the dispenser and wondered if he should wipe Wani's face for him; then he stood and waited, which Wani didn't object to. He thought with bleak hilarity that this was their most intimate moment for many months. He looked at the streaky black walls and found himself thinking of nights here the year before, both cubicles sometimes carelessly busy with the crackle of paper and patter of credit card. There was a useful shiny ledge above the cistern, and they would go in in turn. The nights sped by in unrememberable brilliance. 'Well,' said Wani, grasping his stick and giving Nick a fearful smile, 'no more parfait for Antoine.'

Wani had brought the car to Gusto, and Nick drove him back in it to Lowndes Square. 'Thanks very much,' said Wani, in a whispery drawl.

'That's all right, old chap,' said Nick. He parked opposite the house and they sat for a minute. Wani was taking deep breaths, as if to ready himself for a race or plunge. He didn't try to help Nick by explaining himself – well, he never had, he was his own law and his own licence. If Nick asked him how he felt he was drily impatient with him, both for not knowing and for wanting to know. It was the unfair prerogative of illness. Nick reached a hand over the steering wheel and swept the thin dust off the black leather hood of the dashboard. How cars themselves changed as they aged; at first they were possibilities made solid and fast, agents of dreams that kept a glint of dreams about them, a keen narcotic smell; then slowly they disclosed their unguessed quaintness and clumsiness, they seemed to fade into the dim disgrace between one fashion and another.

'I really must get a new car,' said Wani.

'I know, it's frightfully dusty.'

'It's a fucking antique.'

Nick peered over his shoulder into the cramped back seat, and remembered Ricky, the stupid genius of the old days (which was to say, last summer), sitting there with his legs wide apart. 'I suppose you'll keep the number plate.'

'God, yes. It's worth a thousand pounds.'

'Dear old WHO 6.'

'OK . . .' said Wani, cold at any touch of sentiment.

Nick glanced up and saw Lady Ouradi looking down from one of the drawing-room windows. She held the net curtain aside and gazed out into the browning leaves of the plane trees, the long dull chasm of the square. Nick waved, but she seemed not to have seen them; or perhaps she had already seen them but let her gaze wander, as it was clearly prone to, down the imagined vista of the past or future. He noted her austere wool dress, the single string of pearls. To Nick she was a creature of indoors, of unimaginable exiled mornings and measured afternoons; her gesture as she held the white curtain back was like the parting of a medium through which she wasn't quite supposed to see or be seen.

'You're OK for money?' Wani said.

'Darling, I'm fine.' Nick turned and smiled at him, with the mischievous tenderness of a year ago. 'Your little start-up present has grown and grown, you know.' He put his hand discreetly into Wani's, where it lay on his thigh. A few seconds later Wani withdrew his hand, so as to get out his handkerchief. There was a question in the air, all this week, since he had come back from Paris, and it was only his pride which kept it from being asked: which it wouldn't be in words, but in some brave melting gesture. Instead he said,

'You should really move out of the Feddens'. Get a place of your own.'

'I know,' said Nick, 'it is rather dotty. But we muddle along somehow. . . . I'm not at all sure they could manage without me.'

'One never knows . . .' said Wani. He turned his head away and looked out at the pavement, the ugly concrete planters in the square gardens, a bicycle frame chained to the railings. 'I was thinking I might leave you the Clerkenwell building.'

'Oh . . .' Nick glanced at him and then away, almost scowling in shock and reproach.

'Of course I don't mean you should live there.'

'Well, no, that's not the point . . .'

'I suppose it's a bit odd leaving you something unfinished.'

After a couple of breaths, Nick said, 'Let's not talk about you leaving things.' And went on, with awful delicacy, 'Anyway, it will be finished by then.' It was impossible to say the right thing. Wani grinned at him coldly for a second. Until now he had only had the story of Wani being ill; he had taken the news about with him and brought off the sombre but thrilling effect, once or twice, of saying, 'I'm afraid he's dying,' or 'He nearly died.' It had been his own drama, in which he'd felt, as well as the horror and pity of it, the thump of a kind of self-importance. Now, sitting beside him and being offered buildings, he felt humbled and surprisingly angry.

'Well, we'll see,' said Wani. 'I mean, I'm assuming you'd like it.'

'I don't find it easy to think about,' said Nick.

'I need to get this sorted out, Nick. I'm seeing the lawyers on Friday.'

'What would I do with the Clerkenwell building?' said Nick sulkily.

'You'd own it,' said Wani. 'It'll have thirty thousand square feet of office space. You can get someone to manage it for you and you can live on the rent for the rest of your life.'

Nick didn't ask how he was supposed to go about finding a manager. Possibly Sam Zeman could help him with that. The phrase 'the rest of your life' had come out pat, almost weightless, a futurity Wani wasn't going to bother imagining. For Nick it was very strange to find it attached to an office block near Smithfield Market. Wani knew he hated the design of the building; there was a sharp tease in the gift, even a kind of lesson. 'What are you going to do about Martine?' said Nick.

'Oh, just the same. She'll carry on getting her allowance, at least until she marries. Then she gets a lump sum.'

'Oh . . .' Nick nodded dimly at the wisdom of this, but then had to say, 'I didn't know you gave her an allowance.'

Wani slid him the smile that had once been slyly grand but now had something vicious in it. 'Well, not me,' he said. 'I assumed you'd worked it out. Mamma's always paid her. Or kept her, rather.'

'I see . . .' said Nick, after a moment, thinking how little Wani had taught him about Lebanese customs. He seemed to search for the discreet transaction in the tilted mantelpiece mirror. He glanced at the house again, but Wani's mother had dropped the curtain and absolute discretion reigned: the black front door, the veiled windows, the eggshell sheen of property. 'What a charming arrangement, to keep your son's girlfriend.'

'For god's sake,' murmured Wani, looking away. 'She was never my girlfriend.'

'No, of course not, I see . . .' said Nick, blushing and hurrying to cover his own foolishness, and also feeling absurdly relieved.

'Of course you must never tell Papa. It's his last illusion.'

Nick didn't imagine seeing much of Bertrand in 'the rest of his life'. The little aesthete already felt the prohibition of that closed black door: which opened as he looked at it, to reveal Monique and the old servant woman, dressed in black, ready but not coming forward. 'They're expecting you,' Nick said quietly.

Wani looked across and then almost closed his eyes in droll disdain. All his old habits were there, and the beat of his lashes brought back occasions in the past when Nick had basked in his selfishness. He reached beside the seat for his stick. 'How are you getting back?'

'I think I'll walk,' said Nick, unthinkingly fit. 'I could do with some exercise.'

Wani pulled back the handle and the door cracked open onto the cold blue afternoon.

'You know I love you very much, don't you,' said Nick, not meaning it in the second before he said it, but moved by saying it into feeling it might still be true. It seemed a way of covering his ungraciousness about Wani's will, of showing he was groping for a sense of scale. Wani snuffled, looked across the road at his mother, but didn't echo Nick's words. He had

never told him he loved him. But it seemed possible to Nick
that he might mean it without saying it. He said,

'By the way, I should warn you that Gerald seems to be in
a bit of trouble.'

'Oh, really?' said Nick.

'I don't know exactly what's happened, but it's something to
do with the Fedray takeover last year. A spot of creative
accounting.'

'Really? What, you mean the Maurice Tipper thing.'

'I think you can be pretty sure Maurice has covered his
back. And Gerald will probably be all right. But there may be
a bit of a fuss.'

'Goodness . . .' Nick thought of Rachel first of all, and then
of Catherine, who for the past few weeks had been in a wildly
excitable state. 'How do you know about this?'

'I had a call from Sam Zeman earlier.'

'Right,' said Nick, slightly jealous. 'I must give him a ring.'

They got out of the car, and Nick dawdled across the road,
finding it hard to go at Wani's pace. He kissed Monique and
explained that Wani had brought up his lunch; she nodded,
pursed her lips and swallowed in a funny mimetic reflex. She
was dignified and withdrawn, but as she touched her son's
upper arm the glow of a long-surrendered power over him
came into her face, the animal solace of being allowed to love
and protect him, even against such hopeless odds. Wani himself, with the women at each elbow, seemed to shrink into
their keeping; the sustaining social malice of the past two
hours abandoned him at the threshold. They forgot their
manners, and the door was closed again without anyone
saying goodbye.

16

Nick crossed Knightsbridge and went through Albert Gate into the Park. He swung his arms, and his calves and thighs ached with guilty vigour. There was so much to think about, and the Park itself seemed pensive, the chestnuts standing in pools of their shed leaves, the great planes, slower to change, still towering tan and gold; but all he wanted to do was march along. A group of young women on horseback came trotting down Rotten Row, and he crossed behind them, over the damp, crusted sand. He didn't mind the north-easterly breeze. It was the time of year when the atmosphere streamed with unexpected hints and memories, and a paradoxical sense of renewal. He thought of meeting Leo after work, always early, the chill of promise in the air. Once or twice they met at the bandstand, away over there, with the copper ogee roof: strange that that particular shape should have floated on its slender pillars above the quick kiss, quick touch, odd nervous avoidance of their meetings. He took the long diagonal that went past Watts's monument to, or of, Physical Energy: the huge-thighed horseman reining back and gazing, in a ferment of discovery, towards Kensington Palace. Nick gave it the smug glance which showed that as a critic he noticed it and as a Londoner he took it for granted.

He thought about the Clerkenwell building. What Wani had bought was three narrow Victorian properties making a corner block, one extending deep behind the others into a high iron-and-glass-roofed workshop. They were solidly built, of blackened brick which showed up plum red when they were knocked down. There were doorbells of moribund trades, a glass beveller, a 'Church and Legal' printer. There were boarded-up windows, industrial wiring, the light vandalism of use. Wani had taken Nick to see them, and Nick's whole impulse was to do them up and live in them. He went into the cellars and attics, heaved open trapdoors, climbed onto the leads, and looked down through the steep glass roof into the workshop where Wani was pacing around in his beautiful suit, flipping his car keys in his hand. Nick saw their friends coming to parties and dancing in that room. Something in Wani's impatient, unseeing manner told him this was never going to happen. He felt like a child whose desperate visionary plea has no chance of persuading a parent. And of course the buildings came down – for a month or two the backs of other buildings not seen for a century felt the common sunlight, and then Baalbek House, named by Wani as if he'd written a poem, started to go up. Nick cast about but really he'd never seen a more meretricious design than that of Baalbek House. His own ideas were discounted with the grunting chuckle of someone wedded to another vision of success and defiantly following cheaper advice. And now this monster Lego house, with its mirror windows and maroon marble cladding, was to be Nick's for life.

When he turned into Kensington Park Gardens Nick remembered what Wani had said about Gerald, and started walking more slowly, as if to resist a strange acceleration of trouble. He was shy about meeting Gerald, who could be aggressive when in the wrong and sarcastic when he needed support. The Range Rover was parked outside the house, which might mean he'd come back early from Parliament. It looked significant. As so often, Nick didn't know what he was supposed to know – or indeed what he did know, since creative accounting was just a jocular phrase to him. Behind the Range Rover a man in a reddish leather jacket was leaning on the roof of a parked car and talking to another man sitting at the wheel. He looked up as Nick approached, and carried on talking while his eyes, in one fluent sequence, seemed to find him, hold him, scan him and dismiss him. Nick turned in at No. 48, and glanced back while he felt for his keys: the man was staring at him, and raised his chin as though about to call out, but then said nothing. He smiled unnervingly. His friend in the car passed him a camera through the window and he put it to his eye and took three pictures in two seconds – Nick was mesmerized by the lazy precision of the clicks; and too surprised to know what he felt. He felt victimized, and flattered, pretty important and utterly insignificant, since they clearly had no idea who he was. He thought in dignity he shouldn't answer questions, and was confused by their not asking him any. It took him an age to open the blue door.

In the hall everything seemed calm. Elena was in the kitchen and Nick said hello and waited for a sign from her. She was preparing the 'meal and a half', the separate portion, like a child's or an invalid's, that was made for Gerald when he was going to be late at the House. 'Have you seen what's going on outside?' said Nick. Elena thumbed her pastry expressively, but only said,

'I don't know.'

'Is Gerald here?'

'Is gone to work.'

'Oh good . . .'

'Miz Fed upstairs with his Lord.' Elena radiated resentment, and Nick didn't risk exploring its cause, whether it was Gerald or what was being done to him: it felt large enough to include everyone. 'You take the tray?' she said.

The kettle was coming to the boil, and the tray was ready with two teacups and the little sweet *lebkuchen* that Rachel liked. Nick warmed the pot and put in two spoonfuls of lapsang. It was the set with a pink Petit Trianon in a wreath on each cup and saucer, dull and pale now from the fury of the dishwasher. He poured on the water, gave it a good stir, dropped the lid on, and picked up the tray. Elena looked at him more amiably but shook her head. 'Is Street of Shame,' she said. 'Is Street of Shame, Nick.' It was the *Private Eye* phrase for Fleet Street, which Gerald had once teased Toby with, but Nick wasn't sure if she meant that or if she meant that Kensington Park Gardens itself had been brought down.

The drawing-room door was open, and Nick slowed again before going in. Lionel was saying, 'If he has been a bloody fool then he'll have to face the consequences. If he hasn't, then we have infinite resources to demonstrate the fact.' His manner was as quiet as ever, but without its usual cordiality: he sounded as if he expected the former option, and the stain it would bring on the family. Nick rattled the tray and went in. Rachel was standing by the mantelpiece, Lionel sitting in an armchair, and for a second Nick thought of the scene in *The Portrait of a Lady* when Isabel discovers her husband sitting while Mme Merle is standing, and sees at once that they are more intimate than she had realized. 'Ah, my dear . . .' said Rachel, as Nick came forward with a slight mime of servility, which wasn't spotted as a joke. Lionel greeted him with his eyes, and went on, 'When's he due back?' 'He's got a late division,' Rachel murmured. And Nick, setting down the tray, saw that though he hadn't chanced in on a secret he had caught the note of an older, more unguarded friendship than he'd heard before, the shared intelligence of brother and sister.

'Thanks so much,' said Rachel.

'Did you have your picture taken?' said Lionel.

'I did,' said Nick; and for some reason went on, 'Not my best side, I'm afraid.'

'No, they're awful about that,' said Lionel, clearly resolving to show by his humour and by sitting down squarely and comfortably that there was nothing to worry about. 'I was tipped off, so I came through the gardens.'

'Thank heavens for the gardens,' said Rachel. 'With four exits they really can't keep it covered.'

Nick smiled and hesitated. There wasn't a cup for him, but he longed to be included. He said tactfully, 'Is there anything I can do?'

'Oh . . .' Lionel and Rachel looked at each other, searching for an answer among their own proprieties and uncertainties. Perhaps it was too shaming, even with the press outside, for Rachel to talk about. 'Some rather awful things are being said about Gerald,' she said, in her tellingly passive fashion.

Nick bit his cheek and said, 'Wani . . . Ouradi told me something about it.'

'Oh, well it's out, then,' said Rachel.

'It will come out, darling,' said Lionel.

Rachel poured the tea, and seemed lost in this sombre idea, passing Lionel a cup and the plate of *lebkuchen*. 'And what about Maurice Tipper?' she said.

Lionel sat scrunching his biscuit in a vigilant squirrel-like way, and licked the sugar from his lips before saying, 'Maurice Tipper is a cold-blooded thug.'

'That's certainly true,' said Rachel.

'My guess is that he'll only help Gerald if doing so helps himself.'

'Mm . . . I saw Sophie at lunchtime,' Nick offered. 'I thought she was rather evasive.'

'Thank god Tobias didn't marry that false little girl!' said Rachel, clutching at this out-of-date consolation and laughing with new bitterness and relief.

'Quite!' said Nick.

'Two things you can do,' said Lionel. 'Obviously, don't talk to anyone. And could you bear to pop out and buy the *Standard*?'

'Of course,' said Nick, suddenly more nervous of the photographers.

'And a third thing,' said Rachel. 'Could you try and find my daughter?'

'Ah, yes . . .' said Lionel.

'She's frightfully *up* at the moment,' Rachel said. 'You've no idea what she'll do.'

'Well, I'll try,' said Nick.

'Isn't she taking the pills?' said Lionel, firm and vague at once.

'They can't quite get it right,' said Rachel. 'Two months ago she could barely speak – now she can barely stop speaking. It is a strain.'

They both looked at Nick and he said, 'I'll see what I can do.' He sensed a certain hardness towards himself, a request that he should prove his usefulness to the family. Then he thought briskness might be a mark of confidence. A structure of command, long laid away in velvet, had been rapidly reassembled.

Catherine came home about six. She was thinking of buying a house in Barbados, and had been having a long talk with Brentford about it. Nick could tell from the smell of her hair when she kissed him that she'd been smoking pot; she seemed both elated and spaced out. Flashes went off as she opened the front door, but she treated them almost as natural phenomena, the meteors of her own atmosphere. 'What was all that about?' she said, hardly waiting for an answer. 'Another visit from the Prime Minister?'

'Not exactly,' said Nick, following her upstairs and thinking that whatever was going on made another visit from the PM very unlikely. 'We've been wondering where you were,' he said. Rachel was on the phone in the drawing room, talking to Gerald in Westminster, and seemed to be getting the reassurances she needed; she was oddly placable. She smiled indulgently at Toby's portrait and said, 'Of course, darling, just carry on as normal. We'll try . . . ! We'll see you . . . Yup, yup.' Nick went to the front windows, which looked very large and shiny in the early dusk. It was unsettling to know there were men waiting outside, their patience barely tested. The curtains were never closed, and when freed from the brocaded bands that held them back they still curved stiffly apart. Nick leant in to close the shutters, seldom used, which unfolded with alarming cracks.

When Rachel explained what was going on, Catherine seemed distantly enthusiastic. 'Extraordinary . . .' she said.

'It could be quite serious actually,' said Nick.

'Not prison, you mean?' It was the pot perhaps that gave her this smile of benign speculation.

'No,' said Rachel crossly. 'Besides, he's done absolutely nothing wrong. It's clearly all to do with that hateful man Tipper.'

'Then Tipper can go to prison,' said Catherine. 'Or both the Tippers, better still.'

Rachel gave a twitch of a smile to show the subject of the joke touched her a little too nearly. 'They're only making investigations. No one's been arrested, much less charged.'

'Right.'

'Uncle Lionel's been here, and he was very reassuring.'

Nick murmured endorsingly and said, 'Would anyone like a drink?'

'Anyway, darling, you know your father would never do a thing like that. He's far too experienced. Not to mention dead honest!' Rachel coloured slightly at this affirmation.

'So is it in the paper?'

'It's not in the *Standard* tonight. And Toby says they won't touch it at the *Telegraph* – he's spoken to Gordon. Daddy says it's just the sort of thing the *Guardian* would love to blow out of all proportion.'

'I'll have um . . .' Catherine said, bearing down on the drinks table with a fascinated smile but in the end only managing to think of a gin-and-tonic. Nick mixed her one, juniper lost in quinine: when she was on the up curve it was best to be careful with alcohol, annoyance, laughter – any cause of excitement. They stood with their glasses at their chins and nodded 'Cheers!' in a meaningful way.

'The thing is, darling,' said Rachel, 'we simply mustn't talk to anybody at the moment. Oath of silence, Daddy says.'

'I don't know anything about stocks and shares, so you needn't worry.'

'It's what they make you say, though . . . Darling, or they twist your words. They've got no principles.'

'They're not your friend,' said Nick, which had been Lionel's dry way of putting it.

'They've got the morals of rattlesnakes,' said Rachel.

Catherine sat on a sofa, swayed her head over her glass, and looked from one to the other of them. She started to smile and they flinched, with the feeling they were being mocked; but the smile spread and they saw it was to do with something else, the flowering of a clear belief, just touched with playful calculation, that they would share her happiness. 'I've had such a thrilling day,' she said.

They sat down to dinner in the kitchen. Normally Nick enjoyed the nights when Gerald was kept late at Westminster – the mood of snug reduction and humorously tolerated crisis; if they had guests, or if Gerald and Rachel were due out, there was even a thrill to Gerald's absence: it was a wing-brush of power, the sign of demands and decisions greater than dinner.

Tonight his absence was more critical. It was odd that he hadn't come home. Clearly he attached great importance to carrying on normally.

Catherine said, 'What's Gerald voting about?'

'Oh, darling, I don't know . . . it's obviously something pretty major.'

'Can't we ring him?'

'Well, he's not answering the phone in the office. And if he's in the Chamber, or somewhere else about the Palace,' said Rachel impressively, 'then we couldn't reach him anyway.'

'He'll be back straight after the vote,' said Nick. He knew that Gerald had Penny's new mobile phone; Rachel must be trying to spare him a wild, irrelevant pep talk from his daughter.

'What is a takeover?' said Catherine.

'Well, it's when one company buys up another.'

'They acquire a majority of the shares,' said Nick. 'Then they have control.'

'So are they saying Gerald didn't have these shares?'

Rachel said, as if judiciously filtering the facts for her child, 'I think sometimes perhaps people fiddle with the price of the shares.'

'Make them more valuable?'

'Exactly.'

'Or less, of course,' said Nick.

'Mm . . .' said Rachel.

'And how would they do that?'

'Well, I suppose they sort of . . . um . . .'

'Mm . . .' said Nick, after a bit.

They smiled doubtfully at their own unworldliness.

'It's not the same as asset-stripping, anyway,' said Catherine.

'No . . .' said Rachel, with hesitant firmness.

'Because that's what Sir Maurice Tipper does. Toby told me. Maurice Tipper, Asset Stripper. That's when they get hold of something, it's like an old house, they strip out all the marble fireplaces before they demolish it.'

'And leave everyone on the street,' said Nick.

'Exactly!' said Catherine.

'That, of course, is what Badger's supposed to have done all over Africa,' said Rachel, with a guilty grimace. 'I don't know if it's true.'

'Oh, Badger . . .' said Catherine, indulgent and dismissive at once. 'What's become of poor old Badger, lately, I wonder.'

'He's often away,' said Rachel, as if to excuse her vagueness about him.

'I'm going to get in touch with him.'

'Well, you could.'

'I'm going to catch up with quite a number of people who've dropped out of my life. It's so pathetic to lose touch,' Catherine said, with a lively but disgusted look at her last summer, when everything about her had been pathetic.

'I'm sure he's not expecting a call . . .' said Rachel.

'I saw Russell today, for instance.'

'Oh really?' said Rachel thinly.

'Do you remember?'

'Oh, I do.'

'Me too,' said Nick.

'He was asking about everybody.'

'I should still be a bit careful with Russell,' said Nick, with a supportive glance at Rachel.

'But that was all *before* . . . !' said Catherine, in happy exasperation.

Later, she said, 'If Gerald resigns, you'll be able to come to Barbados with me, that would be perfect, wouldn't it, until things blow over.'

'That's very kind,' said Rachel. 'Though I can't help feeling there's more than one "if" in that sentence.'

'Oh, Mum, this house has got an enormous swimming pool, as well as being right on the beach. You just take your pick!'

'No, I'm sure it's delightful.'

'It could be just what he needs. A complete change of direction.'

'You have the oddest idea of just what people need,' said Rachel. 'I've noticed it before.'

'Well, let's face it, he certainly doesn't need the pathetic little *empee's* salary.'

'What you perhaps forget is that . . . your father wants to serve his country.'

'OK, when you get back, *plunge* into charity work! Probably much more useful than being Monster for Social Welfare and cutting everyone's grants. He could found something. The Gerald Fedden Trust. People often have a complete change of heart when something like this happens. You know, they go into the East End.'

'Well, let's just wait and see, shall we,' said Rachel, folding her napkin and pushing back her chair.

Nick and Catherine went up to the drawing room. 'Will you put on some music, darling,' said Catherine.

'I'm not sure your mother really . . .'

'Oh, just something nice. I don't mean God-dammery. All right, I'll choose.' She went to the record cupboard, and knelt with her head cocked sideways, humming teasingly as she picked out an LP and prepared to put it on. Nick heard the needle drop, the kindling crackle.

'Turn it down a bit, darling . . . ?'

She did so, and tutted, 'Uncle Nick!' Out from the speakers came the sinister little jumps that start Rachmaninov's *Symphonic Dances*. 'There, you like that,' she said.

'Up to a point,' said Nick, knowing how much he didn't want to hear it.

'Oh, it's wonderful,' she said, staring from the stage at an invisible dress circle and raising her arms. It was a piece he'd adored as a teenager, and played all the time in his first year at Oxford to confirm and deepen the regretful longing which seemed now to have been the medium he lived in – it unfolded for him like that endless tune on the alto sax. Now its melancholy felt painful, even vicious. He half watched Catherine sweeping through the room, alarmingly unself-conscious. He had danced to it himself, but by himself, in his room, drunk, at the end of days brightened or not by contact with Toby.

'It is a bit God-dammery,' he said, as a Russian Orthodox chant made itself heard. Catherine waved her arms hectically. 'It's a bit like having a bop in St Basil's Cathedral.' He tried to throw off his embarrassment with these square little jokes. She smiled, stretched out a hand to him, and scowled for a second because he wouldn't join her. He thought of her four months ago, trailing her hopelessness from room to room like a sad child with an inseparable rag; and now, mere chemistry, she was Makarova. She didn't notice the melancholy, the insidious, shifting harmonies; it was movement and therefore life. He said, 'The thing is, darling, there's a bit of a crisis going on. You know, it looks rather odd leaping round like this when your mum's so anxious – well, we all are.' He spoke consciously as one of the family, to cover his private unease, at being both needed and excluded by the terms of the crisis. Catherine didn't pay attention, she hummed, serenely, stub-bornly, and a while later stopped dancing as if on her own decision. She wandered to the big bay window at the back, and stood looking out through her reflection at the lights beyond the trees. They seemed perhaps like elements in a pattern, which, read with the right intuition for shape and meaning, might reveal an instruction. When she turned round she gave

Nick a smile that hovered before various possible cajolements. She sat on the broad arm of his chair and slid in sideways against him.

'I know,' she said, 'let's go out for a bit. Have you got the car here?'

'Um, yes,' said Nick. 'Round the corner. But . . . well, Gerald will be back soon.'

'Gerald could be ages. You know they don't vote till midnight sometimes, if they're filimandering.'

'Or gerrybustering.'

'Exactly! We needn't be long. I've just got an idea.'

Of course the idea of not being here when Gerald got back was very attractive. Rachel came in, and Nick felt he'd been caught larking about, Catherine squashing him like some bolshie teenage attempt at seduction. 'Gerald's just rung,' Rachel said. 'It seems they're going to be really awfully late. It's a bill he's got to, um, you know, keep a bit of an eye on.'

'How is he?' said Catherine fondly.

'He sounds fine. He says really not to worry.' She had a new confidence, an almost pleasurable glow, and Nick felt sure she'd just been told how much she was loved. She moved across the room, looking for some small task to perform; found fallen chrysanthemum petals on a table top, swept them into her open palm, and dropped them in the wastebasket. 'Oh, I like this,' she said. 'Isn't it Rachmaninov?' The sad waltz of the second movement was just catching fire. She stood gazing over their heads at the caprice by Guardi, and perhaps at some memory of her own. Nick thought for a moment she was going to start dancing too – she seemed suddenly very like her daughter. But really it was only in charades or the adverb game that she took the licence to be silly.

Catherine said, 'Mum, Nick and I are going out for half an hour.'

'Oh, darling . . . really?'

'There's just something we've got to do. I'm not going to tell you, but . . . We'll be back!'

'Is it quite the best moment . . . ?'

'Yes, I wonder,' said Nick.

'I'm not going to talk to anyone, don't worry!'

Rachel thought, and said, 'Well, if you are going out, then obviously Nick should go with you.'

'We'll just go in the car,' said Catherine. 'Nick will be with me the whole time.' And she hugged him to her in the chair with a delighted laugh.

Rachel looked rather narrowly at Nick, as the guarantor of this excursion. He thought he might be going to put up more resistance than he did. He gave a half smile, a slow nod, a wearily tolerant closing of the eyes. She said, 'Please don't be long. And take the back way. Take a torch.'

They went out, and as they started downstairs Nick heard the minatory little fanfares interrupt the waltz, and wondered if Rachel would go on listening to it after they'd gone. In the hall it was still quite loud. The whole house seemed steeped in a wilful air of romance.

Catherine wouldn't tell him where they were going, only where to turn. Nick sighed good-humouredly at this, and was half glad she didn't notice his tension as they left the house further and further behind, and Rachel in it alone. When they swung around Marble Arch and down Park Lane he said, 'It looks as though we might be going to Westminster.'

'In a sense,' said Catherine. 'You'll see.' Her seductiveness had hardened to a brightness.

'There's absolutely no point in going to the House of Commons.'

'No, no,' she said.

They went down Grosvenor Place, wound through Victoria, and then headed straight towards Westminster. The floodlit front of the Abbey appeared, and then they were gunning out into Parliament Square, the bright face of Big Ben, always stirring to Nick, like the best picture in a child's book, showing 9.30: 9.30 was striking, iron circles fading in the bus roar. He said, quite relieved, 'I can't go in there, you know.' But she made him turn left instead, towards Whitehall, past Downing Street, and the Banqueting House, and then suddenly towards the river, and into a side street walled right up to the sky by a vast Victorian building. It was a feature of the London riverscape Nick had almost unconsciously absorbed, without ever deducing or being told what it was: he had an image of its roof, like a Loire château. He parked opposite, outside some dark ministry. The whole street was oddly dark, except for the glowing glass canopies of the château's doorways, somehow redolent of gaslight and cab horses, at one of which a porter in a peaked cap was silhouetted. For a moment a London sensation, unnoticed and perpetual as the throb of traffic, came clear for him: of order and power, rhythmic and intricate, endlessly sure of obedience. Then he remembered. 'This is where Badger lives, isn't it?'

'It was just Mum mentioning him,' said Catherine, as if it was an obvious breakthrough.

Nick saw that she was crazy, that the trip was not an inspiration but an irrelevance. He slumped and pursed his lips in tender annoyance. He tried kindly to find a reason in her craziness. 'You think Badger can somehow throw a light on this business? He's probably not here, is he, darling – isn't he in South Africa?' But she had opened the car door, with no sign in her face or voice that she was even aware of Nick's worry, or of any possible objection. She had her certainty, a source of joy and tension, like revealed religion. Nick's objection was mainly that he didn't like Badger, that it was mutual, and that Badger would like him even less for bringing his manic god-daughter round. It was a fuck-flat, in Barry

457

Groom's hard phrase, not a proper home. He had an image of small hotel-like rooms in which Badger conducted strained affairs with much younger women; of Badger shooting a line as phoney as the prints on the wall and the Chippendale cocktail cabinet.

They went in under one of the glass canopies, and through a brown-marble entrance hall; a porter in a cubbyhole was listening to the radio and nodded back at them as if they were always in and out. Catherine, in her dark coat, made up, evangelical, had the confidence to pass anywhere; the sense of getting away with something was all Nick's. The wait by the lift was a reasonable but finite chance to turn back: Catherine smiled and quivered, hands thrust into pockets flashing her coat open. 'Are you sure about this?' said Nick. He knew he ought to be restraining her and at the same time he was trying to live up to her. Her conviction was a challenge to someone reasonably cowardly. He felt a vague intellectual awe of her insights, however mad. He thought her state might be like the capable elation of coke, but more psychic. There was a warning plink, the doors opened, and Penny came tearing out.

'Penny!' said Nick. He dawdled for a moment with a shrug and a helpful half smile. Catherine was already in the lift, narrow-eyed, breathing audibly. Nick, feeling like a silly ass and then also feeling the loose smugness of having discovered something without knowing what it was, grinned, and said considerately, 'How are you?'

Penny had stopped and turned round, with a look both peevish and frightened. She went very white; and then a rich hot pink started up in her round cheeks and spread (in the three or four seconds while Catherine stamped and said, 'Nick, come on!') into her neck and throat and ears. 'Um, Nick,' she said, in bossy defiance of her blush, 'actually, I shouldn't, um . . .'

Nick, confused, reluctant to be rude, but enjoying Penny's blush, in itself and for not being one of his own, had a foot in the lift, and blocked the thrust of the door with his arm – it kept stolidly reasserting itself. 'How's Gerald?' he said.

'Nick, come on!' Catherine said again.

He stood back into the lift and Penny, shaking her head and stepping forward, said, 'He's not here, Nick, he's not here—' as the doors closed.

'Well . . . !' said Nick. He glanced at Catherine, then at the mirror wall, where they seemed to stand like self-conscious strangers. Even in a stuffy old mansion block like this a slanting FUCK had been scratched on the brushed-steel door. He thought of Badger flirting relentlessly with Penny, years ago now, when Gerald had first taken her on. It was that awful, rivalrous straight thing, taking the girl not only from Nick, who didn't care, but from his best friend, who clearly would. He found himself smirking, looked in the mirror, and said, 'God, darling, Badger's going to be furious. We're obviously not supposed to know.' But the lift stopped and Catherine slipped out past him with a mocking frown, as if surely she couldn't have anyone so dim or so chicken as a friend.

He followed her along a red-carpeted hallway past brown-varnished doors with bells and nameplates; on one side brown-and-yellow leaded windows gave on to inner light wells, lit now only by the dim back windows of other flats. A telly could be heard from one flat, but otherwise sound was dampened as by the gravest discretion. The subliminal sense of gaslight, of stepping back through time into the depths of this monstrous building, was oppressive but also, for Nick at least, beguiling: his mind ran away for a moment along the panelled dado, the swan's-neck curves of the light fittings. The last door on the left was slightly ajar, waiting perhaps for Penny's return. Catherine pinged the bell, and they stood looking at the card in the brass frame that said 'D. S. Brogan Esq'. A deeply familiar voice shouted, 'It's open,' and Catherine stared into Nick's face with a gleam of vindication before she put her arm through his. It was much worse than Nick had thought. He didn't want to go in, and would have run away fast if he hadn't been tightly held there. There was a loud sigh, soft thump of footsteps, and Gerald plucked open the door. He wasn't wearing shoes or a jacket and tie, and his front stud was undone, so that the white collar stood up skew-whiff. In his left hand he held a cigarette. Nick said, 'Oh, hello, Gerald!' and Catherine, gleaming with indignation, said, 'Dad! You said you'd given up!'

17

(i)

It didn't take the photographers long to work out about the communal gardens, though they were stretched to cover all four gates. They put up their stepladders and looked over the railings and peripheral shrubbery through binoculars or through their telephoto lenses, dreaming of shots. The falling leaves were in their favour. It was news, but it was also a matter of patience. They talked confidently on mobile phones. They were rivals who'd met so often they were friends, sharing their indifference to their victims in companionable Thermos caps of tea. They toasted them sardonically in milk and sugar. Then the house gate would open and Toby, perhaps, would come out, who for a while had worked with these guys and now was dodging them, making towards one exit and then switching and jogging to another – the photographers went swearing and clattering round the long way; one or two jumped in cars. Soon Geoffrey Titchfield was making hourly patrols of the gardens, after several of the buzzards, as he called them, had simply used their ladders to climb in. 'You are not keyholders,' he said. 'I must ask you to leave immediately.' Sir Geoffrey was deeply vexed by the whole episode. The exposure of his idol, terribly shocking to him, was brought home, like the threat of a larger disorder, by these incursions on the gardens.

At the front of the house the shutters or curtains stayed closed, so that indoors the day had the colour of an appalling

461

hangover or other failure to get up. Electric light combined with diffused sunlight in a sickly glare. All the papers came as usual, in their long, arrhythmical collapse onto the doormat, where they lay like a menace and were approached at last with long-armed reluctance. And there they were, the Millionaire MP, his Elegant Wife, his Blonde, or his Blushing Blonde Secretary. 'Troubled daughter speaks of minister's affair.' It seemed she'd spoken to Russell, and Russell had spoken to an old friend at the *Mirror*; after that there was no holding it. Oddly enough, in all the pictures 'heartbroken Cathy' was smiling with sublime conviction. That was the first day.

On the second day, Gerald, resenting the demeaning scurry through the gardens, where he looked such a fool to the other keyholders, walking their dogs and knocking up on the tennis courts, put on his widest-brimmed fedora and a dark, double-breasted overcoat, and came out of the front door into the film set of the street. Parked vans, spotlights, shoulder-hefted TV cameras, fluffy boom mikes, the ruck of reporters – everything took on life and purpose with his emergence. The freshly whitened house-front reflected the flashbulbs. Gerald seemed as usual to draw strength from their attention. He was the star of this movie, whatever he did. Nick, looking out from behind an upstairs curtain, saw him step on to the pavement and heard him say loudly, 'Thank you, gentlemen, I have nothing to say,' in a cordial, plummy tone. The Press were in front of him in a half ellipse, of which his hat formed the centre. They called him Sir and Gerald and Mr Fedden and Minister. 'Are you leaving your wife?' 'This way, Gerald!' 'Mr Fedden, are you guilty of insider dealing?' 'Where's your daughter?' 'Will you be resigning, Minister?' Nick saw how they enjoyed their deadpan mockery, their brief but decisive wielding of power. He found it frightening. He wondered how he himself would ever square up to that. Gerald moved slowly, with heavy patience, sturdy in the interest of his case and confident of knowing the right form, however humiliating the content, towards the Range Rover; which at last he got into, and drove off, almost running down photographers, to the House of Commons, to hand in his resignation.

Nick let the curtain drop, and made his way carefully around the twin guest beds and on to the brighter landing. Rachel was just coming out of her bedroom. 'Sorry about this absurd gloom!' she said. 'I find I have the greatest reluctance to have my photograph taken.' There was a briskness in her tone that warned off any touch of sympathy.

'I understand.'

She was wearing a red-and-black wool suit, a necklace, four or five rings, and would certainly have looked good in a photograph. Nick glanced past her into the shadowy white room. There was the first door, into a small anteroom with the bathroom opening off it, and then the second door, which had always sealed the couple away in a grandeur of privacy. Nick saw the end of the bed, a round table with silver-framed pictures of the children. He had hardly ever been in there, since his first summer, when he had walked around noiselessly, with his hands behind his back, an intruder in the temple of marital love; his own love fantasies had taken envious possession of it, like squatters, in the married couple's absence.

'Mm, strange times,' said Rachel, again as if talking to someone barely known, and instinctively disapproved of, whom a crisis had thrust her together with: Nick felt for the tender irony which always lined their little phrases, but he wasn't sure he found it. Perhaps she knew that he had known all along about Gerald and Penny, and her dryness was a form of bitter embarrassment.

He said, 'I know . . .' He was painfully sorry for her, but didn't see how to say so; it was a strange inhibition. In a way it was the moment for a new intimacy, and he hoped to bring her round to it. He glimpsed something beautiful for both of them emerging from the wreckage of the marriage: their old alliance, running rings of secret mockery round Gerald's pompous head, would flourish and be a strength to her. He hesitated, but he was ready.

She looked at him, her lips firming and relenting; then she turned away. She went unnoticing past Norman Kent's portrait of Catherine, though to Nick it played its part in the unfolding moment. 'I *wish* you would go and get Catherine,' she said, as she started downstairs.

'Oh . . .' said Nick, following behind, with a nervous laugh that he regretted.

'She ought to be here with her family,' Rachel said, not turning round. 'She needs care. I can't tell you how worried I am about her with that man.'

'Of course you are,' said Nick promptly, 'of course you are,' feeling he needed a new tone to console a woman twice his age. He felt he learned as he spoke, and saw how all her worries found an outlet in this one worry. He said, 'I'm sure she's safe with him, but if you want me to, I'll go over there, gladly,' pressing and then faltering behind her in anxious support and respect. The truth was he was frightened of the reporters and photographers: he didn't know how to deal with them, or with anyone who didn't show support and respect. And he was very wary of Russell, who seemed to have brought about his longed-for exposure of Gerald almost by chance, and now was 'looking after Cath' in his Brixton flat, and declining to let anyone see her.

Rachel reached the first-floor landing. 'I mean, I can't go over there; I'd have the whole press pack at my heels.' It was as if she was in danger even coming down to this level. The world outside her door had revealed itself as not only alien but hostile. And her world within doors had abruptly been robbed of comfort. She turned and her face was stiff apart from her moving lips; Nick thought she might be going to cry, and in a way he hoped she would, because it would be a natural thing to do, as well as a sign of trust – he could hold her, which he'd never done before. He saw the quick sensual crush of his chin against the shoulder of her wool suit, her grey-streaked hair across his mouth; she would clutch him, with a shudder of acceptance and release, and after a while he would lead her into the drawing room, where they would sit down and decide what to do about Gerald.

'No, you mustn't . . .' he said. 'Obviously.'

He watched her blink rapidly and choose a different sort of release: 'I mean, since you're so good at winkling people out!'

Nick didn't counter this gibe, the first he'd ever had from her. He said, 'Oh . . .' almost modestly, looking away at the carpet, the legs of the Sheraton table, the polished threshold of the drawing room. He felt very low, and Rachel went on,

'You know, we do rather count on you to keep an eye on Catherine.'

He tried to think when he'd heard the tone before. It was one of her adorable, unexpectedly funny little moments of exasperated candour about some party official, some simpleton at Conference. 'Well,' he said, 'I have tried . . . as I hope you know.' Rachel didn't endorse this. 'But, you know, she is an adult, she leads her own life . . . !' He gave the soft laugh of sensible conviction, which was all it had ever taken to win Rachel's agreement.

'Well, you say that!' she said, with a quite different kind of laugh, a single hard gasp.

Nick leant back on the mahogany banister, and felt his way into the new conditions. He said, very measuredly, 'I think I always have been as good a friend to her as she would allow me to be. As you know, friends come and go with her – and they all disappoint her. So I suppose I must have been doing something right if she still trusts me.'

'No, I'm sure she's devoted to you,' said Rachel, 'we all are,' in a sharp but conditional tone, as though it didn't much matter. 'It's really the question of your doing what's best for her, I mean, not simply . . . *conspiring* with her in whatever she wants you to do. She has a very serious illness.'

'Yes, of course,' Nick murmured, while his face grew fixed at the rebuke. Rachel was waiting, as if taking the pulse of her feelings; he peeped at her, saw her blink again and draw breath but then only give out a sharp resentful sigh. Nick said, 'I left her with Gerald . . . the other night. That should have been safe enough.'

'Ah, safe,' she said, 'yes. She should never have been there in the first place.'

'I promise you, I didn't know where she was taking me . . .'

'She wasn't taking you anywhere. You were taking her, if you remember, in your horrible little car.'

'Oh . . . !'

'I'm sorry,' she said, and Nick wasn't sure if she was instantly retracting or grimly confirming her remark. His impulse was to forgive her, he frowned tenderly, the reflex of a boy who couldn't bear to be in the wrong. 'You know the state she was in. Who knows what's happening to her now, if she hasn't got her librium with her.'

'Mm . . . her lithium . . .'

'There's just rather a question of responsibility, you know? I mean, we'd always supposed you understood your responsibilities to her – and to us, of course.'

'Oh, well, yes . . . !' He flashed a smile at the sting of this.

'We'd imagined you'd tell us if, for instance, anything went seriously wrong.' Her steady tone, her emphasizing twitches, were new to Nick; they seemed to signal a change in their relations that wouldn't easily be reversed. He was used to her easy assents, her oddly contented demurrals . . . 'We didn't know until last night, for instance, about this very serious episode four years ago.'

'What do you mean?' said Nick, shaking his head. The 'we' was fairly unnerving, the apparent solidarity with Gerald.

'I think you know very well what I mean.' She peered at him, with an effect of complex distaste; which extended in a reluctance to put it in words. 'We had no idea she'd tried to . . . harm herself while we were away.'

'I don't know what you've been told. She didn't harm herself, anyway. She asked me to stay with her – which I did – and she was fine, you know, she'd just had one of her bad moments.'

'You didn't tell us about it,' said Rachel, pale with anger.

'Please, Rachel! She didn't want to upset you, she didn't want to spoil your holiday.' The half-forgotten alibis came back, and the squeezing sensation of being out of his depth. 'I stayed with her, I talked her through it.' It was a bleat of a boast.

'Yes, she said you were wonderful,' said Rachel. 'Apparently, she quite raved about you to Gerald the other night.' Nick looked at the floor, and at the rhythm of the black-and-gilt S-shaped balusters. Then beyond them, and below, he heard the scratch of the front door being unlocked, a voice from the street saying, 'Over here, love!' and the jump of the knocker as the door slammed shut again.

Rachel stood where she was, in her own house and her indignation, and Nick edged away from her, still reluctantly holding the thread of her accusation, and went down a few steps to look over the banister. But it wasn't Catherine. It was Eileen, Gerald's 'old' secretary. She gazed up into the stairwell. She was wearing a dark overcoat and holding a black handbag. She looked like someone who'd come for a smart party on the wrong night. Nick thought she must have wanted to look good for the press. 'Hello, Eileen,' he said.

'I thought I'd better come in and see to things.'

'Good idea,' said Nick.

'I've said I'll keep an eye on things.'

'Well, that's marvellous.' Nick smiled with the real but finite politeness of someone who's been interrupted; he put a clinching warmth into it. The joke in the family had always been that Eileen had a crush on Gerald, who kept up an unseemly mockery of her efficiency and forethought. She was part of Nick's earliest idea of the house, in that first magic summer of possession which Rachel was now turning over like a stone. She'd been keeping an eye on things then. She came forward and put her hand on the tight bottom curl of the stair rail.

'I've brought the *Standard*,' she said. She'd been gripping it in her other hand, almost behind her, shielding them from it. 'I don't know that you'll like it very much.' She came up a few steps and Nick came down, with a vague sense of receiving a summons, and took it from her. He felt he should be specially diligent, and take the brunt of it on Rachel's behalf. He stood capably, with one foot on the stair above, and shook the paper flat. He saw the picture of himself, and thought, I'll come back to that in a second, and looked at the headline, which didn't make sense, and looked at the picture again and the one beside it of Wani. There was hardly any room for the article itself. The words and the pictures crowded out any sense of what they might mean. He felt oddly sorry for Bertrand: 'Peer's Playboy Son Has AIDS'. That was the subheading. 'Gay Sex Link to Minister's House'. Hard to get all that in. Didn't flow very well. Nick had a strange subliminal sensation that the banister wasn't there, and that the hall floor had hurtled up to meet him, like fainting but remaining fully conscious. He could tell it was very bad news. Then he realized where it had come from, and started to read the article, with a feeling like a thump in the sternum.

468

(ii)

'Bloody hell, Nick . . . !' said Toby next morning.

Nick chewed his cheek. 'I know . . .'

'I had absolutely no idea about this. None of us did.' He pushed his copy of *Today* away from him, across the dining-room table, and fell back in his chair.

'Well, the Cat did, obviously. She twigged when we were all in France last year.' He used the family nickname with a sense that his licence to do so had probably expired.

Toby gave him a wounded look which seemed to search and find him back at the manoir, under the awning, or by the pool, where they'd got drunk alone together that long hot afternoon. 'You could have told me, you know, you could have trusted me.' Toby had told his own secrets that day, his problems with intimacy – he'd entered into Nick's realm of examined feelings, it had been a triumph of intimacy in itself for him. 'I mean, two of my best mates, you know? I feel such a blasted idiot.'

'I was always longing to tell you, darling.' Again Toby's face seemed to close against the endearment. 'But Wani just wouldn't hear of it.' He looked shyly at his old friend. 'I know people take it very personally when they find they've been kept out of a secret. But really secrets are sort of impersonal. They're simply things that can't be told, irrespective of who they can't be told to.'

'Hm. And now this.' Toby pulled out the *Sun* from the slew of newsprint on the table. ' "Gay Sex Romp at MP's Holiday Home".' He threw it away from him, with a look of disdain and a hint of a challenge.

'It's really rather sweet their idea of what constitutes a romp,' Nick said, to try and put it in proportion.

'*Sweet* . . . ?' said Toby, incredulously, but with a flinch of regret as well, that he should be speaking like this to some-one he'd always simply trusted. He stood up, and walked awkwardly along to the far end of the table. The mood of an extended morning-after still reigned in the room, with sunshine seeping in over the top of the shutters, and the gilt wall lamps casting a crimson glow. He stood with his back to the Lenbach portrait of – what was he? – his great-grandfather: a stout bourgeois figure in a tightly buttoned black coat. Nick, with his eye for the family line, saw Toby growing into a likeness. Toby himself had on a dark suit, blue shirt, and red tie. He was going to a meeting, and this little chat was a bit like a meeting too. He seemed to share with his ancestor a respect for the obvious importance of business, as well as a dignified failure to anticipate the scandals of this week.

'God, I'm sorry, Toby,' said Nick.

'Yah, well,' said Toby, with a big sigh that seemed to weigh a burden and hint at a threat. Unexpected intimacies were blowing up all around him. He leant on the table and looked at a paper to hide his discomfort. 'First it's Dad and Penny, with this fraud thing going on too, then there's you and Ouradi, with the plague thing . . .'

'Well, you knew Wani had AIDS.'

'Mm, yah . . .' said Toby uncertainly. He squared up the newspapers in a pile, with distracted firmness. They were the astonishing evidence of his situation. 'And my bloody old sis going clean off the rails.'

'She has rather landed us in it.'

'It's as if she hates Dad.'

'It's difficult . . .'

'And hates you too. I mean, how did she get like this?'

It was the long-ago talk by the lake, the solemn explanation . . . 'I don't think she hates us,' said Nick. 'Since she crawled out from under the lithium she's just been in a mood to tell the truth. Actually, she always has been, when you think about it. I'm certain she'd never actually want to hurt us. She's been got at by people who do hate Gerald, perhaps; that's the thing.'

'Anyway, it's a fuck-up,' said Toby, quickly resisting the role-reversal. And Nick caught that startling thing, the stared-out threat of tears, the miserable twitch of the mouth.

'It's a fuck-up,' Nick agreed. He winced at his own readiness to explain Toby's story to him. Poor Toby had been tricked, or not trusted, which seemed a form of trickery, by everyone around him: it was awful, and Nick found a smile creeping out of the corners of his mouth in bizarre amusement.

'I must say the *Independent* has by far the best-quality photographs,' Toby said. 'They've achieved consistently high standards.'

'Yes, the *Telegraph*'s are very murky in comparison.'

'The *Mail*'s somewhat better, though.' Toby snapped back the pages. The Mordant Analyst had been given a double spread to explore the whole situation, drawing on his inside knowledge of 'the Fedden set'. The picture of Toby clasping Sophie on the dance floor at Hawkeswood was one of Russell's. Toby looked away at the floor and still didn't meet Nick's eye when he said, 'I don't know quite where this leaves us.'

'No,' said Nick. 'Everything's rather in the air, isn't it.'

'I mean, I don't see how you can stay here.' Then he did look at Nick for several seconds, and the lovely brown gaze, which had always softened or faltered, didn't do so.

'No, no, of course,' said Nick, with a scowl as if Toby was insulting him to suggest he thought he could.

Toby pursed his lips, stood up straight and buttoned his jacket. There was a sense that, though it could have been done better, he'd performed a bit of business, and his uneasy satisfaction carried him quickly to the door. 'I'm going to have a word with Ma,' he said. 'Sorry.'

Nick sat for a while, feeling that Toby's anger was the worst part of it, the one utterly unprecedented thing; and looking over the papers in which his own image appeared. He was letting himself in at the front door of this house, and also, four years younger, in a bow tie and his Uncle Archie's dinner jacket, looking very drunk. It was fascinating, if you thought about it, that they hadn't got hold of the picture of him and the PM. Still, they had all the rest, sex, money, power: it was everything they wanted. And it was everything Gerald wanted too. There was a strange concurrence about that. Nick felt his life horribly and needlessly broken open, but with a tiny hard part of himself he observed what was happening with detachment as well as contempt. He cringed with dismay at the shame he had brought on his parents, but he felt he himself had learned nothing new. His long talk on the phone with his father, and then with his mother, had been all the harder for his lack of surprise; to them it was 'a bit of a bombshell', it called for close explanation, almost for some countering offensive. He had found himself sounding flippant, and wounded them more, since of course, when it came to it, all their deep instincts were for him, for his safety, and protection. They took it utterly seriously, but rattled him with their clear admissions that they'd expected trouble of some kind, they'd known something wasn't quite right. Nick resisted that, he wasn't shocked, and couldn't capture at all the shock that was fuelling the press. He'd known about Penny, and he'd known about himself and Wani. The real horror was the press itself. 'Greed drives out Prudence,' wrote Peter Crowther, as if nobody'd ever thought of that before. He saw the romance of his years with the Feddens, deep, evolving, and profoundly private, framed and explained to the world by this treacherous hack.

The doorbell rang, and since no one answered it Nick went out and peered through the new spyhole: in which the furious, conceited features of Barry Groom loomed and then fled sideways as he rang the bell again. Nick opened the door, and glanced out past the MP at the now almost deserted street. '*Hello*, Barry, come in . . . Yes, they've virtually all gone now.'

'No thanks to you,' said Barry, stepping past him and frowning his eyebrows and mouth into two thin parallel lines. 'I've come to see Gerald.'

'Yes, of course.' It wasn't clear if Barry was treating him as a servant or an obstacle. 'Come this way,' he said, and went on gracefully, as he turned back down the hall, 'I'm so sorry about all this ghastly business.' There was a strange smooth relish in saying that. For a second Barry seemed to take it as his due, then his face soured again. He said,

'Shut up, you stupid little pansy!' It was a quaint sentence, and somehow the more expressive for that.

'Oh . . . !' – Nick darted a look in the big hall mirror, as though for witnesses. 'That's hardly—'

'Shut up, you little *cunt*!' said Barry, with a biting clench of the jaw, and pushed past him and down the passage towards Gerald's study.

'Oh, fuck off,' said Nick, in fact he only mouthed the words, because he thought Barry might turn back and punch him in the face; Gerald opened his door and looked out like a headmaster.

'Ah, Barry, good of you to come,' he said, and gave Nick a momentary stare of reproach.

'You ignorant, humourless, greedy, *ugly* cunt . . .' Nick went on to himself, in the shocked hilarity of having been insulted. He wandered in the hall, blinking in astonishment at the black-and-white marble squares of the floor. He couldn't quite tell, when he went into the kitchen, if Elena had heard this outburst. She always protested, dimly but sincerely, at Gerald's unguarded *fuck*s – she was serious about all that.

'Hello, Elena!' said Nick.

'So, Mr Barry Groom come,' said Elena. She was a little woman but she occupied the kitchen from wall to wall. She patrolled it. 'He want coffee?'

'Come to think of it, he never said. But I rather think not.'

'He don't want?'

'No . . .' He looked at Elena with cautious tenderness, uncertain what credit remained from his years of diligent niceness to her. 'By the way, I won't be here for dinner tonight.' Elena raised her eyebrows and pinched her lips. The new revelations about Nick and Wani must be amazing to her. It wasn't clear if she'd even taken in that Nick was gay. He said, 'It's all a bit of a mess, isn't it? *Un pasticcio . . . un imbroglio.*'

'*Pasticcio, si,*' she said, with a hard laugh. They'd had a certain amount of fun over the years with each other's Italian. She went into the pantry, and spoke to him without turning round, so that he had to follow her.

'I'm sorry?'

'How long you been here now?' She peered up at the shelved tins.

'In Kensington Park Gardens? – Oh, four years last summer, four and . . . a quarter years.'

'Four years. A good time.'

'Yes, it has been a good time' – he grunted at the little blur of idiom. She was reaching up, and Nick, not that much taller, stretched past her. 'The borlotti?' He put the can into her hands, so that she had at least to nod in thanks; then he followed her out again, as if hoping for another task. She jammed the beans under the tin opener and cranked round the handle, something Nick felt he'd seen her do scores, hundreds of times, with her tomato purée and her *fagioli* and all the things she preferred canned to fresh. And suddenly it was obvious to him. He said, 'Elena, I've decided it's time to hand in my resignation.'

She looked at him sharply, to make sure she'd understood him; then she nodded again, in acknowledgement. She might almost have smiled at his apt phrasing. She moved back to the table, and her busyness expressed her purpose but also perhaps hid some sort of regret at the news. Nick was very shaken by it himself. He glanced at her hopefully. Behind her on the wall were all the family photos, and she seemed to stand, stooped and efficient, in an angled but intimate relation to them – indeed she appeared in one of them, displaying a lordly Toby in his pram: she'd been there from the beginning, in the legendary Highgate days . . . She started chopping some onions, but looked up again and said, 'You remember when you first come here?'

'Yes, of course,' said Nick.

'The first time we meet . . .'

'Yes, I do,' and he chuckled fondly and went a little pink, because of course they'd never been over that minute of confusion in the hall. He saw he was pleased she'd mentioned it. It was hardly even an embarrassment, since all he had done was be charming to her; he'd treated her not as an equal but as a superior.

'You thought I was Miz Fed.'

'Yes, I know I did . . . Well, I'd never met either of you. I thought, a good-looking woman . . .'

Elena squeezed her eyes shut over the onions – it seemed for a moment like a slide into another emotion. Then she said, 'I think to myself that day, this one's . . . *sciocco*, you know, he don't know anything, oh, he's all very nice, lady, but he's you know . . .' she tapped her forehead with a finger.

'*Pazzo* . . . ?' said Nick, taking a last sick chance.

'He's no good,' said Elena.

Nick went up to his room, and stood looking at the window sill. Late-morning, late-October sunlight dimmed and brightened indifferently over it. He was lost in thought, but it was thought without words, pure abstraction, luminous and sad. Then a simple form of words appeared, almost as if written. It would have been best in a letter, where it could have been done beautifully, with complete control. Spoken, it risked tremors and deflections. He went downstairs to see Gerald.

The study door was ajar, and he could hear him talking to Barry Groom. He stood in the passage, as he felt he had often done in this house, as an accidental eavesdropper. Decisions were being made all the time, in an adjacent room, in a phone call half-curiously overheard. He liked the noise of business and politics, it was an adult reassurance, like the chatter of parents on a night journey, meaningless, fragmentary, and consoling to the sleepy child on the back seat. Sometimes of course he did pick up on a secret, a surprise still being contrived, and his pleasure was a very private one, the boosted glow of his own trustworthiness. Barry was saying, 'I can't think how you let it happen.' Gerald made a gloomy rumble and single hard cough but said nothing. 'I mean, what's the little pansy doing here? Why have you got a little ponce hanging round your house the whole fucking time?'

The last words were louder and louder, and Nick's pulse thumped as he waited, four or five seconds, for Gerald to put him right. He was warm with indignation, and a new combative excitement. Barry Groom had no idea of the life they led in this house. 'I suppose I'd have to say,' said Gerald, 'that it was an error of judgement. Untypical – I'm a pretty sharp judge of character as a rule. But yes . . . an error.'

'It's an error you've paid a very high price for,' said Barry Groom unrelentingly.

'He was a friend of the children, you know. We've always had an open-door policy towards the children's friends.'

'Hmm,' said Barry, who had publicly disinherited his son

Quentin 'on principle', to make him learn about money from scratch. 'Well, I never trusted him. I can tell you that, unequivocally. I know the type. Never says anything – always nursing his little criticisms. I remember sitting next to him after dinner here, years ago, and thinking, you don't fit in here, do you, you little cocksucker, you're out of your depth. And I'll tell you something else: he knew that. I could see he wished he was upstairs with the women.'

'Oh . . .' said Gerald, in wan protest. 'We always got along all right, you know.'

'So *fucking* superior.' Barry Groom swore harshly and humourlessly, as if swearing were the guarantee of any unpalatable truth. It was just what he'd done that night, after dinner, with an effect Nick could still remember, of having absolutely no style. 'They hate us, you know, they can't breed themselves, they're parasites on generous fools who can. Crawling to you, crawling to the fucking Ouradis. I'm not remotely surprised he led your poor lovely daughter astray like this, exploited her, there's no other word for it. A typical homo trick, of course.'

Gerald murmured something, with an effect of grumpy submission. Nick stood clenched by the door, leaning forward slightly, as if about to knock, in a novel confusion of feelings, anger at Gerald's failure to support him, and a strange delighted hatred of Barry Groom. Barry was a multiple adulterer and ex-bankrupt – to be hated by him was surely a mark of probity. But Gerald . . . well, Gerald, for all his failings, was a friend.

'Dolly Kimbolton's completely furious about all this, I need hardly say,' Barry said. 'Ouradi's just given another half-million to the Party.'

Nick trod quietly away and sat down at his old place in the dining room. He looked again at the picture of 'Banger' Fedden and Penny Kent embracing, taken from hundreds of feet away and so blown up that the lovers broke down into a pattern of meaningless dots.

Gerald let Barry out and a minute later Nick went back to the study, knocked, and put his head round the door. He looked about quickly, as though checking Gerald was alone, and drawing on some humorous shared relief that Barry had gone. Gerald was standing at his desk, surveying various documents, and glanced up over his half-moon glasses. 'Is this a good moment?' Nick said. Gerald grunted, a loudish dense sound made up of 'what?', 'no', 'yes', and a furious sigh. Nick came in and shut the door, not wanting to be overheard by anyone. The room still seemed to tingle with what had recently been said in it. The low leather armchair still showed where the visitor had sat. A process went on here, there were meetings and decisions, a sense of importance as seasoned and stifling as the odour of leather, stale cigar smoke and polish.

'A good moment,' said Gerald, plucking off his glasses and giving Nick a quick cold smile.

'Yes, well . . .' said Nick, hearing the words bleakly dilate. 'I mean I won't be more than a moment.'

'Oh . . .' said Gerald snootily, as if to say it would take more than a moment to get through the business he had in mind. He threw his glasses onto the desk, and walked over to the window. He was wearing cavalry twill trousers and a buff crew-neck sweater. The effect was of symbolic abasement mixed with military resolve – the strategy for a comeback must already be in hand. Nick had a silly sense of privilege in seeing him in private and in trouble; and at the same time, which was more of a shock, he felt almost oppressively bored by him. Gerald gazed into the garden, but really into his own sense of grievance. Nick wasn't sure whether to speak, it was as hard as he expected, and he stood holding the back of a chair, tensed against what he thought Gerald was preparing to say. 'How's Wani?' Gerald said.

'Oh . . .' The question showed a kind of chilly decency. 'He's terribly ill, as you know. It doesn't look at all hopeful . . .'

Gerald nodded slightly, to show it was therefore typical of a lot of things. 'Bloody tough on the parents.' He turned to stare at Nick, as if challenging him to sympathize. 'Poor old Bertrand and Monique!'

'I know . . .'

'To lose *one* child . . .' They both heard a touch of Lady Bracknell in this, and Gerald turned promptly away from the danger of a joke. 'Well, one can only imagine.' He shook his head slowly and came back to the desk. He had the heavy-faced look, indeed like someone resisting a laugh, that was his attempt at solemn sympathy. Though there was a mawkish hint too that he had somehow 'lost' a child himself: he absorbed the Ouradis' crisis into his own. 'And ghastly for the girl too.'

For a moment Nick couldn't think what he meant. 'Oh, Martine, do you mean?'

'The fiancée.'

'Oh . . . yes, but she wasn't actually his girlfriend.'

'No, no, they were going to get married.'

'They might have got married, but it was just a front, Gerald. She was only a paid companion.'

Gerald pondered this and then flicked up his eyebrows in sour resignation. The facts of gay life had always been taboo with him: he and Nick had never shared a frank word or knowing joke about them, and this was an odd place to start. With a nervous laugh Nick went on, '*I'll* miss him, of course.'

Gerald busied himself with some papers, shuffled them into a box-folder and snapped down the spring. He glanced, as if for approval, at the two framed photos, of Rachel and the Prime Minister, and said, 'Remind me how you came to be here.'

Nick wasn't sure if courtesy really required him to do so. He shrugged, 'Well, as you know, I came here as a friend of Toby's.'

'Aha,' said Gerald, with a nod, but still not looking at him. He sat down at the desk, in the spaceship black chair. He made an exaggerated moue of puzzlement. 'But were you a friend of Toby's?'

'Of course I was,' said Nick.

'A funny sort of friendship, wasn't it . . . ?' He glanced up casually.

'I don't think so.'

'I don't think he knew anything about you.'

'Well, I'm just me, Gerald! I'm not some alien invader. We'd been in the same college for three years.'

Gerald didn't concede this point, but swivelled and stared out of the window again. 'You've always been comfortable here, haven't you?'

Nick gasped with disappointment at the question. 'Of course . . .'

'I mean, we've always been very kind to you, actually, I think, haven't we? Made you a part of our life – in the widest sense. You've made the acquaintance of many remarkable people through being a friend of ours. Going up indeed to the very highest levels.'

'Yes, certainly.' Nick took a deep breath. 'That's partly why I'm so dreadfully sorry about everything that's happened,' and he pushed on, earnestly but slyly, 'you know, with Catherine's latest episode.'

Gerald looked very affronted by this – he didn't want some defusing apology from Nick, and especially one that turned out not to be an apology but a commiseration about his daughter. He said, as though parenthetically, 'I'm afraid you've never understood my daughter.'

Nick flattered Gerald by taking this as a subtle point. 'I suppose it's difficult for anyone who hasn't suffered from it to understand her kind of illness, isn't it, not only moment by moment, but in its long-term patterns. I know it doesn't mean she loves you and Rachel any the less that she's done all this . . . damage. When she's manic she lives in a world of total possibility. Though actually you could say that all she's done is tell the truth.' He thought he'd perhaps got through to Gerald – who frowned ahead and said nothing; but then, rather as he did in TV interviews, carried on with his own line, as if no answer or objection had been made.

'I mean, didn't it strike you as rather odd, a bit queer, attaching yourself to a family like this?'

Nick thought it was unusual – that was the beauty of it, or had been, but he said, 'I'm only the lodger. It was Toby who suggested I live with you.' He took a risk and added, 'You could just as well say that the family attached itself to me.'

Gerald said, 'I've been giving it some thought. It's the sort of thing you read about, it's an old homo trick. You can't have a real family, so you attach yourself to someone else's. And I suppose after a while you just couldn't bear it, you must have been very envious I think of everything we have, and coming from your background too perhaps . . . and you've wreaked some pretty awful revenge on us as a result. And actually, you know . . .' he raised his hands, 'all we asked for was loyalty.'

The strange, the marvellous thing was that at no point did Gerald say what he considered Nick actually to have done. It seemed as natural as day to him to dress up the pet lamb as the scapegoat. There was no point in fighting, but Nick said, as if eerily detached from the very young man who was gripping the chair back, tearful with surprise, 'I haven't the faintest idea what you're talking about, Gerald. But I must say it's a bit steep to talk to me about loyalty, of all things.' It struck him he'd never spoken a word of criticism to Gerald before. It clearly struck Gerald too, from his incredulous recoil, and the grappling way he turned Nick's words on him.

481

'No, actually, you haven't the faintest fucking idea what you're talking about!' He stood up convulsively, and then sat down again, with a sort of sneer. 'Do you honestly imagine that your affairs can be talked about in the same terms as mine? I mean – I ask you again, who are you? What the fuck are you doing here?' The slight rephrasing, the sharpening of his position, loosed a flood of anger, which moving visibly through his face seemed almost to bewilder him, like a physical seizure.

Trembling with the contagion of madness Nick said the thing he'd come to say, but in a tone of cheap sarcasm he'd never intended to use: 'Well, you'll be devastated to hear that I'm moving out of the house today. I just dropped in to tell you.'

And Gerald, furiously pretending not to have heard, said, 'I want you out of the house today.'

18

The Duchess insisted that Gerald and Rachel go to the wedding. Gerald had made a noisily abject phone call: 'Really, Sharon, I could never forgive myself if I caused you a moment's embarrassment on so joyous a day,' and before Sharon, in her robust way, had finished saying that he shouldn't talk nonsense, he had rapidly said, 'Oh good, oh good,' in a tone which suggested he hadn't really meant it in the first place. It was a tiny protocol of self-abasement that he had found himself reluctantly obliged to follow. 'I just thought I should ask,' he said, as if the offer and not its cause might be the social false note. He didn't really believe he could be an embarrassment to anyone. They drove off to Yorkshire on the Friday morning.

Wani had had an exquisite new morning suit and dinner suit made, with narrow trousers and a smaller chest disguised by flyaway lapels. They looked like the formal dress of a little prince, which might only be worn once before he grew out of it. Nick saw them laid out on the ogee bed, with the new Oxfords and evening slippers aligned on the floor beneath. It was as if two people even more insubstantial than Wani were lying back side by side on the covers. He helped Wani pack, and peeked out of habit in his leather stud-box, where there was a flesh-pink paper packet an inch long. He took it out and hid it, with a sense of a new code of honour overriding an old one.

He found Wani lying on the sofa, in front of some heavy-duty video: but his eyes were closed, his mouth open and askew. Nick took a second or two to burn off his horror in the slower flame of his pity. Twice now he had come across Wani dozing and leaned over him not, as he used to, for the private marvel of the view, but to check that he was alive. He sat by him with a sigh and felt the strange tenderness towards himself that came with looking after someone else, the sense of his own prudence and mortality. He thought it might be like parenthood, the capable concealment of one's worries. He hadn't told Wani, but he was having another HIV test in the afternoon: it was another solemn thing, and even more frightening than it need have been for not being talked about. From the corner of his eye, the video seemed to pullulate, like some primitive life form, with abstract determination. It was an orgy, unattributable organs and orifices at work in a spectrum of orange, pink, and purple. He looked more closely for a moment, with a mixture of scorn and regret. It was what they were already calling a 'classic', from the days before the antiseptic sheen of rubbers was added to the porn palette – Wani had hated that development, he was an aesthete at least in that. Turned down low, the actors grunted their binary code – *yeah . . . oh yeah, oh yeah . . . yeah . . . oh . . . yeah, yeah . . . oh yeah . . .*

'Is the car here?' said Wani, still waking, with a look of dread, as if he longed for his word to be challenged and the trip to be cancelled. His father's chauffeur was to drive him to Harrogate in the maroon Silver Shadow. A nurse was travelling with them, a black-haired, blue-eyed Scotsman called Roy, whom Nick felt pleasantly jealous about.

'Roy will be here in a moment,' he said, ignoring Wani's weak sulk of resentment; and then, to encourage him, 'I must say, he's very cute.'

Wani sat up slowly, and swung his legs round. 'He speaks his mind, young Roy,' he said.

'And what does he say?'

'He's a bit of a bully.'

'Nurses have to be pretty firm, I suppose.'

Wani pouted. 'Not when I'm paying them a thousand pounds a minute, they don't.'

'I thought you liked a bit of rough,' said Nick, and heard the creaky condescension of his tone. He helped Wani up. 'Anyway, four hours in a Rolls-Royce should smooth him out.'

'That's just it,' said Wani. 'He's madly left-wing.' And the ghostly smile of an old perversity gleamed for a moment in his face.

When the bell rang, Nick went down and found Roy talking to the chauffeur. Roy was about his own age, wearing dark blue slacks and an open-neck shirt; Mr Damas wore a dark grey suit and funereal tie and a grey peaked cap. They stood at an angle to each other – Roy candid and practical, fired up by the crisis of AIDS, throwing down his own bravery and commitment like a challenge to Mr Damas, who had driven the Ouradis since Wani was a boy and looked on his illness with respect but also, as a creature of Bertrand's, with an edge of blame. The recent newspaper stories had brought shame on him, and it struggled with the higher claims of loyalty in his square face and leather-gloved hands. He straightened his cap before accepting the two suitcases that Nick had brought down.

'So you're not coming, Nick,' said Roy, with sexy reprehension.

'No, I've got a few things to sort out here.'

'You won't be there to protect me from all these dukes and ladies and what have you.'

The sudden reassurance of being flirted with, over Wani's stooping head, was shadowed by a flicker of caution. He was still getting used to the interest of his own case, something extrinsic to himself, which he registered mainly in the way other people assumed they knew him. 'I think I'd need protection from them myself,' he said.

Roy gave him a funny smile. 'Do you know who's going to be there?'

'Everyone,' came a wheezy voice.

Roy looked into the back of the Rolls, where Wani was fidgeting resentfully with a rug and the copious spare cushions. 'Just get yourself settled down in there,' he said, as though Wani was a regular nuisance in class. There was something useful in his briskness; he seemed to take a bleak view and a hopeful one at the same time.

Mr Damas came round and shut the door with its ineffable *chunk* – it was the sound of the world he moved in, a mystery in his charge though not his possession, the tuned precision of a closing door. Wani sat, looking forwards, lost in the glinting shadow of the smoked glass. Nick had the feeling he would never see him again, fading from view in the middle of the day. Such premonitions came to him often now. He made a beckoning gesture, and Wani buzzed down the glass two inches. 'Give Nat my love,' Nick said. Wani gazed, not at him, but just past him, into the middle ground of ironic conjecture, and after a few seconds buzzed the window shut.

Nick went into the deserted office on the ground floor, and started going through his desk. He didn't have to move out of Abingdon Road, in fact he was staying upstairs while he searched for a flat, but he felt the urge to organize and discard. It seemed clear, although Wani wouldn't say so, that the Ogee operation was closing down. Nick was glad he wasn't going to Nat's wedding, and yet his absence, to anyone who noticed, might seem like an admission of guilt, or unworthiness. He saw a clear sequence, like a loop of film, of his friends not noticing his absence, jumping up from gilt chairs to join in the swirl of a ball. On analysis he thought it was probably a scene from a Merchant Ivory film.

The doorbell trilled and Nick saw a van in the street where the Rolls had been. He went out and there was a skinny boy in a baseball cap pacing about, and some very loud music. 'Ogee?' he said. 'Delivery.' He'd left the driver's door open and the radio on – 'I Wanna Be Your Drill Instructor' from *Full Metal Jacket* echoed off the houses while he piled up big square bundles on his trolley and wheeled them into the building. He'd taken over this bit of the street for five minutes – it was an event. It was the magazine. 'Thanks very much,' said Nick. He stood aside with the ineffectual half smile of the non-worker, longing to be left alone with the product. The boy pounded in and out, breathing sharply: it was as if this delivery was keeping him intolerably from another delivery, as if he'd have liked to have made all his deliveries at once. He stacked up the bundles, a dozen of them, in four squat columns. Each packet was bound both ways with tight blue plastic tape; Nick scratched at it and broke a nail. 'Sign, please,' said the boy, whisking a manifest and a biro from his jeans pocket. Nick hurried down a loose approximation of his signature, and handed the paper back, to find the boy looking at him with his head tilted and eyes narrowed. Nick coloured but hardened his features at the same time. If the boy was a *Mirror* reader he might well recognize him – he sensed a latent aggression muddle and swim towards a focus. 'Want to see?' said the boy, and before Nick understood he'd whisked out a Stanley knife from his other pocket, thumbed the blade forward, and ripped through the tape on the nearest bundle. He pulled off the loose paper wrapping, slid the first glimpsed shining copy out, turned it in his hands, and presented it to Nick: 'Voilà!' Nick held it, like the winner of a prize, happy and unable to hide, sharing it courteously with the boy, who stood at his elbow working it out. Nick felt very exposed, and hoped there wouldn't be questions. 'Yeah, that's beautiful,' said the boy. 'That's an angel, is it?'

'That's right,' said Nick. Simon had done a wonderful job – clear glossy black, with the white Borromini cherub on the right-hand side, its long wing stretching in a double curve on to the spine, where its tip touched the wing tip of another cherub in the same position on the back, the two wings forming together an exquisitely graceful ogee. No lettering, except at the foot of the spine, OGEE, ISSUE 1 in plain Roman caps.

Nick thought he'd rather not open it, he was teeming with curiosity and hot-faced reluctance; he needed to be alone. The boy shook his head admiringly. 'Yeah, fucking beautiful,' he said. 'Pardon my French.' He stuck his hand out, and Nick shook it. 'See you, mate.'

'Yes . . . thanks a lot, by the way!'

'No worries.'

Nick smiled, and watched his first critic bound out of the office.

'Right . . .' he said, when he was alone, and even then he smiled self-consciously. He sat down at Melanie's empty desk, the magazine squarely in the centre, and turned back the cover with an expression of vacant surmise. And of course what he saw was the wonderland of luxury, for the first three glossy spreads, Bulgari, Dior, BMW, astounding godparents to Nick and Wani's whimsical coke-child. He went quickly to his name under the masthead on page 8 – 'Executive Editor: Antoine Ouradi. Consulting Editor: Nicholas Guest' – and blushed, out of pride and a vague sense of imposture. He thought how relieved his parents would be to see that, to see his name in print as a distinction, not a shameful worry. It fortified him. He went on through, stopping for a moment on each page – he'd read every word of it ten times in proof and passed the pages for the printer but he felt they had undergone a further unaccountable mutation to become a magazine . . . he blurred his eyes against the impossible late mistake.

His own article, deferentially far back, behind Anthony

Burgess on brothels and Marco Cassani on the Gothic revival in Italy, was about the Line of Beauty, illustrated with sumptuous photos of brooches, mirrors, lakes, the legs of rococo saints and sofas. He read it with a beating heart, going back once or twice to ride the slide of an elegant sentence again. Beside him as he read were other admirers . . . Professor Ettrick, his trust in a little-seen student restored . . . Anthony Burgess, in Monaco, brought to a marvelling halt as he skimmed his contributor's copy . . . Lionel Kessler, relaxing perhaps on a Louis Quinze day bed, garlanded all round with lines of beauty, seeing welcome proof that his clever maligned young friend was a mensch. Nick went on, with a confident smile, through the latter pages, the glowing short features on mah-jong sets and toy soldiers of the Raj. The inside back cover, to his satisfaction, was an ad for 'Je Promets'. And after that the answering angel with its lifted wing. Nick took the highest view of it all, his initial timidity was flooded out by its opposite, a conviction that they'd produced a masterpiece.

Strange teetering mood of culmination. Five minutes later he wished he had it to read through fresh again; but that could never happen. He took a copy upstairs to the flat, and opened it at random several times – to find that its splendour had a glint to it, a glassy malignity. No, it was very good. It was lustrous. The lustre was perfected and intense – it was the shine of marble and varnish. It was the gleam of something that was over.

How he wished Wani could have been here to see it – he'd missed it by five minutes. He could have taken it with him to Yorkshire, given copies to the guests, to Toby, to Sophie, to the Duchess, to Brad and Treat. Nick pictured Roddy Shepton, huge in tails and top hat, casting a wary eye over it as he waited for a drink. He pictured Wani himself, shuffling through the rooms in chilly defiance to show them the one beautiful thing he had managed to make out of his millions – it would confirm or confound their slight expectations that he was or wasn't going to do something. The reflex acclaim for anything published by a child of the fellow-rich would be loud, but tempered by disgust at his illness and remembered unease about his origins. Copies would be left behind in bedrooms and lavatories. Nick sighed over their fate and then thought how silly he was, since Wani hadn't taken the magazine with him; and really there were worse things to imagine. He was afraid, for instance, that he hadn't been careful enough in checking Wani's bags – he could easily have had other wraps of coke in his pockets or in his rolled socks. The crisis in May had forcibly broken his habit, but the reprieve, the return to London and its suddenly finite pleasures, must have pulsed with temptation. Nat himself was clean now, but his friends included half a dozen steady users, who could easily and carelessly offer Wani a line. And his heart was very weak. It would be a kind of suicide. Nick stood at the kitchen window, hardly seeing the house-backs opposite as he lived through the phone call, from Sharon perhaps, or from Gerald himself, tersely dutiful: a massive heart attack. There was nothing they could do.

When he went into the sitting room, there was the magazine on the table. It was a weird sort of launch, when there was never going to be a second issue. It would be good if people knew that, and prized it as itself, not as a portent or pilot of something to come. It was the only *Ogee*. Lying there, in a room in his house, at noon on a mild autumn day, it might have been Wani's memorial tablet, with the angel's wing sheltering the blank where his name and achievements should go.

Next morning Nick drove up to Kensington Park Gardens to collect his things. There was intermittent drizzle and he wondered if the wedding hats were being spoiled in Yorkshire. The wide street was empty, with that accidental vacancy of a

London street, a momentary lull in which the pavements, the house-fronts, the rain-striped windows have the aura of the déjà vu. He let himself in at number 48, hasty in the new skills of avoiding notice: which he countered needlessly by slamming the door shut.

Inside, in the hall: the sound . . . the impassive rumble of London shrunk to a hum, barely noticed, as if the grey light itself were subtly acoustic. Nick felt he'd chanced on the undisturbed atmosphere of the house, larger than this year's troubles, as it had been without him and would be after he'd gone. The gilt lantern burned palely in the stairwell, but in the dining room the ordinary shadows deepened in the corners and hung like smoke in the coving of the ceiling. The boulle clock ticked, with mindless vigilance. He went up the stone stairs and into the drawing room. It was really just a matter of finding his own bits and pieces, the CDs mixed in family-wise with theirs, a book that he'd lent them and watched filter slowly and unread to the bottom of the pile. He stood by the piano and thought about giving the Mozart Andante a final go; but the effect would have been maudlin as well as laughably inept. Toby's portrait looked out at him, an emblem of adolescence in its hormonal glow and expectant frown. It added an urgency to the need to move on. Nick stood in front of the fireplace, holding his possessions against his chest. A lorry passed outside, and the windows throbbed in their frames for a moment, in sympathy with its roar and the rattle of its tailgate, and then the broad quasi-silence disclosed itself again. And something else, what was it?, the smell of the place, tapestry smell, polished wood, lilies, almost churchy – he felt his senses seize and resign the thousand impressions he'd grown used to.

And it all reached back. It spoke of Gerald and Rachel without visible interruption. He went down to the kitchen, where the tidiness and profusion, the jars, the noticeboard, the draped dishcloth, were signs of a wide, deep system. He was already an intruder, glancing up at the photos of these absent celebrities.

He went down again, to the basement, to fetch some cardboard boxes from the *trou de gloire.* This lumber room under the kitchen was where the gilt ballroom chairs were stacked and interesting old tables and bleary mirrors abandoned; and where Mr Duke kept his paints, ladders, and toolboxes, along with a kettle and a calendar – it was his den, and Nick almost expected to find him there, in the subconscious of the house. He pressed down the light switch and got the shock of the wallpaper, which was purple with a pattern like black wrought iron, only partly hidden by all the junk. It always amazed him. It spoke of a time before Gerald and Rachel, and a different idea from theirs of what was great fun. Like his own parents they seemed to have avoided the '60s, with its novel possibilities and worthwhile mistakes. Perhaps in the Highgate days they'd had a joss stick and a floor cushion, but here the purple room was the junk room. Nick found some old wine boxes, and took them awkwardly upstairs. He wondered who'd lived here before the Feddens. There might well have been only three or four owners in the years since the whole speculation rose up out of the Notting Hill paddocks and slums. It was a house that encouraged the view its inhabitants had of themselves. Nick thought of Gerald's showmanship, the parties, the pathetic climax of the PM's visit. That had been just a year ago, another drizzly autumn wedding . . .

He stopped on the second-floor landing, set down the boxes and went into Gerald and Rachel's bedroom. From the window there was the view of the gardens, in slanting rain, the large brown leaves of the planes dropping and blowing. It was a grander but closer view than the one he'd grown used to upstairs, the treetop view, with other rooftops and a spire beyond. The gardens grew smaller at this time of year: you saw the far fence and the street outside. He turned and walked softly on the pale carpet towards the bed. Who slept on which side? – Rachel here, clearly, with the novels and the earplugs. The little Gauguin landscape Lionel had given them hung opposite. On the round walnut table, with a bowl of lavender, and china boxes, stood the photographs in silver, ivory, or red-velvet frames.

He picked up the one of Toby as a Lord of Tyre – Nick couldn't remember his name. He was the trusty minister who looked after things while Pericles went on his travels; he only came on at the beginning and the end, and spent the middle acts lounging restively around the cricket pavilion, which was used as the green room for these open-air plays. It was June, the smell of the lake and cut grass outside, creosote and linseed in the stuffy pavilion. Toby took off his heavy tunic, and blocked imaginary deliveries with a cricket bat as he waited for Sophie, who was playing Marina, to come off. Someone had photographed him then. He wore dark tights, and his own suede shoes. His naked upper body looked very white against the line round his neck where the make-up ended. His face was feminine, over-beautiful, a dancer's face, his body muscular and jutting enough to cause amusement in others. Nick had the brief but memorable role of Cerimon, the Lord of Ephesus who revives Queen Thaissa when she's washed ashore in her coffin: it was one of the intensest experiences of his life: 'I hold it ever / Virtue and cunning were endowments greater / Than nobleness and riches . . .', his heart slamming, tears in his eyes; and then it was over, he made his dignified exit – a sense of floating and thinness, a forced adaptation to the scene outside the circle of lit stage and dark audience, who were already attending to what came afterwards. He peeled off his grey beard, twirled off his cloak, and had a jealous bottle of Guinness while Toby 'unconsciously' flexed his biceps for Sophie – they were preoccupied by each other and by having

493

still to go on. Toby wasn't a very good actor, but the role was only a bit of rhetoric, quite unpsychological, and he was warmly applauded – there was something right about him. He did it as if there was no more to acting than to rowing or passing a rugger ball. He was neither modest nor vain.

Nick knew he would never see the picture again, and found it hard to put it back on the table. It gleamed in the rainy light as an emblem of why he'd come here. It wasn't clear with Toby, any more than with Leo and Wani, if fantasy could hold back time, if this sleek second-year with his sportsman's legs and marvellous arse could still excite him when he knew the fat Toby of five years on. Well, not in the mind, perhaps, but in an image, a photo: it took a certain aesthetic nerve to fly in the face of the facts. He did something silly and solemn, and left on the glass the light, blurred imprint of his lips and the tip of his nose.

Up in his room he pulled handfuls of books from his shelves and thrust them like bricks into the boxes. He hardened himself against his taste for nostalgia – the long-breathed leisure of the old days was over, matters were more urgent and unsure. The week ahead was already shadowed by the wait for his test results. The boost, the premature relief of taking charge and agreeing to learn the worst, waned steeply in the following days; already when he thought of it he felt unreachably alone. It was the third test he'd had, and that fact, and the mysterious number three, seemed by moments to shrink and to swell the chance of a positive result.

The boxes filled immediately, in proof of the ungraspable formula relating shelf-length to box-capacity. He carried one of them down, and as he dumped it in the hall he heard the sound of the back door being unlocked, feet scuffed on the mat, an umbrella shaken. Elena? Or Eileen again? Whoever it was was very unwelcome. He was annoyed by their furtiveness as well as their confidence. He went into the kitchen with a bored look.

'Oh my god!' said Penny in a breathy rush. She held the pink bundle of her umbrella in front of her chest. Then, furious to have been frightened, she said, 'Mm, hello, Nick,' and went to the sink with a bored look of her own. 'I thought you'd gone,' she said.

'I think I thought you'd gone,' said Nick, quite gently. They'd both been in the wars, and he felt they might finally have found some ground to share. There was an outside chance she might give him some sympathy, which so far he hadn't had a taste of; and to him commiseration was always easy.

She settled the wet brolly, like a blown flower, and came back across the room. 'In five minutes I will have. I'm getting my things.' He seemed almost to be blocking her way. 'You're not at the wedding,' she said.

'I thought I'd give it a miss.'

'Yes. Well, I don't know them, of course.'

'Oh, Nat's awfully nice.'

'Uh-huh.'

'I don't think anyone really knows Beatriz yet. Hardly even Nat actually!'

'She's Argentinian, isn't she?'

'Yes, she's a rich widow. Her first husband broke his neck playing polo.' He hesitated and said, 'Apparently she's four months pregnant.'

Penny made a grim snuffle. 'At least I avoided that,' she said, and with this tiny sarcastic self-exposure she edged past him and out of the room.

He hadn't seen her since the night at Badger's flat, and he had to admit she had an interest, a bleak unanticipated glamour. A week ago her name was known only to her family, her school and college friends, and her work contacts;

now millions worldwide had heard about her sex life. He watched her march off along the passage; his mocking sense of her as a busily ambitious little person with no sense of humour rather faltered. He stood with a thin smile of remorse, and a minute later went after her into Gerald's study. She was standing reading a yard-long fax, which she clumsily folded and put down. She said, 'So where are you going to go?' crisply, almost as though she were despatching him herself.

'Oh, I'm staying at Wani's. Yup.' He gave a rueful smile over the ramparts of his own scandal, but no answering wave came from within hers. 'Then I'm going to start looking for a place of my own.'

'You're not worried about money.'

Nick shrugged. 'I've done all right, actually, in the past year or so. With a little help from my friends . . . How about you?'

'I don't have much.'

'No, I mean, where are you staying?'

'Oh, I've gone back home for a bit.'

'Right . . . How's Norman taken all this?'

'Well, how do you imagine? Very badly indeed.' She moved some papers on the desk and put them down as if inadvertently on the looped fax. 'He detests Gerald, of course, and always has.'

Nick shook his head slowly, as if this was beyond his grasp. 'I never really believed that. Just because he's a Tory.'

'Fiddlesticks. He took Rachel off him – that's what he's never forgiven him for.'

'It was an incredibly long time ago,' said Nick, turning towards the window to cover his surprise.

'Well, Dad's like that. When he was young he thought he was going to be very happy and very rich. And then Gerald came along.'

It was clearly an arrival she could vouch for the force of. Nick laughed for a second and was vaguely touched. He said, 'We all know how competitive Gerald is.'

Penny searched in a drawer for a while before saying, 'Mmm . . .' It was more than competitive, it was pathological – to steal the girlfriend and then fuck the daughter. Clearly he wasn't called Banger for nothing. He said, with a little whine of incredulity,

'You've heard about his new directorship.'

'Yes . . . yes, I have.'

'It's rather amazing, isn't it? With the share thing hanging over him . . .'

'Oh, they'll want him,' said Penny.

'Yes,' said Nick. He remembered her when she first came here, with nothing but a good degree behind her, innocent, pliant, a little complacent at the candlelit table; now her eyes looked tired and guarded from the glare of the lights. 'It's rather amazing to resign in disgrace one day and be offered a job at eighty thousand a year the next.'

He was afraid she resented his word 'disgrace'. 'That's how this world works, Nick. Gerald can't lose. You've got to understand that.' She sat down at the desk and looked around it. He had the sense of her clearing it of any scraps of sentiment – it was a secret raid.

'I expect you'd like to be left alone,' he said. He came and stood in front of her so as to glance at the fax, which he saw was in Gerald's impossible handwriting: it ended with that breezy ideogram that might have been 'Love' or 'Yours' or 'Hello' and a big 'G' and a line of crosses. Then he found Penny was looking at him tensely, with a look that acknowledged the writing and the kisses, and with hurried blinks as she decided.

'I'm not giving him up, Nick.'

'Oh . . .' said Nick.

'I'm not.'

'I see.'

'I don't care what Dad says, or Madam, or the Editor of the *Sun*.'

Nick stared respectfully, but said, 'I thought he'd virtually been given up for you.'

'What . . . ? Oh, I see – well, publicly, yes. That's what we want people to think.'

'You say "we".'

'We're very much in love.'

Nick looked at the floor, perhaps impatiently. It seemed everything was going to go stubbornly on: first it was Rachel who wouldn't leave Gerald, and now Penny wouldn't either. He must have something extraordinary, Gerald, something Nick had been incapable of understanding. He saw the story reaching on through an obscure futurity; innumerable articles by the Mordant Analyst. He said, 'But how can you bear the secrecy?' with a real curiosity as to how someone else would answer this question.

'Perhaps it won't be a secret.'

'Hmm . . .' Nick's raised eyebrow and dry chuckle made her blush but not apparently change her mind.

'Anyway, I don't care,' she said.

'Well . . .'

'Catherine's always mocked and jeered at Gerald,' said Penny, as if not quite able to bear the line of talk she'd started.

Nick said hesitantly, 'I think it's pretty mutual.' Penny's world seemed only to make sense to her as a forcefield of detestations.

'I know she's always hated me,' she said, with a grim laugh that didn't quite spare Nick either; she didn't come out with it, but she seemed to know what he'd thought and said about her over the years.

'You know that's not true,' said Nick, in a mutter at the pointlessness of saying it. 'I think it's herself that she hates most at the moment.'

Penny tucked her chin in, and gave him a very old-fashioned look. 'She was revelling in the whole thing, I would say.'

'That's not revelling, Penny. At first it seems thrilling, but then it becomes a kind of torment to her, being manic.' He realized that Penny's main source of views on Catherine would be Gerald; just as his own, besides a friend's intuition, was the strenuous prose of Dr E. J. Edelman.

'Well, it's nothing to the torment she's caused,' said Penny unrepentantly.

Nick shook his head at her in astonishment, and thought he might as well leave her to it. She was too excited to look at him as she said, 'I assume it was you that told her, was it?'

'Absolutely not!' said Nick.

'Well, that's certainly what Gerald thinks.'

Nick said, 'You see it's typical of Gerald to think she couldn't work it out for herself. Actually she's the cleverest one of us all.'

'I could tell you suspected something when you were with us in France,' Penny said.

'I was very worried about Rachel,' Nick said. 'She's an old friend.'

'Well, I wonder if she feels the same about you.' Penny gave him a short sharp smile, and then sat forward, with her elbows on the desk. 'And now, if you'll excuse me,' she said, 'I have things to do,' and found a chance after all, in the dullest of formulas, for a further dismissal.

Nick pulled the blue front door shut, double-locked the Yale locks and the Chubb lock, and stood fiddling the keys off his ring. He held open the letterbox and flung them through and heard them tinkle on the marble floor. Then he peered through the letterbox himself and saw them lying there inaccessibly. There was also the back-door key, so in fact he still could get in, but he soon threw that in too. The one he was most reluctant about was the sleek bronze Yale for the communal gardens; it had a look of secrets to it. He could probably keep it, no one would remember; it would be nice to be still in fact, if not by rights, a keyholder. His eyes moved in lazy twitches of indecision. He hardly saw himself coming back, haunting the place, gazing up at the Feddens' windows for glints of the life they were leading without him. Painful and pointless. He pushed up the flap and put his hand through with the key in it, held it for a second before letting it drop onto the mat.

The little car was jammed full of boxes and curled heaps of clothes on hangers. It sat low on its springs, under all these possessions heavy as passengers. Nick stood by it, still thinking, and then drifted unexpectedly down the street. The pavement was dry now in patches, but the sky was threatening and fast-moving. The tall white house-fronts had a muted gleam. It came over him that the test result would be positive. The words that were said every day to others would be said to him, in that quiet consulting room whose desk and carpet and square modern armchair would share indissolubly in the moment. There was a large tranquil photograph in a frame, and a view of the hospital chimney from the window. He was young, without much training in stoicism. What would he do once he left the room? He dawdled on, rather breathless, seeing visions in the middle of the day. He tried to rationalize the fear, but its pull was too strong and original. It was inside himself, but the world around him, the parked cars, the cruising taxi, the church spire among the trees, had also been changed. They had been revealed. It was like a drug sensation, but without the awareness of play. The motorcyclist who lived over the road clumped out in his leathers and attended to his bike. Nick gazed at him and then looked away in a regret that held him and glazed him and kept him apart. There was nothing this man could do to help him. None of his friends could save him. The time came, and they learned the news in the room they were in, at a certain moment in their planned and continuing day. They woke the next morning, and after a while it came back to them. Nick searched their faces as they explored their feelings. He seemed to fade pretty quickly. He found himself yearning to know of their affairs, their successes, the novels and the new ideas that the few who remembered him might say he never knew, he never lived to find out. It was the morning's vision of the empty street, but projected far forward, into afternoons like this one decades hence, in the absent hum of their own business. The emotion was startling. It was a sort of terror, made up of emotions from every stage of his short life, weaning, homesickness, envy and self-pity; but he felt that the self-pity belonged to a larger pity. It was a love of the world that was shockingly unconditional. He stared back at the house, and then turned and drifted on. He looked in bewilderment at number 24, the final house with its regalia of stucco swags and bows. It wasn't just this street corner but the fact of a street corner at all that seemed, in the light of the moment, so beautiful.

picador.com

blog
videos
interviews
extracts